—GRIPPER—

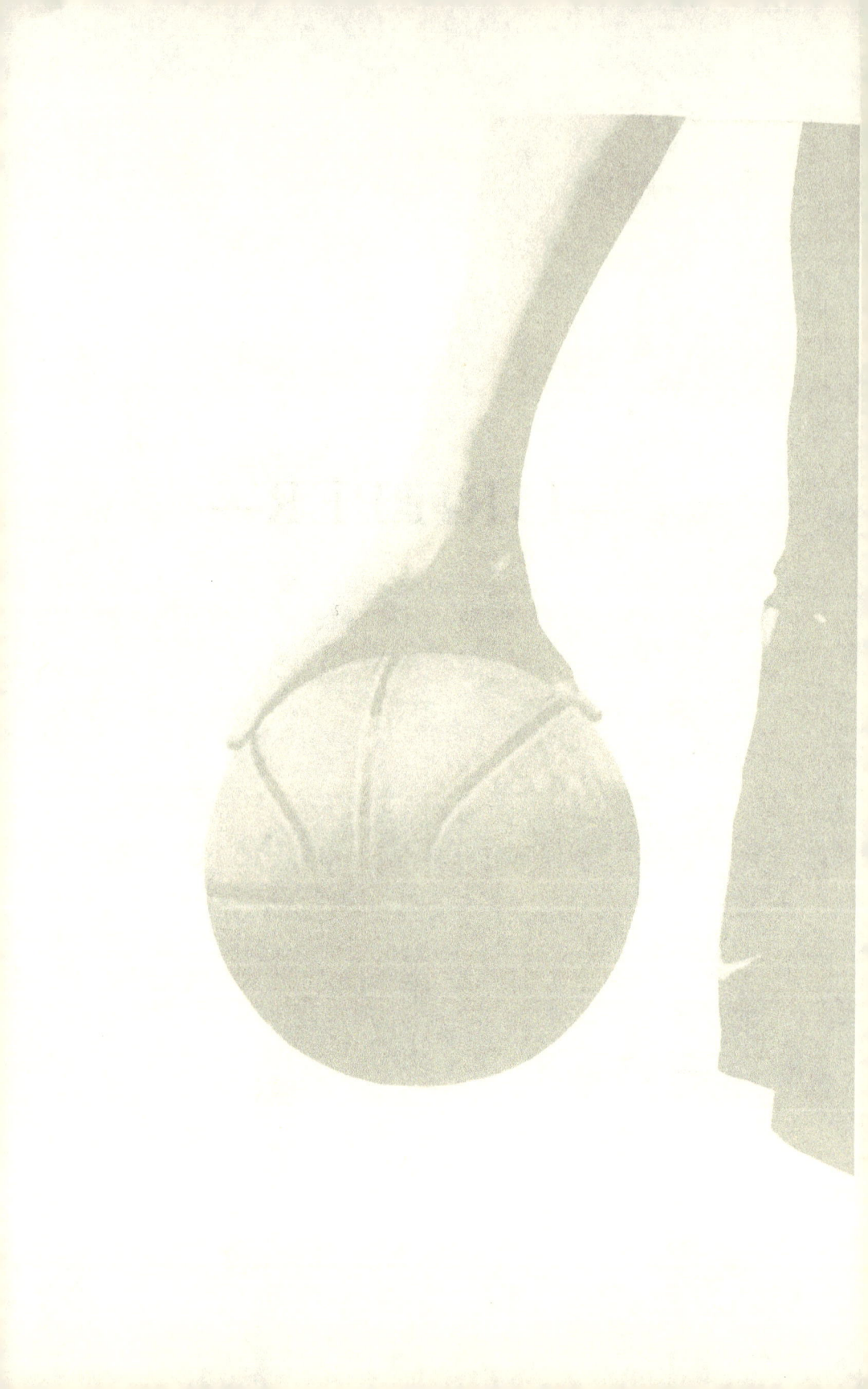

GRIPPER

ASHNA GRAVES

LYCHGATE

GRIPPER

Lychgate Press

Distributed by Partners West
Bellingham, Washington

ISBN-13: 978-0-9882887-8-2
ISBN-10: 0988288788

Library of Congress control number: 2016932985

LYCH☩GATE

www. lychgatepress. com

Cover design by W. Lee Gilroy

*For Scott, my dear brother and
a steadfast Jeneva Leopold fan*

CHAPTER
1

"Murder. Right here in River City." The editor savored the words, watching her with a look of happy expectation.

Neva tried but failed to control a yawn. She had to be patient, had to let him talk this thing through so she could get back to the coffee and Sunday morning paper she'd left behind when he called. "Murder," she said.

"Murder. Of a young man."

"A young man."

"Not just any young man. A basketball player. And not just any basketball player. Miles White."

The name meant nothing to her and she didn't try to pretend that it did.

"Terrific," he said. "Just what I hoped, though it's pretty hard to believe that even you could live and breathe in this town and not know about Miles White. The Boomers' star forward and starter for three years. Conference MVP for two years running. An NBA shoo-in. He put the team on the cover of *Sports Illustrated*. Not once but twice last season."

Starter? MVP? It was sports lingo and nothing to do with her. The yawns were really uncontrollable now. "Sorry," she said. "Not a good night and I didn't have time to finish my second coffee. As far as I'm concerned, a boomer is a mountain beaver—not even a real beaver, mind you."

"Mountain beaver, river beaver, stuffed beaver, doesn't matter. The point is, White is dead. Murdered on a jogging trail. Now get this. He's been missing for a week and no one reported it. A week, Neva. And no one said a word. Their star player. At the start of the season."

Where Ambrose was going with this she had no idea, and she could not even begin to guess why he'd called her rather than the sports editor on a weekend morning. She was a columnist, not a reporter, and her indifference to organized sports was no secret in the newsroom.

"He was found early this morning. He went out jogging last Sunday at Calapooia forest and didn't come back. A week ago. A star player goes missing for a full week and no one reports it, not to the police, not to us, not to anybody. Okay, so Miles was known as a loner, not really a team man in the general sense of the term, but a week? How many assaults of any kind have we ever reported in that park? Nobody randomly mugs a jogger—what are they going to steal? His Nikes? So a premeditated murder is what we've got here. And that's not all. That, my friend, is just the tip of the iceberg."

The editor patted a red file folder, the only object other than a telephone on his broad oak desk. "We've got trouble, big trouble. And I've thought so for a long time. This is the wedge I've been waiting for. This is our big opportunity."

Neva looked steadily at the editor, expecting enlightenment, but he appeared to be waiting for some signal from her. "Ambrose, what am I doing here?"

Rather than answer, he leaned back in the old swivel chair, laced his fingers behind his head, and regarded her for a long moment before announcing with confiding chumminess, "You know what I think? I think you're a snob."

"I'm too old for games, especially on Sunday morning."

"Not a game. Did you know it was because of the Boomers that I took this small-town job? It certainly wasn't a promotion to come here. You do know that the Boomers were rated number one in the nation last year?"

"I was aware that they're a pretty good team."

"Pretty good! They're red hot and rolling. What do you think keeps this town going? What puts Valley State University campus on the map? Not apple maggot research, I can tell you that. Or robotics. Or climate research. Or etc. etc. With your contacts in the community I'm surprised you haven't picked up on all this yourself."

"Of course I'm aware of the general situation. I'm just not interested. The world is full of things that do interest me but competitive sports ain't one of 'em. I simply don't care."

"That brings us to the snob part. You dismiss the importance of sports without knowing anything about it. That's plain arrogant, in my book. No doubt you didn't bother to look at that AP story a while back about traffic accident rates going up all over the country on Super Bowl Sunday? The really interesting bit is that they go up most in the state of the losing team. Just mull that over, okay. As a sort of significance indicator."

Ambrose lifted the flap of the file folder, removed a single sheet of paper, slipped it across the desk. "And there's this. It came in two months ago. Unsigned."

Dear Editor Ambrose,

I'm writing this letter as a sports fan, not somebody that wants to see trouble. But I've been watching the Boomers for too long to play dumb anymore. I'm worried they're going too far and it will hurt the program, which would be a terrible loss to this community. Ask your sports reporters. They know what goes on in the locker rooms and hotels and private homes, and worst of all some businesses, including banks. Or maybe you're afraid to do anything about it? I see you at all the games. If you really care about the program, why don't you do something before it goes too far? For starters, ask Franklin Budd who really owns that nice sports car he drives with the BUDD license plate. And ask Joey Field how he pays for that nice apartment. And Dashiel Clemente where he goes on weekends and how he gets there and what he's expected to do when he's there. And Miles White—what is Miles White up to? Something stinks in Denmark. Need I say more? I'll be watching.

Neva slid the letter back across the desk. "What? No sex with kiddies in the shower?"

"So you do notice sports news."

"Penn State wasn't sports news. It was news news. This stuff in the letter sounds like standard drill for college sports programs. Even I know that."

"Standard drill. Well, well." Ambrose's chuckle was deep and relishing. "Okay, let's walk through this. College sports is big business, a multi-billion-dollar industry. Some say we should stop pretending it's amateur and treat these guys like the pros they are. But the fact is college players aren't considered pros and aren't supposed to be treated like pros. The NCAA are the cops of college sports. They make the rules about recruiting and what a school and boosters are allowed to do for the players. Most of all, though, what they aren't supposed to do for them. Now consider what would happen if nobody was making rules. Schools would go out and buy the best high school players they could get, and fly them around in style, and pamper the hell out of them. Because if you have a winning team, you make more money. But it's more than money. Everybody wants a winning team. It puts a school on the map, everybody feels good, the alumni love it, the town loves it. Everybody loves it. Everybody concerned walks tall. Look what happened in College Station when they fired Paterno. Riots. That tells you something right there."

"Did you play basketball in high school?"

The editor nodded.

"Did you play in college?"

"Just pick-up games. I wasn't good enough to be recruited."

"Are you a booster?"

"God no. I never miss a game but I don't go near the players. It's a game to me, not a lifestyle. But some of these fans, well, you'll see for yourself. It's not pretty. I don't know why the NCAA hasn't caught wind of this yet, but they will. White's death may trip their alarm the way it's tripping mine. We need to get this story, Neva. This is our story. It's nobody else's story. A hometown paper can't let itself be scooped on something like this, which is just what will happen if we don't get on it. Besides, it's a damn good story, a potentially great story that will rattle a lot of cages."

"If you love it so much, why do you want to rattle cages? Just out of curiosity, old friend."

"You would ask that, wouldn't you? But here's the thing. For some of us, it's all about quality. You can't really believe in quality on the court if there's corruption all around it, even I can see that."

The editor looked down, shook his head in what looked to Neva like genuine sorrow or regret, but the next instant was burbling over again with newshound glee. "To top it all off, there's the almost unbelievable imbalance in money, in pay. The athletes are supposed to be amateurs, in other words poor and honest. Meanwhile the coaches and ADs are cleaning up. Some top coaches pull in more than $6 million, and that's just base pay—they win and even more pours in. For a little perspective here, the president of this great nation of ours gets paid $400,000 to lead the free world. Coach Krzyzewski at Duke scored over $9 million in 2014. Are you hearing this?"

"Of course, but the real question is why are you telling me? Where's Cal? He should be able to write this kind of thing out of his head." She and sports editor Cal Humphrey rarely had reason to talk beyond pleasantries, but he knew his stuff—at least, he gave every indication of being a journalist on top of his material.

"That, in a nutshell, is the problem. Cal's too close to the forest, Neva. All the sports guys are too close to see the trees. I've talked to Cal about it in the past and he said it's no big deal, 'no different from anywhere' as he puts it. No, this story needs a fresh eye. Your eye, in fact."

"Oh, no. No no no. Nope. No way."

The editor held up his hand. "Whoa."

"For starters," she went on, "the murder's a crime story. I can't believe White was killed by a booster so you get Charlie working on the murder. Since there's nothing actually criminal about pampering basketball players, that would be a higher ed story."

"Maybe the murder's separate, maybe it's not. That's one of the things we have to find out. We also need to know the extent of this thing, how far it's gone. You've got a dozen guys out there, most of them black in a whitey town, built like gods, playing basketball like angels. You've got a bunch of fat rich old men who want to get next to them and a university administration that depends on a winning team, on the big money that comes with it. A lot could go wrong in a picture like that. You might think it bothers me that you don't know diddlysquat about basketball, but that's exactly why I called you. Well, that and your working style. I'm asking you to go out there, snoop around all big-eyed and innocent like you do, and come back and tell me what's going on."

"Sorry, Ambrose. I can't do it. You know how I work. If I don't care about something, if it doesn't give me a chill or make me laugh, I don't do good work. And believe me, this subject leaves me about as cold as cold could be. You need someone who cares, really cares. And it's not column material. If I put in the time and energy it would take to run this to ground and write some news stories—that's what you want, right?—I won't be able to do the column."

"Take a week off the column. Two weeks. Hell, we'll run wire copy or rerun some of your oldies. The change might even be good for you. Let's just say I have a hunch. I think you're wrong about not being the right dog for the bone. The players won't have a clue where you're coming from, while on the other hand, the boosters all know you, at least by name. Oh, yes. I've got a list of the most visible boosters here, and every one will ring a bell."

He took another single sheet from the folder and slid it over. Without picking it up, she glanced down the list. Hal Richter (lawyer), Jasper Luce (developer), Vern Varney (car dealer), Lyle Crisp (insurance), Bill Tunney (gas station), J.P. Cornish (jeweler), Tucker Reilly (court club). She recognized all but Cornish and Luce, although the only one she actually knew was Lyle Crisp, an energetic and personable man who had coached her son Ethan's soccer team the last year he played with city league.

"Another funny thing," said Ambrose. "Jasper Luce is, or was, a big-time land developer but the word is he left town in a hurry not long ago. It may mean nothing but on the other hand. . . Here, I dug these out for you."

This time he handed her the folder itself. In it was a manila envelope full of smaller envelopes, each one clipped to a sheet of paper covered in type. Written on the outside of each small envelope were a name, a position, and a year. Each one contained a mug shot.

"Those were taken when they were freshmen. The bios are there too. Positions, standing in the conference, all that."

Neva scanned one of the bio sheets. "It's gibberish to me. I'd have to learn a whole new language to do this right."

"I suggest talking to the players first, before tackling the boosters. Start with the guys who've used up their eligibility. They'll have less at stake in protecting people."

"I don't even know what you mean by 'used up their eligibility.' You see how crazy this is."

"Eligibility to play. Each player gets four years of active scholarship support, plus a fifth year after they're done playing."

"Then they graduate?"

Instead of replying, the editor opened the top drawer of his desk and took out a five-by-seven photo of a tall young black man in blue cotton pants and shirt. On one hand he balanced a broom, on the other a basketball.

"Joshua Gifford, blue chip guard and starter for three years, but not quite National Basketball Association material. He played like he was born to be a Boomer. For four years he played his big heart out. Now he's a janitor at a grade school in East L.A."

He played his big heart out...It was a calculated shot on Ambrose's part but even knowing this Neva could not duck the impact. Refusing to show the hit, she said, "He was a student at the university for five years with a scholarship, which is more than a lot of students get. Surely, he could have made better use of it."

"That's fine, that's just fine," Ambrose said as though encouraging a child on training wheels. "It's good to start with the basics so you get the whole picture. It may take a while to grasp this, but these guys aren't really students. Most of them haven't been real students since they were little squirts and somebody noticed they could get the ball through the hoop nine times out of ten. They've been passed from grade to grade whether they could read or not. Then they end up in college, functionally illiterate, stuck into remedial classes and no time to do homework even for those who are interested. Some schools, like Chapel Hill—look it up—set up a whole system of bogus classes with bogus grades to make sure they wouldn't get suspended. No one realistically expects them to get a degree in four years while playing. Just the away games would kill them. So they get the fifth year and suddenly they're supposed to be full-time, serious students. By that point they've got maybe half the credits needed to graduate, and only a year to finish, and rotten study habits. How many do you think actually make it? We don't know, never been able to get the figures. The NCAA has a rule that at least 50 percent of conference athletes have to graduate. Fifty percent! A few go on to the pros but most don't make it. The university has no more use for them and they have no more use for the university, so they go home and get a job sweeping hallways."

Neva looked steadily at the editor, waiting for the significance of his words to hit her *I care* button again. It did sound like a bad business, but the athletes, at least, had been given a big chance. The country was full of kids who were lost before they reached middle school.

"You see?" Ambrose urged. "Tell me what you're thinking."

When you don't know what to say, repeat what you've been told.

"Well, let's see. We have a dead basketball player, murdered in the park. We have rumors that the school and certain boosters are way out of line according to college basketball rules. We have players who are on the team for four years and then end up janitors. We have an anonymous letter saying the rot extends into local businesses, including banks. You think this is all related and you want me to go out and piece it together and write some news stories instead of my column."

"You got it. Don't worry about the basic story on White's death. The newsroom can handle that. Focus on the big picture. Plan on starting today and we'll shoot for running the first story two weeks from now. Unless, of course, you think you can do it faster? It's early in the season, the players are mostly in town now. I suggest you start with Clayton Perle. He played his final season last year but has stuck around for another year of school, and I hear from the sports guys he's having some problems adjusting to his new status as Mr. Nobody. And he lives just down the street. Convenient, eh?"

She had not said she would go along with the editor's plan. The words she spoke were automatic, stalling for time to think. "Wouldn't it make more sense to start with the police?"

"That's part of the basic murder story, finding of body, cause of death, etc. The booster trail is the one you should follow. It wouldn't hurt to go over to the cop shop tomorrow and read the police reports on White, but the guys you want to talk to are eight feet tall and black, or wearing business suits and a drooling grin."

"Okay then, if we're starting with a player, wouldn't it be better to go for one mentioned in the letter?"

"I thought of that, but the only one mentioned who's no longer on the team is Franklin Budd and he has disappeared, literally dropped out of sight with no forwarding address. Like Jasper Luce, come to think of it. Cal wanted to do a final feature story on him and couldn't find anyone willing to admit knowing where Budd's got to even though he's still a student. Now get this. Since he left the team, Budd usually ran on Sundays with Miles White, but it seems he didn't go along last Sunday. One dead, one disappeared. You see why I'm a little worked up? You'll find Budd an interesting character. He's damned smart and I hear he might even graduate. As for Perle, I'd be willing to bet he'll be history by June. He never did shine for brains, but my god could he dance."

CHAPTER
2

Long powerful arms. Big hands hanging empty next to polished ebony thighs. Glossy blue and white shorts and tank top.

It was Sunday morning. Perle was no longer on the team. Why was he dressed in full Boomer colors as though about to play?

He never did shine for brains, but my god could he dance.

"Clayton Perle?"

"That's me." Perle filled the open doorway, his head barely clearing the top.

She had to look up, way up, to find his eyes. "I'm Neva Leopold, from the *Willamette Current*. Do you have a few minutes to talk? Sorry not to call first."

"I already talked to the cops."

Walking the six blocks from the newspaper building to the basketball player's studio apartment, she had tried to find a way to do this without using the murder to get through the door. But now Perle had brought it up and this was just fine. With a smile, she said, "Police and reporters are interested in different things. Could I come in, please?"

Stepping back without another word, Perle pivoted and sat down on the foot of a bed that was directly in front of the door. Facing him and only a few feet away against the wall was a television tuned to a basketball game with the sound off.

Neva closed the door and stood in the half dark waiting for a clue to tell her what to do next. The room was narrow, with no way around the bed other than by squeezing between Clayton's bare knees and the dresser that held the television. On this side there was nothing but a band of empty carpet between the bed and the heavily draped window next to the door. Beyond the bed was a small living area with a table, two straight chairs, and a counter with kitchen built-ins. To the right of the counter the open bathroom door showed a toilet with the seat up and towels on the floor. A sweet smell of shampoo lay heavy on the air with a sharp note under it, possibly urine.

The bed was heaped with laundry, dirty laundry, mostly boxer shorts and wadded athletic socks. Using her thumb and one finger, Neva drew the corner of a limp sheet over the laundry and sat down behind Perle with her right leg folded and the left extended so her foot was off the bed but not on the floor.

At first, Perle watched the game in silence, sitting as though frozen, but then his right arm swept up, hung a moment, and dropped. His torso twitched and he leaned sharply forward, grunted, and sat upright again. Shifting for a clearer view around his left shoulder, Neva saw a swarm of players and above them a ball arcing toward a basket. The ball hit the rim and bounced out of sight. Perle blew through closed lips and hit his thigh with a balled fist.

One team was dressed like Perle in Bloomer blue and white, the other in maroon and gold.

"What game is this?" she said.

"Last week. Arizona."

"Oh, right. Arizona."

Minutes passed. Riveted on the small screen, Perle seemed to forget her existence. Shifting again so she could see without leaning, Neva studied the action. Powerful legs and arms flashed, the ball slammed down through the hoop and net, huge feet thundered—soundlessly—down the golden surface of the court. It was all close-ups and confusion. The scoreboard showed 68 to 42. The Boomers were ahead. Had they won? This she could not ask.

Her attention shifted to the monochrome tattoo that ran across the back of Perle's shoulders. The beads of a rosary draped with surprising grace into the hollow between his heavy shoulder blades and encircled a three-dimensional cross. Under the cross in looping print were the words *Life, Love, Faith.* The pious message was not quite what it seemed, however, for the 'o' in love was a devil's face with tiny horns.

"Clayton?"

"Uh."

"Do you always watch with the sound off?"

"Uh-huh."

"Why is that?"

"Makes me sick."

"What's that? What makes you sick?"

"Coach yelling."

Neva's hand went to her jacket pocket and her fingers curled around the narrow notebook. But she did not take it out. She looked around, perplexed. This was one of the pampered athletes, wooed and won by recruiters, paid by scholarship to be on a campus where other students went into debt for the privilege. He was healthy, strong, in college, and in his short life had already enjoyed more kudos and adulation than most people get in a lifetime. Yet here he sat alone in a cave-like apartment dressed as though he should still be loping back and forth across the screen rather than watching the action in pantomime because the coach—his own former coach—made him sick to hear.

"Clayton," she said gently. "I really do need to talk with you. It won't take long."

"Talk then." The words were flat rather than rude, a statement rather than an invitation.

"Okay. In all honesty, I have to say I don't know a lot about basketball but I've been asked to help out on some stories. Stories about what it's like to be a star player in a town like Willamette."

No response.

"I'm hoping you can tell me what this whole experience has been like for you. Moving here from Los Angeles and living in this small community as a sports celebrity."

No response.

"The thing is, most of us are never famous in our whole lives, not even for four minutes let alone four years."

Clayton let out a low snort that might or might not have signaled amusement. Choosing to take the reaction as encouragement, she said, "I've heard about certain kinds of things that happen with athletes, especially the star players, and I hope you can help me understand, most of all tell me if the things I've heard are true."

"What things?"

"For instance, that some players get free clothes at some of the stores in town."

"Free clothes."

"Yes, clothes and other things as well. Did anybody in the community ever help you out in special ways?"

"Friends."

"Friends?"

"Athletes need friends, too."

"Of course they do, but were some of the friends not students? Were some of them community members?"

"Community members?"

"Sure, community members. You know, business people, fans, townspeople."

Slowly, almost ponderously, Clayton turned on the bed to study her, frowning. "Who are you again?"

"Jeneva Leopold. From the newspaper, the *Willamette Current*. I thought I explained."

"What are you asking me questions for?"

"I'm interested in what it was like to play for the Boomers, to go to this school as an athlete and live in this town. Now that you're finished playing, I thought you might have some interesting things to say about what it's like to come here from another city and live as a student, but a sort of famous student who attracts a lot of attention. And support. Quite a lot of support."

Clayton shifted to sit sideways, not quite facing her. His knee, the biggest knee she had ever seen close up, was inches from her own puny knee in faded olive pants. "Are you asking me did anybody give me stuff they weren't supposed to?"

"Well, yes, actually, that's just what I'm asking. Did they? Special favors, clothes, dinners, you know."

"Friends, friends of mine, friends bought me dinner. I am an athlete. I am an athlete but I am also a person. If anybody ever did anything for me, bought me stuff or gave me money or took me places, it was because they were my friends, they cared about me. About *me*."

"And are they still buying you things now that you're no longer on the team?" Her glance swept the comfortless room.

Clayton sat in silence, his face without expression.

"Speaking of giving, you gave this school a lot. Are you going to get a degree out of it?"

Waiting through the next silence was almost more than she could manage without trying to soften it. *Of course you have friends. It must be really strange to sit here watching the team that used to be the center of your life and now you have no part in it* . . . but she was not his mother.

"I've got to go to the library." He turned away from her and again put both feet on the floor. Reaching without having to lean forward, he grasped the handle of an athletic bag that sat on the dresser next to the television and swung it toward him easily despite the books that bulged out the open top. He let the bag drop hard onto the floor at the foot of the bed.

Neva waited but he didn't pick up the bag and didn't respond when she thanked him for the conversation. He looked at the screen until she let herself out.

CHAPTER
3

Okay, it did look dismal. She could see that. Clayton was frozen, stuck in place, unable to move on from being a Boomer star. Everyone else had moved on—players, fans, coaches, boosters—leaving him stranded in ugly apartment limbo.

But he didn't have to sit in his own dirty laundry on Sunday morning watching television. He didn't have to keep wearing his numbered jersey. He was a student. His bag was full of books. He was still supported by scholarship money. There were a lot worse situations to be in.

As for the interview, it didn't even deserve the name. A bust, a total bust. She had learned nothing and had failed to connect with Perle in any way. This was a charade, a pointless charade. She didn't care one bit what happened to athletes as a group, though she could not help feeling a bit sorry for the big droopy character she'd just left to his own gloom.

Walking, absorbed by her thoughts, Neva found herself approaching the newspaper building and stopped abruptly. Ambrose was waiting for her. If she tried to quit the story now he'd say it was too early, that one bad interview doesn't mean defeat. And he might not see it as a failure. He might be intrigued by the silent television, might nod in satisfaction over Clayton's confession that "friends" had done things for him. Even the miserable apartment might look like evidence—today you're a hero, tomorrow you're a bum.

It had been a long time since she'd left an interview feeling so dissatisfied. That she knew nothing about college basketball was not sufficient excuse. Over the years, she had taken on many new and difficult subjects, had tracked down and won over sources far tougher and more daunting than a mute young athlete. Her very first story had put her on the scene where a man had been eaten by his pet lion, nothing left but the chewed skull, and she hadn't flinched. . . Had she lost her edge? Two decades ago, as a reporter in San Diego and then Seattle, she'd done hard time on the investigative rock pile. Maybe life as a small-town columnist was so easy and safe she'd forgotten how to find the vulnerable spot and go for it. Her questions had been direct but they'd lacked strategy, lacked the necessary finesse to steer Perle into indiscretion, into spilling the beans without realizing he was giving himself away.

On the other hand, maybe her initial reaction had been right and this was not a story she could work effectively. Why get excited over free dinners for ball dribblers? Especially when it was a story repeated all over the country for decades. White's death was something else altogether, but that was not her territory, not the ground she'd been asked to plough.

She had turned around while musing and was walking toward downtown now, toward the river and, yes, why not? She would go to the Beanery to continue mulling things over. Since taking up home coffee roasting, she had got out of the habit of frequenting coffee shops—even her worst roasts were generally better, and certainly fresher, than what was available by the cup—but she sometimes missed the friendly café hubbub, especially of the old Beanery on First Street, favorite haunt of the underemployed, internet addicted, activist youth, Valley State faculty oddballs, and what remained of the old Sixties radicals.

One of the popular small tables by the front window was free. She draped her jacket on a chair and joined the line at the counter. Soon back at the table again, she opened her notebook but could think of nothing to note. She should at least have asked about Miles White, which Clayton had clearly expected. It might have got him talking. Really, it had been her worst interview in years, maybe forever.

"Jeneva! At long last." A short, tight-knit man with the ruddy cheeks of an all-weather outdoorsman—in this case, a runner—

pulled out the chair on the other side of the table. "Mind if I sit down? I never drink unless I'm alone or with somebody."

Laughing obligingly at the hackneyed line, Neva waved a welcome as he set down his mug with the strainer full of sodden tea on top, chamomile by the look of it. Gerry Farnes was a plant physiologist, a small man crackling with big energy. They had met some years before, here in the Beanery, when the only empty seat had been at Neva's table. Settling into it, he had glanced at her and done one of those double takes she knew so well.

"You're Jeneva Leopold! I'll be damned. I never miss your column. Really. If it doesn't make me laugh it makes me think and sometimes both at once. And, listen, I've got a great idea for you." And then he had proceeded to tell her all about the idiots in state government who couldn't tell a university from a microchip manufacturer. "It's all cash in and product out to them. Size, that's all. If we're not big and not growing we're failing. Never mind what's actually happening to students. Or the community, for that matter."

She never had discovered specifically what he wanted her to write about, and maybe just getting it off his chest had been enough. Though after that day he'd sat with her a number of times before she gave up the regular Beanery habit he'd never raised the subject again. He did, however, pass along tidbits of campus gossip that were always welcome. Now she said, "Are you a Boomers fan?"

"Does a bear shit in the woods? What are you doing, going after the basketball boys?"

"Do you know of anything to go after?"

"You bet. I mean, you get heroes like that, nothing but overgrown kids, and you're bound to have trouble. It's an old story, not just here but all over the country. I'm not talking about Penn State stuff, you understand, no kiddie sex, at least as far as I know. And no paying big bucks to players for crippling the opposition. But I hear about other things all the time. Just this morning I heard two guys in the locker room. One was Jake Something-or-other from economics. The other guy I think is on the faculty senate but I don't know his name or department. Anyway, Jake says to the other guy, 'You have any players this term?' And the other guy says, 'No. How about you?' And Jake says, 'I've got Joey Field in my 300 level.' 'Joey Field!' the other guy says, and whistles. 'Is he passing?' Now, this is the good part. Jake says, 'He flunked the midterm the first time but passed on the second try.'"

Gerry waited so visibly for a reaction that she said almost sheepishly, "You'll have to explain, I'm afraid."

"Ah, Neva, you've been out of school too long. Think back. Did you ever get a second try at a midterm? Field was the only student who got to take it again, all by his little self—like a special film showing. It's not like he was out of town. It seems he was tired from the Stanford game when he took it the first time. He made the winning shot in that game, in case you forgot. I don't have anything against the players. Hell, I'm a jock myself, and I watch the games. But this is supposed to be an institution of higher learning. I'm on the Academic Deficiencies Committee and I can tell you it's a rare day in hell that a scholarship athlete gets the boot. In fact, I've never seen it happen. They say everybody fudges grades for athletes so we have to do it too, to be competitive. Though, come to think of it, you see fewer athletes in regular classes these days, since they built that new academic assistance center or whatever they call it. Where they spoon feed them. Wonder if they get crackers and nap time, too?"

"Would you say they're capable of doing real coursework under the right circumstances? Or are they dumb jocks?"

"Don't tell me you buy that brawn and no brains bullshit. Do you have any idea how hard it is to be a good basketball player? I mean really good. You can't be stupid. You have to think as fast as the ball's moving. You have to have synapses that won't quit. These guys are no dummies. They mostly don't have the time or the skills to study. But they could."

"Do you know Clayton Perle?"

"Everybody knows Clayton Perle. He's better known in this state than the governor, if you want to be honest about it. What about Clayton?"

"I just tried to talk to him about being a scholarship athlete."

"I didn't know he was still in town."

"He stayed the extra year to finish his degree."

"Is that supposed to be funny? He's been up before the deficiencies committee so many times we call him the Bouncer.

He was in my general botany class one year. I don't think he ever bought the book. They tried to talk me into giving him a D for showing up. They said they could find me some good seats for the next home game."

"They?"

"The usual mafia—athletic director Rex Gregorio and a couple of assistant coaches. I told them to go buy somebody else's soul. Anyway, the Boomers were losing that season. So what is your interest in all this?"

"I've been asked to do a little poking around, see what I can turn up about possible NCAA violations."

"Did you ever go to practice?"

"I've never seen a game."

"For chrissakes, Neva, how can you expect to understand anything? You have to see a game. You won't believe the energy in that coliseum. These guys are like dancers, like gladiators doing ballet, if you will. First go watch a game, and then go to practice and see who comes in."

"Who comes in?"

"All the fat cats who run this town. It always struck me as a little sick the way they suck up to those boys."

"So you're a regular at practice yourself?"

"That's right, but I'm there for the beauty of the game, nothing else."

"Funny. That's exactly what my editor said."

"Well, maybe we do get some thrills, some vicarious something or other just from being in the same room with that kind of physical perfection. But I wouldn't cross the street to talk to a player. I have to get going now but I'll tell you what. You go see a game and I'll keep my ears open. I'm sick and tired of suspending athletes for flunking out and having the committee's decision overturned by the president. One word of caution. The Boomers didn't get where they are on sugar and spice. Rex Gregorio doesn't really answer to anybody, not even President Havesham. He's capable of just about anything to keep the Boomers in the national spotlight."

"Including murder?"

"Of course not—Neva, what are you saying?"

"Miles White is dead. Shot through the head. It'll be in tomorrow's paper."

Farnes stared at her for a long silent moment. When he spoke it was with more wonder than shock. "Miles White. Miles White. He was so *big*, so really *big*, if you know what I mean. So packed with life. I can't picture him dead. I can't really believe it. Who'd do such a thing? It's going to change things. Really, really change things."

CHAPTER
4

Getting her car out of the *Current* parking lot without being seen turned out to be easier than expected. Before approaching the car, she stood briefly behind a rhododendron bush across from Ambrose's office window and studied what she could see through the glass. She was in luck. The editor was not at his desk.

Moving briskly, not looking again at the building, she got into the car and was out of the lot within seconds and around the corner where she pulled over to fasten her seatbelt. It was absurd to play hide-and-seek with Ambrose, but far easier than reporting back to him before she had anything to say.

Joey Field's apartment was on the west side of campus in a small, well-kept complex enclosing three sides of a swimming pool that had been drained for the winter. Number 6 was on the ground floor facing the pool. Neva parked on the opposite side of the pool with a view of the apartment door through cyclone fencing. She did not get out of the car.

So Clayton Perle was *better known in this state than the governor* . . . Clayton who was washed up high and dry in a pile of laundry, Clayton who was stuck in front of a Boomers rerun on a Sunday morning dressed in full Boomers colors, Clayton who thought the people of Willamette were his true friends, Clayton who had *been up before the deficiencies committee so many times we call him the Bouncer.*

And Joey Field got to take the midterm twice . . . *all by his little self—like a special film showing.*

Maybe she should ask Field how he'd done on that exam?

No. No way. You just don't ask about grades—these days it was easier to ask about religious faith or even sexual orientation than about grades. Or income. Or personal weight.

Funny thing about taboo subjects and how they change over time. She had opened the door to get out of the car but paused to write a note: *taboo subjects of conversation, change with eras*. It would make an amusing column subject when she got back to her proper role again.

Before ringing Field's bell she stood for a moment on the tidy porch to consider his cheerful red door. Of course, the choice had been the property owner's and not Joey's—every door in the complex was a bright color—but still she felt the warming effect and smiled as she pressed the button. Chimes sounded within and the door sprang open. A beaming young man stood with his arms spread wide as though to embrace her.

"Oh," he said and laughed. "I thought you were a friend."

"I may not be a friend but I like to think I'm friendly," Neva managed to quip and laughed in turn.

"Are you a friend of Vera's?" He stepped back to let her in without waiting for a reply. Poised and handsome in tan slacks and a cream turtleneck, he might have been an actor playing the role of an athlete relaxing at home. Shorter than Clayton, his body made almost ordinary by clothing, he stood at ease with his hands in his trouser pockets, smiling with expectant interest as she introduced herself.

"I didn't know the paper had a new sports reporter." He gestured toward a leather couch and settled across from her in a matching recliner.

"I'm not really a sports reporter. That is, I don't generally write about sports."

"So what's up?"

Field's look of intelligent interest demanded a straightforward response, and without taking time to consider whether it was strategically wise, Neva said, "I'd like to talk with you about something that isn't actually basketball, not directly anyway."

The change in Field was dramatic. His smile vanished, his shoulders hunched, and the self-possessed man gave way to the anxious boy. "Not sports? What then? What about? Oh, I know, oh, my god, what an idiot." He slapped his forehead and sat up straight again. "It's Miles. You're here about Miles. It's so terrible, really unbelievable. But I'm afraid I can't be much help. He didn't show up for practice Monday and we all wondered, but you have to understand. And this is what I said to the cops this morning. Miles was Miles. He did what he wanted. He disappeared before, a couple times actually. No explanation."

"Didn't he have any close friend on the team, someone who might worry?"

"Miles was only close with one person, his girlfriend. You better talk to her. Talk to Annette."

"I will, thank you for the suggestion."

"Sorry," he said with what sounded like genuine regret. "I wish I could be more help. It's pretty shocking. We're all still processing it, if you know what I mean. They've called a meeting for this afternoon."

"Of course." She let a moment pass. What had alarmed this pleasant young man if not White's murder? Something was on his mind, something he did not want to talk about. Casually, with a smile, she said, "I'm afraid it's my job to ask awkward questions. But you can handle it, right?"

"Sure. I mean, I hope so. What questions?"

"I'm not actually here about the murder. Another reporter is working on that. This probably sounds trivial given the news about Miles, but what I came to ask you about is the rather serious situation with some rule violations. I realize you might not want to say things you think would hurt the team, but letting the situation go on as it is could hurt the team more in the long run than getting the truth out in the open now."

Self-possessed again, speaking calmly, Joey said, "I'm afraid I can't help you much on that either. I'm only aware of the circumstances surrounding my own situation. I did something wrong, and I think the decision they made for me was more than fair because I'll still get to play when it really counts. I should have said, 'Excuse me, sir. This is against the rules.'"

"Ah, yes." What had she stumbled onto here? Not just getting to take his exam over again, this much was clear. Matching his easy tone, she said, "That sounds like a very reasonable attitude."

"Well, I got caught red-handed, and we'd been told. Only I didn't know Coach Leonard was going to tell the paper about it. He only talked to me yesterday. How did you find out?"

"Well, you know how it is in a small town. The newspaper's tapped in."

"Did they tell you how much I sold the tickets for?"

"Not exactly. A lot, it seems."

"Well, yes. But I'd rather not say how much. That's the private business of the people who bought the tickets. At least the suspension's only for two games. It's early in the season."

"That's a very mature attitude, Joey. I'm not sure which is worse, selling tickets or accepting some of the other favors athletes receive from boosters. What do you think?"

"I'm not the one to point a finger at anyone. I don't know anything in depth about past players, although you do hear of this kind of thing at all schools, don't you? You couldn't compare the number of boosters here with the number at some places I've seen, and I mean in our conference. And the school with the most boosters and other bennies gets the best players because they have the most to offer. To some people, that's a good thing."

"It sounds as though you think there's nothing wrong with people giving players free clothes or rent or whatever it might be. Is that right?"

He nodded.

She mentally checked off *clothes, rent.* "Do you think the rules are unreasonable?"

"I don't think I'm at the point in my life to evaluate what should be in the rule book. These men in their fifties and sixties have made the rules and if we don't follow them, we suffer the consequences."

"You talk like a lawyer in the making."

"Thank you. I'm a speech communications major."

"Do you think they make sense, though. The rules? Do you agree with them in principle?"

Joey fixed his gaze on a wall clock made from a smooth circle of golden wood. "I'm not so much questioning the rules but what I did was not against any godly law or even government law. They're just basketball rules." His gaze shifted to the dark leather shoe on his left foot. "Of course, they were made up by some intelligent men so they must make sense, and I mean they do change them sometimes, like what recruiters can do and everything. I mean you have to have rules, right? I have to accept them like everyone else."

"But does everyone accept them? That's not what we hear. I hear that some players get free shopping accounts at local stores for pretty much anything they want." She kept her eyes on Joey and did not look at the elaborate entertainment center that took up the end wall. She remembered the lumpy sofa and board shelves she had used as a student way back when.

"Most guys jump at it," he said and then stopped, frowned, shifted in the chair. "I think at every school in America there's at least one."

"One what?"

"One person who breaks all the rules. I mean, anybody could be tempted. And I think we deserve it. I deserve it."

"Deserve what?"

Joey stood and walked to the kitchen doorway and back again, his hands moving up and down in his pants pockets as though rubbing his thighs. "Friends. I deserve friends. Who's to say if I wasn't an athlete that a certain person wouldn't do a nice thing for me? Most of the people I know here I've met through athletics, but that's because that's what I do. If they do something nice for me, it might be because they like me."

"Certainly. What nice things might they do for you?"

"I didn't say they did. But if they did, and were caught, it wouldn't be the older people getting in trouble because these aren't community rules. It's the players that get identified and that isn't fair. In that way, the rules stink."

Wet streaks on Joey's forehead caught the light from the window—he was sweating. Ten minutes of conversation about NCAA rules and this star athlete was dripping wet.

"I agree," Neva said, feeling like a cheat. "That's why I'm trying to find out who the community members are, and what they do, so it doesn't all come down on the players. Who bought your tickets?"

"No." Again Joey paced to the kitchen and turned to face her from the doorway. "I've said too much already and it's not important anyway. I'll be playing again soon and this will all blow over. I don't know why your newspaper wants to make a mountain out of it. I'm sorry but I've got to go now, I've got something to do. You'll have to leave."

He strode to the door and snatched it open. A woman stood just outside with her hand raised to ring the bell. "Vera!"

Petite in white stretch pants and a yellow sweater that looked bright as a lamp against her dark skin, Vera let her slender hand drop to rest on a white bag that hung from her shoulder. She looked at Joey, eyebrows raised. "I hope I'm not interrupting?"

"We're just finishing an interview," Neva said, amused and instantly liking the young woman. "One last thing. Do you know where Franklin Budd lives? I understand he just moved."

With his original poise in place once again, Joey gave a firm shake of the head. "He's done playing and he's just a student like anybody else. I don't see him much."

"And good riddance!" Vera said, but at a quick gesture from Joey she put a hand over her mouth and winked at Neva.

"Isn't it going to be hard on the team to be without you and Miles?"

"No kidding. I didn't think I'd be suspended. Of course, that was before we found out about Miles. And like I said, it's early in the season."

"Can I talk to you again?"

"I don't have anything to say."

"You could talk to me," said Vera. "I have plenty to say. What are you interested in?"

This time Joey clapped a playful hand over Vera's mouth and Neva left to the sound of laughter.

CHAPTER
5

A sweet pair, really, she liked them both very much. Still caught in the warmth of the young relationship, Neva stood again for a moment outside Joey's door. She was glad Vera had arrived at that instant; it would leave Field with a happier aftertaste from the interview, and also allowed her to feel easier about making him sweat. They would talk again no doubt, and as for the beaming Vera, if only she'd thought to get her last name. She must remember to get it from Cal.

And what a contrast between the two athletes—Field confident, talkative, well-dressed and well-housed, Perle stunned and mute in his drab den. Ambrose would certainly find the differences

Approaching her car, she passed a convertible parked two spaces over that she hadn't noticed when she arrived, and given that it was the same bright yellow as Vera's sweater it would be a hard one to miss. She glanced back at the apartment, then circled to peer in the driver's side window. Nothing. Not even a used to-go cup. The car was clean enough inside and out to have come straight off the sales lot.

She'd never attempted to find a car owner by checking the license number with the Department of Motor Vehicles in Salem but it might be the simplest and most discreet way to get Vera's last name and address. She wrote down the number, returned to her car, and headed back toward downtown on Boomer

Boulevard, the broad avenue that bordered the south side of campus.

The street passed right next to the coliseum and its vast parking lot, which was almost empty today. On game days, whether football or basketball, the lot was packed, a sea of cars, trucks and campers jammed among barbecues, camp chairs, coolers, portable fire pits and rain shelters. Drifting smoke, music, laughter. She tended to avoid the neighborhood on such days because of traffic, but sometimes forgot and found herself in a suddenly strange country where all the cars flew snappy flags and the people were decked out in every kind of blue and white getup imaginable, including face paint and feathers.

On sunny days, she had sometimes felt a wistful sense of exclusion, of missing out on the best party in town. On rainy days, she thought they were all nuts. The mass tailgaters made more sense in fall, and hadn't the ritual once been only for football? She could not recall when it had happened—maybe when the Boomer basketball boys started appearing on the cover of *Sports Illustrated* regularly—but now the partying raged even through February downpours.

With an abrupt swing of the steering wheel, she turned into the lot. Gerry Farnes was right. If she did not understand the huge attraction of competitive college sports, how could she grasp what was wrong with the scene? It was midafternoon on Sunday, only a handful of cars clustered near the door. Did the Boomers practice on Sundays—but this was not a normal Sunday. They were all "processing" the murder, Joey had said, and a meeting had been called for later.

It was not a good day to get the feel of the place, but even so she drove across the wide lot to park with the other cars near the side door. For ten long slow minutes no one went in and no one came out of the coliseum. At length, she drew her notebook from her coat pocket where it had remained for the whole of her visit with Joey Field, as usual for touchy interviews. Now she tried to recall exactly what he had said. Years of practice had given her a near verbatim memory for the important bits and she easily filled three pages.

She had set the notebook aside and was wondering whether to venture into the building or wait for a more active day, when the double doors opened and a man and woman stepped out—and what a woman. Masses of bright red hair above a white face, a long body strategically zipped into a snug green jumpsuit. She would have been striking anywhere but appearing through a doorway that should have produced basketball players turned her into an apparition.

She spoke to the man, a sporty figure in down vest and skinny jeans, and pointed toward the street that ran past the front of the coliseum. As though on command, he strode up the walkway to the front corner of the building, peered around it, and sprang back in cartoon-like alarm.

Evidently alarmed in turn, the woman sprinted toward the parked cars with long athletic strides and leaped into the driver's seat of a dark blue van. The van was already rolling when the man reached it and yanked open the passenger's side door.

Neva started her car as well, intending to follow them out to the street, but the van swung in a tight circle and sped west across the empty lot toward the most distant exit. Unprepared to make a high-speed chase just out of curiosity, she drove instead toward the exit closest to the coliseum. Slowing down as she reached the corner of the building, she eased forward until she could see the main entrance where the public crowded in by the thousands on game days. Now the wide entry was deserted apart from two police cars parked in the passenger loading zone. The cars were empty. There was no sign of anything in the least alarming, nothing to make a man leap backward and flee—unless it was the mere sight of the police cars themselves?

Ambrose met her at the office door rubbing his hands in such theatrical anticipation that she protested, "I'm not delivering chocolates."

"Five hours with Clayton Perle!" he crowed. "You must have got his whole life story."

Neva sank onto the visitor's chair and dropped her bag to the floor. "Sorry. He was tight as a clam. I left after an hour with nothing to show for it. Then I went to see Joey Field but didn't do much better there."

The editor went behind his desk and sat down with no sign of disappointment. Folding his hands on the desk rather than leaning back in his usual listening pose, he said, "Shoot," and didn't say another word until she reached the bit about selling tickets.

"Whoa, wait a minute there. Did you say Field was *suspended*?"

"For two games. He thought I already knew about it and that's why I wanted to talk to him."

The editor laughed, shook his head, stood up to peer toward the sports corner, rubbed his hands again, and sat down. "Well, well, well. That's going to rattle some cages. Cal's crew would have got it eventually, for sure when Field didn't play, but this way, we've got the jump on Leonard and might be able to surprise something out of him."

"I thought Leonard didn't take the rules seriously. Now we find out he suspended Field just for selling a few tickets."

"*Just* for selling tickets? That's a serious no-no. Every player gets free tickets for his family, good seats, worth a lot. In other words, easy money. As for Leonard—" the editor shrugged "— I'm sure he takes the rules seriously. Coaches have to or the NCAA would come snooping around. It doesn't mean he thinks the rules are right or cares whether players toe the line, only whether they're caught. Probably enough people knew about this one that he thought he'd better react, but suspension is just cosmetic. It's a slap on the wrist to remind the players to be more careful. And you can bet they'd never have suspended him if it wasn't the start of the season. And they didn't know about White at that point. I'll bet he's kicking himself hard right now. They're down two important players. This will be on the front page tomorrow."

Neva shook her head, slowly, quizzically, studying the editor. "It's out of proportion, Ambrose. It's off balance. Selling tickets has no meaning at all compared with the death of a young man. And yet both are considered front page news. I just can't connect with this in any real way. I worked all morning and didn't get anywhere."

"What do you mean? You made Joey and Clayton nervous. Both admitted that rules are violated but they don't plan to be the ones to tattle with specifics. You beat sports to the news of Joey's suspension. For half a day's work, I'd call that rolling."

"Well, it doesn't feel like much." There was more, there was Gerry's story about the president rescuing suspended players, but she needed something stronger than say-so on that one. When she had facts, documents, verification from officials, she'd pass it along.

Through the glass wall behind the editor, Neva could see city editor J.D. Shelby pouring water into the top of the coffee maker. She was chewing her lip and staring furiously at the empty pot waiting below. In a moment she would snatch the pot off and thrust her half-gallon mug under the drip—she looked up, caught Neva watching, and rolled her eyes in Ambrose's direction.

Neva's thumbs-up made Ambrose turn to look through the glass and wave for the city editor to join them. She came only as far as the open doorway and shook her head as she addressed Neva, "I just hope this isn't contagious."

"You think I'm off the deep end on this but we'll see who has the last laugh," Ambrose retorted. "You'd better leave room for a single column head next to the White story. Joey Field's been benched for selling tickets."

"Since when do we know that?"

"Since Neva came back from talking to him."

"Too bad it's Sunday, I could use a few more hands."

"Call them in."

"I already got Charlie out of bed. And listen to this. He got a call at home last night. It seems one of our local developers isn't really a developer. The caller wouldn't give his name, or say what the real business is, but he said it's worth looking into."

"Not Jasper Luce?"

"No, not Luce. This—"

Ambrose cut her off with an impatient sweep of his hand across the desk as though wiping away a spill. "Just a pissed-off employee making trouble. I get those calls all the time. I hope Charlie's not taking time to work on that today."

"Hear that?" J.D. looked at Neva and again shook her head. "A week ago he would have been all over this. Now it's just a worker with his nose out of joint. Don't you want to know who the developer is, or have you gone off the deep end too? Never mind, I can answer that myself. It's your old pal, Mel Pascolini."

"Oh, lord." Neva had tangled more than once with Pascolini, most recently over his attempt to get the zoning changed from single family to high-density residential on three lots he owned in the city's oldest neighborhood. She said, "If he's not a developer, he's putting on a terrific act."

The city editor went back to her coffee operation and Ambrose went back to basketball as though there'd been no interruption. "Budd's address," he said, sliding over a half sheet of lined paper. *324C Carters Green* was scrawled on it in red ink. "Cal got it but he can't tell us who gave it to him. That's how bad this thing is. My own reporter's forced to keep secrets. Anyway, you've got Budd now."

"Could you tell me again why this matters? It happens all over the country."

"Murder also happens all over the country. That doesn't make it status quo."

"This is not murder, well, aside from White, which I'm accepting for the moment—for the moment—is not a sports issue. As far I can see, the rest of it, the favors and recruiting and so on, is a victimless crime that's a crime just because of convention, or a set of rules, rather than for any intrinsic reason. Joey Field actually put it very well."

"This is a complicated subject, Neva. Enough for now to say it's important because anyone getting caught for serious violations faces real trouble. Like losing conference titles and getting fired. The absolute right and wrong of it is not our business. Our business is to pin down what's happening in this program that shouldn't be happening."

He picked up some printed pages and handed them across the desk. "Notes from Cal. I got him going on the phone while you were gone, things he's seen or heard about. I must say, it's quite an earful for a guy who says he doesn't see much wrong. We'll chew it over in the morning, and you can give me your notes then too. That leaves you free to see Budd on the way home."

"Are you kidding? I haven't had a proper breakfast yet."

"Then eat, and call me after you see Budd."

Though it was afternoon, she fried three eggs in olive oil and topped them with black pepper and freshly grated Romano cheese. In no hurry, she finished reading the Sunday *Current* and most of *The Oregonian* as she drank a rare third cup of coffee for the day. At last, revived, she drove to Budd's triplex south of campus. Apartment C was on the north end. The front walkway was flanked by early yellow primroses and the knocker was decorated with dried lavender.

Neva had to ring twice before the door opened with a sharp crack as though it had stuck on tacky paint. A burglar chain kept the opening to a slit just wide enough to show a shriveled little face topped by fine white hair.

"Franklin Budd? Franklin Budd?" The woman's voice was rasping but eager. "No dear, there's no Franklin Budd here. I've lived here twelve years and three months and I never knew anybody like that, not in A or B either. Maybe your friend lives on Mansion Green instead of Carters Green. Just a moment, I'll get the directory."

A hand spotted with freckles pushed a telephone book through the crack. Knowing it wouldn't help, Neva looked up Budd anyway and, as expected, found his old address on Abigail. "I don't understand it," she said with a puzzled shake of the head. "Are you sure he doesn't live in one of the other units?"

"Oh, perfectly sure, dear. No one lives there. They've been empty these six months now for remodeling and I don't know what's taking so long. I don't like being here all by myself. That's why I picked a triplex, you know. It's like a house but you have company on the other side of the walls. Maybe your friend was going to move in when they're done? Did you try the police? They know where everybody is with these new computers. You can't get away if you want to."

Back in her car, Neva sat for a moment savoring the fact that the sports editor had been duped. Someone had gone to the trouble of feeding him false information. Franklin Budd, the player who had not gone jogging with White on the day he was killed, didn't want to be found and had taken steps to cover his tracks. It was the most interesting thing that had happened all day.

CHAPTER
6

Clouds and heavy rain descended, bringing early darkness as Neva returned to the house. She built a fire, poured wine, and settled on the couch with her skimpy notes and laptop. Her first Web stop was the NCAA "public" site. Clicking into it she eventually reached *Role of Boosters*.

"Boosters play a role in providing student-athletes with a positive experience through their enthusiastic efforts. They can support teams and athletics departments through donations of time and financial resources which help student-athletes succeed on and off the playing field."

Well, talk about an open door…but the door soon shut with a list of "impermissible" activities, a nice long list spelling out what boosters were barred from doing not only for current players but prospective recruits to the team. No more than eight hours had passed since Ambrose's morning telephone call and yet the violations were already familiar enough to make her nod. *Tickets, travel, charge accounts…*

Next she read the section on "permissible" activities, which was brief and tidy—and unmistakably distinct from the no-no's. Clearly, ignorance was no defense here.

A general Web search for NCAA violations brought up a list of the worst offenders in NCAA history, the "all-time dirtiest programs." Topping the list of the most notorious cheaters was Arizona State—the maroon and gold team on Perle's TV screen—followed by Southern Methodist University. There followed a list of seven-time violators (Auburn, Florida State,

Texas A&M, California, Memphis, Minnesota, Oklahoma, Wisconsin and Wichita State), six-time violators, five-time violators and so on. Valley State was not on any of the lists.

Among the many hits for violations was one that made her smile—the NCAA itself had been investigated! And, in fact, had admitted to having paid for information it wasn't legally allowed to have as part of its own case against the University of Miami.

The world of college sports was a veritable carnival of transgressions, no question about that. But what did it really matter in this earthly vale of woe?

In the morning, Neva woke early and got up immediately to retrieve the *Current* from the front porch. Sliding the paper out of its thin plastic bag, she stuffed the bag into her bathrobe pocket rather than taking time to put it with the recycling in the hall closet. She unrolled the paper, looked at the headline, and flinched as though it were actually news to her as it would be to thousands of stunned fans.

Star forward found shot to death

The words spanned the front page. Below it was a classic photo of a young man caught in midair, a basketball arcing between hand and basket. His face was turned away from the camera but his soaring body and powerful outstretched arm shouted *Life!*

Studying the picture, Neva slowly sat down on the chair next to the hall telephone table. Yesterday she had taken her cue from Ambrose. She had accepted his newsman's distance and his interest in the killing as primarily a piece in a puzzle, an incident tangential to the booster story.

Now the force of White's vitality hit her hard. A week ago he had been a physical masterpiece. Now he was nothing. This was about murder, not about sports.

She folded the paper and sat for some time thinking, then stood up wearily as though at the end of the day rather than the beginning. Still deep in thought, she crossed the living room to the kitchen and gazed out the window above the sink. The sun was up but little light reached the soggy garden through the clouds. Not a good day, not a good day at all.

She turned on the cold-water tap and left it running to get rid of the taint of old pipes and reached for the coffee bean jar.

The jar was empty.

Hell! She was barely twenty-four hours into this story and yet already it had disrupted her routine. She always roasted coffee in the evenings but last night she had not given it a thought.

The roaster was in the basement on the old workbench along with a dozen jars of green beans. Her hand moved along the row, hesitated at the Mexican Organic Chiapas, moved on to a new Brazilian coffee she hadn't had much success with yet, and then settled on beans from Yemen. Three scoops into the small glass roasting chamber, heat on high, fan on high, timer punched up to eight minutes. Beans bounced around in the chamber.

Generally, she didn't allow herself to be distracted by anything while roasting, but now she ran back up the stairs, retrieved the paper, and returned to spread it out on the workbench. The byline on the White story included both the sports editor and police reporter Charlie Frank. The story took up the entire front page apart from the short piece about Joey Field, which had not run next to the murder story, as suggested by Ambrose, but was in the bottom left corner. The White story was complete, with no jump to an inside page.

The body of star forward Miles White was discovered early Sunday morning in Calapooia forest… A pair of ecology students working in the university research forest had spotted the body behind a heavy clump of ferns about thirty yards off a jogging trail and had called 911. Police said he had been dead for a week, killed by a single shot to the head. According to roommates, he had left the house the previous Sunday morning as usual to run, though he had not gone with his usual jogging companion, Franklin Budd. He had taken a sports bag. The bag was missing, nothing had been found near the body or in his car, which had sat unremarked all week near the trailhead. There was no evidence of a struggle. The bullet had passed through his head and had not yet been found.

In response to questioning, athletic department members had said no one had been alarmed at first by White's absence as he had vanished for brief periods in the past, though he had never missed a game until that week. He lived alone so there had been no one to wonder at his failure to return from the run.

The death was under investigation as a homicide.

The story about Field's suspension was brief, the headline low-key: *Field sold tickets, barred from play.* Field's transgression had consisted of selling two complimentary tickets to an unnamed buyer for an undisclosed price "rumored to be $1,500 each." Field was described as contrite. "I let my team down and I'm deeply sorry."

It was easy to picture Joey in his slacks and turtleneck speaking these earnest words to the good-natured sports editor, but surely Cal could have discovered at least who bought the tickets. Wouldn't the buyers have been sitting in Field's reserved seats at last week's game? Or maybe the tickets were for a future game?

The coffee beans had entered the second cracking phase and were a glossy brown. She pushed the cool-down button and returned to the kitchen to put water in the kettle and a filter in the drip cone.

Soon settled with coffee at the kitchen table, she skimmed the rest of the *Current*, then set it aside and turned to Cal's notes. Typed and single-spaced, they filled three pages. And they were an "earful" indeed. Cal had not only fleshed out what Ambrose had already told her, he had added rumored details of favors to athletes that included fancy cars and fat monthly allowances. And most interesting of all, he had linked booster names with specific players.

Hal Richter—Julian Loomis
Vern Varney—Dashiel Clemente, Jim Borden
Lyle Crisp—Joey Field, others
J.P. Cornish—anybody who's hot
Bill Tunney—general booster
Tucker Reilly—general booster
Jasper Luce—Frankie Budd

Apart from the unfamiliar Luce and Cornish, she knew all the boosters at least by name through their involvement in Rotary, the Chamber of Commerce, United Way...But where was Miles White in all this? The star players attracted the most goodies, he had been a star forward for the last two years, and yet he wasn't mentioned.

Neva made a note and read on.

Julian Loomis and Jim Borden were former Boomers, now playing in the NBA, Borden for the Mavericks and Loomis for the Lakers. Did this mean Richter no longer had a favorite player? Was it Crisp who had bought Field's tickets? If she could find Luce would he lead her to Budd?

She made more notes, shoved the papers away, stood up, stretched, made toast with almond butter, poured milk, and returned to the table. Either she had to accept Ambrose's approach—the murder and the rule violations were two different worlds—or she could not continue pursuing the story.

Though to step away from it now would not be easy given that the editor was on fire about it as she'd never seen him on fire before. "Watch your step with Budd," he had warned as she left his office yesterday. "He's smart, maybe the smartest Boomer yet. He could charm the hair off a dog, but he won't tell you anything he doesn't want to."

Heading for the triplex, she had braced for a contest of wits and had found only an ancient woman with lavender on her doorknocker. Budd had not gone jogging with White. Budd had disappeared and someone was trying very hard to cover his tracks.

She wouldn't recognize Franklin Budd if she tripped over him

The envelope Ambrose had given her lay under Cal's notes. She pushed away her empty plate and pulled the bio-sheets and mug shots out of the envelope. The pictures were 2-by-3-inch black and white prints taken when the players were freshmen. The faces were mostly sweet in a tough-kid sort of way, wistful and young—with one striking exception. Franklin Budd. Even as a freshman, Budd had shown the world a man's face. Carved, controlled, alert, the image returned her scrutiny with calculating interest: What's in this for me?

Suddenly she was glad not to have found him at the triplex. She would not have been ready. She needed to be well armed before facing this boy/man in the flesh, well-armed with information he could not dismiss. And the best source of such information was likely to be his booster, Jasper Luce. And if she could find Luce, he might lead her to Budd.

Ambrose had put together a contact sheet with the known addresses and phone numbers of both boosters and players. Budd and Luce were not on it, of course, but she picked it up anyway and found herself studying the name Tucker Reilly. Reilly was the CEO of LandMark, the largest high-tech firm in the area, and president of the university's Court Club. As president, he was responsible for seeing that boosters didn't violate NCAA rules and thereby jeopardize the program. And this, Ambrose had pointed out with relish even if without originality, was like the wolf watching over the sheep.

Listed as a "general booster," with no specific player attached to his name, Reilly should be able to give her an overview of the situation—the official version—and best of all, he would be easy to find. She would start with Reilly rather than Luce, give herself a chance to practice on someone whose name at least was already familiar. And maybe luck would be on her side and Reilly would know where his former fellow booster had gone and would save her the trouble of tracking Luce down.

The newsroom was quiet at the early hour of eight. Neva reached her office without having to engage with anyone apart from a passing good morning to one of the night cleanup crew in the coat room. Her office was small, no more than a large closet with a narrow window onto the parking lot, but at least she had a door to close behind her, which was more than anyone else in the newsroom could boast apart from Ambrose.

She had no more than closed the door when a light tap sounded on it. The editor stepped in without waiting for an invitation.

"Budd?"

"Did you spend the night here?" Laughing, Neva waved him to the small armchair that just fit in the corner next to the window, but the editor shook his head and leaned back against the closed door with his arms crossed.

"I'm fine here. That chair's made for midgets. How'd you get on?"

"Bad news. The address was bogus. An old woman lives there and has lived there for twelve years, and says she never heard of Franklin Budd."

"Well, damn. Maybe I will sit down." One stride took him to the chair. Folding downward like a stiffly jointed doll, he said, "Oof, remind me to find you a real chair. Cal's going to be ticked off about this, though it raises some interesting questions. When tracks are that worth covering they're well worth uncovering. I'd bet a dozen donuts you're more excited about the false trail than anything I've said about boosters. Am I right or am I right? Did you notice what was missing from the Joey Field story?"

"A lot, actually. Did Cal check on who was sitting in Joey's seats at the Arizona game?"

"He was able to find out they were empty. The buyer must have been warned off. Do you suppose he got a refund?" The editor chuckled without appearing genuinely amused. "But that's not what I meant. There were no quotes from the coach. When Cal tried to talk to Leonard he got his head bit off. Mostly they want to know how we found out. Imagine what Leonard's going to be like when you get to him."

"He won't talk to me, I'm sure of that." Neva had never met the coach but sitting in Clayton's laundry pile watching close-ups of Leonard's snarling mug had been warning enough.

"He'll have to talk to you."

"No he won't, Ambrose. No one ever has to talk to the press, remember? A lot of people forget that, but you know it's true. We're not the police. Leonard will never talk to me except to tell me to go to hell. If I get this story, it will be despite him, not because he cooperates or even pretends to cooperate. I feel it in my bones."

"If you don't talk to him before then, you'll see him in action on Thursday."

"How's that?"

"The game. I thought we'd go together."

"Will you treat me to a hotdog?"

The editor's laughter was explosive in the tiny office. "That's *baseball* food, Neva. Christ, you are an innocent."

CHAPTER
7

The brick and glass complex that housed Willamette LandMark, leaders in GIS technology, sprawled over five acres of green swale dotted with native oak and maple trees. Though it was too early for blooms, tulip trees with fat buds promised a fine spring display along the walkways, and under them crocuses were thrusting up by the hundreds. A genteel factory for a genteel town.

Neva pushed through heavy glass doors into a lobby of soaring windows, potted tree ferns, and an open set of curving stairs with a chrome railing that gleamed like a vintage Chevy bumper. A young woman receptionist in black telephoned Tucker Reilly's office. In less than a minute, elevator doors opened to reveal a short, round man in a blue suit jacket that strained across his middle as though he'd suddenly inflated. He coasted toward Neva with his right arm extended and his left arm curved snug against his rounded side like Tweedledee.

Neva offered her hand and smiled with extra sparkle to cover her surprise. She had expected Tucker Reilly—the name, the position as head of a sports booster club—to be tall, a little beefy, a former athlete maybe, a hearty fellow with a big laugh and prone to winking.

He drew her into the elevator where they stood side by side to go up a single floor. "You have beautiful grounds," Neva said. "The trees make it look like you've been here forever."

"Don't they though? The bulldozers almost got them but one of our people came by in the nick of time. It was in the plan to keep them. We like to think they make us better neighbors."

The elevator delivered them directly to Reilly's office and a wide view over hills and treetops. Reilly led the way to a cluster of upholstered chairs near the floor-to-ceiling windows. The room was airy, sparely appointed, and would have been entirely impersonal except for a basketball covered with looping signatures that hung above a basketball hoop mounted on the wall.

Neva stopped to consider the hoop and the tight wads of paper in the wastebasket below it. "Do you always get them in?"

"Don't I wish." Reilly chuckled. "I cheat and pick them up before anybody sees. Coffee?"

"Thank you but I've had my limit for the morning." It was her usual line to avoid drinking bad coffee.

"It's decaf. Local roast, water extract. In short, the best."

"Well then, terrific."

Reilly opened what looked like a wooden filing cabinet, took out a bottle, and poured dark streams into two teal and white LandMark mugs, followed by steaming water from a brass spigot. He reached again into the disguised refrigerator. "Cream?"

The coffee was good enough, the chair fit nicely against Neva's back, the unaccustomed lofty perspective on the town was absorbing. She could have sat for some time in appreciative silence but a gusty sigh burst from her host as he settled across from her, followed by mournful words.

"A sad day for the Boomers, a sad day, indeed. Joey will do his little penance and go on with his life, but Miles—ah, Miles." Again Reilly sighed, shook his head, sipped from his cup, swallowed with a pensive air. "I've always wanted to meet you but I would have chosen a less sad occasion. It's very appropriate for you to do a column. I don't believe I've seen you write about athletics before. I never miss a column, you know."

Oh lord, Reilly was a Leopold fan as well as a booster! How she hated letting friendly readers down, even the smarmy and the suspect—best to get it over with, best to launch right into the tough questions…and yet, he had given her an easy opening and there was nothing to lose by taking it. He was going to feel double-crossed soon anyway.

"You're right, my only sports writing was about a hundred years ago when I did a column on my son's losing soccer team, if you can call that sports writing." She waited for the chuckle before going on. "It is so terribly sad about Miles, and so hard to believe he was killed." Another pause as they shook their heads, and then, "It's just so hard to believe, and I have to say I'm also really puzzled by another thing. I talked to some of his teammates yesterday and they seemed remarkably unemotional about it."

"That doesn't surprise me. First off, they're young. And White never really was one of the boys. He kept to himself from the start, had his own life. And you have to remember there's competition on a team, any team. With Miles gone, everybody moves up a notch. He was headed for pros, you know, a first-round draft pick for sure. He's hands down the best since Julian Loomis. A very fine player and a very unfortunate turn of fate."

"Fate? You think it was random violence?"

"There's no question about that, surely. I understand the police suspect robbery."

"Who would choose a jogging trail to lie in wait for a robbery victim, and what would a jogger have that could be worth stealing? Runners don't carry anything except water, and often not even that."

"Are you going to mention deliberate murder in your column?"

Neva set her cup on the empty coffee table that stood between them, took the notebook from her jacket pocket, looked thoughtfully at Tucker Reilly for a moment, and said, "I'm not really here in connection with my column. Or White's death, not directly anyway. I've gone back to working as a reporter for a few weeks. This isn't an easy subject, but there's no reason to beat around the bush. I'm following up on rumors about activities of certain Court Club members. We hear that NCAA rules are being violated regularly and I'm hoping you can give me some perspective on the situation."

Rather than showing dismay or indignation, Reilly smiled, and his eagerly persuasive words flowed as though he'd prepared for just this conversation, and even welcomed it. "You like good things, do you not? A good car, nice house, well-made clothes. Good coffee." He raised his mug in a confirming salute. "You feel good when quality is high. We all feel good when quality is high. We all strive for excellence. It's a natural human impulse to reach for the best. Quality is a human value, a high human value. It's no different with athletics. A university must strive for excellence in athletics as well as academics. You have to look beyond the university to the community and the state, to what it means to the whole to have a successful team."

Reilly waved with an expansive sweep of his arm toward the tall windows. "When you have a nationally recognized team, it creates benefits well beyond the sphere of athletics. A good team is a thread that ties all the elements of a college or university together. It gives an identity. It makes it easier for graduates in botany and engineering and such to feel a commonality that the more heady subjects just don't give. You've seen them, the kids camped on the ramps to get tickets. Kids—heck, I've seen adults out there, back before tickets went online. They used to wait all night to get a seat. It's the most positive single influence on campus life. You know of course that I'm an alum? Loyalty isn't just a word to me."

"Is the Court Club primarily a fundraising organization?"

"Yes and no. Without us, there would be no athletic program as we know it, not in this state. The state money just isn't there, not for gold-star facilities anyway. And television earnings have to be shared with other programs, at least to an extent, though as everyone knows they've skyrocketed with the cable contracts. Still, we play an important role. We raised money to remodel the coliseum, install the digital screens and so on. We raised money for the new workout rooms. We contributed to the new taping and instant replay video equipment. Those improvements benefit the university as a whole, not just the basketball program. Consider all the other sports, women's athletics, for instance, that don't bring in money but use the facilities. By building up the basketball program, we benefit the minor sports as well by providing better facilities and raising the level of interest in the athletic program. We hold awards banquets. We pay every winning coach a salary bonus that's part of the hiring package. And so it goes."

Neva knew it was not a useful direction, but still she had to say, "I can't help thinking how much the library could benefit from that kind of help, direct help, I mean."

Unfazed, apparently even pleased, Reilly chuckled. "Don't think you're the first to say that, but believe me, this kind of effort wouldn't work for a library. You don't have the same network of loyalties there. Honestly now, how often have you screamed and cheered over a book?"

Fortunately, Reilly did not wait for an answer but chatted on in a pleasantly confidential tone. "Our efforts do help the library indirectly because a successful program raises the profile of the entire university. You may get donors who decide to leave money to the library because they love the Boomers. It happens. And believe me we don't just build up the facilities. We take good physical care of the athletes, too. You might say we keep our rolling stock in good running order. We help provide dental and medical care, on a trade-out basis, of course. In other words, community members and alumni can give goods and services instead of cash donations to the Court Club. A doctor, say, could not give money or anything straight to an athlete but a donation of medical care made through the Court Club is permissible. Giving money directly to athletes can be easily abused to attract certain talented individuals to the program, as I'm sure you're aware, and I am adamantly opposed to that."

"Is that rule generally followed in this community?"

Reilly uncrossed his short legs, tipped forward, set his cup on the coffee table precisely opposite hers. "We in the Court Club cannot answer for the actions of every community member. Now and then we do hear rumors of behavior that the club would never condone and neither would the university. We ask our members to abide by the rules of the NCAA and the conference and I would hope that they would honor that request. I have been involved with the club for perhaps ten years and in all fairness, I have never been asked to do anything that was not in accordance with regulations."

"You feel confident then that Court Club members are not violating NCAA rules?"

"No. No, I would not go so far as to say no members ever do anything out of the way. Human nature being what it is, I would expect that now and then someone, some peripheral member most likely, would overstep the bounds of what's allowed. But, as a club, we do not condone it."

"Do you have any knowledge of boosters giving athletes cars, or clothing accounts, or paying their rent, or giving them espresso machines or sound systems?"

"Heavens." Reilly's eyebrows arched. "Those would be grave violations indeed. May I ask who you've been talking to? Assuming you didn't just pull that out of the air? Or maybe you assume that, because this sort of thing has occurred elsewhere, at other schools, it's happening here?"

"Several players have indicated to me that certain things do go on along this line."

"Which players?"

"I'll be happy to give you that information at some point before I finish this investigation but I can't right now, I'm afraid. It could get the players in trouble."

"Investigation? That sounds rather more serious than you indicated at first. Am I under 'investigation?'"

Neva smiled and shook her head. "That word is a little melodramatic. I'm basically just poking around to find out if there's anything behind what we're hearing. Naturally, anything you say to me will get the same protection I'm giving the players."

"I can't imagine that anything I say would need protection. I have nothing to hide and neither does the club. What we do is in the best interests of the university and the athletes alike. It's good wholesome fun for everyone, fun that also does a lot of good. But I must say I don't like the sound of what you're saying. If too much attention is paid to rumors, a good deal of trouble may follow. We don't need the NCAA nosing around. Wherever they go, there's bound to be trouble. It never fails. The NCAA, or some such watchdog, is obviously needed but some of us view it as a necessary evil."

"Does the club play any role in what happens to the players academically?"

"Absolutely. We believe in the whole person. We're involved with the entire well-being of those boys. We think the athletic department's commitment to making better students out of them is highly commendable."

"You remember Clayton Perle?"

"Of course. A fine player, very controlled."

"He's finished his four years of play, as you know, and is in his fifth and final scholarship year, as you know, but what you may not know is that he has only two years' worth of usable credits."

"I'm very sorry to hear that. These young men give a lot to this institution and it's a shame that some don't take better advantage of the opportunities here. But you find that in every program. Some make it and some don't—remember, you can only lead a horse to water."

"Did you know that more scholarship athletes fail academically at this university than make it? We don't have exact figures yet, but it's clear that fewer than half the basketball and football players graduate, which is a lower rate than the latest NCAA rules require."

Reilly frowned, shook his head, laced his stubby fingers. "That is not a figure I've heard before. Did the athletic department give you that figure? Did Rex Gregorio verify it?"

"No. Our librarian calculated it by comparing team lists and graduation records. I haven't talked to the athletic director yet but of course I will before anything's published."

Reilly's face relaxed and he released an audible breath. "Ah, you had me worried there. You realize that many of these boys go on to other programs, not playing here their full four years, or they get drafted by the NBA before they graduate. That would make for a highly misleading graduation statistic, would it not?"

"We thought of that but it doesn't add up any better. In the past six years, only Julian Loomis and Jim Borden and two others whose names I've forgotten have been drafted into the NBA. Next year, Miles White would have been, and maybe Joey Field. Nearly every other player during that time played the full four years here, but more than half didn't get a degree and didn't go to another school. What happened to them?"

"Well, you seem to know so much, you tell me," Reilly snapped, and then visibly collected himself before resuming in an even voice. "I see the point you're trying to make and I agree it sounds like a pretty low academic success rate. But I think you're overlooking some key points. VSU purposely takes in students who would not otherwise go to university—"

"Athletes, you mean?"

"That's what we're talking about. Let's be frank. Many of these boys would never see the inside of a college classroom if it weren't for sports. In bringing these kids here, the college fulfills a civic obligation to provide opportunities to the disadvantaged. It's all done through the Minority Advancement Program. Over the long term, there's no question but what this experience—even without a degree—will have a significant impact on how they conduct their lives.   And I assure you these young men are perfectly intelligent."

"I'm not talking about ability. I'm talking about getting an education, something lasting out of college such as other students expect and generally achieve. But to go back a bit. It seems that certain community members have established close relationships with specific players, for instance, Jasper Luce with Franklin Budd. Which reminds me, Luce has evidently left town. Do you know where he went?"

"I'm afraid not. Of course I knew him but, well, let's just say we weren't really friends and I have no idea where he's gone or why."

"What can you tell me about Miles? I understand he was an exception to the pattern, that he was not only a loner on the team, but he didn't have a personal booster. Do you have any idea why?"

"I'm not comfortable with your term 'personal booster'. It has implications...Actually, Ms. Leopold, I have to get ready for a conference call. It's been an interesting conversation but I urge you to keep something in mind and maybe you'll be able to see all this a little more clearly. You're stuck on the idea that a university's sole concern is to produce graduates. It isn't. A university is a complex organism. To have good academic programs, you have to have money, a good reputation, alumni support, community support, school spirit. That all comes from sports. A strong, competitive athletic program is like a huge, on-going endowment. What do players get out of it? They get a completely different perspective on our society than some of them grew up with. They get admiration from thousands of fans. They surely learn something sitting in all those classes even if they don't get a degree. And some do get a degree just like some make it into the NBA. What do the players lose? Nothing. I urge you to keep that in mind."

CHAPTER
8

Let's be frank, many of these boys would never see the inside of a college classroom if it weren't for sports.

How matter-of-fact Reilly had sounded, as though any old fool should understand that this is how things work in the real world. It wasn't so much what he had said but the shimmer of implications. If only she had used a recorder! There was no way to get it all down during the interview even with the personal shorthand she'd developed over the years, but now she needed to fill in as much as possible from memory while it was still fresh.

Before leaving the LandMark parking lot, she sat in the car scrawling rapidly, filling page after page beyond what she'd noted while Reilly talked. Finished at last with every worthwhile detail she could remember, she closed the notebook and reached for the key. A sporty black car pulled into the lot and stopped with a jerk in the handicapped spot. The driver got out in a hurry, a phone clamped to his ear. Gesticulating forcefully with his free hand, he strode into the building.

Neva had never met athletic director Rex Gregorio, but she must have seen pictures because his name flashed across her mental screen before she was fully out of the car for a better look. She reached the glass doors as he stepped into the elevator on the far side of the lobby.

Reilly had said he had to get ready for a conference call, not an appointment. For Gregorio to show up here fifteen minutes after her visit had to be more than coincidence.

Approaching the receptionist with a distracted and slightly embarrassed air, she said she had forgotten to ask Reilly an important question but didn't want to disturb him if he was with someone—had that been his next appointment just heading up?

"Rex, I mean Mr. Gregorio, doesn't make appointments," the young woman said. "But Mr. Reilly told me to hold calls so I guess you'd better not interrupt."

"Oh, certainly not. I'll call him later, no need to mention it. You certainly have a nice view from here."

"I guess so. But I'd rather have a little privacy, you know what I mean? Talk about a fish bowl."

Back at her desk, Neva typed up the notes, filling in yet more details as she relived the hour in her thoughts. Reilly was extraordinarily sure of himself, and highly experienced at touting the glories of college sports—men's college sports—but could he really be unaware of how loaded his observations were in these times? Again she wished she'd taped the interview but she had rejected such technology years ago. Recorders tended to make sources wary, plus she found it far easier to flip back and forth through a notebook than to search recordings for specific quotes. Still, in this case, the exact wording was the giveaway.

Done with the notes, she peeled a banana, and turned to her action list. The next job on it was to find Jasper Luce but after the hour with Reilly she was not in the right mood to tackle another booster. A player then. Was she ready for Budd? Not really, but most likely she never would be, so now was as good a time as any, if she could find him. Maybe he would tell her where Luce had gone and save her the effort of that search. No doubt Cal had already tried the obvious methods for finding the elusive basketball player but, just to be sure, she had to cover the same ground.

The people-search function on the university website brought up dozens of links but they were all to sports news. She tried the campus activities office and met a blank—neither of the young foreign students who passed the phone back and forth had heard of Budd. She even called the athletic department without giving her name. No they didn't have Budd's current address and did not hand out student information in any case.

The online local telephone directory had no listing, which wasn't surprising given that he no doubt used a cell phone. A general Web search brought up the predictable sports news going back to his high school years, but no contact information. Next she called all five property management offices for the major off-campus student housing complexes. Nothing.

Stumped, she went down to the staff room for a cup of hot water and a ginger tea bag. J.D. was there taking a plastic bowl of leftover Thai curry out of the microwave. She stuck her finger into the middle of the sauce, scowled, and shoved the bowl back into the microwave. "Damned thing needs a tune-up. So what's new?"

"I'm trying to find a missing basketball player. Not missing, just moved with no forwarding address. Any brilliant ideas?"

J.D. had been in the "news biz ever since I could pick my own nose," which was only a bit of an exaggeration given that her mother had edited a weekly broadsheet in eastern Oregon for as long as J.D. could remember. "Campus library," she said. "Call them and say you have a book he left with you and you want to get it back to him in time to study for a test."

"That's lying."

"You've been off the beat too long, Leopold."

"How long since you lied to get information?"

J.D. made a show of looking at her watch. "Three hours. To be honest, it wasn't to get information. I called animal control and reported my neighbor's dog. It barks all night and the way I look at it, better to lie than kill the bitch."

"What was the lie?"

"I gave a fake name or she might kill me. My neighbor, I mean."

"That's not really the same."

The editor shrugged. "Call the library. Won't hurt anybody."

The moral struggle was over though not resolved by the time she got back to her office. J.D. was right that some lies are harmless—she only wanted to talk to Budd—but the ol' slippery slope was real, and there was no way to miss the obvious irony in fudging the truth in the name of catching rule breakers.

When the ploy failed—*we don't use that kind of contact information at the library, just the student's ID number, and that's not public information*—it only seemed right.

The next moment, inspiration struck.

The university no longer put out a yearly student directory in printed form but the switch to streamlined online listings had occurred only a few years ago. It was just possible that Budd's home address would be in an early volume. She had to kneel to look through the old directories lined up on the bottom of the newsroom shelves. State blue books, a couple of atlases, city directories, ancient AP stylebooks. And, at last, the final paper issue of the student directory—published during Budd's sophomore year.

Back in her office, she closed the door and flipped through the pages with a slightly furtive air. She found the B's and skimmed down to the Bu's and then back up again. No listing for Budd. The disappointment was sharp. Unable to accept the dead-end, she continued to turn pages to the P section and checked for Perle. No listing even though Clayton would also have been a student that year. She continued to the W section. Miles White was not there.

It made no sense.

Were the athletes considered too precious to include in a public directory?

The answer lay a few pages beyond the end of the alphabetical listings. Here she found separate sections for student government officers, club presidents, and, at last, scholarship athletes. These were arranged by sport, with Franklin Budd at the top of the basketball page: name, class, local address, and family information. His parents were Milton and Arlene Budd, 947 North Redfern Drive, Seattle, WA.

She copied the information into her notebook, turned to the computer, and searched the Seattle phonebook for Milton Budd. Within seconds she had the telephone number and was dialing.

After just two rings a child's voice squeaked "Hi?"

"Hello. My name's Jeneva. I live in Willamette, Oregon, and I've found a book with the name Franklin Budd and this telephone number on the cover. Is he your brother?"

"Yes. I have a cold. I'm very sick."

"I'm sorry. Were you resting?"

"No. I'm too bored to rest. I rested yesterday. Frankie moved."

"Did he? Do you know his new address?"

"Oh, sure. It's on the phone book."

"Could you read it to me, please?"

There came a rustle of paper and several thumps. "Tell him I'm sick," the girl said, and then carefully read out a street address and telephone number.

"Thank you. And I will definitely tell him you're sick."

And she would, too. The very moment she met Budd she'd confess to the underhanded maneuver. Lying to a sick child! Really. Even J.D. might flinch at that.

So why was she smiling as she hung up? Why did she feel so very very pleased with herself?

For a moment she tried to think seriously about her actions, tried to let feelings of proper guilt cast an internal shadow, but then a second brilliant idea broke in—now she knew how to begin the search for Franklin Budd's booster.

Luce was a building contractor. He had reputedly moved to Washington State. He would need a state license to pursue his business.

She turned again to the keyboard, found the Washington State Department of Labor & Industries, clicked on "Trades & Licensing," followed the links to a contractor search function, and typed in Jasper Luce. His name and contact information popped up so fast she sat back with an exclamation. No one seriously interested in disappearing would register online in his own name. He could have used a family member's name, a partner's name, the dog's name. It looked like Ambrose had been given misleading information yet again, told that Luce had "disappeared" when in fact he had simply moved out of the area for his own reasons.

Strangely disappointed, Neva turned in the swivel chair and looked out the narrow window. She was into this now, wasn't she? Hot on the trail and let down that a supposedly tough quarry was hiding in plain sight. She hadn't felt like this in years, not since her days as an investigative reporter on the *San Diego Union-Tribune*. She had forgotten how much fun it was to be on the scent, and then what a letdown it could be when the scent failed.

But the scent hadn't failed. She had Luce's number and the big challenge was still ahead; getting him to talk.

"You have reached the Jasper and Candace Luce residence," a recorded woman's voice answered after six ring tones. "Please leave your name and number."

A home phone! She hung up without leaving a message.

Budd's new apartment was north of campus in a neighborhood that had recently been invaded by blocks of three-story townhouses wedged in among older family homes. Developers had taken quick advantage of a change in the building code that favored high density construction, also known as "infill." But just about everyone, including city planners, had been stunned by the speed and impact of the change. Neva had written several columns about it but they'd been of the unsatisfactory, waffling variety—on one hand, it made sense to contain sprawl but on the other, the townhouses looked like cutouts stuck in among the lovingly kept Cape Cod and craftsman homes.

The townhouses were almost certainly as generic inside as out and she would soon see this for herself...but she did not get out of the car. She sat where she had parked across the street, turned on the radio, and watched Budd's blank front door and curtained windows. The windows were strangely uniform from floor to floor, without the usual size range from big living room window to small bathroom windows. All were identical, bedroom-size, aluminum framed, with colorless curtains that had clearly come with the place because they were just like all the others in the row.

Cars lined the curb, but the special BUDD license plate mentioned in Cal's notes was nowhere in sight.

Ten minutes passed. Nothing happened. What was she waiting for?

She was waiting for courage to knock on Budd's door.

Courage to face a basketball player!

She wasn't afraid of anything in Willamette. The town regularly ranked among the top ten safest and most livable communities in the country. She walked alone at night without a second thought. Property crimes were common, bicycle and laptop thefts leading the list, but violence was rare and almost never random—White's death was no casual assault, she felt sure of this. When she'd first moved to Willamette twenty years ago, some wag had said *If you slept out in the park downtown all night you'd wake up okay in the morning but your watch would be gone*, and it was still true, though now it would be your cell phone.

Even nature was nice here. The floods, typhoons, earthquakes, tsunamis, and droughts that plagued so much of the world were unknown in Willamette apart from an occasional rise in the river that set pumps going in basements. Mount St. Helens had erupted a good decade or more before her time, but only a dusting of ash had reached town.

The sensation of fear was so unfamiliar that she didn't recognize it at first, not until she wondered why her mouth was dry and why she continued to listen to All Classical Portland even after the pledge break came on.

Pull yourself together, Leopold. He's only a basketball player.

Clayton Perle and Joey Field had proven perfectly docile. Ambrose's warning to watch out for Budd had included nothing about temper, only quick wits and manipulative charm. The worst he could do was slam the door in her face.

But when she steeled her nerve and crossed the street it wasn't Budd who opened the door. She knew this from the mug shot that still lay face-up on the passenger's seat of the car, though the powerfully built and thickly tattooed young man who looked her up and down was surely an athlete.

"Is Frankie at home?" She said, casual and smiling.

"Who wants to know?"

The line was such a cliché, even in the way it was delivered, that she might have assumed it was playful in other circumstances. But there was nothing playful about the speaker, not even a remote glint of humor in his deep-set eyes.

Still, she could not give a fully serious answer. "I do. Which is why I'm standing here."

"What if he doesn't want to see you?"

"He's not even going to know I'm here if you don't tell him."

He looked at her without any change in expression for so long she nearly spoke again, but then he shrugged, stepped back, and bounded up an open flight of carpeted stairs, leaving the door

open. She stepped inside, closed the door, and moved well away
from it before taking a good look around.

The room had no clear identity. Too small for a living room,
too large for an apartment entryway, it seemed to be a sort of
catch-all for active students coming and going. There was no
furniture and the walls were bare, but the heavily tracked beige
carpet was littered with the sorts of things that generally get left
on porches—enormous shoes, knapsacks, a scooter, a bike wheel,
a quart of Pennzoil in a paper bag, a set of jumper cables coiled
in a laundry basket. This, at least, explained the absence of a
ground-floor living-room window.

One of two doors at the back end of the room stood open, and
as she was trying to see what sort of space lay beyond it, she heard
a sound on the stairs, turned and discovered Franklin Budd
halfway down. He paused like a model on a runway, the muscles
of his bare torso above the black sweatpants as crisply visible as
in a da Vinci anatomical drawing.

"Well," he said, continuing downward. "Lamarr was right for
once. He said a little lady wanted to see me. That's you."

"I'm Jeneva Leopold. From the *Current*."

"I know that. Your picture's in the paper almost as much as
mine." He was standing close now, so close she had to look
sharply up to meet his gaze as he complained, "Seems like every
time I pick up the paper you're staring at me. Just like now."

"I don't know where else to look. You're standing on my foot."

It wasn't true but still Budd snorted with amusement. He
turned away, then half-pivoted in her direction again to crook a
finger. She followed him through the open doorway into a large
room with a kitchen at one end and a sitting area that evidently
served as the living room at the other, though it was so sparely
furnished with just two recliners and a coffee table that it seemed
to be waiting for occupants rather than already housing at least
two young men.

Budd crossed to the small kitchen table, planted a bare foot on
one of the two chairs, and propped an elbow on his raised knee.
They studied each other in silence.

"You've been talking to people," he said at last. "Clayton and
Joey. Why do you care who does anything for us? That's a nice
jacket you have on. I like it. Did you buy it? Where would you

get a nice jacket if you didn't have money? You're paid for what you do, right? And how did you find me anyway? Nobody knows where I'm at and anybody that does wouldn't tell."

"Your sister told me."

"Like hell."

"I told her I'd found a book with your name in it. She said to tell you she had a cold."

"Well, shit." He dropped his foot from the chair and cleared the space between them in two strides.

She stiffened but he stopped short of impact and stood, tense and angry, his chest inches from her face. The apology jammed in her throat. With an abrupt expulsion of breath, he turned away and fell with perfect control into a recliner.

"Shit. Maybe I'll be a reporter when I grow up. Come here and sit down." He waved at the other recliner.

For a moment longer Neva continued to stand where she was, returning his hard look. Then she picked up one of the dining chairs, moved it closer to Budd, and sat down. She no longer felt afraid but every nerve ending was on alert. To wait in silence took powerful self-control but it was the right strategy.

Budd played with the gold chain that banded his powerful neck. He drummed his fingers on his chest. He hiked his eyebrows, sucked in his cheeks, studied her with his head dropped back on his neck. After several minutes of this, he stood, picked up the other kitchen chair, and set it down close to hers. He sat on it, matching her pose, and after another interlude of silence, he said mildly, "What do you want?"

"I want to know whether you're really going to graduate in June."

"You bet I am. What do you really want?"

"I want to know who bought that fancy car for you, who paid your clothing account at Dutton's Menswear, what your relationship with Jasper Luce was like, what you were promised when you were recruited to play here, and why you didn't go jogging with Miles White on Sunday."

At the name Jasper Luce, Budd was on his feet and looking fierce again, but once she finished speaking he screwed up his face like a puzzled kid. "God, you've got balls. You really are something else." He paced a circle around her, came up close behind, put his large hands around her throat. Though he did not squeeze, the heat from his hands spread down her shoulders and upward into her face.

Dropping his hands, he said, "Come here." Without giving her time to stand, he pulled her to her feet and hustled her across the room to the kitchen. Still holding her arm with one hand, he yanked open the refrigerator door.

"Look. Look at that."

 She saw a bottle of ketchup, a piece of dry pizza on a plate, and a package of hotdogs.

"You call that living good?" Budd's voice throbbed with anger. "You call that being a pampered athlete? What do you have in your fridge? Steak? Beer? Ice cream? Good food and plenty of it. Nobody gives me a god damn thing and that's all I have to say." He slammed the door and faced her with his arms crossed, his head reared back.

Neva, too, stood still and said not a word.

"Damn!" He pivoted, walked three paces, and then turned and strode back as he snarled, "You want to know how many times a day I jerk off? You want to know what's in my sock drawer? You want to see my marble collection?"

"I want to know everything about boosters."

His hand came down on her shoulder, forced her back against the refrigerator, and slowly tightened. "They want to touch us," he said with harshly mimicked desire. "They want to put their hands on us, to feel our muscles. They grab us." The hand cinched hard on her shoulder and pulled her close. "That's why we call them grippers."

Releasing her, he turned away but stopped to add, low and fierce. "That's why I hate the bastards. That's why I took everything I could get."

Neva took a long breath, released it slowly, and said with determined calm, "So then. Tell me about it."

CHAPTER
9

Rain flooded the windshield faster than the wipers could clear it. Neva slowed, gripping the wheel and hunching forward to peer into the night. It was just ten miles from town to the interstate and the 24-hour restaurant where she was to meet Jasper Luce, but tonight it was a long ten miles.

This was a bad idea, a very bad idea. She shouldn't have called him after leaving Budd, she should have waited until tomorrow, but momentum has a way of overwhelming good sense and she'd felt elated when she got back to the office. She was on track, really on track, and Budd was on her side. *You tell him I said to talk to you. He can tell you everything, I don't care anymore.*

But that had been hours ago. She was exhausted now, worn out by the pure force of him. All she wanted was a nice fire and some wine, something red and heavy. And she was worried about Jasper Luce. He had agreed to this meeting far too readily.

"I'm driving south to Ashland and will be on the road most of the night," he had said. "Why don't you meet me at Tony's Truck Stop around one?"

For a man who had supposedly left town in a hurry with no forwarding address, he had been way too easy to find and now way too easy to meet. Could Budd have set her up? Had he called Luce as soon as she was out the door? Her confidence of the afternoon had plummeted, but there was nothing to do except go ahead with the meeting and trust her instincts, if instinct could function at all at such an hour on such a night…And yet, she could not quite believe Budd had been putting on an act.

Finished with the dramatics, he had offered her a beer—"We have another fridge in the garage, ha ha"—and started talking.

"You say you want to get the grippers, well, I'm giving you everything you need to get going on it but you'll have to fill in the blanks. Ask Jasper. He's got a bee in his bonnet. He'll tell you. If he likes you. I can tell you one thing. If it wasn't for Jasper, I'd be at the same dead-end as Clayton. He told me way back in the first year that I wouldn't make the draft. That pissed me off. I knew I'd make draft. I was hot and I still had three seasons to play. We all knew we were headed for pro ball. Only 1 percent of college players make NBA, did you know that? But nobody ever tells you. Leonard's an asshole, a real butthead, but he makes you think you're the greatest and that he's chewing your ass to give you the final polish instead of just beating you up to win games for him. You might think we could figure it out for ourselves, but when you've been a star since you could tie your own Nikes, you don't think about that. You don't think about anything but getting there. But Jasper told me. He said I was good but not good enough, and I better knuckle my ass down and get a degree so I'd have something to show when this circus was over. 'Don't waste yourself, Frankie,' he told me so many times I got sick of it. 'You live in an educated world. If you expect to get anywhere, you have to get your ticket. You have to learn to talk white.' He made me study."

You're saying he was an exception, that he wasn't a gripper?

"Like hell. He was one of the worst, if not the worst. He wanted to crawl right inside my skin. But at least he said so straight out. He said he'd give his house, cars, business—shit, even his wife—to play ball like me. Crazy dude."

Why had Jasper moved away if the Boomers were so important?

"Lots of reasons, mainly work. He had some problem with his partner. And his wife wanted out of the scene here. She thought it was sick. She didn't like it and she didn't like me. She thought Jasper had some kind of sexual thing for me but she was wrong. She was right about the money, though. Jasper spent a lot on basketball. I mean, a lot."

What about Miles? She'd asked at last.

"Miles? Listen, that whole deal sucks, just sucks. I've got my own ideas about it. And that's all I have to say, for now anyway. You ask Jasper about Miles. He can tell you a thing or two."

Jasper's voice on the telephone had been responsive but hushed, as though to keep from being overheard. "Look, meet me, okay? At Tony's, it's out on the Interstate. I'll be there by midnight. I'm big. You'll see me."

Budd had told her a lot, but everything he said raised new questions. She needed Luce to make sense of it, but why should a grown man with a family, a business, and a reputation to guard give her information that would implicate himself in rule breaking and general scurvy behavior at every step of the way? There was simply no reason for him to do it, and the chance of his turning up to meet her now seemed about zero.

The parking lot was solid with trucks hunkered around the lighted box of the restaurant like great beasts crowding a fire. Forced out to the edge of the lot where gravel ran off into black fields, she listened for a moment to the drumroll of water on the metal roof, zipped up the thin parka, pulled the hood over her head as far as it would go, took a breath as though about to dive, and got out of the car. She ran, jumping puddles when she saw them and splashing through when they were too dark to see.

Wide awake by the time she reached the entryway, laughing, she pulled off the sodden jacket and shook it at arm's length over the wet floor. Her shoes squished as she crossed to the inner door of heavy glass. She heaved it open and stepped into steamy heat and a happy roar. Laughter, clattering plates, shouted orders, wailing jukebox. Every driver on the interstate must have ducked in here to get out of the storm. They were mostly men, burly and pale under the lights. None sat alone, and not one was watching the door.

The climax of a wild goose chase?

A couple vacated a booth. She hurried to it and slid onto the warm vinyl as a waitress swept debris from the table into a plastic tub. "Coffee?"

"Tea, please. Earl Grey, if you have it."

She checked the clock on the far wall; 12:20. Twenty minutes late. Had he come and gone?

She looked back at the door and there he was. He'd spotted her already and now began making his way to the table, not directly as she had come, but circling to avoid having to squeeze between chairs. As he'd said, he was big, big all over, every piece of him cut from a giant mold, head, neck, shoulders, arms, chest. Towering over her and the booth, breathing loudly, he enclosed her hand with a hand as warm and enveloping as bread dough on the rise. Unzipping his dripping jacket, he slid into the space across the table that had suddenly become small and tight.

"You're older than your voice, but nice enough," he said as though passing along a significant tip. "Tell you what, though. I've been wondering all the way down here why I agreed to this. I almost drove on down the road." And then to the waitress, "I'll take milk and a piece of that cream pie from the cooler case. No, no coffee, I get heartburn." And then again to Neva, "I don't know what you said on the phone to talk me into this. I talked to Frankie after, and he said you're something else. If it wasn't for Frankie, I wouldn't be sitting here."

Jasper looked hard at her from deep-set blue eyes. His bulk was made up of muscle overlaid by solid flesh that was just heading toward fat. He pulled the plate of pie close and bent over it to eat, washing big bites down with slugs of milk. Neva waited for him to finish and didn't have to wait long for the pie to disappear.

"I suppose you heard I was the king gripper," he said, pushing away the empty plate. "I know what they call us. It's not flattering but what the hell, it's true. I won't try to hide anything. Well, not much. I'm not proud. It's just the truth." He finished the milk in one long pull, wiped the lower half of his face with a handful of napkins from the dispenser, and shoved the wad into the empty glass.

"Can you imagine walking down the street with Madonna? Well, I guess she's old news, but then I'm getting that way myself. Anyway, that's what it was like. I mean fame and glory. I didn't start out with any idea it would go so far but you get caught up in it, caught up in the glamor. These guys are the greatest, they're on TV, on magazine covers, and they're your friends. It's a real high. We all need to put someone on a pedestal. For a while, I actually believed the players were my friends, that they would like me even without my money. The whole country's watching this kid make the winning shot and he goes home with you. You have a big screen and rerun the game. Everybody wants to be there, it's where it's at. You have a swimming pool and these guys are out there. Anybody who's anybody is at your place. You're the center. Can you see that? It sucks you in. You begin to think it's real, that everybody's your friend, that these guys like you, and your friends and clients envy you—hey, I'm not proud of this. I look back and it's some kind of bad dream. No, it wasn't all bad. There were good times, times like I'll never see again, but you can't live like that. It gets to you. It gets to your family."

This was not information; it was a confession. Jasper wanted to bare his soul, to ease his burden. It was not what she'd hoped to hear, though one line stood out as a strange echo of what Clayton had said, and Joey Field as well: *For a while, I actually believed these guys were my friends.*

"Frankie was different," Luce said in a new voice, warm and slightly wondering. "Frankie changed me. There won't be any more Frankies, and that's another reason I got out. It was the end of something, something real. Back before Frankie, there were others. Daren Johnson. Packard LeMott. You'll remember them. I bought Daren's tickets, that's how it started. His folks were out in Detroit and couldn't make the games so I got his tickets. But then I started flying his folks out so they could see Daren play. Is that bad? Is that a bad thing, to fly a kid's mom and dad out to see him play? I didn't give a damn for the rules. It didn't make sense. I still don't give a damn for the rules. But that's not it, that's not what gets to you."

Jasper pulled a bandanna from his pocket and swabbed his shiny face. "My wife would be out of her mind if she knew what I was doing. She hated Frankie. If she only knew he got me out of it. Women." He shook his head. "No offense. Are you married?"

"Widowed. For many years. One son in college."

"I have two girls. Nice kids, anybody would say so. They deserve better than me for a dad."

"Did you do sports?"

"Are you kidding? I was the next Joe Montana. Then I got too big. Yeah, that's right, too big for football. I grew right through it. One year I was king and the next I kept falling over my own feet. That was high school. You know, I was quite the disappointment. To everybody. Wouldn't a shrink have fun with that one? That's the good thing about girls. If I don't expect anything, they can't let me down, right?"

Neva said nothing.

"I sound like a chauvinist shit. I am a chauvinist shit. Even Frankie says so. Do you mind?"

"No," she said, controlling a sudden urge to laugh. "Not personally that is. That's your wife's problem. And your daughters'."

"That's funny. Candy says it's my problem. She's a lawyer and nobody's fool. Did Frankie tell you I cover the loan for his car?"

"I gathered that, but he said he wanted to give you the privilege of relating the details."

"He said that? I can just hear him saying that. He'll go far, Frankie. I like to think I made a difference in his life. Did he tell you how I made the payments? We set it up in his name but it came out of my account every month. Give him a good credit rating and so on. They're very cooperative at Valley Savings and Loan, they're used to it. How about his trips home for holidays? Did he tell you I flew him in my plane?"

Frankie had said nothing about a private plane, but she nodded anyway. "Would you mind if I made some notes? I'm pretty tired and I might not remember things correctly."

"You're going to write this? In the paper?"

"I thought I'd said that."

"I guess I just thought maybe it was background. But why should I care? What's it to me anymore? I know plenty in town that've done worse and they'll know who they are. It's the system. I don't care what you write as long as it's true. The truth sets you free, right?"

Over the past three years, he said, he had bought Frankie so many things he couldn't remember them all. A sound system, TV, laptop, iPhone, mountain bike, gold jewelry, most of his clothes, a couple of vacations, things like that. "I'm not even talking about cash or meals on the road or that sort of thing. You just did that. Everybody did that. Like you do for your own kid."

"I can't help wondering where it all went. His townhouse has hardly anything in it."

"Maybe he shipped it all home because he's graduating soon. Or it could be in his room, the garage, I don't know. Wherever it went you can be sure it was no accident. Frankie thinks things out. Now anyway."

"Did anyone ever say anything to you, the coaches or university officials, about violating rules?"

"Oh, for sure. Lots of times. That was part of the game. They do their bit by talking like everything's being monitored and you're the only one being bad but everybody knows, and they know, that these guys aren't buying sports cars on their piddly scholarship allowance. The so-called scholarships aren't even enough to cover costs, not at Valley State anyway. Who do they think they're fooling? You should see the hotel scene on road trips. Ask your sports guys. I mean, it's a feeding frenzy. We all stay at the same hotel, players, coaches, boosters, media, girls. After a game, especially a big win and they always won, there were parties like you see in movies. By the pool. In the rooms. Hey, it was golden times."

"You were always there on your own? Without your wife?"

"Why take a sandwich to a banquet?"

Despite her distaste, Neva almost laughed. It was a very good line, even if despicable. "Sounds like a great relationship."

Like everything else about him, Jasper's shrug was big. "Candy's okay. Anyway, like I said, she hated the whole scene."

"Did the players drink a lot? How about drugs?"

"There's always some of everything, but they have to be a little careful. They're athletes, they have to keep in shape. But not the rest of us. And believe me, those boys really pull in the fancy chicks. That's an extra you might say. For all of us. No, I'm not young anymore. I couldn't keep that up now if I wanted to. I don't know how some of those old farts keep doing it. Or wanting to."

"When I talked to Tucker Reilly, he said the Court Club members are careful not to break rules."

Jasper's hoot was loud enough and long enough to make heads turn. "Good old butter-won't-melt-in-his-mouth Reilly. God. He keeps his paws clean in public but I happen to know he has some very objectionable little habits of his own—oh, nothing like Penn

State, not little boys anyway. At least I was up front, I never pretended. How about Vern Varney, you talking to him? Or Hal Richter, Lyle Crisp, Bill Tunney. They're all in it up to their mythical jock straps. What you have to get is the linkups. Richter's big thing was with Julian Loomis. He wanted to manage his career so bad even I could taste it. But that boy had better sense. He's playing for the Lakers now. And Vern Varney goes with Jim Borden. Ask Vern about Jim's taste in cars—this is kind of a joke. Vern's just a wee bit tight, even with his players, and he used to give Jim used cars. Borden always wrecked them on purpose, hoping the next one would be new. Borden's playing for the Mavericks now. Are you getting all this down? Don't quote me on it. This is just telling you where to look."

"You seem ashamed of having been involved in being a gripper even though you think the rules are stupid. What bothers you about it?"

"I'd rather start with what I'm proud of. I'm proud that Frankie's getting his union card and when he crosses that stage in June, I'll be there. And that gets me to what I hate most. Those kids are nothing more than fucking prostitutes, excuse my French. Underpaid prostitutes at that. You get right in there in the thick of it and you don't see it. You think they're having a good life, high old times, fame, glamor, chicks. But when you get out in the fresh air again, like I am now, it's enough to make you sick. I've thought about this a lot the last two months. They're exposed to a Rolls Royce lifestyle and then the Rolls is taken away. They're bodies. That's all they are. Famous, fabulous bodies. You get close to them and you feel the heat of their fame and vitality and you bask in it, you think it's for you, too. You buy that thrill with stuff, cars, TVs, clothes. And then it's over. Your player's through, he doesn't make pro, you have to stand out in the cold or try to get tight with another player. And your old player? He leaves the country to play for some wannabees in Timbuktu. Or he goes back to the old neighborhood and gets a job coaching the next crop of little Jordans and Magics at the local Y. What does he have? A pile of press clips and a closet full of old Nikes."

"Like Joshua Gifford?"

"Exactly. You talk to Josh?"

"I will."

"Good kid, Josh. I still send him a check at Christmas. Forget I said that. I don't know about you but I've got to hit the road. Look, I'll call you in a few days. It's better if you don't call the house."

"One last question, please. What can you tell me about Miles White?"

Already on his feet, Jasper looked down at her for a long, silent moment before speaking in a new tone, subdued and regretful. "Of course it made the Seattle papers. I was shocked, but you have to realize these kids aren't virgins when they arrive. Some of them have been working the system since they were eight years old. You can't have corrupters without corruptees, right? White didn't have a gripper. He didn't need one. Suggestive, isn't it? One other thing. He and Dash Clemente have been competing ever since they were recruited the same year. Dash's good but he's played in White's shadow for three years. Without White, he'll be Numero Uno. Have you talked to the girlfriend, Annette Octavian?"

"She's on my list, though our sports editor heard she left town to stay with her family somewhere. I haven't found out where yet."

"You'll find her," he said with sudden amusement. "You found me—and Frankie. He told me about your lost book trick. Taking advantage of a sick little girl. Naughty, naughty. At least I never did anything like that. Just kidding. Listen, I'll call you."

It was 3:30 a.m. when Neva pulled into her short driveway. The rain had eased off but the night was black with heavy cloud cover, and she had stupidly forgotten to leave the porch light on. Exhausted beyond thought, she trusted her feet to take her up the familiar stone walkway and front porch steps. Halfway across the porch her foot struck something, throwing her off balance. She caught herself with a hand against the door jamb, stood for a moment listening to her body to see if anything had been torqued, then opened the door and flipped on the light.

The object she'd kicked nearly to the end of the porch was a shoebox. To find offerings outside her door was not uncommon, though it was early in the season for the usual overflow zucchinis and eggs from her urban farmer neighbors. The box was light. She carried it inside, set it on the hall table, and lifted the lid.

In the box, nestled on white tissue paper, was a dead kitten with a single pin stuck into the middle of each eyeball.

She stepped back, closed her eyes, and waited for the revulsion to settle. Who had done this? Why? What recent action or writing of hers had triggered such an appalling act? Never in all her years…but she could not think it through now, not at this hour, not after such a day. Now she must simply deal with the sad and disturbing object itself.

Gently, without looking closely at what was under her hands, she removed the pin from each eye and dropped the pins in the hall wastebasket. She replaced the lid, set the box back outside on the porch and locked the door, using the bolt as well as the button lock.

The house was icy. Moving with deliberation from room to room, she turned on the heat and every lamp on the ground floor. Upstairs, she turned the shower to the hottest water she could tolerate and stood under it until she was sweating. Only then did she let herself think, and the first solid thought was that it had to be more than coincidence that the dead kitten had been left two days into her sports snooping.

Had the tiny creature been killed to upset her? Or been found dead and abused to make certain of the shock? She could not imagine Clayton, Joey, or Budd having anything to do with such nastiness. Who then? Tucker Reilly? Absurd. Jasper Luce? Ridiculous—and she and the contractor had only just met.

Nothing would come of reporting it to the police but not to report it could bring its own problems, especially if there were further nasty pranks. In the morning, she'd submit an online incident report, for the record, and leave it at that for the time being.

She was out of the shower, dry, and heading for her bedroom when the telephone rang in the hall below. Pulling on her robe she went down the stairs, resolved to answer only if it was her son.

It was not Ethan. The Caller I.D. said "Unavailable." The phone rang on, ten times, fifteen times. What if someone needed help?

"Hello?"

Click.

CHAPTER
10

"Luce was on the record with this stuff? You aren't kidding me?" The editor's hand lay lovingly on Neva's five pages of notes as though caressing a holy text.

"He said we could print anything as long as it's true, which I guess is up to us to determine." Neva controlled yet another yawn. She had slept hard despite the kitten episode, but for only four hours, and then had spent an hour typing the notes on her Luce interview. The effort had exhausted what little energy the sleep had restored.

"And Budd, he really calls them 'grippers'? That's a new one on me."

"He said 'we,' that's why *we* call them grippers. And Luce knew about it, and even referred to himself as the 'king gripper.' Cal must have heard it."

Ambrose nodded but his attention remained on the notes. "So Luce said White didn't have a booster. And then, 'Suggestive, isn't it?' He really said that? Suggestive? Like he knows the score and it's for us to find out."

"I'd say he doesn't know or he wouldn't have been able to keep it to himself. More like he's wondered about it before and figures there must be something going on."

"Some business on the side? Drugs?"

"Could be. Did White's family have money?"

"Far from it. The usual story. Single mother who died two years ago, public housing, he was the only kid in the family to finish high school let alone go to college. What we need now is facts. You get enough people saying the same things, and it begins to look like a fact, but still you need documentation. Check into the Valley Savings and Loan connection right away. You've already got the texture for a great story, plenty of usable quotes, why grippers grip and so on. I've jotted down some thoughts, where to go next."

He was planning a series of stories that would explore the whole question, what a full-ride athletic scholarship really meant in terms of money and other support, and every conceivable aspect of boosterism, from sex to bank loans. In between were questions about how scholarship athletes from the non-glamorous sports manage to survive without the "extras" provided by boosters, and who really benefits from a successful team, and how this program compares with others around the country in terms of recruitment and booster activity. As for the murder, that would continue to be reported by Charlie drawing mostly on information from the cop shop.

"I don't want Charlie knocking on players' doors and sniffing after boosters," he said. "Nothing against Charlie. Just too many dogs on the trail. And like I said, this needs your touch."

Neva merely nodded though she could not help wondering yet again over the editor's blatantly unbalanced approach, in which the murder was treated as incidental. It would be covered in a routine fashion while he poured resources into the gripper chase.

"Anyway, he's doing fine where he is," the editor continued. "Good story for tomorrow. They found the bullet. Buried in a tree—but get this. There were two bullets in the tree. Two. The first one they dug out had been there for years. The second one was the real deal."

"Good grief, too weird. Hunting? I think there's a short season, though I thought it was just bow hunting."

"Now it is. But that's not all. Looks like White was killed by a sniper rifle. That means long range. Whoever did it was taking no chance of being seen if they happened to miss. It's really pushed the search out."

"How long is long range?"

"Charlie says there's a record of more than 2,000 feet by some Navy SEAL in Iraq. Same kind of gun. He's checking it out."

"That wouldn't work in the woods." Calapooia was a dense forest of mostly second growth Douglas fir, though there were clear patches here and there from fires, old logging, research plots . She really should look at the scene even if she wasn't handling the murder stories. "Presumably he wasn't shot in one of the open spots if the bullet was in a tree?"

"You're quick, Leopold, you're quick. But as it happens it was open on one side so that's where they're looking now, around the edge of the clearing. Charlie says sniper rifles are pretty common so that may not help much, but it's interesting."

Neva managed to hide another yawn by turning it into a cough.

Changing gears without appearing to notice her condition, the editor said, "Back to the boosters. Cal and his crew are focusing on the institutional aspects, like scholarships and how the girls in volleyball manage. We can't just assume it's because they're mostly white and middle class and have some family money on top of what they get from the program. I figure we'd better get as much information from the athletic department as possible before they figure out that the Leopold Express is bearing down on them. Cal said Leonard wants to know why you're talking to his players. Word's getting around and people are getting nervous. The academic situation may be the hardest nut to crack. Student confidentiality and all that. Makes it easy to hide what's really going on with graduation rates and so on. You've got some good contacts on campus. There's got to be somebody willing to talk."

Was it time to tell Ambrose about Gerry Farnes? And certainly the kitten.

"Knock, knock. Hello?" The Dragon Lady of the Front Desk— aka Verlene—stood in the editor's open doorway and waved a pink message slip. Looking at Neva with a particular set to her red eyebrows that they all knew to take seriously, she said "Caller left a note for you. Looks like a hot one."

The caller was Farnes. The message: "Meet me at ten at the Beanery. It's good, really good."

"What's this about?" Ambrose demanded.

"It's Gerry Farnes, plant pathologist, on the Academic Deficiencies Committee. I was just going to tell you that I ran into

him at the Beanery and he said he might be able to get us some
goodies on special treatment of athletes. Sounds like he's got
something."

"See what I mean? You've set the landslide in motion and
we've only seen the start."

Gerry was waiting at the same table as before though now the
table was covered with sheets of paper.

"Check these out," he said as she sat down without taking time
to get coffee.

They were grade reports with the student names blacked out.
Except for sports grades, all were D's, F's and Incompletes.

"Athletes, every single one. All were referred to the Academic
Deficiencies Committee. We had a breakfast meeting. God, what
a pack of jellyfish. I managed to bully them into suspending
Dashiel Clemente because he's always on the list, but they put the
rest of these guys on probation for a term. One term! You know
what that means? Nothing, absolutely nothing. They'll keep
going to class as though nothing happened and when they fail
again, nobody will have the guts to suspend them. They talk a
good line about special tutoring but talk is cheap. It makes me so
damn mad. I've just had enough. I don't know what you'll do with
these, but just remember they didn't come from me or it'll be my
head on a platter."

"Are there other basketball players here besides Clemente?"
Neva leaned to read the sheets upside down.

Turning the top several papers in her direction, Farnes said,
"Two. Look here. And two from football. And get this. I checked
with the admissions office this morning. They said sixty-six of
our scholarship athletes were let in under the Minority
Advancement Program and thirty-four of them were deficient last
term. That means more than half couldn't handle it. Academically
deficient means they failed to keep a C average. A C average! A
donut could get a C average."

Coach Gregorio was boiling over about Clemente's
suspension, he said, and they would no doubt appeal the decision
to President Havesham today.

"I'll let you know if he's reinstated. I'm sure he will be, especially given the situation. I mean, Field can't play and White's dead, to be blunt about it."

"What kind of student was White?"

"Not so bad when you use these guys for comparison. He might have graduated after a fifth year like Frankie Budd. Except that he would have been recruited. He seemed a little more mature than the others, or focused maybe. They lost a good statistic with White as well as a good player. They can't afford to lose another player right now. If Clemente is reinstated, I think you should go ask Havesham what he thinks he's doing. Sure, he's president but does that give him the right to override his own committees? Maybe I'll ask him myself. It's pure charade."

"You really can't attach names to these sheets? It would make them far more powerful."

"Sorry, no can do. I'm going out on a limb but I don't plan to fall off—and isn't that a crock? The players and athletic department honchos get away with anything but if they knew I gave you this stuff, I'd be out on my ear, tenure or no tenure. Now I'm out of here before anybody notices."

Neva decided on tea rather than coffee, and stayed for a bit after Farnes had gone, mulling over what to do if President Havesham did override the committee's decision on Clemente. It wasn't easy to imagine herself or anyone else from the *Current* marching into his office to demand an accounting. She had talked with the reserved and somewhat formal university president on various occasions but never about a contentious issue.

His public record so far was spotless.

Her strongest image of him came from a day some years past when she had seen him striding up Martha Avenue, his head high, his arms swinging in precise counterpoint to his long legs, his grey hair thick as a knitted cap. He had stopped at a lemonade stand set up by two young girls, reached ceremoniously into his pocket, and pulled out some change that he set on the card table. He accepted a paper cup, held it to his lips, and drained the contents before shaking hands with the girls and walking on.

Neva, too, had stopped at the stand.

"Did you know that was the president of the university?" she had asked, digging for coins in her bag.

"What university?" the older one had responded even though the campus buildings were easily visible two blocks away.

"He paid more than anybody," said the younger one.

Neva had considered their grubby hands and then carried her cup of lemonade around the corner to empty it onto the grass.

Dignity can be tougher to face than anger. No, she did not relish the thought of having to confront President Havesham. With luck, the showdown wouldn't happen today when she was feeling so ragged.

No such luck.

The message from Gerry was waiting when she arrived back at the office. "The sonofabitch reinstated Clemente. Go get him."

CHAPTER 11

President Havesham ran the university from a workmanlike office on the top floor of the administration building. His desk faced away from the bank of windows that looked out over the heart of campus. The desk was covered in orderly stacks of papers. In front of the desk stood two visitors' chairs that promised to be at least as hard and comfortless as the one in Ambrose's office. Beyond them, four chairs with dark green upholstery visibly worn on the arms clustered around a spindle-shanked coffee table.

Compared with Tucker Reilly's swank quarters it might have been a prison warden's office. It wasn't that the university was poor or stingy with its top administrator but rather that Havesham valued frugality above all, or so said rumor. Faculty who deplored the trend to model universities on businesses never faulted the president himself.

Neva settled in an armchair at Havesham's urging while he stood with his hands on the back of her chair as though seating her at dinner, and only when she was arranged with her bag on the floor and the notebook in her lap did he step around to look down at her.

"I'm a faithful reader, I hope you know," he said, his blue eyes bright in a ruddy face worthy of the Scotsman he was.

"I'm so glad to hear it, really. Thank you. Unfortunately, it makes my job today more difficult. I suppose it's best to come straight out with it."

She paused, regarding him with open regret until he nodded with no sign of wariness or concern, which only deepened her reluctance. Such a decent man, and yet the world was full of decent souls in positions of power that were dirtier than their hearts.

"This concerns the athletic department," she said, watching for a change in his eyes. "I'm working on a series of stories, mainly about rule violations by boosters but also looking at certain questions about athletes and academics. I understand that, earlier today, you overruled a decision by the Academic Deficiencies Committee to suspend Dashiel Clemente even though he has essentially failed every term since he got to campus. Could you please tell me why you reinstated Clemente?"

"No."

The simple word, spoken quietly, hung in the silence that followed. President Havesham had moved toward the opposite chair as she spoke but now remained standing. They observed each other, Neva with mild surprise and Havesham with a calm but possibly redder face than before.

"Is there anything further you wished to ask about?" His tone and manner were gravely polite though the look of warm interest was gone.

"Quite a bit, I'm afraid." Again a pause, a breath, and then she launched into it full blast. "I know that the committee suspended Clemente. Clemente and Athletic Director Rex Gregorio were here just a little while ago appealing the decision. If Clemente remains enrolled, it will verify that you overruled the committee. I understand that student records in general must be confidential, but athletes live in the spotlight. When unusual academic exceptions are made for them, it becomes news. We're hearing more and more about this kind of thing on campus, from both faculty and community members who are deeply concerned."

"The academic standing of VSU students is the business of this university, not the business of the public or the daily press. Athletes are students and to suggest otherwise is outrageous. I don't know who your sources are but if they work on this campus I will find them."

"Are you saying my information is wrong?"

"I'm saying you're making some very unfortunate assumptions. What I may or may not have done has nothing to do with athletics and everything to do with university retention policy for students with special academic needs. Students are suspended and reinstated every term, yet I've never known it to be of concern to the local press."

"Are they reinstated regularly by the president?"

"Not regularly, of course not. But it has happened."

"Students other than athletes?"

"Certainly."

"Could you tell me how many non-athletes you have reinstated in the past year?"

"That kind of information is never shared with the public. Those are internal decisions and they are made with the greatest care for the well-being of the student and the institution. I can only assure you that there have been others besides athletes, although I don't pay all that much attention to such details."

"I understand that you reinstated two athletes last year and two last term. The only other student you reinstated during that time was a man who was in a farming accident and couldn't keep up with his studies."

Havesham had remained cool beyond her expectations but now he gripped the back of a chair with one hand, extended the other hand toward her, and spoke with deep fury. "How do you know this? I demand an answer."

Sudden sweat streaked Neva's back. He was going to throw her out. He was going to run her out of his office, right in front of the assistants and vice presidents whose offices opened off the reception area. She had been in the news business long enough to grow a thick skin but she could still be deeply embarrassed in some situations, and this was one. The choices were to make an exit now under her own steam or press on and hope he didn't blow his top all the way. To leave would be easy and made good sense—she was unlikely to get anything substantive out of Havesham today, and if this meeting didn't blow sky high she would have a better chance with the president next time around…But a vivid image rose and filled her mental screen, an image of Clayton Perle hunched, solitary, and marooned in his laundry.

"Fewer than half your football and basketball players reach graduation," she said calmly.

Now it was Havesham's turn to mull alternatives. He released the back of the chair, circled it, clasped and unclasped his bony hands, and at last sat down and said with matching calm, "You are mistaken."

"I don't think so. We compared player lists with graduation lists for the past ten years. It looks as though it could be as low as thirty-seven percent, and definitely lower than the fifty percent required by the NCAA. That's why I'm interested in what happened with Clemente. I'm not saying, or even thinking, that you consciously allow athletes to stay here and play with no regard for whether they earn degrees. But there does seem to be a problem, a pattern. I can say with confidence that the people giving me this information are doing it only because they have reached a point of severe frustration with the system."

Looking beyond her at the unadorned wall, the president spoke with somber precision. "I have been assured that these young men are getting all the help we can provide them. I realize, we all realize, that some of these athletes come from disadvantaged homes. They need special help and giving them that help is a sacred charge considering all that the athletes do for this school. Without a winning basketball team, I assure you, we would be a good deal poorer. I also assure you that no decision I have ever made about an individual athlete has hinged on money. Or success on the playing field." His gaze shifted to her face. "At the same time, you must realize that we belong to a very competitive conference, the winningest conference in NCAA history. Some have suggested that we drop to a lower level conference, but there is no comparison in the prestige, the alumni excitement, and the gate and television receipts when you stop playing schools like UCLA and Arizona. We have to remain competitive."

"Would it concern you if my graduation statistics are correct?"

"Of course it would concern me. This is first and foremost an institution of higher learning. Bringing disadvantaged young men here and letting them play for four years on a scholarship and not doing our best to educate them would be using them. I do not see this university as a user of youth, poor black youth or any other group. The well-balanced individual should be the goal of every educator and has always been my guiding principle." Again he stood, crossed to the desk, picked up a small framed plaque that stood beside the telephone, and handed it to her. "From Plato, 'The Republic,' in case you don't recall the words."

The brass plate bore a brief inscription: *Excessive emphasis on athletics produces an excessively uncivilized type, while a purely literary training leaves men indecently soft.*

"Forgive the 'men' reference. We can blame the times."

"Of course. And please believe me, I don't doubt the sincerity of your intentions." Handing back the plaque, Neva continued with open puzzlement, "But our records check has come up with a shockingly low graduation rate for athletes who, I would think, should have a higher rate than average because they're fully supported for five years. This statistic must be known to at least some people on campus as it was very easy to calculate. I've just met a basketball player in his fifth year who has only two years' worth of credits. I've been told about others in the same boat. I learned this morning that thirty-four of the sixty-six special admit athletes were academically deficient last term. You just reinstated a star basketball player despite the recommendation of one of your own committees that he be suspended. And yet you tell me that the university has a moral obligation to see that these kids get an education."

"I insist on knowing your source. This is not public information and must not be printed in your newspaper."

"I'm afraid there's no polite way to put this, but I can't tell whether you're more upset by the substance of what I'm saying or by the fact that I know it."

This was too much even for Havesham. He strode to the door as though to fling it open but then paused for a rigid moment before pivoting and pacing to the window. He looked out in silence. When, at length, he turned to speak he was again in control of his voice but his face remained a furious red.

"Please forgive me. I am not accustomed to being brought up short and made to feel foolish by reporters or anyone else. You realize, I hope, that you're saying things that are very painful for me to hear and I fervently hope—and believe—are not true. We have put considerable resources into the tutoring center. I have questioned the athletic director repeatedly on this point and he has assured me that progress is being made with the athletes. I have accepted his word on that but, perhaps, it is time to look deeper."

Returning to the opposite chair, he rested his hands on its tall back rather than sitting again, and regarded her with open appeal. "I do hope you will refrain from publishing this information. I would hate to see students embarrassed, and you can feel confident that I will begin my own inquiries."

"I wish I could promise you, but this is just part of a larger story we're working on about what happens to athletes in this community, on campus and off. Naturally we will be as respectful of all individuals as possible while trying to paint an accurate picture. Obviously, what triggered this was White's murder—"

"You don't think that has anything to do with the team!"

"I've found nothing to suggest it does, but meanwhile other information is surfacing that raises serious issues, most having to do with NCAA rule violations. But it's the academic situation that's at question here, the reinstatement of students like Clemente with consistently terrible grade records."

"Enough! I am not aware of NCAA rule violations and I am not going to discuss individual students with you and that's that. All I can say is that in each case, the student was strongly represented to me as deserving of special help and I made that judgment. Sometimes, being a university president is like being a father to twenty thousand kids. We live under a complex set of rules here but human beings are all different, all with different needs. Sometimes it falls to me to step outside the rules to find a human solution to a painful problem. I have done this for some kids who were also athletes and I do not apologize. I will, however, look closely into the areas you've mentioned."

"Will you discuss your findings with me?"

"I will not."

CHAPTER
12

"Where did you get these?" J.D. handed the grade sheets to Ambrose but kept her eyes on Neva. "These are highly confidential. We've never been able to get student records like these. For any reason. Even with the names blacked out."

"I have a mole, a very angry mole. He's in a position to know about student suspensions and probation. They suspended Dashiel Clemente but—"

"What's that?" Ambrose looked up sharply from the papers in his hand. "Are you sure? Who said so? That would mean the three top players are out."

"You didn't let me finish. Havesham reinstated him. Instantly."

Ambrose's whistle was long and low. "You have some explaining to do."

Despite the no-smoking rule, J.D. lit a cigarette as Neva launched into a detailed account of her meeting with Havesham, while Ambrose listened without the usual interjections and questions. When she finished, they continued to sit in silence as though stuck in place until J.D. said abruptly, "Right," and stubbed out the cigarette in the drip tray of Ambrose's potted African violet. "The immediate question is, do we have a story?"

"Of course we have a story, a humdinger of a story," Ambrose said. "Hot damn. Talk about hitting the fan—this is going to splatter in all directions. Neva can handle the main story and Cal can do a sidebar on whatever else we can dig up about historic graduation rates."

"No, Ambrose." Neva had prepared for this on the way back from campus and now put the case into precise words. "No story yet. This one incident was only that, an incident. It means nothing unless we can document the big picture. The only thing we'll accomplish by printing this is to drive everyone farther underground. Before printing anything, we need to talk to Clemente, the committee members, and somebody in admissions. And all by itself the academic special treatment doesn't mean much. Again, it's old hat, it happens everywhere. Look at Chapel Hill—yes, I've been doing my homework. To mean anything, or maybe to have fresh meaning, it has to be tied to an overall pattern of pampering athletes for four years and then putting them back out on the street to fend for themselves. No NBA, no degree, nothing but memories."

"Getting kind of bossy, isn't she?" J.D. addressed Ambrose but crooked her thumb at Neva. "Kind of big for her britches."

"I hate like hell to hang onto something like this." Ambrose threw himself back in the chair, swung his boots onto the desk, clasped his fingers behind his head, and scowled at the ceiling. "Damn. Damn damn damn. You make good sense but, well, I hate like hell to sit on hot news. And this is hot, you know it's hot."

The chunky old black telephone on his desk rang. "What?" he barked into it. "What!" The boots came down and he stood up to peer out the wall of windows toward the front desk. "Tell him she'll be right out." And then turning to Neva with a look of unabashed glee, he crooned, "The great Franklin Budd's here to see you."

Budd leaned on the reception counter with the morning's sports page spread out flat under his scrutiny, as casual as though he stood at his own kitchen table. "Hey," he said, and she thought for a moment he was going to wink. "You doing anything?"

Before she could answer, Ambrose came up beside her and reached for Budd's hand. "We miss you on the court. What are you doing to keep in shape these days?"

"I spend a lot of time over at the rec center. Weights. Swim. Jog. The whole bit. But I'm getting tired of it. I'm thinking of becoming a fat person just for something different."

Ambrose chuckled but Neva was more interested in what was happening in the newsroom. Every reporter and editor within sight of the front counter had managed to turn their way. Over in the classified department the saleswomen didn't bother to pretend they were busy. She thought of Jasper Luce: *It was like walking around with Madonna.*

"Can you come out to play now or is it too early for recess?" Budd said with perfect seriousness.

"Did you bring the jump rope?"

The only one who laughed was Ambrose. They left him beaming in the foyer as Neva led the way through the heavy glass door to the entry courtyard. It was cool out but Budd headed for a bench and looked at her sidelong when they were seated at either end. "Did you hear about Dash?"

"That he was suspended?"

"So you know that already." He didn't hide his disappointment.

"And that he was reinstated by Havesham an hour ago."

"Hooey. You must have spies everywhere. I hadn't even heard that yet. No surprise though." Budd stretched his long legs out straight and leaned against the brick wall behind the bench as though settling in for a nap.

"Havesham told me he did it because Clemente needed help, not because he's an athlete."

"That's probably true. The prez is a soft touch. I went to him my second year and he asked me all about my family, my plans and everything, and then gave me another term to bring up my grades. I did, too. I was only on probation that one time. I think he might do the same for any students, except they're scared to go see him. Or they don't think of it. Athletes aren't scared, and we have Gregorio to go with us if we want. Did he go with Dash?"

Neva nodded but her thoughts had turned in a different direction. "Do you know where Annette has gone? White's girlfriend?"

"Beats me, but I'll ask Lamarr."

"Who?"

"Lamarr. My roommate. You met him. He always had a thing for her but was too scared of White to do anything about it. Maybe now he's got a chance, though between you and me, she's way out of his league. Did you talk to Dash?"

"I was thinking of trying to catch him at practice this afternoon."

"Good luck. But you really need to talk to the guys that don't get so much good stuff. They get jealous. Dash is pretty jacked up right now, now that he's king of the court."

"People keep saying that. About the competition between Clemente and White. Do you think that could have anything to do with White's death?"

"Of course not. That's bullshit. Just talk. Speaking of which, anybody you want to talk to on the team, you better do it. Leonard told them to keep clear of you, but you just work a number on them like you did on me and it should be okay. Journalism must be a trip."

"Maybe you should try it. What are you going to do?"

"When I grow up? Business most likely. That's my degree. So. You got a dose of Jasper. I told you he'd talk. He said he spilled his guts like a fool but he isn't sorry. It's something new, he said. You never can tell with Jasper."

"You talked to him already?"

"He called me right after, from the road. What did you think of him?"

"That he really cares about you but feels pretty disgusted with himself for how he carried on with the players in general, and he wants to relieve himself by confessing."

"That sounds about right."

"He told me a lot of interesting things but, like you, he left holes and said I had to fill them in myself. I have to say, I feel as though you two are playing some kind of game with me, having some sport of a different kind, you might say."

"You have a funny way of putting things. Do you learn that being a journalist? Or the other way around?"

"The other way around, I think. You know, I'm finding this more and more interesting, particularly the academic stuff. But I can't quite believe White's death has nothing to do with the rest of it, which seems to be the general assumption. Jasper didn't give a straight answer when I asked him about it but he said you guys aren't virgins when you get here."

Budd laughed, delighted. "Virgins! He's right. Miles more than most, I guess."

"Can you tell me what you mean by that?"

"Did you know I'm a suspect? I've been questioned three times. Why didn't I go jogging, did anybody else know I wasn't going that day, why did he call me before he died, where was I all day Sunday."

"White called you?"

"About something personal. Had nothing to do with anything. I didn't go because I partied all night and couldn't get my butt in gear. I mean, I was out, really out. I can tell you one thing—I wish to hell I had gone. I keep going over it in my mind, how I almost went and then didn't because of one little thing. And now Miles is dead and I'm a suspect. I mean, shit. I actually liked him. Of course, if I went there might be two of us dead. No, forget that. If I was there Miles wouldn't have got shot."

Neva turned on the bench to give Budd a long look. "You know things you aren't telling, don't you?"

He slid his hands into the pockets of his unzipped warm-up jacket and smiled. "Sure I do. And I'm not going to tell because it wouldn't get anybody anywhere. I don't know what's going on, don't get me wrong, but I've got some ideas I'm following up myself. Don't you go messing around in it. This is bad shit. You just stick to the gripper thing."

"Wouldn't it be better to tell the police what you know, or even just suspect? It could be dangerous for you, too."

"Life is dangerous for me. I'm a young black man, remember? Statistically, we're at the top of the death by violence list."

"You've already beat that statistic."

"Let's just say life is more of a contest for someone like me than you. I'm either on the defensive or attacking. There's no middle ground. One thing I've learned in this place is to pretend there's middle ground, but that's bullshit. I've been trying to get Clayton to talk to you again but he's got his head up his ass as usual. He still thinks everybody loves him because he's Clayton. He thinks they're all ignoring him now because he moved and they don't know where he's at. He doesn't hear me yet. But he will."

"Jasper told me about the Valley Savings and Loan connection but didn't mention any names. Who do you work with there?"

Budd shrugged. "Jasper's the paperwork guy. Ben something? Bart? It starts with B, I think, but better ask him."

"I will but if you remember could you let me know?" A quiet moment passed and Budd moved restlessly. She said, "Wait, please. There's one more thing. I haven't told anyone else about this yet but I'd like to hear your reaction. Last night when I got back from talking to Jasper I found a shoebox on my front porch."

He looked at her with curiosity but no sign of knowledge, not that she suspected he was behind this but some rumor could have reached him, someone bragging about the dirty deed.

"Someone left it to shock me. Inside was a dead kitten with pins in its eyes."

Budd's flinch was genuine.

"You don't have any idea who might have done that?"

"Somebody sick. Or like middle school. Shit. Maybe I won't be a journalist after all. I don't even like cats alive and purring. I'll ask around, okay? Don't forget about Dash. Red Camaro, can't miss it."

Crossing the newsroom to her office, Neva ignored the quizzical looks and was particularly careful not to catch Ambrose's eye. She had a lot of calls to make before heading over to the coliseum to try to intercept Dash Clemente at practice. Besides Farnes, the Academic Deficiencies Committee included four members—these were the "jellyfish" he'd browbeaten into suspending Clemente. They were unlikely to talk to her but she had to try, and maybe Havesham's prompt pardon had pushed other members over the tolerance line. All she needed was one more, even if they refused to be named; quoting multiple well-placed anonymous sources saying the same thing shifted the ground from hearsay to serious allegations.

The committee chair did not answer and she decided against leaving a message. Next on the list was Gene Fouchette, from agricultural economics. Fouchette cut her off after the first sentence about athletes and suspension.

"This is no business of the newspaper's," he snapped. "It has to do with internal campus affairs and confidential records and is no one else's business. In regard to President Havesham's action, let me assure you it has nothing to do with the student in question being an athlete. The president has a great deal of sympathy and commiseration for all students, not just athletes, and to even hint otherwise is offensive. Now surely, the paper can find a subject of greater interest than the study habits of a basketball player? Or maybe there's nothing else inflammatory enough for your taste?"

Neva stood up, blew out a long breath, rubbed her eyes, muttered *stupid jerk*. Tonight, after talking with Clemente, she would give herself an evening off to read by the fire. And she needed to restock on green coffee beans and also could do with a haircut. She sat down again, made a note to call Northwest Hairlines, then dialed committee member Bob Coker, from computer science. She caught him heading out to play tennis but he could spare a few minutes to talk, he said.

"Is this for attribution or background?"

"Preferably attribution, but not if you're worried." Neva never said "afraid," because that could be insulting, but she did try to convey the impression that speaking anonymously carried a taint of cowardice. This rarely failed to shame reluctant sources into letting their names be used, but it didn't work with Coker.

"Let's see how it goes and if I say something that I think better of afterwards, that I'd rather not see in print, if I say so will you cross it out?"

"Of course."

"We're all frustrated about this," he said, not waiting for her to finish her set speech about athletes and academic progress. "We're not the college gatekeepers. We don't decide whether these young men will be admitted but we have to deal with them once they're here and failing, and sometimes it's not easy. I don't mean just athletes but all of them, the marginal ones. It's hard enough when you read their stories on paper, the money problems, the family problems, the health problems. But we have a job to do, which is to keep up academic standards. First we give students a warning with probation and then, if their grades don't improve, we send out a suspension notice. And then, most of the time, we forget about it. We don't see them face to face.

"But it's different with athletes. We know as soon as we see an athlete on the list—a scholarship athlete specifically—that we're in for a lot of noise, a lot of hassle. Probation isn't so bad but any time we try to suspend one of these guys, we get landed on. The athletic department sends a delegation. The student, Gregorio, sometimes Leonard or one of the other coaches. We've had them call emergency meetings at seven in the morning. We've had them take an hour telling us why a kid should be given another chance. Frankly, after a while, it's just not worth the fight. I admit it. We'll use any excuse not to bump a star player. No, wait. Scratch that. That wouldn't sound good, would it?

"Let me say it another way," he continued after a moment's thought. "Athletes are different. You can go in there determined to be tough and after listening to some kid tell about his broken family, his dreams of the NBA and hoping to earn enough to put his kid sister through college, you don't feel so tough. I don't know if Gregorio makes up the stories for them, sometimes I think so, but they get to you anyway."

"What happened with Clemente?"

"In his case, we had to draw the line. He had been given so many chances we couldn't in good conscience give him another. The president has a right to overrule any committee but this kind of thing does damage morale—why bother to have a committee? We take our job seriously and he dismissed our efforts as though they were meaningless. Don't quote me on that, please. Just say I am gravely concerned about the effectiveness of committees. And it does bother me that, though it was due to an act of the president's, Clemente's reinstatement goes on record as a committee decision. By the way, I have heard the president say, 'Do you want to be pure or have money for buildings and salaries? A good team brings money.' He's right of course, but that can't be the bottom line for our committee. And now I've really got to run. Good luck with this. It's about time."

Sheila Toosian, from anthropology, was pleasant but apologetic. "I understand what you're asking but I'm up for tenure this year. I realize that shouldn't influence me in such a matter but this place is a lot more political than you may realize. We learn not to rock the boat until we have a lifetime ticket. Then, of course, we're in such a habit of not taking sides, we've forgotten how."

Neva made understanding murmurs, but then said mildly, "Not making it into professional ball must be like failing to make tenure, the end of a dream. And so many don't have a degree to fall back on."

"I'm not too up on sports, actually," Toosian said, sounding more uncertain than cautious. "I've never heard any graduation figures on this. My understanding has been that things are improving, that with counseling and study halls and whatnot the players are doing better. On the committee, we've come to think of it almost as an act of social work to keep these guys on board. What are the other members saying?"

In the end, she agreed only to be quoted to the effect that she was concerned about helping disadvantaged students complete their studies and that committee members had been assured that athletes are a safer bet than most other academically handicapped students because of the support system provided by the athletic department. If that proved not to be the case, she concluded, the committee would have to take a harder line on suspensions.

Half an hour later, parked outside the coliseum door, Neva mulled over the different responses, marveling at how much people give away without meaning to, including these thoughtful and educated faculty members. Such transparency—and yet, so little she could use, though two had agreed to be quoted as expressing "concern" about the situation. It was easy to see why Farnes called them jellyfish. When she wrote the story she'd have to remember to include Farnes in some innocuous way or it would be too easy for the others to spot the mole. She opened her notebook to the page where the interview with Toosian ended and made a note to check with Farnes on how he'd like to be quoted.

The radio was on, the window down a few inches, her view of the door where players would soon emerge unobstructed. She did not expect Clemente to talk, especially out in the open parking lot, but she didn't want to put off the meeting any longer, not with the players warned against her already. It was unlikely that Dash knew that she knew about his suspension and reinstatement, putting the surprise factor on her side.

Two players came out and headed for the lot, both too short for Clemente. *He's a giant even for basketball*, Ambrose had said. And the mug shot beside her on the passenger's seat might actually prove useful this time; Clemente's long face was distinctive but the real clincher was the Nike swish tattoo on his left check.

Another player she didn't know appeared talking on the phone. A group of three followed. If Clemente was with others her job would be tougher—but there he was, alone, a regular giraffe just as Ambrose had said. Leading with his head as though walking into the wind, he made for the glossy red Camaro beside her.

She got out of her car as he stooped to unlock his door.

"Dash," she said.

He glanced at her, looked toward the coliseum, and shook his head.

"I'm Jeneva Leopold from—"

"I'm not talking to anybody from the paper." He slid into the driver's seat and drew his legs in after him like trawling lines, but she managed to get hold of the door before it closed.

"Please, it will only take a moment. I'm really concerned about the basketball players."

"Concerned? What's that supposed to mean?"

"Only thirty-seven percent of scholarship athletes manage to get degrees from this school. You guys play for four years and get nothing out of it, except for a few who make it to the NBA. Only one in every hundred college players makes it into the NBA. You might make it, but none of your teammates will. If you care about them, you'll talk to me for a few minutes."

"I've been told to keep away from you." He shook his head and released a snorting laugh. "They said you're trying to screw the team but you don't look dangerous to me. If you promise to keep your head down—oh, shit, I've got to get out of here." He shoved in the key, gunned the engine, and reached for the door. "Let go before I catch hell."

She looked toward the coliseum and discovered Rex Gregorio bearing down on them and scowling ferociously. "Sorry," she said, turning back to Clemente and letting go of the door. "Let's talk another time."

The car backed away and sped for the exit as Gregorio came within snarling distance. "What are you doing here?"

"Trying to get details about what happened this morning in President Havesham's office."

"Nothing happened. What did he say?"

Gregorio stopped at a good arm's length from her but still she could smell mint on his breath and see the individual tips of dark hairs that spread a fashion-worthy shadow across the lower half of his face.

"He didn't say anything, nothing at all. He's well trained. Why are you so worried about the players talking to me?"

"I don't understand what's got into you people. There's nothing happening, nothing different going on."

"Are you saying it's business as usual for basketball players to be killed in parks? Or academically suspended and then rescued the same day by the president? Could you please explain to me why Clemente was reinstated when he has straight D's and F's in academic subjects, and has had for two terms running?"

"You don't know that. If you want the real picture, I suggest you come in for a little talk."

In the thin light of early evening, Gregorio looked older than she'd expected, but what Ambrose called his "gangsta glamuh" remained potent. No way did she want to be shut up with him alone. She said evenly, "I'd rather talk right here. When was the last time the president reinstated a suspended basketball player?"

"I have no intention of talking in the middle of a parking lot. Either you come with me or take no comment for your story."

"Are you going to give me anything more than no comment?"

"Come in and find out."

The athletic director turned and strode away, and after a moment's hesitation, she followed. They walked without speaking in through the double doors, down a deserted corridor, through a reception area, and into Gregorio's office. The door was blocked open by a straight chair piled high with magazines, folders, wadded clothing. Gregorio shoved the lot onto the floor, dragged the chair sideways, kicked the door shut and turned to face her.

He did not bellow with rage or shake a threatening fist. He smiled. "There. That's better. A little privacy and all kinds of nice things can happen. Let me build you a happy."

In a ritual that echoed Tucker Reilly's, he opened a sliding wood cupboard and took down two heavy glasses, talking over his shoulder. "No need to say it. You're a gin and tonic girl. Can you name my poison? I'll give you a hint. Anybody that doesn't drink it neat or on the rocks is a Philistine."

"Scotch?" She didn't want a drink and she didn't want to play his little game but the dramatic change in the famously ferocious athletic director had thrown her off balance. What kind of Jekyll and Hyde was she dealing with here? Wary, watching him, she chose a chair that stood away from the others. She left her notebook in her jacket pocket and kept the jacket on.

"Scotch is my vice, all right. No ice." Gregorio prepared the drinks with experienced speed. Neither tall nor short, he had a springy, slim-muscled build that wore clothing well. Today it was a cream blazer with a Boomer-blue tie over a pale blue dress shirt. Handing her a sizable tumbler, he raised his in salute but did not propose a toast. "Well, now, that's better. I think best with a glass in my hand. And before I forget, you've got a complimentary seat for Thursday's game. Stanford. Right up front. No need for thanks. You may not believe this, but you and I are on the same side. Oh, yes we are. I'm sure you want only what's best for our program and you think what you're doing is in our best interest. Isn't that right?"

His look was warm and encouraging but he did not pause for a reply. "Of course, we're all in shock over Miles. When I said nothing unusual had happened I wasn't talking about that. That's still so far beyond belief you can't talk about it like anything else. This place has been like a church all week. We couldn't get through the team meeting Sunday, really, I'm telling you."

Nodding, Neva thought of Joey and Clayton and Budd. Plenty of dry eyes there.

"When I came here ten years ago, the program was in decline," the athletic director continued in a tone that suggested a well-worn speech. "Low morale, crappy facilities, inept coaching. It was a challenge, a real challenge. You have to go slow, you have to build it piece by piece, first a good coach, then some good players, then you get more fans and more money, more good coaches, morale starts to climb, you start winning games and all of a sudden you find yourself with a winning program and everybody in the world wanting a piece of it." Gregorio tilted his head, drained his glass, looked at hers. "What's the matter? Did I make it too strong? Too weak?"

"It's fine, thank you." She hadn't tasted the drink yet but now sipped, realized she was very thirsty, and half-drained the glass.

It was an excellent G & T, made no doubt with the best gin. And what a performer he was, and no wonder he got his way with everyone from Havesham on down.

"I get interviewed all the time," he said, refilling his glass while managing not to look away from her. "Magazines. TV. One thing they always want to know is the secret. How do you build a winning program from scratch in ten years? That's what they want to know. You know what I tell them? 'People,' I say. 'You have to know people. You have to understand what makes them tick. You have to know what they're going to do before they do it. Before they even know they're going to do it.' That's what I tell them."

He waited, expectant, until she said, "Really?"

"That's right." His smile was big. "It's bullshit, of course. You want to know the real answer? Do you?"

She nodded and felt a sudden slippage inside her head. Had Gregorio poisoned the drink? Ridiculous—he had made it strong, that's all, and she hadn't eaten for too many hours, and was not a regular drinker of hard liquor.

Speaking each word and letter separately and with equal emphasis, he said, "I've got balls. B.A.L.L.S. That's all there is to it."

He crossed the carpet on light feet, took her glass, and turned toward the bar.

"Thank you, it was very good but one is enough," she said. "I haven't eaten much today."

"So much the better. The gin works faster that way. Aren't you enjoying our little talk? I'm enjoying our little talk. You're not in a hurry are you? Nobody expecting you? No sexy date waiting for dinner? Good. It's not every day I get to talk to a woman like you."

He handed her another full glass and let his fingers brush hers, lightly, carelessly, but even so the touch was like hot wires on her skin. She stared at her hand wrapped around the glass. She wasn't used to this. A glass of wine before dinner, that was her ritual, sipped over the course of an hour. She hadn't been tipsy in a long while, and she wasn't interested in hot wires, at least not from the likes of Gregorio.

"Balls," he said, drawing the word out and pulling a chair up close to hers. "That's all it is. You've heard that expression. When the going gets tough, the tough get going. That's not me. I'm always going. Ask anybody around here. Sure I get tired, sure I get worked up and depressed and pissed off. I'm human, hey, did I ever say I wasn't? I was born that way. I took this little piece of trash of an athletic program and turned it into a powerhouse. Do you know how many million dollars we've brought into this university in the last five years? Do you? No. Scratch that. I can't remember numbers but it's a hell of a lot. Have I taken any for myself? No way. Do I expect special favors? No way. Do I ask for a gold medal? No way. It's the program, that's what it is, the beginning, middle, and end. You know what I mean?"

Gregorio was going down fast. Whether he turned out to be a careless drunk or a mean drunk remained to be seen. Either way, her only hope of getting anything out of this was to steer the monologue in a useful direction before he was too far gone to talk straight. "You have built an amazing program. Everyone respects that, very much. But aren't you just a little worried sometimes that what has happened in some other places will happen here? That boosters will get out of line?"

"You don't give up, do you? I told you I didn't want to talk about that stuff. We're having a nice little talk about the athletic program. I don't give a shit about boosters. Is that what you're bothering my boys about? Boosters?" He threw his head back and laughed. "Well, I'll just say this. If you want to see boosters in action, don't hang around here. We're minor league. These guys are amateurs." He paused, took a breath, looked at his empty glass.

"You know," he said, his tone suddenly flat, "I think you better mind your own business. How does that sound?"

"I'm afraid my job is to nose into other people's business rather than minding my own. Especially when it's of public concern."

"Public concern? Are you kidding? The only public I ever see is the thousands of fans cheering their heads off at games. What public concern? Look, this is my show here. I'm trying to tell you, I know what's good for it and I won't stand for any interference from candy asses. Concern? What concern? What do you think it would do to Dash's career? You publish anything about this business today and he's down the tubes. He won't play this term and that means his last year is a waste and he won't make draft.

You talk so holy about saving the program from the boosters and then you want to wreck a kid's career."

Gregorio was on his feet now, pacing and scowling. "You don't know crap about basketball. Not crap."

"What about all the players who don't make a career in basketball and don't get a degree either?"

"What about them? They have it good while they're here, better than they ever imagined. Why don't you look at the kids that get degrees that wouldn't even have gone to college if we didn't bring them here? That's what I can't stand about the press, always looking for the crap. Why don't you print the success stories? What about Julian Loomis and Jim Borden? From housing projects to the NBA in four years. Now that's a story. You ever heard of Pahokee? Pahokee, Florida? No, I didn't think you did. It's a little shit-hole outside Palm Beach where I grew up. Palm Beach, not Pahokee. They used to grow vegetables there. Now they grow football players. If it wasn't for the NFL those boys'd rot there like everybody else on welfare and crack. You think that's cynical, don't you? Well, I'd like to see you go down there and tell them all about it, tell them they're being used. Exploited. That's the word. Right? Am I right? Tell me I'm right."

"What about Joshua Gifford?"

"Mistake. Never should have brought him here."

"Clayton Perle?"

"What about him?"

"He's into his fifth and final year on scholarship and has only two years' worth of usable credits. He's going to leave here with no future in the NBA and no degree."

"Something you have to get through your head. Some of these boys just aren't college material. They—" Gregorio stopped and bent his head as though listening to a replay of his own words. He picked up his empty glass, set it down, moved some papers on his desk, unwrapped a piece of gum but started talking before putting it into his mouth. "Let's just say some can handle it better than others. It takes a lot of work to play ball and go to school at the same time and some kids just can't handle it. You can't tell until they get here who's going to make it but there will always be a few that just can't hack it."

"A few? Sixty-three percent?"

"Where did you get that number? If you've got such accurate figures, I'd love to see them."

"You mean you don't keep track?"

"Not in just that way, but I can tell you that's a ridiculous figure."

"How do you know it's ridiculous? You just said you don't keep track."

"You really know how to make yourself lovable, don't you?"

The sudden nasty edge in his voice made her stand up. He circled the desk and came close enough for her to smell his breath again, whiskey this time rather than mint. "I thought we could work this out but you're determined to make trouble. I want you out of here and if I catch you talking to my players again, I'll get security to throw you out. As far as Clemente goes, if you print anything from me except no comment you can expect trouble. From me personally to you personally. With pleasure. Are we understanding this?"

Neva strode to her car through deep twilight, slid in behind the wheel, locked the door. She crossed her arms on the steering wheel and let her head drop forward. The man was insane. Unbalanced. Not at all what she'd expected. Smarmy for starters, then a cheap drunk, then aggressive. Had he really thought his little performance would satisfy her? Charm her into docility? All the while he dropped little revealing gems . . . *If you want to see boosters in action, don't hang around here. We're minor league. These guys are amateurs. . . Some of these boys just aren't college material.*

She sat up, pulled out notebook and pen, and felt a sudden sense of being watched. The coliseum's double doors and porch were lighted and pole lamps around the parking lot were coming on as daylight vanished. Gregorio had not followed her out and no one else could be seen around the building or the handful of cars that remained in the lot.

Had he continued tossing down whiskey?

Called his friendly local assassin?

Ha ha.

Drinking had been a very bad thing to do. She set the notebook aside and started the car.

The house was dark and as she pulled into the driveway she made a mental note to leave the porch light on around the clock in future, at least until this business was done. And the lack of a garage—particularly a garage with an automatic door opener—suddenly seemed lamentable.

All was quiet as she went up the front walkway, not even the usual evening breeze stirring in the shrubbery and trees. Pausing, she considered the bulky camellias that flanked the porch, the black shadows where the small lawn met the laurel hedge, the dark windows of the house. She returned along the walk to the driveway and continued down the driveway to look up and down the street.

Over the years, she had received her fair share of hate mail, along with the predictable raspberry awards from local rightwing groups, and once even a nicely wrapped container of rat poison in response to an appreciative column about possums in her garden shed. A few messages had carried mild threats, but nothing in the past had affected her like the kitten with pins in the eyes. The kitten was now buried in a flowerbed but her sense of invasion remained fresh. There was more to come, she felt certain.

Returning to the porch, she studied it before crossing to unlock the door, then stood for a moment in the hall to listen and test the air for unfamiliar smells. Nothing was obviously amiss and yet the house did not feel right. Moving now with determined confidence, she went through each room, flipping on lights, looking behind doors, opening closets. The back bedroom was undisturbed, the living room was as she'd left it, the kitchen was tidy apart from her breakfast plate and mug on the counter.

She was halfway across the kitchen when she felt cool air moving against her face, just the suggestion of a breeze carrying the smell of outdoors. The window over the sink was closed. She focused on the dark doorway to the utility porch and waited. No movement. No sound. Easing forward, she reached the opening and stopped in the current of fresh air that now clearly was coming through the window in the back door. That window did not open.

She felt for the switch on the wall to the right. Light blazed. The utility room floor sparkled with glass fragments. She blinked and focused on an object sitting in the broken glass. It was a basketball. A knife had been jammed into the ball, skewering a piece of paper to it.

For a long moment she stood simply taking it in—the black hole in the door window rimmed with jagged glass, the littered floor, the half-deflated ball and scrap of torn, impaled newsprint.

Stepping through the glass with care, she squatted for a closer look at the paper and discovered her own face neatly split by the blade. It was one of her columns from last week with the usual mug shot at the top, a mug shot now sliced from left eye to right shoulder.

"Hell," she said, and pulled out the knife.

CHAPTER
13

In the morning before making coffee, Neva checked the plywood she had nailed over the broken window. Of course it was solidly in place—she had used a handful of nails—and the floor was cleared of glass, just as she'd left it. Although she had searched the house thoroughly after cleaning up the mess, she now went again from room to room, listening and feeling as well as looking, and concluded for a second time that the ball had been shoved through the window. No one had entered her house.

And whatever they had used to break the window must have come with them as a thorough search of the area around the back door turned up no blunt object suitable for smashing glass.

Maybe it was time to get a dog. A large dog.

When she arrived at the *Current* half an hour later, she went straight to Ambrose's office to report the incident and tell him, finally, about the kitten. But the words that popped out instead were, "What's the occasion?"

For the editor was waiting with an entire box of donuts, a rare, even unprecedented offering. "Meeting at 9 with Cal and J.D. You didn't get my message? We'll start with how you got on with Clemente. Ah, there's Cal now."

The sports editor came straight across the newsroom rather than veering right to the sports section. Tall, rangy, and affable, Cal had been on track for an athletic scholarship out of high school when a bad knee injury "slapped me down." Always said with a shrug. Neva had worked within whistling distance of him for more than a decade but the last three days had brought more interaction between them than the rest of the years combined.

Before Cal managed to sit down, Ambrose said, "Okay, Neva, let's have it."

"What about J.D.?"

"She's late."

"Of course she's late. It's the middle of the night for her."

"I got her donuts, didn't I? Now, what did our Dash have to say for himself?"

"He didn't get time to say anything, though I think he was ready to. Gregorio must have been on the watch because he caught us before we got started."

"That must have been fun," Cal said.

"It was just the opening move. He refused to talk in the parking lot and we ended up in his office. Door shut, just the two of us." Her account was detailed and was not interrupted once by either man. "So I've been warned," she concluded. "If he catches me talking to his players it's big trouble—from him personally to me personally, with pleasure."

"Christ, you got the full-Gregorio right out of the chute," Cal marveled. "I've only had to deal with the half-Gregorio myself, and that was bad enough. We must be barking up the right tree."

"That clinches it. I want a story for tomorrow on Clemente's suspension," Ambrose said and slapped the desk.

"No—"

"I don't think—"

Neva and Cal looked at each other with sudden complicity. United they might actually stand against Ambrose. The sports editor had made a slow start on the booster saga but now was under full sail. The murder, Budd's anger, the ugly picture painted by Jasper Luce, the leaked documents from the deficiencies committee…just what had changed Cal's tune after years of telling Ambrose *It's no worse than anywhere else* Neva didn't know but she was glad to have an ally.

"After you, ma'am," he said with a grave nod.

"Thank you, sir," she replied with equal solemnity. And then to Ambrose, "I thought we'd settled this yesterday. Clemente might still talk if I can catch him alone, but not if we've already blown the story open. He seemed willing until Gregorio came tearing across the parking lot."

"I'm surprised at you, to be intimidated by a petty thug like Gregorio."

"That's not what she's saying," Cal protested. "You know that's not what she's saying. We have a situation here, a very delicate situation that for the time being has been resolved. It's an isolated incident that nobody would really understand out of context. It will have a lot more effect as part of our series. We're working hard to make this all hang together and I, for one, don't want to see it dribble out in pieces."

"Cal's right. Why weaken our own punches with a preview? None of this is going away any time soon."

A knock at the door was followed by a rumpled J.D. who cast a mournful look at the pastry box. "That pitiful excuse for a donut's mine, I take it?"

Ambrose pushed the box with its lone remaining donut—not only the smallest but with no chocolate topping—across the desk toward the city editor. "You missed Neva's rundown on Gregorio but you'll get the notes."

The confab that followed, mostly a rehash of Ambrose's overall plan, failed to hold Neva's attention, though she did hear Cal vow to call in every chip that was owed him by anyone affiliated with athletics. A powerful picture of the relationship between grippers and players was emerging, but she had to get documentation. That fancy red car of Dash Clemente's—who really owned it? And that comfortable apartment of Clayton's and his preppie clothes, and all the rest of the goodies and favors that appeared to be routine bennies for players…there must be paper trails and it was time to find them.

As the meeting was ending at last, she said, "There's one more thing. Well, two actually. A dead kitten and a dead basketball."

Her quick account of the incidents was followed by three different reactions in perfect character.

J.D.: "Bastards!"

Cal: "What kind of basketball was it?"

Ambrose: "You've punched their buttons, Leopold. Keep it up. Better file a police report for the record. Send me a bill for the window. No, better yet, leave it to me. I'll get someone over there today."

Back in her office, pleased to have got through the meeting without committing to any particular line of action, Neva opened the Willamette law enforcement website and filed the first incident report of her life. It took no more than five minutes to give the details of both episodes. She had planned to call Jeb's Window & Glass to get the repair going as well, and now wished she'd turned down Ambrose's offer to take care of it. No telling when he'd actually get around to making the call.

Next on the list was Valley Savings and Loan. This was a bit tricky in that she knew only to look for a loan officer with a name that began with "B." Happily, the answering message included a staff directory option. The third name listed was Benjamin Bailey. She was jotting it down when the voice said Burt Thomson. She wrote that as well, but when the list ended with Barry Trueman, she had to laugh. Ben? Burt? Barry? Looked like she'd have to walk into Valley Savings and Loan and ask to speak to the person in charge of issuing dodgy loans on cars for athletes.

And just what did she hope to learn if she did find the right man?

Job one was to find out whose name was on the car registration. Was a lending institution really the right place for this? What mattered was who owned the vehicle, not whether they'd financed it. But what if it were possible to finance a car in someone else's name? Hadn't Budd said as much?

Musing, she flipped through the notebook on her desk and came to a page with numbers. License plate numbers. From the yellow car that she suspected belonged to the elegant Vera. If she could get the plate numbers for all the big-name players then she might be able to check the registration information with the department of motor vehicles. But how to get the license numbers, especially for players like Jim Borden who were long gone?

Maybe the names would be enough.

Maybe the DMV would have traffic ticket information on the players that would say what car they'd been driving at the time.

The Oregon Motor Vehicles Division office was in Salem only forty minutes up the freeway, but best to begin with a phone call to see whether this kind of information was available for the asking. Expecting the usual series of recordings, she was surprised to hear a live human voice answer, the voice of a woman who turned out to be more than cooperative. "No need to drive all the way up here. I can take the names by phone. I'll look them up when I get a chance and if there's anything on them I'll let you know."

Julian Loomis, Jim Borden, Dashiel Clemente... She spelled carefully, added the license number from the yellow car, then hung up with a sense of triumph. The next moment she felt uneasy. Apart from her name, the woman had not asked for her identity or why she wanted the information. Apparently, anyone could call the office and get a traffic history check on any driver along with vehicle ownership names. Her life, like the lives of the basketball players, was as open to scrutiny as the life of an ax murderer, should anyone care to follow the paper trail—not that anyone would bother.

She had no secrets, not after writing three columns a week for almost twenty years, columns that used her personal experiences as entry points for exploring everything from city planning to single motherhood. She had created a public Jeneva Leopold that was not quite the same as the private woman, but even so, the shape of her life was known to thousands of regular readers who thought they knew her like a family member.

Sudden discomfort made her look around at the narrow window, but there was nothing to see apart from the usual stretch of parking lot and gray sky. The sense of exposure persisted. Being so visible had never truly bothered her before, but then, no one had ever invaded her life so physically and repulsively before. That the attention could escalate to violence against herself she considered very unlikely. Dead kitten, knife slash to her face on a basketball—these were nasty gestures, that's all.

Even so, they were more disturbing than she would have admitted aloud. Should she move to a hotel until this was over?

No way.

So then, what next?

She yawned, stretched, reached for her notes. So many strings to follow, and so hard—so very hard—to know which were important. Her thoughts drifted. What was Rex Gregorio doing right at this moment? What would he say or do if she turned up at the game on Thursday expecting her free seat? Out of the question, of course, but, well…gradually her thoughts collected around a name.

Joshua Gifford.

What had Gregorio said? Gifford was a mistake? *Never should have brought him here.*

Gifford was on the list of contacts that Cal had put together, no address apart from Los Angeles, but both a cell number and work number. The former Boomer worked nights as a janitor and slept days, according to what he'd told Cal when they'd run into each other at a Bruins vs. Boomers game six months ago. If she woke him up he might be cranky—or, with luck, mellow and communicative.

"Hey, Sweetie Cakes. You're late," a very unsleepy male voice crooned after two rings.

"Not Sweetie Cakes, I'm sorry to say. A nosy reporter from Willamette."

Gifford laughed merrily. "Trust me to call a reporter Sweetie Cakes. Maybe you guessed it but I'm expecting a call from my fiancé. We're getting married in May and she was supposed to call before lunch. But you got me first, so shoot."

Neva kept the explanation simple, maybe too simple, because Gifford seemed to think she wanted to know what it was like playing on the team, and launched into fond recollections. "We were definitely a family, relaxed, comfortable, like being at home. We played high-pressure basketball for Leonard, don't get me wrong, but that was on the court. When you're number one it means every other team wants to get you, bring you down. You can't stay number one forever but you got to try. I'm real calm off the court but when I get on court I get excited, keyed up. You know you can be beat but you can't let it affect the way you play. You play like you never can be beat. It's hard to be that intense all the time but that's what it takes to be number one. You can't win a game by yourself but if you play your hardest, and the team loses, well, you know you did your best. It's all you can do."

This was good stuff, great for a column on the psychology of high-competition team sports, but she wasn't writing a column, or even a feature piece. "How about classes? Was it hard finding time to study?"

A brief silence was followed by a nervous little hum, before Gifford said, "Sure. An athlete's got it harder than other students. It takes more physical ability and stamina to do two things at once. You have to concentrate on your books and the teacher when you're in class, then you change and go to practice and put your mind on basketball, nothing but basketball. I had to go to summer school to keep up my eligibility. They talked about putting me on probation. They have tutors there in the department but, looking back on it, I guess they didn't help too much. They couldn't go to class for you and nobody could take the tests for you."

Listening hard, typing fast, Neva thought of Clayton Perle. He, too, would have been tutored, and very likely had gone to summer school. Did all the athletes have to put in this kind of extra time? And why didn't it help more of them graduate? "How much longer would you have to go to get a degree?"

"A year, maybe two, but I don't guess I'll ever finish. I'm taking a heating and refrigeration class at El Camino Community College. Just for backup, you know. For security. As a married man."

"That sounds useful. What kind of work do you do now?"

"I work for the L.A. Unified School District, in maintenance. Summers I lifeguard."

"Do you still do sports?"

"Well, sure, of course I do. I'm still aiming for the NBA. I work from six-thirty to three-thirty, then I work out at the gym from four to six, only now I'm doing it for myself. In college, I did it for the school. It makes a difference. I know what I'm doing now, and with prayer and a little luck, I'll make it."

"How can you still hope for a place in the NBA? I thought they drafted out of college."

"Mainly, but that's not the only way. I have a tryout in June with the Nuggets. I play in five city leagues and I fooled around in the CBA for a while so I put in a lot of time at it."

"CBA?"

"Continental Basketball Association. Kind of a farm league but what the hell, it's basketball. It kept my hand in. At least I'm not playing in China. Not yet anyway."

"It must be a pretty big letdown. Not to be drafted."

Again the pause, followed by careful words. "You aren't kidding. I had a plan to make a career out of basketball. It was a priority I set to make pros. Not just for me but for my mom, to give her a better life. It was the only thing I ever did. I had a lot going my way. This may sound kind of dumb but, you know, most of us think we'll be one-and-done."

"I'm sorry to be so uninformed, but what is one-and-done?"

"Drafted after you've been out of high school for a year. Doesn't happen all that often but, well. I still don't know why Leonard didn't give me a better rec. I started for the last two years. I thought it was in the bag and when it wasn't, I thought it was the end of the world. I wanted to die, to tell the truth. Just die and be gone. But you can't do that. You go on, and maybe I needed to do some more growing up. It's a big change from high school to college. I didn't have my priorities straight, I guess. I didn't think about the long run."

"How do you feel about not getting a degree?"

"I felt bad at first, like it was one more thing I failed at. I was bitter for a while. But now I see I'm a lot better off, a lot more aware of things, than if I didn't go to college for four years. I got to travel, met a lot of good people, made friends. It makes my life better today."

"Did you make friends in town, here in Willamette?"

"Oh, sure. After a certain amount of time, they see you on TV, they begin to like you. It depends some on how you get along with people. I never had a problem with that. There was mutual respect. I met a lot of people who made me feel at home. I'd never stayed away from home by myself before where I had to take care of all my own stuff, if you know what I mean, and at first I was lost. But people in the community really play a part in helping you relax, make a family-type atmosphere. It was the first time I was ever accepted into an all-white environment. I worked for people, did yard work, painted garages just to help out and give them back something for what they gave me, but I never let them pay me. I wanted to keep myself clean, keep them clean."

"You weren't allowed to accept pay because of the NCAA rules?"

"That's right. I hate the NCAA, that's one thing I do hate. The athletes are used by the school, you know—I guess that's why you're asking me these questions. Sure, we're used. They make a lot of money off us, I mean a lot, especially now, and they don't pay us enough to live comfortable, or even to live at all. If it wasn't for community members, a lot of players wouldn't make it. The NCAA is too strict. I'm for the wellbeing of the player, the well-disciplined player being able to get help when they need it. If you want to give me money as a community member, well, that's your money. Nobody should be able to tell you that you can't. Nobody should be able to tell you whether you could be my friend or not just because I play basketball. When I played for the Boomers, I gave a hundred and ten percent whether I was on the court or studying or whatever. And that's more than other students have to give. No, I don't blame the university. It's not their fault. It's the NCAA."

"Some players have told me they were given things like cars, charge accounts, gas and repairs, cash, big screen TVs. Was that how it was for you?"

"I guess I'd rather not talk about particulars. I was always pretty careful, more careful than a lot of guys, but I was only a kid, really, and I never had much practice resisting temptations, if you know what I mean. I can tell you one thing. I've got nothing to show for it today, so it's like one of those things in the desert. A mirage. Only you can actually feel it and taste it for a while and then it goes away."

The sudden feeling of affection for the young man at the other end of the line took her by surprise. Talking with the other players—Clayton, Julian, and even Budd to a degree—had left her feeling puzzled and uneasy rather than truly sympathetic, as she so often felt when engaging with subjects for her column. Most people, in her experience, were worth talking to and most had at least one good life story to tell and some good heart in them somewhere. Josh was the first Boomer to stir her feelings in this familiar way and for a moment she didn't know what to say.

Then, warmly, she said, "You amaze me. You're so philosophical and calm about it all, about what had to be a deeply wrenching change in your life and expectations."

"I don't blame anybody anymore. I'm not bitter anymore, even when I found out they were using me in some video game, my face, team number, everything, making more money and me still not getting any of it. I'm just working hard every day, keeping myself in shape. My fridge is full of food, I'm getting married. I'm settling my life down. I've been wanting to come back up there and thank all the people that helped me."

"Does anyone from here still help you?" she could not help asking.

"Hell no—why would they want to do that? I'm nobody now. I do understand that much." A pause. "Well, I suppose it won't hurt to say I still get a small check sometimes from one guy."

"That would be Jasper Luce."

Gifford's chuckle was deep.

"Just one more thing, Josh, if that's okay. Miles White."

"I was wondering when you'd get around to Miles."

"Do you think the murder could be connected to the team? Anything you know that makes you wonder?"

"No way. I mean, it's sports, you know? People get all riled up about it but not like that, not like killing people. I've been thinking about Miles and I can't figure it. I only played with him one year and we didn't hang out but he was cool. Tell you what, though, I'll ask around. There might be something serious coming down since I left. I doubt it, but I'll let you know."

CHAPTER
14

Neva set the receiver down gently, as though closing a door on going out of a room where something tender should not be disturbed. Joshua Gifford. A broom balanced on one hand, a basketball on the other. About to be married, studying refrigeration, still believing in his future in the NBA…It changed things for her, it did change things. This was not a basketball story she was chasing, it was a human dilemma story, like so much of her work over the years. She must keep Joshua Gifford in her thoughts.

For all his talk of being squared away, Gifford seemed the most wistful Boomer so far. Clayton was in such limbo there was no telling how he would land when he finally came to his senses and realized it was over, done, finished, that he was not a national star and never would be again. Budd was plain angry and determined to succeed in the world beyond sports. Julian and Clemente were still playing, still counting on a future in the NBA.

Every one of them had spent a childhood, the teen years, the early twenties preparing for an almost impossible future. Athletes weren't alone in spending their young years preparing to excel; musicians, dancers, even some actors put in long early apprenticeships learning their craft. They might or might not make it to Juilliard, Carnegie Hall, the Big Screen—but if they failed to reach the top, they still had lives, still had a future. They didn't vanish overnight like athletes rejected by pro scouts.

Neva let her head sink forward onto her folded arms. She had not slept well—yet again—after cleaning up the broken glass. She had put the basketball and knife into a box in the spare bedroom closet out of sight. Now a powerful impulse to go home, to reclaim her territory in the friendly light of afternoon, made her stand up with resolution and collect her bag and folders. She headed out without letting anyone know she had no intention of returning that day.

As she was about to pull out of the parking lot she changed direction, and headed downtown to the coffee bean store. Oregon Coffee & Tea occupied half a block of storefront on Elizabeth Avenue between First and Second, and was run by three generations of the Collett family. Casey Collett was behind the counter today.

"What's new?" Neva said, her routine greeting for this coffee maven whose knowledge had added flavor to every one of her mornings for the past decade. "I'm really enjoying the Ethiopian Kaffa Forest."

"How about the Yemen Sana-ani Haimi? Very deep flavor. It's not always available, and hardly ever from the same supplier two years in a row. Dennis has to watch for it. And now with the political situation, well, that may be the end of it for a while."

Casey led the way to the shelves at the far end of the store and handed Neva a one-pound zip-lock bag fat with green coffee beans. "They let this one dry on the tree. A bit spendy but worth trying. Now tell me why we're reading old Leopold columns, if that's not too nosy."

Neva kept the explanation simple and concluded by teasing, "I don't suppose you keep open charge accounts for caffeine-addicted basketball stars?"

Casey laughed, a true peal of merriment that sent Neva on her way cheerful once again.

At home, she checked every room, every window and door, before changing into jeans and a sweatshirt. She collected gardening gloves, a trowel and a basket with handles and set to work on the back planting beds. Most years, she cleaned them up in late fall but the season had changed so suddenly, had gone from balmy October to bitter November so fast, that she'd left the corpses of tomato plants standing inside their cages. Dead bean vines still clung to the twine.

For hours she worked with absorption, and got an extra reward in the discovery of some young kale and mustard leaves, enough for a dinner salad. And the garlic was well up, she noted with delight, the spear-like tops bright green against black earth. She was trying six different types bought from a stall at the farmers' market in September, though as sprouts they looked identical.

The sun was well down when she quit, reluctantly, and carried the tender leaves indoors just in time to pick up the phone.

"So what's up?" said her son's voice without a greeting. "What's with the old column? You wrote that five years ago when I was still home."

"I didn't know you were a regular reader." Neva carried the phone to the living room and settled on the couch, the same old couch that Ethan had jumped up and down on as a small boy and turned into a lumpy relic that was on her list for replacing. Someday.

"I'm not," Ethan said cheerfully. "I was downloading something and to pass the time I decided to see what you were up. You haven't been sick?"

"Not a bit. Your mother has turned into a basketball groupie."

"Whoa, March Madness, I never would have thought of that in a hundred years. Not that it's March yet."

"What do you know about March Madness? You hate sports."

"So do you. I still feel guilty for making you stand in the rain every Saturday morning."

"Kid soccer ain't sports, honey."

"What is it?"

"Parental obsession. Which I suppose is what it all boils down to—obsession." She sketched the week's action so far, starting with Ambrose's call on Sunday and ending with Joshua Gifford. Naturally, she left out the kitten and the speared basketball as any sensible parent would. "I've been feeling my way into this, trying to understand, to figure out what's going on and whether it matters."

"Nothing to figure, Mumsie. It's all about the marketplace. The university buys players with scholarships and under-the-table extras, the fans buy them with expensive tickets, the boosters buy them with stuff and favors. When they get past their due date, it's over, off the shelf. Pretty simple, really."

"How do you know so much?"

"I'm just repeating what you told me. Guess where I learned that trick? Maybe I'll go see the Boomers next week. They're playing here, you know. I could skulk around, see if any cash gets tucked into their G-strings, so to speak."

The rain started again as she hung up and returned to the kitchen and turned on the lights. Closing the window over the sink, she noticed the wheelbarrow at the edge of the patio. She had forgotten to stand it upright against the shed. What's more, her garden gloves were draped over the handle. One wet night wouldn't hurt the wheelbarrow but her gloves would be sodden by morning. And what had she done with the trowel?

She flipped on the back porch light and felt pleased all over again by the pleasantly diffuse glow from the ceramic shade she'd installed some months ago in place of the plain bulb that had done the job—glaringly—for years. Why the simple improvement had taken so long to do was just one of those small puzzles in an essentially orderly life.

Not bothering with a jacket, she went down the three steps to the patio and over to the wheelbarrow. Her hand was extended to gather the gloves when the sound of a distinct and human sneeze stopped her cold. Gravel crunched on the path beyond the planting beds and the back gate slammed.

Rooted in place, listening with her whole body, Neva waited through a silence before rasping out, "Hello?"

She did not expect an answer and there was none.

The gate went nowhere. That is, it led only to the yard on the other side of the fence. The yard sloped up to a house built against the hillside above and occupied for two years now by students. For anyone walking from campus, the shortcut would be considerable compared with going all the way up Spring Street and around, and whenever she saw her young neighbors cutting through the yard with a furtive air she let them know they were welcome.

The sneeze had sounded innocent and even childlike in the night, and not in the least bit alarming in itself. A week ago, she would have called out again. Now she continued to stand in silence, feeling the night.

She had created every square inch of this garden, built the raised beds, laid down the gravel for paths, meticulously pieced the patio flagstones, shored up sagging cedar fences, transplanted shrubs and bulbs, fashioned picturesque seats to get the best views as the light changed by day and by season. This was her outdoor home and she'd never felt a moment's uneasiness in it before.

She did not intend to start now.

Firmly, she walked up the path through leafless lilacs to the gate. It was hanging open as though it had rebounded rather than latching when slammed. Through the opening she could make out the long steep yard with the dark house above. Since the house had become a rental, no one tended the yard, which, in summer, grew thick with grass, Queen Anne's lace and chicory.

The soggy grass and old flower stalks of winter left nowhere to hide, but it was just possible for a student to have covered the ground to the house in the time it took her to reach the gate. The current renters were new. She would let them know in the morning that using the shortcut was just fine.

She shut the gate and returned down the path, resisting the urge to hurry or look over her shoulder, though she did not take time to move the wheelbarrow after all. She plucked up the damp gloves as she passed and took them inside to dry on the bathroom towel rack.

The new Yemen coffee beans had roasted nicely, popping vigorously and turning a good though uneven brown before going into the cool-down cycle, and her first sip in the morning made her stop short in the middle of the kitchen. The first roast with a new coffee was often a disappointment, which made the pleasure even greater when the result was good. This was more than good, possibly one of the best ever. Rather than sit down immediately with the paper, she let herself simply enjoy the miracle of flavor.

Her pleasure was eclipsed in the next moment by a rehash of White's murder on the front page, with added details about the gun, a Remington 700 .338 Lepua Magnum.

"It was designed for law enforcement and military use," said Gale Marcum, assistant chief of police, "but is easily available to civilians and is cheaper than a lot of the fancier sniper rifles."

Quoting Wikipedia, Charlie had reported that the rifle had been used by Christopher Kyle "the most lethal sniper in American military history with 160 confirmed kills out of 255 probable kills" when he'd fired "the longest kill shot of his career."

Neva got up from the table and moved restlessly around the kitchen, emptying the dish rack, swapping out the dirty dish towel and rag for clean ones, but it was not enough to push this information away from the front of her brain. "Kills" means people.

She returned to the story with an effort, and was surprised to read that White's gym bag had been found in the woods late yesterday. In the bag were a lone pair of dirty cotton socks.

The rest of the news sections failed to hold her interest for long. Today, for the first time in her life, it was the sports section she pored over, mainly the basketball stories. The Boomers had started the season with a losing streak, for a change, and it was being blamed on White's absence for the past two weeks and now the loss of Joey Field for two games.

She hadn't realized they'd lost the Arizona game by two points, and this was with Field still playing. Tonight they would face Utah—oh, lord!

Again she stood up and began to pace. It was Thursday, game day, and Ambrose expected her to join him for it in the evening. Of course she should see a basketball game. In fact, she realized abruptly, she now wanted to see the Boomers in action. A week ago she would have said such a desire was impossible and would have laughed at the very suggestion.

Returning to the paper, she skimmed sports stories that meant very little to her and then was caught by a headline at the bottom of an inside page. *Imperfect NCAA remains valuable.* The brief piece was a reprint of an editorial from *The Kansas City Star* that laid it out in the first line: "Given the well-known problems of college sports—where money and influence peddling corrupt the world of student-athletes—a referee is needed to set and enforce fair rules."

So here it was again, the well-known corruption of "money and influence peddling" in college sports, openly stated as casually as talk about the weather. The focus was on the NCAA's dicey tactics in that investigation of the Miami coach she'd read about online but still, the underlying point of the editorial was that the situation was so bad, even an imperfect watchdog had to be kept on the scent. "The NCAA must continue trying to rein in the excesses that plague college sports, but it must do so with higher ethical behavior."

Chasing down college sports violations was like the old journalism days of exposing corruption in city hall—it was the same old story around the country, but, as Ambrose had put it, "this is *our* corruption, which makes it new. Or at least news."

Without stopping by the newspaper office first, Neva headed for the south end of town where car lots, new and used, were strung out along the highway. It was time to tackle a hard-core gripper, and car dealer Vern Varney appeared to fit the bill.

Varney was a longstanding member of the Court Club and, according to Jasper, a regular provider of cars and repairs to favored players, mainly Jim Borden until he was drafted, and now Dashiel Clemente. It was almost nine when she arrived. The hours posted in the window were 8:30 a.m. to 6 p.m. but the glass door was locked.

Hell.

Half an hour later she was back, and this time a plump young man hurried toward her across the showroom, beaming and holding out his hand. "Hey, how about that sun out there?"

"Marvelous," she said. "Almost blinding. Is Mr. Varney in?"

"You bet. Follow me."

He led the way down a green-carpeted hall to a small waiting area, knocked once on a closed door, opened the door just enough to put his head in. "Vern? Lady to see you."

A muffled reply sounded within.

"He's on the phone and says please to have a seat."

The indicated seating consisted of a pair of straight-backed chairs padded with flowered cushions, more like side chairs from a bedroom than office furniture. She just had time to pick up the December issue of *American Driver* when the door opened. A gaunt man, possibly the thinnest she'd ever met, waved her in with a sweep of the arm that appeared to upset his balance. Staggering backwards, he landed hard in his desk chair.

The only other seat faced the desk. Neva took time settling in it, removing her coat, putting her bag on the floor, adjusting her crossed legs, and only when Varney seemed to have pulled himself together did she look directly at him with a smile. The attempt at an answering smile made him look all the more cadaverous.

Alley cat, not fat cat.

In fact, the entire set-up was out of keeping with the fat cat image, from the powerful reek of alcohol to the imitation pine paneling and green industrial carpet. The room was a modular add-on, with the same sort of seedy impermanence as a badly kept mobile home.

Varney coughed, cleared his throat, and spoke with exaggerated formality. "What can I do for you, Ms. Leopold? I take it you are not looking for a car?"

Neva launched into what already felt like a set-piece about rumors of booster behavior, keeping her tone mild and even offhand, as though it were a routine subject and she was merely double-checking the facts. She'd already decided to focus on Jim Borden rather than Dash Clemente and his red Camaro, at least to begin with. Far easier to admit to past indiscretions than those of today.

Listening in silence, Varney bowed his head, closed his eyes, and lightly pinched the bridge of his thin nose between his right thumb and forefinger. When she was done, he looked up with an almost puzzled air.

"Sure, I loaned Jim a van," he said, his face muscles contracting under tight skin. "It was his birthday and his old two-door broke down. Wouldn't you lend somebody a car in that situation?"

"But Borden drove that car for a year, and several others from your lot during the rest of his time here, or so I understand."

"You understand wrong. He drove it now and then, whenever his broke down, and it always was breaking down, a piece of junk he got from his dad. It was no more than I do for any customer."

"Anyone who brings you a car for repairs gets another one to drive in the meantime?"

"Not everybody—I'd run out of cars. Regular customers and friends, sure. Jim was both. And a good kid. I'm a Boomers fan, that's no secret, but I know the rules as good as the next guy. What's with the paper anyway? Was it you that wrote that story about Joey's suspension for selling a few measly tickets? You have any idea how much money comes into this town every home game? That money circulates a long time around here, round and round and into the newspaper's cash box, just like any other business. I wouldn't think you'd tear down the Boomers, no, I wouldn't at all."

Varney's words were argumentative and even accusatory, but they were delivered with no punch. Slightly aggrieved and distant, the tone was that of a man talking to himself, a man lost in fog.

"Reporting on what's happening, whether it's at the City Council or with sports, is not the same thing as tearing something down," Neva said, still mild and gentle in tone. "If rules are being violated then that could mean trouble for the university and that is legitimate news. You must see that."

"If you don't go digging it up, there won't be any trouble, will there?" This time the tone was vaguely triumphant. He picked up a pack of Camels, fumbled out a cigarette, pulled open the right-hand desk drawer, and felt for a lighter. Leaning over the drawer, he snapped the lighter repeatedly before getting a flame.

"You don't mind?" He took a long pull on the cigarette, then flicked ash into the open drawer as he spoke, the smoke and words coming out together. "You've been talking to a lot of people."

"And I've heard some interesting things. According to the players, they could get free gas, clothes, rent, fancy electronics, meals, just about anything from the boosters."

Varney grinned with sudden delight. "Bunch of spoiled brats, okay? They never asked for nothing, did they? Everybody just rushed up and emptied their pockets at their feet." He bent his head in silent laughter, shoulders twitching. "It's not a bunch of angels we're talking about here. These guys are streetwise. They know how to get the goodies. 'You did it for Jim, why won't you do it for me?' Listen, I'm not made of money. Everybody thinks a guy owns a business is made of money. They all come around, United Way, handicapped raffle, Jumprope-for-Heart. A bottomless pit of money, that's what they think. Price of gas is going down but not so it counts. So who gets screwed? Car dealers, that's who."

He stubbed out the half-smoked cigarette in the drawer and sagged back in the chair, eyes closed, as though suddenly too weary to remain upright. Neva waited in silence until he opened his eyes and said as though there'd been no break, "Nothing against Jim, you understand. Or Dash, or Joey, or anybody. Sure I like basketball. I never missed a game in eight years. I'm not kidding, I go to all of them, clear in Arizona, Southern Cal, you name it. I love the Boomers, goddamn it. I miss that bastard. Never see him anymore. Dash and Joey are okay but Jim, he was king, king of the court, Jesus could he handle a ball. You ever take a good look at his hands?"

Varney held up his own bony hands, the fingers splayed. "Make mine look like toys. I used to tell him, 'Jim, if I had a body like yours, I wouldn't sell tin cars for a living.' You know what he said? 'Shit, man, what would I drive if you didn't sell cars?'" Varney started to laugh, stopped, sat up straight and spoke with sudden business-like crispness. "Basketball is important to this town. I guess that's all I have to say."

"It sounds as though you were really fond of Jim Borden. Did you know that when he left here he didn't have a degree?"

"What does he need a degree for? It's just a piece of paper. He's hot shit in the NBA."

"What about when he's finished with the NBA?"

"If he's smart, he's saving his money and won't have to do a thing for the rest of his life. Anyway, those guys always find something to do. Sportscasting, advertising, something slick. Like I said, they aren't babes in the woods."

"What about all the players who don't make professional teams? They leave here with nothing."

"I don't have a degree. It never stopped me from getting ahead."

"You didn't grow up poor and black."

"These guys aren't black, they're athletes, if you get my drift. Anyway, whether they get a degree or not has nothing to do with me."

"Okay, then let's talk about whether they get special favors from the community. I don't know why the players would tell me they got the use of cars—"

"I didn't give them a thing. Nobody can prove I did because I didn't. I'd like to see you put it in the paper that I did. I'd like that very much. I have a damn good lawyer, Ms. Leopold, and I wouldn't think twice about calling on him."

"One more thing, please. What can you tell me about Miles White?"

Again Varney laughed, and this time didn't stop himself. The explosion left him gasping. He opened a different desk drawer, took out a half bottle of clear liquid that might or might not have been water, and drank with his head back and his throat convulsing. "Sorry. Sorry about that. Must look funny, laughing. Right. Miles. Hooey, what to say. Not like the others."

"No cars for Miles?"

"No, he never—listen." Varney sat up and looked straight and hard at her for the first time. "One thing I hate, it's a showoff. Jim, he never showed off. When he made Most Valuable Player he didn't brag, he kept playing his guts out. You get guys bragging, talking too much, taking advantage of people, you have hard feelings, you bring down the whole damn team. And everybody else too. I guess if I was a Boomer, I wouldn't mind seeing Miles at the bottom of the ocean."

"What do you mean, taking advantage of people? I've heard that Miles was independent, didn't have relationships with boosters."

"Listen, what does it matter now anyway? Why don't you forget the Boomers and go write a column about your garden? Nice column about flowers. Look, I've got an appointment. Don't quote me or I'll sue, okay?"

CHAPTER
15

Driving back to the *Current*, Neva could not settle on what to think of the car dealer, how to categorize him in the mental picture she was beginning to form of boosters. He was clearly lying, he was a drunk, he was unpleasant, his smoking had left her hair smelly, and he had laughed at the mention of Miles White. *If I was a Boomer, I wouldn't mind seeing Miles at the bottom of the ocean.*

Vern Varney was detestable.

And yet, there was also something deeply sad and pitiable about him.

What had he meant about White talking too much and taking advantage? It didn't square with other accounts, not a bit.

She parked in the lot and was heading toward the staff door when a silver car turned in from the street and swept toward her. The license plate said BUDD loud and clear.

"Hey, you doing anything?" Frankie called through the open window. "I've got somebody here for you to talk to."

A muffled cry of protest came from the back seat. Neva looked in and discovered Clayton Perle sitting hunched in the cramped space with his knees up.

"I told him I was picking up a friend but I didn't say who." Budd looked pleased with his prank. "Well, are you coming or not?" He leaned to open the passenger's side door.

Without having said a word, Neva found herself settled in the bucket seat next to Budd, her feet in a midden of crumpled food wrappers. Clasping her hands in her lap to keep from grabbing the armrest as Budd accelerated out of the lot, she said, "I just talked with Vern Varney."

"The Walking Dead. I don't know how Borden could stand him. Or Joey or Dash. Did he deny everything?"

"He probably thinks he did, but he'd obviously had a lot to drink and kept giving himself away. There's nothing I can use directly, but it confirmed everything you said. He claimed he loaned Borden the van for only a few weeks for his birthday."

Even Clayton hooted at this. Encouraged, Neva shifted to sit sideways, and smiled at him. "I gather you didn't expect to see me today. This wasn't my idea either, though I'm glad to see you."

Clayton's answering smile was wary. Neva noted that he looked the same dreamy, detached young man of Sunday's laundry pile, but she felt a real difference in herself from that day. Since then she had suffered a crash course in gripperdom and knew now that Clayton could tell her a good story, if only he would.

"I'm starved." Budd said. "I'm for a Big Mac. Is that okay with everybody?"

It was impossible not to think *And I'm to pay for it naturally.* These boys aren't innocents when they get here…They know how to work the system…But, as it happened, Budd treated them all. "An early graduation check," he said with a wink.

With burgers, fries, and drinks in hand, they headed south out of town to Willamette Park. Budd pulled up near a picnic table at the lip of the steep riverbank. He sat with his back to the river while Neva and Clayton settled on the bench facing the wide curve of muddy winter water. Comfortable in the mild sun, they ate in silence apart from the whisper of the current. It wasn't easy for Neva to keep quiet but she knew enough now to wait.

Budd ate his burger in a couple of bites, as though it were a cookie and a small one at that. "Clayton has something to tell you," he said.

Clayton continued to chew without speaking or making eye contact with her or his former teammate across the table. A string of geese flew over, heading for the wildlife reserve south of town. The smell of earth and water came and went with a movement of air too small to be called a breeze. Budd mused, "It sure is peaceful here. Sometimes I wonder what my life would be like if

I grew up in the country. Maybe I would be a brain surgeon or a professor instead of a jock. You ever think about that Clayton?"

Clayton shook his head.

"I think about it. I like the country. We used to go for drives when I was a kid. I never wanted to go. I just wanted to shoot baskets. You know the weirdest part of my life now? I have to buy my own shoes. I haven't bought my own shoes since I was in middle school."

"Who bought them?"

"First the coach, and then the sporting goods stores just gave me whatever I wanted. Later, different companies try to get you to wear their shoes. It's not like my parents couldn't afford to buy shoes. I don't really know why people buy shit for players. It's an investment, I guess. They feel like they have a piece of you, of your career. The bigger your career, the bigger their piece is. It's like the grippers. They can't be you so the next best thing is to own you. Those people got a pretty good deal out of me, if not the top." He lobbed his crumpled burger wrapper toward an open trash can. It fell short and landed on the concrete pad at the base of the can.

"Well, shit."

Clayton retrieved the wad, added his wrapper to it, and pitched it into the can with a looping shot behind his back.

"Show-off."

"That's what I did best in school." Smiling properly for the first time, Clayton returned to the table but now sat next to Budd facing out on the bench, his long legs stretched over the grass, his gaze on the river.

"Did people buy shoes for you when you were young, Clayton?" Neva addressed his back.

"Shoes. Shorts. Socks. Whatever."

"Clayton was poor folks, not middleclass like me," said Budd. "He's going right back and be poor folks again, only he's seen a different life and it's going to eat at him and eat at him, and he'll have a bunch of little snotnoses and beat them all except the one that can shoot baskets. Isn't that right, Clayton?"

Clayton laughed and nodded, but said, "Depends."

"Sure. Clayton says he's going to graduate but I never see him crack a book. Nobody ever saw him crack a book yet. That's why

I talk mean to him. If I can make him mad like Jasper made me mad, maybe he'll get off his butt and do something. His problem is he still thinks the Fairy Godmother of Basketball is going to come down and touch him with her magic wand."

"Sounds like Joshua Gifford," Neva said, deeply amused despite the ring of painful truth to it all. "He told me on the phone last night that he's still working out and going to camps, and thinks he has a chance at the NBA. But just in case, he's taking refrigeration classes."

"That's something useful, at least. Hear that, Clayton? Refrigeration. That's like parts, and tools, and shit. That's what's waiting for you, son. Wrenches. If you're lucky." Budd stood up, yawned and stretched like it might be the last yawn and stretch in the world. "Whooey. Don't know where that came from. Well, now that you've had this informative little talk with Clayton, I guess I better get back to work."

Not moving, watching the ponderous flow of the river, Neva said, "Did Clayton really have something to tell me or were you just hoping something useful would come up?"

"Well, Clayton?"

Clayton nodded with sleepy agreeability, but said only, "I don't guess it matters what anybody says."

"Oh, good one," Budd said, and stooped to pick up a stone. With a powerful snap of the arm he hurled it out over the river with more force than Neva had ever before seen go into the throwing of a rock. It seemed an angry gesture but his face remained pleasantly composed as he turned back to them. "So, I guess that's it for our little picnic."

"Miles didn't go by himself," Clayton said.

"What's that?" Budd said. "What did you say, man?"

"Miles didn't go by himself. Running out there. Somebody went with him."

"Who went with him? Who, Clayton? How do you know?"

That Clayton might say something about Miles hadn't crossed Neva's mind—it was boosters that he knew about, surely, and it must have been boosters on Budd's mind as well because now he stood tense and straight, staring at Perle.

"Who?" he said again.

"Lamarr."

"No way! Lamarr was home. I was there, I saw him. Eating breakfast."

"Is he on the basketball team?" said Neva.

"Football. Was anyway. Now he's just like me. I tell you he didn't go, Clayton."

"Ask him," Clayton said, still sounding offhand and sleepy. "Anyway, you didn't get up."

"Well, shit. I got up. I mean I slept in kind of late, I had a headache, but I got up. I don't get this. You didn't tell the cops. Did you?"

"No way."

"Did Lamarr see who did it?"

Clayton shrugged, stood up, stretched, not ferociously like Budd but like a lanky cat in the sun. "I didn't ask him. You could ask him."

"Well, shit. This is great, just great. Now what are we supposed to do?"

The question remained unanswered when they arrived back at the *Current* ten minutes later. They agree that, even if he didn't take back his story, Lamarr was very unlikely to tell the police about it. Neva insisted that someone, logically Clayton, must report the claim. Budd agreed but suggested that Neva should do the talking. Clayton said very little, though he did make it clear that he had no intention of going anywhere near the law enforcement building or anyone connected with it. "I'm just a black dude to them," he muttered.

That he had trusted Neva with the information was confusing. She could not possibly keep it quiet, and yet to go to the police herself could bring even heavier attention down on Perle than if he stepped forward voluntarily. When Budd stopped at the curb rather than pulling into the parking lot, she didn't get out. This could not be left hanging.

"It will just get worse," she urged. "You two could go in together."

"I'm going home," Budd said. "Right now. I need to talk to Lamarr before anything else. I mean, he was there on Sunday when I got up. I heard him in the shower."

"Would you call me right after? Maybe you should take Clayton with you."

"Listen, I don't know what's coming down here, something weird. I'll be in touch but no promise when. Okay?" He reached across and opened her door.

What she would have done with Clayton's information was never put to the test. Wrestling with the question, she heaved open the heavy staff door and even before crossing the coatroom she knew by the uproar from the newsroom that something had happened.

J.D. spotted her first. As usual, her communication was cryptic, as basic as it could be. "Another murder. Football player this time. Duffy. Lamarr Duffy."

Neva went straight to her office, closed the door, and sat in the corner chair. She had to do something, but what? Think and think carefully, for starters. Was it really a coincidence to have been told less than half an hour ago that Lamarr had gone running with Miles? Lamarr was now conveniently dead and could not be questioned about whether he had or had not been with White that day in the woods. If she took this tale to the police, would she be playing an expected role? Was she being used?

Her head was moving back and forth. No. Budd's surprise had been genuine and Clayton was not clever enough to engineer such manipulations. Someone else, then? Had someone put Perle up to it? And if so, why?

A light tap sounded and the door opened. Ambrose closed it behind him and sat on her desk chair without a greeting or any of the usual jokes and pleasantries. "You heard?"

"J.D. told me. Where did they find him?"

"Two blocks from here."

"What!"

"They stopped his car. Just now."

"Whose car? What are you talking about?"

"Budd's. I thought you knew. He's been arrested for the murder of his roommate, Lamarr Duffy. They found Duffy's body this morning. In his own bed."

Jasper Luce had said not to call him at home but as soon as the editor left, Neva dialed the number. This time Luce answered and before he could object, she said, "Frankie was just arrested. He's

been charged with killing his roommate, Lamarr. Lamarr Duffy."
The silence at the other end of the line lasted so long, she finally
said, "Jasper?"

"I'm here. I'm just—well, Christ. It's beyond getting hold of.
He didn't do it. He couldn't do it. I mean, Lamarr was a pain,
more than a pain, and I told Frankie he was trouble. But kill him,
no way."

"How was Lamarr a pain?"

"Just bad news, you know what I mean. A chip on his shoulder.
Fights. Trashed hotel rooms at away games. You know the kind
of thing."

"I don't know, actually. Do players often trash hotel rooms?"

"Sure. They come back to the rooms all wound up and that
energy has to go somewhere. Gregorio picks up the bill. Listen,
do you think they do bail in a case like this? I'm going to call
some people down there. Let's keep in touch, okay. I'll call you."

It was a bad afternoon in every way. Clayton was not to be found
and at last Neva gave in to the demands of simple responsibility.
She went to see Police Chief Kitty Fiori. Fiori had run the
Willamette Police Department for enough years to change the
good ol' boy culture, institute bicycle patrols on and around
campus, and generally bring an atmosphere of reasonability and
cooperation to law enforcement. But she also was a master at
seeming to give out information while managing to get more than
she delivered. She and Neva were cordial, even friendly enough
for an occasional drink together, but this had not made their
professional interactions casual.

Now she said Neva could not see Budd until certain official
steps had been taken, and she proved more interested in Neva's
lunch with the suspect than Clayton's information about Lamarr
Duffy.

"The timing was pure coincidence," Neva insisted. "I've been
talking with Franklin Budd a lot for a story about grippers."

"Grippers? Am I supposed to know what that is?"

The meeting left her more worried about Budd than before,
and irritated with the police chief. It was deep twilight when she
left the bunker-like law enforcement building and headed for
home without returning to work. Before going inside, she circled

through the yard and checked the back gate. Nothing appeared amiss. Once inside, she made a thorough pass through all the rooms, checking windows, even looking in the closets, more for peace of mind than because she expected to find anything. Or anyone.

The only surprise came, again, in the utility porch and it was a dilly. Her plywood window patch was gone—and so was the door. A solid wood door now stood where her door with the old-fashioned multi-paned window had been. A heavy deadbolt had been installed and secured.

Ambrose! He'd not only done what he'd promised but overdone it...and yet, looking at the sturdy barrier between her and the darkening yard she could not feel entirely regretful at the loss of her charming door that let in the afternoon light so pleasantly. This was temporary, and when the situation cleared up she'd reinstall the old door.

Already she was dialing the editor's office number.

"I guess I don't need to ask how the locksmith got in," she said.

Ambrose chuckled. "It was so easy we decided to go for the new door. He just punched the plywood out with his fist and put his hand through the hole."

"Where's my old door? I will put it back when this is over, you know."

"I figured as much. It's in the shed. I wanted him to do the front, too, but he said people don't break into front doors that way because of the street. Anyway, the front door locks with a key instead of that feeble latch you had on the back. Feel better?"

"Actually, I do. Thank you."

"Good. And make sure it's still locked when you leave for the game. How about we meet by the trophy case in the lobby."

"Oh, good grief! The game. I'd forgotten, completely forgotten. I can't imagine, I mean really, I'm sorry, but I don't see how I could, not tonight. I'll go on Saturday."

"No problem. To be honest, I'm not up for this myself. But I always go." A pause and then, in a rare tone of understanding, "I know you think the booster business is small change compared to two murders, but we don't know they aren't linked. We're not detectives here but we can do news and you're on the heels of hot news for this town. You won't help Frankie by wimping out."

Was she wimping out? She still had time to eat a quick dinner and get to the coliseum…but it really was out of the question. Even fixing a meal was more than she wanted to deal with. She built a fire, poured wine, and curled into one end of the couch.

She had spent a night in the county jail once years ago as a stunt, her identity known only to the jail supervisor, and the experience had been far worse than the simple, austere, even Zen-like confinement she had expected. She had spent less than twenty-four hours behind bars but the ordeal had shocked just about every nerve-ending in her body. Ugly, cold, noisy, nauseating. Now it was all too easy to picture Budd in the tiny concrete cell furnished with a lone concrete bunk. His stained orange jumpsuit was no doubt too small, the sleeves ending above his wrists, the pants short enough to show the tops of his white jail-issue socks. Every half hour, day and night, when the guards did a prisoner check, the security gate would clang open and crash shut with the violence of an explosion, murdering sleep.

In the morning, exhausted, he'd get no coffee or tea—caffeine is a drug and they dry you out for two days whether or not your offense involved substance abuse—and the other prisoners in the pod of four cells would start the day with fits of coughing and spitting. They'd all be handed buckets reeking of Pinesol and made to mop their fragment of floor before the breakfast of tepid oatmeal and cold toast with runny margarine in squeeze bottles.

Her stomach heaved at the memory. She sat up, breathed deeply, sank back again on the couch.

And then there was Lamarr……she had not taken to him in the least during their brief meeting, but to imagine him dead was impossible, just as those who had known White had reacted with shocked wonder to the destruction of such vitality and power. And now the great, strapping, muscled Lamarr also had been stopped forever.

One was a basketball player, one football. One a star, one a run-of-the-mill quarterback. Lamarr Duffy was not a contender for booster favors and never had been. And yet the two deaths must be linked.

Linked by grippers?

By some athletic department issue?

Or something that had nothing to do with sports?

And how strange that tonight's game would go on despite the murder of a second athlete and the arrest of a former Boomer charged with the killing. Would there be a moment of silence at the game, a prayer, flags lowered…She dozed, woke to the sinking fire, dozed again.

When she came abruptly and fully awake it was 9:30. The fire was out, the room cold. It would be hours before she could sleep again and the thought of food was repellent. The wine—her glass still nearly full—was also unappetizing. She carried the glass to the kitchen, checked that there were enough coffee beans roasted for morning, and returned to build up the fire.

Most of her old copies of the *Current* went into the recycling but there was always a small stack by the kindling box for fires. She picked up a section, started to wad it, and was arrested by the picture, a sports action shot. It showed Dash Clemente at the top of a jump, his arm extended, the ball dropping at the end of its arc toward the basket. The photographer had also caught the faces of half a dozen players looking up to watch the ball plummet through the net.

The faces were strikingly composed, neither eager nor anxious, just intently watching. They were nice faces for the most part. Intelligent faces. Determined faces with strong bone structure under tight black skin.

Her bag lay within reach. From it she pulled the manila envelope and, yet again, spread out the Boomer mug shots. They spanned the coffee table, seventeen of them. Seventeen Boomers, fifteen of them black.

What was the percentage of black students at VSU? Ten percent? Five? She reached for her laptop. A quick search yielded a set of charts showing "Ethnicity in Oregon Colleges and Universities" and matching each school with the racial breakdown for its surrounding community.

Her guess had been way off. Black students at Valley State University accounted for just 1.5 percent of the total; the black population of Willamette itself was 1.2 percent. The black portion of the team stood at—a quick calculation—88 percent.

The extreme imbalance would not be news to anyone. But even so it had to be part of the story, part of what was wrong with the picture.

The two white players were not particular stars, as far as she knew. Neither one had been mentioned in connection with a booster. Did this mean they were entirely cut off from the goody shower? Or just out of the main gusher?

She studied the two faces and settled on Kit Mosely, a horse-faced farm-boy type with freckles and a big Adam's apple. Though the pictures were not in color she'd have bet that his cropped hair was red. He was unlikely to be home so soon after the game, and telephone interviews were rarely as good as face-to-face, but she had nothing else to do.

"Yo?" a slightly hoarse voice answered after the second ring. And then in an almost confiding tone after her brief introduction, "We're not allowed to talk to you. They say you're trying to get the team in trouble."

"I don't know why they're so worried," she said, turning to sit sideways on the couch with her legs out straight and her notebook on her lap. "How'd the game go?"

"Don't even ask. I mean, no Miles, no Joey. And we're playing Southern Cal on Saturday."

"I'll be there," she said. "Was Clayton Perle at the game?"

"Clayton, well, I don't know. I never see him at games anyway. I heard you already talked to him. They told us you were looking for dirt."

"What I'm actually interested in is the relationship between players and boosters. You know, I suppose, that if things go on as they are the NCAA will get wind of it and investigate, and then the program could be in big trouble."

"Won't it be in trouble if you report about us in the paper?"

"Possibly. But it seems better to get it out in the open now rather than waiting for things to get worse. Are you comfortable with the level of violations going on?"

"Well, no, but—hey." His laughter was abrupt and robust. "You really are tricky. You got me to say that without half trying. Leonard would have my ass if he knew I was talking to you. I'd like to talk to you, I really would, but I think I'd better hang up."

"Just give me a moment, please. You know I can't make you tell me anything you don't want to, but look at it this way. It's the boosters I'm concerned with. They're adults, responsible community members, or should be anyway. They're supposed to set an example rather than making athletes their partners in breaking the rules. It's very uneven. Some players get cars and unlimited clothing accounts and so on while other players only get crumbs. The players I've talked to say they know they're being used by the university and they don't mind because they enjoy a good life for four years, but when I ask them what they're going to do next, they don't know. Most of your teammates won't graduate. Did you know that? And most won't make the draft. What then?"

There was a sound of brittle popping—knuckles cracking?—then an expulsion of breath. "I never heard anyone put it like that before. I mean, you're right, and at some level we all realize it. Maybe not the first year, or even the second, but after a while you have to see it if you're not blind and stupid. I mean, I'll graduate if it takes six years. My grandmother will kill me if I don't." A pause was followed by the tentative question, "What was it you wanted again?"

"Information about the relationship, specific relationships I mean, between boosters and players."

"You're really after the boosters and not the players? Some of the boosters really care about the players. But, to be honest, some give me the creeps. They're there for you when you're up, when you're hot, but the minute you stop doing so good they're gone. Most players don't really like boosters. When I first came here, I was amazed. They come at you like flies. People would offer me money—people I never saw before in my life. Men and women. I don't know which are worse. The men just want to hang around you, but some of the women, well, you know."

"So far I've heard mainly about the men."

"That's because they've got the money. But the women are in there. Some are wives. Not for me, mind you. I'm not an attraction for them, and I guess you know what I mean. Look, I'll tell you what. You tell me what you heard from the other guys and I'll tell you whether it's true but I'm not going to rat on anybody."

"Fair enough. Give me a second to find the right notes." She thumbed through the pile of printed pages until she found her cheat sheet, a summary of who was said to be getting what. She read down the list, pausing after each entry. Kit denied them all, emphatically. "No, that's ridiculous. No way."

"How can you deny everything? You've made it clear you know about serious violations."

"You didn't mention any of the things I know for sure. I hear about some things, but there's an unwritten code that you keep your mouth shut. If you've got a good thing going, you don't brag about it. You know, really, compared to what I've seen at other schools, this place is pretty clean. We never find money in our shoes when we get back to the locker room. Nobody ever handed me the keys to a car after we won a game like I've heard about other places."

"Are you sure that kind of thing doesn't happen to other players here?"

"I can't say for sure. I know I'm not the hottest thing going. Like I said, they like the flashy players, the ones that get all the press. You can figure out who that is. Some of them drive fancy cars and it's true I don't know where the money comes from. I couldn't afford it. I have a Toyota pickup that used to be my dad's. Coach Leonard tells us at the start of every season that we aren't supposed to accept presents but he can't babysit us all the time, can he? I don't want to make a race thing out of this, but one thing looks pretty obvious. This kind of stuff is going to be more tempting to somebody poor, and the white players aren't poor, mostly anyway. That's just a fact, not prejudice. You know, I'm feeling pretty uncomfortable. I don't guess I want to talk about it anymore."

"Just one more thing, if you don't mind. Have you known players to trash hotel rooms after an away game?"

"Well, yes. It happens. I never was part of that but I've known of it. You get pretty worked up for a game and after, sometimes, it's hard to come down from the adrenalin. Sometimes you feel like smashing something. I've felt that. But the team has to pay for it."

"The team or the department or someone else?"

"Can't say. I mean I never thought. I never paid anything but then I control myself. Mostly." A pause and then, "I guess you know about Lamarr and Frankie. It's pretty weird. I thought you'd be asking about that."

"Instead of boosters? Do you think there's a connection?"

"Shit no. Excuse me. I just meant murder, you know, being a lot worse than free cars and stuff."

"I certainly agree with you there, but other reporters are working on that part of it. And Miles. Did you know him very well, that is, outside the team?"

"Not much. Drank a few beers. Played cards on the road. He was kind of a private dude."

"I hear he had some kind of complicated life outside basketball, something going on the side."

"No surprise there. I mean he was always on the make, you know what I mean, the only one that seemed to already know people wherever we went. Sometimes he'd go off with them, I don't know where."

"Someone told me this morning that you, his team members that is, were probably happy that he was dead because he was a show-off and talked too much. And 'took advantage,' whatever that means."

"Who said that? That's really dumb. You have to be a show-off to do sports at this level. Nobody's glad he's dead, nobody I know, anyway. We're dying without him, for one thing. Look what happened tonight. Look, for me, the whole deal is that I love basketball. I always will love basketball. I won't make NBA but I figured that out two years ago. I'm a sports education major. I plan to teach high school sports, and coach. I've had a great time and I don't regret anything—except for times I didn't give a hundred percent for the team."

CHAPTER
16

The newsroom was quiet when she arrived in the morning. Even Ambrose's office light was off. He must have returned to work after the game, and no doubt they would all be at it late again tonight as more information about the murder and Budd's arrest came in—or they were forced to pad the little information they already had to keep the momentum up.

The two stories filled the entire front page, along with a picture of Lamarr Duffy, an action shot that was mostly helmet and padding and looked heavily earthbound compared with basketball photos of airy jump shots. Duffy was pitching forward, trapped at the knees by an opponent's clenched arms.

The Budd arrest story ran with a file photo, not the raw freshman mugshot but a more cheerful head and shoulders picture that must have been taken toward the end of his years on the team.

The stories consisted mostly of background about the two athletes, with little else apart from the basic finding of Duffy's body in bed, evidently suffocated, possibly after being drugged. No specific reason was given for Budd's arrest, no details on fingerprints, witnesses, or other telltale circumstances provided. The bylines on both stories included Charlie and Cal Humphrey, and naturally they had mentioned White's murder, and that Duffy was believed to have gone jogging with Miles on the day he died, but this had not been confirmed. No one had suggested outright that Budd might have committed both murders but this shouted from between the lines.

As usual when Neva arrived at work, the message light on her phone was blinking, and as she listened to the brief recording she smiled for the first time since yesterday's impromptu picnic. The driving records she had requested were ready and would be waiting for her to pick up unless she called back to have them sent by regular mail.

Regular mail? Not a chance. She was out the door and heading for Salem in mere minutes. The state capital was a bit more than half an hour up the valley via the Interstate but it took another fifteen minutes to locate the DMV office and find parking in the packed lot. Mercifully, the telephone message had said not to take a number and wait in line, but to go to window number 7 and ask for Gina.

"Plenty of tickets for these guys," the young woman said cheerfully and handed over a large envelope. "Nothing too serious though."

"Could you please do one more?" Neva had not included White's name in the traffic records check because he didn't have a booster as far as anyone knew, but when there are no leads, any path could be the right one.

"You want me to fax it to you this time, since it's only one?"

"That would be terrific."

Too impatient to wait for the privacy of her car, she opened the envelope as soon as she got out the door and flipped through the pages. A glance was enough to make her whoop. She had them. She had them just as surely as though she'd discovered a stack of signed and witnessed confessions.

There were ten traffic tickets. Three for Julian Loomis, three for Jim Borden, two for Dash Clemente—and two for Joey Field, issued for the yellow car she had thought was Vera's. That car was registered to Lyle Crisp. The vehicles Borden and Clemente drove were in car dealer Vern Varney's name. Loomis's car had been registered to lawyer Hal Richter. The tickets had been issued over the course of four years. There was no coincidence here, no chance that these vehicles had been borrowed for the day.

A breeze of relief swept through her. This little game, at least, was over. The cars belonged to the boosters but were in possession of the players. Period. With such evidence, she could go back to Vern Varney and insist on the truth, not only about the cars but other goodies as well, for this verification gave credence to all the other claims of favors. Now she could face even the famously clever lawyer Hal Richter—in fact, she'd do that right away, as soon as she got back to town.

"Don't let Richter go off the record," J.D. had warned. "He'll want to go off the record and if you agree you'll end up walking out of there thinking he's done you a great favor by telling you the sun comes up in the morning."

Hal Richter was standing behind his desk when she was shown into his office. He was homely, remarkably homely. Short, round, and pug-faced, sheathed in a fine suit, he suggested a pit bull dressed for the Oscars.

He did not walk around to meet her or offer his hand. He sat down, folded his hands on the desk, and observed her without speaking.

Neva, too, remained silent.

At last, as though granting a child permission to recite for the grownups, he said, "You can start whenever you're ready."

"I'm quite ready, now that the silent appraisal stage is done," she said and regretted it instantly. What had been meant as an easy riposte sounded defensive, and her prepared spiel came out flat. Aware that she was speaking too fast, but afraid he would break in if she slowed down or paused for breath, she concluded with a direct accusation. "Your name is openly connected with several players, particularly Julian Loomis. It is said that you supplied Julian with a clothing account, rent money, weekends at your house at Black Butte, an allowance, a car. I have documentation that the car he drove for three years was registered to you."

"You are making a serious error," Richter said mildly. "I suggest we go off the record or you'll make mistakes you'll regret. I can guarantee that."

"I'm afraid I can't go off the record."

"Then I suggest you check your facts."

"Of course I check facts. In the case of the car, the state has given me copies of every traffic ticket Julian got during a lengthy period and in every case he was driving the same car, which was registered to you. It is the car that other players and boosters have referred to as his in conversations with me."

"Things would be very simple if we were to go off the record."

Without J.D.'s warning, Neva would have agreed to his urging, and even now her curiosity to know what Richter had up his sleeve was almost more than she could withstand. And what could she lose? He was unlikely to tell her anything if they continued as they were, but if she let him talk she might at least glean some tidbits and get a glimpse of his game.

"Are we off the record?" he said, noting the hesitation.

It was the wrong move. It was too eager in an otherwise uninflected performance. "No. I'm not going off the record. I need information on the record."

"Then all I can say is you had better check your facts."

"As I said, I have checked my facts. These records are as clear as anything could be. They're indisputable."

"Then there's no more to be said."

"You have nothing to say about any of the activities I described, all of which are serious violations of NCAA rules and could subject the program to penalties and fines?"

"Do you know who killed Miles?" the lawyer demanded. "And Lamarr Duffy?"

"Of course not."

"Then I suggest you stop wasting your time on trivia and solve those tragedies." He pushed a button on the phone and said without taking his eyes off Neva, "Julie. Ms. Leopold is ready to leave."

It was a spectacular failure. Despite being armed with irrefutable paperwork she had got nothing out of Richter, not one single tip or hint, not a sign even of worry or a guilty conscience.

The lawyer had spoken with the conviction of the innocent, or at least the well justified, but he was famous for this, famous for winning cases no matter the odds or the truth.

Really, she had handled it badly, very badly indeed. Leaving the car where it was parked outside the lawyer's office, she set off walking fast, hands shoved into her pockets, thinking furiously. She had been too hasty in rushing to see Richter, too confident about the power of the tickets. Her strategy had been all wrong. She had shown her hand too clearly. She had failed to prod his curiosity or make him uneasy in any way.

Striding along, heading for nowhere in particular, she went through the downtown business district and was approaching the riverfront when she heard singing. It was strange singing, unaccompanied and harsh but somehow appealing. Turning left up Second Street, she followed the sound to The Mixer, Willamette's oldest music store. Over the years, the store's quirky proprietor, Benji Slocum, had figured in more than one of her columns.

But it wasn't Benji who was perched on a stool behind the counter, or Benji who had chosen to play the music. "He always goes to Mexico for two weeks this time of year to dry out," said the thin young man, sliding off the stool. "Weather, I mean. Not drinking."

"Of course. A very sensible thing to do. What is that music?"

"Sacred harp singing. Weird but cool. It grows on you."

"Well, I'm in the mood for something different."

"You want it?"

"I do."

"Do you mind buying the one that's on? It's the only one. I opened it this morning."

"That's fine."

He retrieved the CD from the player, snapped it into the case, rang it up. "Sorry," he said when she handed him a check. "I need ID. Credit card would be better."

"That's fine," she said, fishing for cards. "You must get a lot of bounced checks in here." The last time she'd been asked to verify her ID in Willamette was too long ago to remember.

"Mostly from the jocks on campus."

She looked up sharply. "Is that athletes or just the regular jocks?"

"Football players mostly, with some basketball."

"It must be hard on business to get so many bounced checks."

"It's okay. We have an arrangement with the coaches. They cover it so we don't actually lose anything. And it doesn't happen so much anymore, with iTunes and so on. Except for that guy that was killed."

"What? Lamarr Duffy?"

"No, the basketball dude, Miles. He was in here all the time. Cool guy but I bet you couldn't guess what he bought. Not rap, I will say that."

"Girl groups?" She hazarded. "Bagpipes?"

"Ha ha. Sinatra. Not kidding. Everything we had. Old guy music, you know."

"His checks bounced?"

"Not his, not that I know anyway. I just meant he still came in sometimes."

"Did you talk to him much?"

"Not much. I'm not into sports, but one thing I noticed, those guys aren't so big, not like they look on TV. Don't forget your CD."

The entire news operation at the *Willamette Current* occupied one large room, with editorial and general news filling the whole space except for the southwest corner, which was sports territory. The line between the two areas was invisible but palpable. Rarely had Neva crossed it over the years, and never with real purpose such as drove her now. Acutely conscious of entering foreign territory, she was prepared for puzzled looks, at least from the two young sports reporters hunched over their keyboards, but they didn't appear to notice, while Cal greeted her affably and offered a chair.

"How's the bloodhound business?"

"Amazing, as it happens. It makes me wonder where I've been living for the last twenty years. With my head in a sack, obviously."

"There's lots of different sacks around for heads to stick in," the sports editor said with an amused nod. "Shoot."

Thinking about their interaction later, Neva understood that she had not really expected Cal Humphrey to be surprised by her music store tale about bad checks being covered but even so his laconic reaction was disconcerting.

"I've heard rumors about some such account but never could get particulars," he said. "I wonder if it's the same account as they use for bail."

"Bail?"

"You know, the usual, DUIs and assaults mostly. Gregorio usually lets them cool their heels overnight before bailing, but I don't think it's much of a lesson myself. It's not the basketball players so much, it's the hotheads in football."

Cal's manner was offhand as though his words were unlikely to be news to anyone, but Neva observed him for long enough in quizzical silence that he finally said, "Right. We'll check into it tomorrow. I suppose there must be records somewhere. I suppose they have to keep books, they're a public institution, unless they use Court Club money. That would be hard to track."

"I wonder if that's also how they pay for the hotel rooms they trash on the road?"

"Could be."

"It's no surprise to you that they beat up hotel rooms and don't have to pay for it themselves?"

"It never seemed a big deal as long as it was paid for. I guess I never thought to ask where the money comes from. They come out of those games with a hell of a lot of steam to work off. Sorry, Neva. This all sounds pretty bad but you have to remember—"

"Don't. Please don't say it. Everyone from President Havesham on down keeps saying that to me. 'What you have to remember is.' I'm supposed to remember that sports brings in money, that every school's guilty, that most of these guys are from poor families, that it's better to go to college and not graduate than not go at all, that the coaches aren't to blame for the grippers, that the corruption starts for some of these guys in third grade, and that what happened to Miles and Lamarr has nothing to do with any of it. Now, if you have something different you think I should remember go ahead and say it. If not, please spare me."

Surprised by her own outburst, Neva felt a moment's deep satisfaction—so this is what it was like to sound off! Then the blood swept up her back and she had to control an urge to pat the sports editor's knee. "Oh hell, Cal. Sorry sorry. That was out of line, really out of line. Please go on with what you were saying."

"No harm done, ma'am. As a matter of fact, you got it just about right except for one thing." A pause, a wry smile. "Coach Leonard wins games. He wins big, and that changes the whole equation."

Neva spent just enough time in her office to check messages before heading out again, this time to the county courthouse to follow up an idea that had come to her during the drive back from Salem. A steepled white wedding-cake classic, the courthouse dated back to the 1880s, certainly a stripling by European or even East Coast standards but venerable for Oregon. Leafless elms cast lean shadows across the lawn on the south side. In the past—that innocent era before 9/11—she would have gone in the back door, which led directly to the basement rooms where records were kept. Now all visitors had to use the front door, pass through the metal detector, and offer up their bags for scrutiny. The new ritual was painless but still mildly dispiriting.

The stairs to the basement were of gray stone, like the walls of the underground corridor and offices. The assessor's office, one door past the elections office, had proven a treasure trove over the years, a well-organized wealth of land deeds. Anyone could mine them for information without so much as a how-do-you-do of explanation, just like the motor vehicles records. And now that everything was digitized, she could just as easily have done this search by computer, but she was not ready to give up the tactile satisfaction in pouring over big platting books in a vault-like room overseen forever by the same elderly lady clerk.

Ordinarily, she would have chatted with the helpful Roseanne James, but now she said, "Roseanne, nice to see you. I'm afraid I'm in a bit of a rush. Just need to check a few property ownership details."

That it took less than ten minutes to match the players' addresses with the owners of the properties they occupied, and that the results were so predictable, should have been highly satisfying. Instead, she felt let down again, like finding Budd and Luce so easily when she'd been led to expect that they'd vanished.

Here, once more, were the familiar names: Luce owned the townhouse where Budd lived, Richter owned Clemente's duplex, Lyle Crisp owned the apartment complex where Julian Loomis stayed...but here was a surprise, a very great surprise. Mel Pascolini was one of two partners controlling the complex where Miles White had lived.

Coincidence? Someone had to own the rental housing in town, and who more likely than a property developer. White didn't have a gripper. Pascolini had not been mentioned anywhere as a sports booster. The boosters flaunted their ties to players, they didn't hide them, though Pascolini's name had come up recently in some context—ah, the anonymous tip to Charlie that the development business was merely a front for something else. Something connected to sports?

"Not what you were looking for?" Roseanne said, handing her the last of the photocopies and not waiting for a reply. "You look disappointed. Say, I thought you must be sick or on vacation, running those old columns. Are you going to repeat the one about the two kinds of people in the world, map people and non-map people? I loved that one. I'd be lost in my own back yard without a map."

Neva said she'd ask the page editor to resurrect that one, though it was a bit outdated now with GIS.

"Same difference," Roseanne said. "You can get just as lost with gadgets as you can with paper. Worse, even. Over-confidence, you know. Like those people that think they've found a great shortcut through the mountains that turns out to be an old logging road and they end up stuck. Or worse. I'll take a good old-fashioned map any day."

Neva had walked the four blocks to the courthouse from the *Current* but did not walk directly back. She turned into Azalea Park and sat down on a bench to think. The property records were reasonable evidence of gripperism but not quite enough in themselves. It was possible the players paid some portion of the rent, if not all. Surely, Joey Field could not afford that pleasant apartment without a serious subsidy but she needed confirmation.

She pulled out the sheaf of property papers, found the phone number for Shady Grove Apartments, and reached the manager after ten slow rings. Sorry, the young woman said, there were no vacancies at the moment, but she would add Neva's name to the waiting list. One bedroom was it? They were going now for $850 but that was likely to go up a bit because of the new carpets they were putting in.

Cal had told her that Joey had been raised by his aunt along with her three children and his two siblings. He was a scholarship athlete with no other documented support, yet he lived alone in that $850 apartment that just happened to belong to his rumored booster, Lyle Crisp. And that lovely yellow car was registered to Crisp.

She knew Lyle Crisp, knew him better than any of the other boosters on Cal's list, and in fact, his presence among the boosters had surprised her. A notably pleasant man who had coached her son's AYSO soccer team, he was no Vern Varney or Hal Richter. If Lyle Crisp wanted to go off the record she wouldn't hesitate to say yes.

CHAPTER
17

Lyle Crisp wouldn't have dreamed of going off the record.

Smiling like a shy but eager schoolboy, he took her hand in both of his and drew her into his office as though she had come to deliver good news. "You probably won't believe this, Jeneva, but I've been feeling neglected," he said, steering her into a metal and leather armchair. "After I heard you cornered Vern and the others I kept expecting a call. I even had the crazy idea yesterday of calling you but I didn't know what to say. 'Hi, I'm a booster, too.'"

"You *want* to talk to me about being a booster?"

"Yes, yes I do. Because it's not what you think. I mean, it does have its down side and I gather you've been hearing about that. But some people could make an angel look bad. Some people go sour and then that's what you get, sour grapes."

Lyle was her first fit and athletic gripper, with a springy walk that propelled him around the desk to his own chair, where he leaned back with an air very like Ambrose's when the editor was in a chatty mood. He said in a quick shift of subject but with apparently genuine interest, "How's your boy doing? Ethan, quick on his feet as I remember."

"He's at Berkeley and seems to love it. He gave up soccer for rocks, as it turned out, both climbing them and studying them. Are you still coaching?"

He shook his head with a look of regret. "Too busy but I'll get back to it. Did you know I was raised here in Willamette? I went away to school like Ethan but I love this town. I'm not one of those people that badmouths the home town. But it was different when I was a kid, more like the fifties even right up into the seventies or eighties. We used to say if the rest of the world blew up in a nuclear holocaust, we'd have another fifty years left to catch up. Well, that's still true. In a lot of ways, the good ways, we're still living like the fifties, strong family values, safe community, all that sort of thing. But it's also true that the Boomers changed things here. They put this place on the map."

Though sparely furnished, the office was cluttered with sports memorabilia. Like Reilly, Crisp had an autographed basketball, but unlike Reilly's, which stood in solitary state, Crisp's almost disappeared in the jumble of signed shoes, caps, posters, photos, and other team mementos on the shelves and walls. Noticing her cataloging look, he said, "Quite the show, eh? Like a kid with baseball cards, only better. I'm not ashamed of my feelings for the Boomers. I love the Boomers. They add excitement and meaning to life. Look, you work for a living, you have a kid, a house, a garden, friends. Right? But it gets old. Everything gets old. You love your wife, you love your kids, you do the husband thing, the dad thing, the Scout thing. You see it through. Right? You do good work for your clients, you get a solid reputation, you help raise money for the new youth club and so on. You have a comfy retirement income building up."

He paused to watch her pen slash across the page. She got the words down almost verbatim, as usual, though it was unlikely she could use this homey outpouring in a story. A shame, really, as it was good material, good column material at any rate, like Jasper Luce's confessional outburst and Josh Gifford's heart-felt portrait of a player's life. But she was in news mode now, she needed facts, and soon she would have to bring him up short by asking the real questions.

"But," he resumed with a sigh and a regretful shake of the head. "But. It gets old. Everything gets old. I don't know about women, but we men need more—we need life. You know what I mean? Life. Something more, something on the edge, uncertainty, risk, gamble, something that gets your heart going and your guts in a knot. That's what the Boomers do for me, that's why I love the Boomers, because they make my guts churn like a mountain river. I owe so much to the Boomers. You get so the team is like a family, a second family. You know what I mean? That's what I want you to understand, Neva, what you have to understand if you're going to write about this."

The outpouring ceased, and in the sudden silence, they regarded one another with mild surprise. Neva said, "Well. Very interesting."

"Umm," said Crisp.

"Well, yes, thank you for telling me what it's like. I think I understand a little better why fans can get so obsessive."

"Good. I really do look forward to reading what you write. Can I do anything else for you?"

With an almost off-hand air, Neva said, "As it happens, I do have a few questions."

"Oh, right. About presents and that kind of thing. I heard you were interested in that. Yes, I'm afraid I broke at least a few rules. A spot of cash here, a dinner there, but really, between you and me, the rules are a sham and everybody knows it. I'm not the cheating sort of man. You can ask my wife. I'm regular at church and I believe in the Commandments, I mean literally. Thou shalt not etcetera. But nobody takes the NCAA rules seriously. I mean, you couldn't, the program would fold."

"Everyone blames the NCAA," Neva said, nodding agreeably but then adding, "As though this absolves the rest of you, coaches, players, boosters. But these are the rules for now, and the violations I'm learning about could bring heavy consequences."

"Violations such as?"

"Such as you letting Joey Field live at Shady Grove."

"Letting him?" Crisp wrinkled his nose. "I also 'let' three old ladies, half a dozen other students, a young couple, and a one-legged man live there."

"For free?"

"Ooh. That's it, is it? Well, I'm sorry to disappoint you Jeneva, old friend, but no, he doesn't live there free."

"What portion of the $850 does he pay?"

"Where did you get that figure?"

"From your manager."

"Did you say you were from the paper?"

"No. If asked, I would have given my real reason for calling but the information was freely given, as it would be to any caller, I suppose."

"Did Joey say he gets a special deal?"

"I reached that conclusion myself based, among other things, on the fact that he couldn't afford such rent on his scholarship, he doesn't have a student job, and he has no money in the family."

"What other tidbits did you dig up?"

"The yellow sports car he drives is registered in your name."

"He drives it some. He doesn't own it. What else?"

"Players say you provide them free car insurance."

"They say that? Who says that?"

"Franklin Budd—"

"Budd! Now, that's just what I was trying to tell you. He's one of the sourpusses. I don't know what he's got to grouse about considering that he got more than his share out of all of us—" Crisp paused and frowned in a way that was becoming familiar in these interviews with players and boosters. They'd hang themselves one by one if given enough rope.

Drawing his hand through the air in front of him as though to erase his last remark, Crisp said, "Well, this is all very interesting. What else does bad Lyle do?"

"You regularly buy players' tickets at very high prices for business associates from out of town."

"And?"

"You provided all the furnishings in Joey's apartment, except for the plants, which came from Vern Varney's wife."

"Ah, Elaine and I are in this together, I see. What else?"

"You bought Christmas presents for Joey's family the last two years and flew him home to deliver them."

"Wasn't that nice of me. Keep going."

"When you have parties, all the players who hold free insurance policies have to be there."

"Sort of like blackmail, you mean? No party, no policy?"

"That's right. You seem to be enjoying this."

"I am, I am. I love hearing about myself."

"It's all true?"

"True? Good lord. Did I say it was true? Truth is a tricky thing."

"Do you give players free insurance?"

"You just said yourself that I make them pay in my own way. What does free mean? Nothing's free. I've never given away anything free in my life, even to my children."

"Lyle, could we please get our feet back on the ground here? Did the players pay you money the way other clients do for their car insurance?"

"Now you're asking about the private business of my clients and I never talk about that."

Neva let silence stretch to the point where he shifted in his chair before she said, "Are you prepared to talk to me frankly about the details of what it means to be a booster, a gripper, or do you just want to play games? You said you wanted to tell me what it's like and you gave a vivid account, but of only one aspect. You don't really expect me to leave it at that."

Crisp leaned back in the chair again, laced his fingers across his chest, and considered her with a thoughtful gaze that was not unfriendly despite his uncooperative responses. "There's a part of me that would like to be completely straight with you. Believe it or not, I do see some problems with the system. But part of me says no way. You're good at this and you'll get your story, and I don't doubt I'll be in it and catch hell from my wife, but why should I spoon feed you? It's not just me, it's other people. I can't talk about me without involving other people."

"But if you're so attached to the Boomers, doesn't it bother you that so many players don't graduate and don't make pro?"

"That is exactly what bothers me."

"Does it surprise you to hear that the graduation rate is only thirty-seven percent and has been close to that for the past ten years?"

"Of course not. They're not here to be students. They're here to win ball games."

"Well, congratulations. You're the only person so far who hasn't expressed great shock at that figure."

"The people you've been talking to are my friends and I'd trust my life to them. Well, some of them. But, you know, if I had a kid that wanted to play pro ball, I'd lock him in the garage and throw away the key until he turned twenty-one. And you can quote me on that."

"I might very well quote you. It's a good line. But now for a different subject. Two murdered athletes. They arrested Franklin Budd in connection with Lamarr's death but as far as we can tell, without any real evidence. Do you know anything that could help explain what's going on? Is there a connection to the athletic program or is it something outside sports?"

Without having to think, Crisp said, "These deaths are tragic and if I knew anything useful I'd gladly tell you, but I really don't, especially about Lamarr Duffy. I'm not really a football man. It's common knowledge that White and Dashiel Clemente had a fierce thing going, more than the usual competition, and both were hot-tempered, but not killers, not murderous. I wasn't close to Miles, although I did like him."

"You liked him? That's also something new. He wasn't very popular with the team or the other boosters, as far as I've heard."

"Ah, I think I can explain that. Miles was a performer, more than a basketball performer, a general performer. He could charm the horns off a bull, but only if he chose to, and frankly, he didn't usually choose to. I happen to know his charming side because I talked him into helping with a community fund raiser one time and it was truly amazing. We put on a mock casino night, with all the winnings going to United Way. It was legal because it wasn't real gambling but people really got into it, and I credit Miles with that. He was the dealer, of course, and believe me he was like something in a movie, suave and funny, buttering up the old ladies and joshing the men, a sort of playboy type one minute and a mock gangster the next. I finally asked him if he was in theater arts and he said no, he learned to act on the streets."

"On the streets?"

"To survive in a tough environment. We never made so much money before. I tried to get him to do it again the next year but he said no, he was too busy, and he wasn't very nice about it. And that's what I mean. He could pour on charm or be a rude bastard, forgive my language. Even though he was probably the only player, maybe outside of Dash, that would have made NBA next year, I never had the impression that he really enjoyed basketball. Win or lose, he'd trot off the court and disappear, and you'd never see him at the parties, like at Jasper Luce's or anywhere."

"Where did he go?"

"I don't know. To see his girlfriend? A real stunner, by the way. He also had an older friend I saw him with sometimes, a former football player, I believe."

"The friend wasn't a booster?"

"No way. Just a friend as far as I ever knew. I never saw him at a game or club event."

"You said old. How old?" She was thinking, *Sinatra music old?*

"Not actually old. Younger than me. Maybe mid-forties."

"Not a booster, just a friend. So White really had no strong personal relationship with a booster?"

"No, no booster. I never really thought about that. Makes you wonder how he could afford that car—" Again he stopped in confusion and then laughed. "You must get a real kick out of it when people stick their foot in their mouth like that."

"It's a mixed feeling. It's something you learn to do in journalism because you have to. You also have to be tenacious, so back to the subject. If Miles had no booster, what was his relationship with Mel Pascolini?"

"Mel? Why do you ask?"

"Just a hunch."

"Don't quote me on this, but Mel and I don't get along and never have. I don't know anybody around here you could call a close friend of his. His friends are from out of town. You hear stories about parties with the guests flown in and everything. He has two planes, you know, and a yacht and I don't know what all."

"Was Miles his friend?"

"There was some kind of connection, you're right about that, but I think it had more to do with the girlfriend. I remember—she was a pilot. I think she used to fly for Pascolini. I heard she left town and I can't blame her. Well, how are we doing? This has been fun, even though I know I'll wake up tonight and curse myself for a jabbering fool. I don't suppose I could read it before it gets printed? No? Well, you can't blame a guy for asking."

CHAPTER
18

As usual during interviews Neva had turned off her phone. Walking back to the paper, she checked messages. Only one was of interest.

"I hope this doesn't sound dumb," said Josh Gifford's voice, "but you said to let you know if I thought of anything. I mean anything about Miles. Here's the thing. I was at a game last year, Arizona, I think, just hanging out with some of the guys I knew from the team. Julian was there, and I think Budd. And some other dudes. Not White. He was never around. Everybody was feeling good, I mean, they won easy. Then I heard somebody say, 'I never knew he was such a spy. Doesn't he even care about the team?' I wasn't really paying attention, but then somebody else said, 'They'll know who did it.' I actually forgot all about it but something kept bothering me after you called, and then I remembered that I thought they might be talking about him, about Miles, since he wasn't there, I mean. That's all I've got to say but you can call if you want."

Neva played it through three times to be sure she had the exact words. *Such a spy…They'll know who did it…*Did what?

Maybe Cal would see some sports significance that wasn't apparent to her.

But when she arrived at the newsroom, the sports corner was deserted though it was well into the afternoon.

Settled at her desk, typing up notes, she left the door open to watch for Cal and also for Charlie Frank. First to amble into view was Charlie, yawning mightily. Before he could sit down, she whistled and waved. Like a ship changing direction, he swung slowly round, eyed Neva, eyed the empty pot sitting on the coffee maker between his desk and her door, and shook his head dolefully. No matter how long he had to wait, he never made coffee for himself.

"Bunch of lazy dogs around here," he said, drifting her way. "I wish you drank the common stuff. We'd never run out."

"Tell you what I'll do. I'll make a pot just for you."

Charlie stopped, straightened, and gave his head a mind-clearing shake. "Whoa, something's up. What's your price?"

"Something easy."

"Okay, but what about making me one of your special brews?"

Neva had been about to tear open a foil coffee packet but stopped to regard the young man speculatively. Did he know she brought only enough home-roasted coffee each day to drip one cup in her office? To make that cup for Charlie would be a high price to pay.

"I might do that," she said. "Depends what you can tell me about Mel Pascolini and his other business."

"Oh, that." He slumped again and slid his hands into his pockets. "It was a bust, a no-go. Either I'm asking the wrong questions and poking into the wrong corners, or he's a legitimate contractor. He's got the license, he bids projects, he even does some of them. I didn't see a shred of evidence of any other business. He hasn't got the greatest reputation among the builders in town but that's a matter of style as far as I can tell. He did the Silver Creek Addition, and Acorn Park, not my favorites but then I prefer a good honest slum over house-cloning. Why do you ask, anyway? What did you hear?"

"Not much, really," she said. Charlie was young and had come straight to the *Current* from journalism school two years ago, but he was a fast learner, plus being on the cop beat made him a particularly useful inside source at times. From the first, she had served as his mentor—his word, not hers—but he was restless these days, and ambitious to get stories that would boost him out of here to a major daily. She knew the symptoms. If he caught a hint of her suspicions he might go after the Pascolini/White connection himself, and it would be hard to blame him. He had already put time into checking out the contractor, and as the crime reporter, the murder was his territory. Even so, he could be hasty and blunt, and she didn't want heavy tracks all over this before she could get a clear view herself.

"Given his general character and affluence, I've been surprised not to see him in the list of big-time boosters," she said.

"You're getting as fixated on boosters as Ambrose. No, I'd say Pascolini operates on a different level. He's one of those people who use this town as a home base rather than a home, you know what I mean. One of those airplane people. Two-airplane people. I even snooped around at the airport."

"Where does he go in the planes?"

"I don't know where he goes, but he seems to have business contacts all over and flies them here. Not him personally, he has a pilot to do that, a nice older guy who hangs around the county airport."

"I'd heard his pilot was a woman."

"So you knew about the planes? What else do you know? What about my coffee?"

"Okay, special brew it is."

He followed her to the office and leaned in the doorway to watch as she switched on the small electric kettle.

"You never served me coffee before," he said and handed over his mug. "Now I'm really really suspicious."

"Good. Never trust anyone in this business. Did you talk to Pascolini's neighbors?"

"What do you take me for, a preschooler? First I chatted up the mailman. Nothing there. I found one neighbor at home, an old lady with a bunch of white dogs. She said it gets pretty noisy on weekends but nobody complains because Pascolini's gardeners or landscapers or whatever they are keep the whole street tidy. I hung around the airport this weekend hoping to see what sort of clients he's flying in but his planes never left the ground. Seems Pascolini's on vacation. So? So nothing. If you want him for a booster, you can have him."

"Thank you very much. Anything happening with Frankie?"

"I'm headed over that way next but I don't expect anything. Any surprises, I'll let you know."

Alone once again in her office with the door closed, Neva sat for some time thinking. She knew Willamette as well as anyone, but there was a slice of life here that she'd never penetrated.

Willamette County had more millionaires per capita than any other county in Oregon, and the wealthy here were divided in a highly interesting way, or so she'd been told by a professional fund raiser. Many of Willamette's wealthy citizens, maybe the majority, were a deliberately unpretentious lot. They tended to be indistinguishable from other community members, to dress casually, even to drive older cars unless they favored the latest thing in hybrid, electronic, solar. And then there were the flagrantly wealthy, the mansion and private plane set, and Pascolini, it appeared, was one of these.

His house was a showplace on a hill, a fit scene for movie-style parties, with the pool—if he had a pool—full of champagne and guests flown in from around the country. Could giving them a good time include free Boomers games? But there it was again; his name had not been mentioned even once as a basketball camp follower and he was not known to attend games. It appeared he had a relationship with White, but his link might be no more than the pilot girlfriend.

Aware that she still had not finished typing the Crisp interview notes, she hesitated, and then clicked on Google. It was time to put serious energy into finding Annette Octavian. And Vera, too, while she was at it.

At least Annette Octavian was an unusual name, and sure enough, her first try got multiple hits, though none useful, as it turned out. The phone listings offered just one number, the same she'd already called repeatedly. The only address listed was the airport, and everything that related to Octavian and not Funicello or some other Annette had to do with the airplane business. Octavian taught flying lessons, she had run a sky-diving school for a couple of years, she had participated in various fund raisers for airport improvements.

That was it.

Next she tried Vera, pairing the name with Joey Field, and while plenty of sites came in, none that she was able to access included Vera's last name or any contact information.

She dialed the athletic department number, got a young-sounding woman on the line, and said with hearty goodwill, "Hello, I'm trying to reach Joey Field's girlfriend, Vera, but I've misplaced her phone number and can't remember her last name. Could you please remind me so I could look up the number?"

The response was a giggle.

"Hello? Do you know Vera?"

"Who is this?"

"Just an acquaintance."

"I don't know any acquaintances that talk like you."

"Excuse me? Are you Vera?"

"That's me. Only I'm not Joey's girlfriend anymore. We broke up last night. I thought he was different, that I could trust him. But, well, those boys get way too much attention, if you know what I mean."

"Oh, I am sorry to hear that!" And she was. They had seemed such a light-spirited couple. On the other hand, maybe this was the opportunity of opportunities, if only she played it right. "And now I have to be more honest with you. I'm not really an acquaintance, though we have met. I'm Jeneva Leopold, from the newspaper. You arrived—"

"Yes, we did order ink cartridges," Vera broke in, her voice loud and businesslike. "Thanks for double checking. If I can be of further help, you can reach me at this number or after working hours on my cell at 780-266-9095. Have a good day."

Taken by surprise, Neva scrabbled for a pen, jotted down the phone number with the dial tone humming in her ear, and put the folded paper in her pocket. She had been right about Vera X, a quick study for sure, and clearly willing to talk though not to be overheard. Had someone walked up to her desk? Whatever had triggered her caution, it was no surprise that anyone working for Rex Gregorio should be nervous about getting caught talking out of school. She'd call the girl this evening from home.

This still left Annette to track down, and the obvious next step there was a trip to the little airport. But first, the Crisp notes. Resignedly, she resumed typing and was nearly done when the phone rang. Word's tumbled into her ear with no introduction, but it took only a moment to recognize Gerry Farnes.

"Neva? I haven't seen any stories yet on this travesty up here but I guess you're working on it. You said you were doing a series. Anyway, there's more. I hope you're ready for a good one. I've just been talking to a buddy from admissions—sorry, no names—and he says athletes get in here all the time before they even apply. Really. It's true. Gregorio or Leonard or one of the other ball barons phones them in."

"What do you mean, phones them in?"

"From recruiting trips. They go out on the road and find who they want and call back and say this guy has to be let in. No paperwork or anything. That comes later. Christ. They don't even do that for geniuses. I don't know about you, but I'm blown away. Are you going to talk to Emanuel or do I have to?"

"That would be Joe Emanuel, the admissions director?"

"That's right. Not that I think Emanuel himself is to blame. I hear he's decent. I'd bet a hundred bucks he's just bursting at the seams with all this and ready to pop. Don't let him know you're coming."

The university admissions office was on the fifth floor of the six-story administration building. She took the stairs rather than the elevator, and argued with her conscience all the way—she should have talked with Ambrose and Cal before heading to campus, should have asked whether it was okay to trespass on Cal's part of the story. Athlete recruitment was supposed to be his territory. But she was certain that she would get more out of Emanuel than anyone else could at this point. The sports editor was embedded in this stuff up to his eyebrows, and yet she'd had to lead him by the hand to recognize significant transgressions like the slush fund for covering players' vandalism and bad checks and heaven only knew what else. No, she was not misbehaving in following up Gerry's tip, she was not failing to be a good team player…Not much, anyway.

The waiting room was large, as though it often had to accommodate a mob, but today only a scattering of students sat transfixed by their phones. She chose a seat facing the bank of windows but had barely settled when her name was called. This was fast even for accommodating a journalist.

The director's office was down a short, mauve-carpeted hall. Large and airy, it did not contain a single item of Boomer memorabilia, a good sign. Emanuel took her hand with a cordial but watchful air. "I've been wondering why the paper's running your old columns," he said. "After so many years it's part of my life, like Dear Abby or the comics."

"Thank you," she said, smiling at the mention of Abby. Twenty years ago such a comparison would have seemed like an unintended insult but now she knew it was a great compliment. Everyone reads the advice columns. "As it happens, I'm taking some time off the column to work on a subject that has to do with the university and I'm hoping you can help me out. This is a bit awkward so it's best to plunge right in. I'm working as a reporter for a while rather than a columnist. The subject is the athletic program, specifically the low academic success rate of the players, the fact that they manage to stay in school despite failing to progress toward a degree, the special treatment they get such as having their bounced checks paid by the athletic department, and the massive violations of NCAA rules by local boosters. What brings me to you, of course, is curiosity about how some of these near illiterate young men make it into the university in the first place. Rex Gregorio himself told me that many of them are not really college material."

Emanuel's expression had run the gamut from surprise to indignation, but her last words made him exclaim with undisguised amazement, "Rex said that? Not on the record?"

"No, not on the record. He got carried away and out it popped. Now before you say anything, let me tell you what I know and have heard." When she finished, Emanuel did not answer right away and did not try to hide the fact that he was undergoing an intense inner struggle that left him looking embarrassed and sad. At last he said as though the words hurt to speak, "There's much truth in what you've said. How could I deny it? But I bring a different perspective to this. I grew up in the barrio, I know the life these kids are trying to escape, and that has made it easier for me to accept the situation."

"But you got out of the barrio, Joe. You got an education."

"I got out, yes. Many of our athletes do, as well."

"But many don't. More fail to get degrees or go pro than make it. The university brings them here, uses them, and lets them go. It's that simple."

"That sounds harsh. Very harsh." He pulled a tissue from the dispenser on his desk and wiped his face, then folded rather than wadded the tissue and tucked it into his breast pocket. "It's a question of opportunity. Poor or not, I was lucky enough to have a mother who read books. I didn't watch TV, I read books. But most of these kids don't have books. They have basketballs."

A mournful quality in his discomfort made Neva regret having to put him on the spot even as she realized that Gregorio and Leonard weren't browbeating him into accepting the athletes. He thought he was doing good.

He said, "This is difficult in more ways than you may realize. It is impossible for me to discuss particulars with you because of student confidentiality. I can't even verify that athletic staff do call on behalf of new recruits, as you say you've heard. I can tell you that this kind of thing is a great dilemma for any admissions staff that cares about young people. Standards are necessary, the bottom line for academic quality, but is it right to let standards eliminate people who have special talents, whether it's music or athletics?" A pause, and then, "But, you know, times are changing, even in athletics. They're cracking down, raising standards, and right now there are ten-year-olds living in projects and inner cities who would have had some hope of getting out on an athletic scholarship, but they haven't got a hope now because of the new rules."

"But the teams will still need players," she persisted. "Won't the new standards mean they'll have to bring in better qualified students who have a better chance of succeeding in college? In other words, their lives will be improved for real, just like yours, instead of going back to the bad dream after the years of fantasy."

Emanuel was shaking his head. "No, no, you just can't understand about shut doors. They shut early on for these kids. If we take only the ones who have the academic standing, we'll only be getting the ones who had some opportunities already, the ones from private schools and stronger families. No one has the right to keep someone from a chance to grow as a person. Think of what is being wasted. I'm the gatekeeper here, and I like to think that the gates are open to some people who never knew any other open gates."

"It's hard not to sympathize with your good intentions, I mean I do sympathize and think I understand. But doesn't this also mean that you regularly ignore the rules that most faculty and students think are being followed?"

"That's where this is such a difficult business. I know that as well as anybody. But in the end, we have to act on our beliefs. I don't think admissions is the problem. I think the problem is the people who are supposed to make sure these kids do something besides dribble balls while they're here. We need to give these kids more, not less. I don't mind saying this to you but I don't want to be quoted on any of it. We work along in our own quiet way to change the system and raising a lot of heated debate won't help. It will just drive the whole thing underground until the storm blows over. You do understand me? I count on you to understand what I'm talking about, and to respect it."

"I do understand, in a way, but here's another aspect to consider. Our analysis shows that, from 2009 to 2015, VSU's spending rose by 48 percent for athletics but only 34 percent in all other areas. It's true that sports brings in a lot of money, but again our findings show that expenses for athletics have grown even faster than earnings. You see what this means?"

Emanual was nodding but she supplied the answer anyway.

"It means sports are heavily subsidized by the university, including student fees. This involves millions of dollars a year, dollars that could do a lot toward helping disadvantaged students."

She paused, then said with a sense of strange embarrassment, "I feel like I'm preaching."

Their laughter was rueful, followed by an eloquent shrug by Emanuel.

Neva could have spent another hour prodding and pulling but without learning anything more from him, she was certain. She couldn't help liking and respecting the admissions director, and was so preoccupied by the moral uncertainty of the situation after they said goodbye that she got into the elevator rather than taking the stairs.

The doors closed and though she pushed the button for the main floor the elevator went up. At the next floor, the doors whooshed open and President Havesham stepped in.

Betraying no sign of the anger that had ended their last meeting, he offered his hand and half bowed over hers in an old-fashioned way that seemed more a matter of nature than manners.

"How goes the chase?" he said as though discussing butterfly hunting.

"It goes and it doesn't go. I've done some fairly surprising interviews with players, boosters, and officials, including Joe Emanuel just now, but documentation isn't easy. It turns out to be a very complicated issue."

"As I said. You deserve to know I've started some inquiries of my own. There's no question you'll run stories?"

"No question. Maybe starting as soon as this weekend."

"Well, I'd rather have kept it internal but if it must be, it must be. You've opened a can of worms, it seems, and now there's nothing to do but watch them crawl. I'm as loyal to this institution as anyone but after forty years in public service, I also know how to face facts."

"Are you aware that Rex Gregorio and Barry Leonard regularly call Joe Emanuel and get him to admit recruits who haven't even applied yet and aren't academically qualified by any stretch of the imagination?"

Havesham's smile was grim.

"Rex told me essentially the same thing this morning. I'm not prepared to comment on it yet, so you can hold your breath on that one. All I can say is, please keep it constructive. There's always room for improvement in any institution."

Things were moving, no doubt about it. Neva left the administration building with an energetic step, though she was not entirely comfortable with her blatant manipulation of the university president. She had implied that her information came from Joe Emanuel, and Havesham had done what nearly anyone does at such a moment—he had assumed what she wanted him to assume and thereby confirmed that athletic department personnel flagrantly disregarded application procedures as a matter of routine and the admissions department went along with the charade.

Neither Havesham nor Emanuel had admitted it for print, but with two confirmed official sources she could safely report it as fact, without direct attribution.

If challenged, she had her evidence, but it was not the way she liked to do things. By implying to Havesham that Emanuel rather than Gerry Farnes had told her about the phone-in admission of athletes she was skating close to a lie—stated outright, it would be a lie. Was skirting so close to dishonesty justifiable for getting at the truth, or was it merely a variant on the same sort of flimsy moral rationalizing that university officials, players and grippers took for business as usual?

CHAPTER
19

Momentum rather than any expectation of success carried her onward across campus to the coliseum rather than back to her office. She expected to get nowhere but she had to try, and delaying her visit to Coach Leonard would not make it easier. She was not afraid of the famously explosive coach but she didn't like temper and didn't like providing opportunities for tantrums to bad-natured grownups who should know better...Well, she was nervous. Definitely nervous. Gregorio had been thoroughly unpleasant but, by all accounts, he was an amateur ogre compared to Leonard.

No one came out of the coliseum and no one entered as she stood within view of the door steeling her nerve and studying the huge, domed, windowless edifice. The coliseum was as mysterious in its way as the ancient temples of Chichén Itzá, also a site of ritual, sacrifice, and ferocious hierarchy. But rather than deities, the object of worship here was a game—a game that was a very long way from a playground.

At last she went in but only as far as the entryway and the wall map of the building's layout, which showed the playing court and stands in the middle, with offices and other rooms around the outside. A broad hallway ran between the two. The shortest way to Leonard's office was to the right but that also would take her past Rex Gregorio's door.

She headed to the left.

Leonard's door was closed. She knocked with brisk energy.

"Come in," said a deep voice.

The office was small, the man big. He no doubt recognized her but gave no sign of it.

"Coach Leonard?"

"That's me."

"I'm Jeneva Leopold from the *Willamette Current*. I'd like to talk to you about a couple of things. May I sit down?"

"No. But you can leave any time."

Unfazed, her strategy ready, Neva kept a mild but determined tone. "We're going to be running a series of stories soon about your program, specifically about your players and their relationships with boosters. We're also looking into the special arrangements for players who don't qualify for regular admission and also the special treatment they get when they fail their classes. I'd like you to have a chance to comment on all this before it's in print."

"You'd like that, would you? I'm not a bit sure you'd like my comments. As it happens, there won't be any comments. I'm not interested in your stories. Or in you. Now you can leave this office or I will."

"You don't care that serious rule violations are common in your program? When these stories go out there's sure to be an NCAA investigation."

Leonard stood up, walked around the desk, strode past her with military rigidity, stepped out of the room, and closed the door. He did not slam it.

Neva breathed, listened, waited.

The man was extraordinary. His self-control was more than impressive, it was disturbing, and more unnerving by far than anger or threats. She had not expected to succeed with Leonard but neither had she expected an ice wall.

No wonder he won games.

She shifted on her feet, listening intently while studying the lair with a sharp eye now that the beast was gone. It was stark, like a room newly moved into or about to be vacated, the shelves nearly empty, the walls bare apart from a lone poster of a player she didn't recognize. The desk, too, was nearly bare. Telephone, coffee-streaked mug, pen jar, campus directory folded open…she shifted to see what page was uppermost but the type was too small. A deep breath, a moment to listen, then she stepped around the desk and studied the page. It was midway through the "L" section with at least fifty names of faculty and staff with rank and contact information. None struck her as significant.

The edge of a sheet of paper showed under the directory. With one finger she slid it into view. It was blank apart from a decorative doodle in the center around the number 22.

The afternoon was drawing to a close, the light dimming fast. It had been a long day and far too full already, but she didn't want to end the day—the week—with a flat-out failure, even an expected one. A quick and easy task was needed. Valley Savings & Loan? If she could just identify the loan officer who was handling the booster/player car loans it would be enough for now. She could arrange to meet him on Monday.

The bank occupied a low brick building on the corner of Fourth and Hannah. An information desk inside the door was a welcome sight, and the young man behind it greeted her like an old friend.

"I'm doing just fine, thank you," she replied, resisting the ritualistic *And how are you today?* "This may seem like a funny question," she said, and managed a sort of chuckle. "I'm trying to identify a loan manager who was recommended to me but I can't remember his name. All I remember is that it begins with a 'B' and he's a real Boomers fan. Do you know who that could be?"

"Easy one." He beamed. "That would be Burt, Burt Thomson, no 'p'."

"That's it! Thank you very much."

"I never went to games until I started working here. He gets good seats. Only, I mostly go for the barbecue but don't tell him."

Their laughter was conspiratorial.

"I'll let him know you're here. That's his office over there. You can go on in." He picked up the phone.

She glanced at the wall clock. Not quite five yet. She had not prepared for a meeting but sudden powerful curiosity about how an official in an institution such as this could pull off dodgy practices made her say, "Thank you. That would be great."

Burt Thomson was a surprise, indeed. For starters, he was gay and open about it—the marriage photo on his desk clearly showed him as the bride.

"So thrilled to meet you," he said, holding her hand rather than shaking it.

Almost as surprising as Thomson himself was the absence of Boomer memorabilia, not even a signed basketball. Did he feel the need to keep such obvious devotional signs out of sight to help cover his tracks? Or was it simply a matter of interior decoration, of sticking to a color scheme with no place for Boomer blue and white in the subtle rosy palette?

"Lovely office," she said, aware that her inspection was noticed.

"Adam's doing. He has the eye. I'm hopeless at colors—he even chooses my socks! Mother thinks it's a scream. 'I just wish he was around when you were in high school,' she says. Really, I used to be such a slob. And now, my curiosity is just too much. Are we a potential subject for your column? Or is this a business call?"

"Both," she said, seizing the opening. "Though in honesty it's mostly something businesslike that brings me here. Once that's done, though, I could see a very interesting column about an insider's view of the loan world, maybe focusing on the odd things people need money for, and maybe the regret in having to turn down good people. I assume there is sometimes regret?"

"Of course. It happens. We try to work with everyone but sometimes you just can't turn a leaky tub into a yacht. Or even a good rowboat. Oh, dear, that doesn't sound nice. Don't write that."

"I'm not writing anything—yet." Neva's smile was easy and genuine. Never would she have thought of doing a profile of a loan manager but she could make this one work very well. Already Thomson was tucked away in her mental file of future column subjects. "But now to the tough thing, and it is rather tough, I'm afraid. I understand you're a big Boomers fan."

"Oh, yes, love the Boomers. Except for last night. I did feel sorry for them. And how about that awful murder business? And now Franklin Budd in jail? Between you and me and the lamp post, that's a crock of you–know–what."

"You think Budd couldn't—or wouldn't—have done it?"

"No question. I mean, excuse me for saying it, but he's so self-centered. This might sound funny, but he'd never think enough about somebody else to get around to killing them."

Neva laughed with sudden delight. Of all the imaginable reasons for assuming someone an unlikely murder suspect, this had to take the prize. "I wouldn't have put it like that but I have to agree. You must know him pretty well?"

"Mostly business. He, well, he's a customer here."

"Ah, yes. A customer. With a car loan, I believe."

Thomson nodded, a sudden wary look in his eye.

"And your fellow boosters, you also have some of those as clients."

Again the nod.

"Such as Jasper Luce."

This time the nod was the merest dip of the head. Neva paused, waiting for the inevitable *I don't know how you know who our customers are but their business is confidential and I can't talk about it.*

But again Thomson proved a surprise. He stood up, closed his office door, and leaned one shoulder against the bookcase with his arms and ankles crossed. "I know where you're going with this but it's not how it looks."

"Could you just tell me about it in your own words?"

The moment hung. Thomson folded and refolded his arms, looked at the ceiling. "It gets better," he murmured.

"Better?"

"Dan Savage's project, 'It Gets Better.' You must know it. We're bullied in school. I mean, really bullied. Gay teens are five times more likely to commit suicide. That includes lesbian, transgendered and bisexual. You think you're dirt and always will be dirt so what's the use. 'It Gets Better' gives kids hope. It shows that school isn't the world."

"Did it help you?"

"It didn't exist then though I'm a member now. Anyway, I didn't need it so much. And that's the point. I had protection and now I'm paying back."

"Yes?"

"My brother played in high school. Basketball. He was team captain and I could have had three eyes and one leg and they would have defended me. No way were they going to let his little brother get pushed around. Nobody dared to look at me cross-eyed because word would get back to the team. I went from the hell of middle school to walking free in high school and I'm here today because of it."

"And now you're returning the help by setting up loans in players' names that someone else actually pays?"

He nodded.

"Do they know why you do it?"

"Are you kidding? These guys are probably gay bashers from way back. I do it because I'd probably be dead today without that protection. And maybe, knowing me and the risk I'm taking for them, these guys might change their attitude a little bit. Doing it this way has some long-term advantages, you know, like giving them a decent credit rating. It's not against the law and it's not cheating Valley S & L in any way. All they care about is the bill gets paid. I don't know what more to say."

Neither did Neva. It was difficult enough when Joe Emanuel had told her he was breaking rules because he knew what it was like to be without hope. Now this self-possessed and immaculately turned out young man was saying he broke rules because he owed basketball players his life. None of it was particularly logical but it made emotional sense.

"I don't know where we go from here," he said. "I can't give you any names or even confirm names you might have, like Jasper Luce. I'm not a good liar so you got the truth. But I can't admit any of it publically. It's their private business. Like I said, it's not against the law. Anybody can pay on a loan, only usually the loan wouldn't be in the name of somebody without a good credit rating and source of income. So you see it could backfire on clients. On the players. I can't do that."

"I appreciate your honesty. Very much. But it does put me in a tough situation."

"What if I said it won't happen again?"

"That would be good, but it doesn't solve my need for information for the stories we're putting together on the larger subject of rule violations. This has been mentioned by other people or I wouldn't know about it."

"Could you write in general terms, like no names?"

"Possibly. We do sometimes use unnamed sources. It weakens the story to do that but it might work if I had the numbers. How many players, how many loans, over how many years."

He'd been nodding but now shook his head and began to pace. Neva remained silent, watching the struggle. At length, he said, "I need to talk to Adam. Can I get back to you?"

"Of course, but please do it soon."

"Tomorrow. I'll tell you tomorrow. You'll be at the game? Come early. We've got a booth in the southeast corner, fundraiser for sports camp. We smoke our own links, local organic pork, gluten free. They're simply killer."

Rather than subject herself to an hour's grilling by Ambrose, Neva went straight home, typed her notes for the day, and sent them to the editor by email. It was 5:30, well past university working hours. She pulled Vera's phone number from her pocket and dialed. After six rings the message system kicked in. She almost hung up but then said, "This is Neva. I'd love to talk. Any time is fine."

Dinner was fried rib-eye steak with chard cooked in the meat dripping, which she devoured while listening to the news on NPR, including a segment on new NCAA regulations that would relax certain recruiting rules. "Big Ten athletic directors and football coaches say they have reservations about loosened NCAA rules that would allow unlimited contact between recruiters and high school players." The coaches expressed "serious concerns about whether these proposals are in the best interest of high school student athletes, their families and their coaches." High school coaches were worried that their players might be "overwhelmed with phone calls, texts, and mailings."

If athletic directors and coaches opposed the new rules, who was pushing for the change? *Whoever stood to earn more money, of course.* These games were, indeed, a long way from the playground.

CHAPTER
20

Ambrose telephoned in the morning before she finished coffee. "Great stuff, really great," he said. "I forwarded your notes to Cal. Are you coming in? I know, I know, it's Saturday, but he'll be here and we need to talk."

"Is there any word on Budd?" she said rather than answer directly.

"Yes and no. Still nothing beyond circumstantial evidence as far as we know. In other words, living with Duffy and having the greatest opportunity. He died during the night but Budd claims to have stayed with Clayton and Clayton backs him up. No motive. There are fingerprints everywhere, of course. His, Lamarr's, Clayton's, everybody and his dog. No bail set yet. Charlie thinks they want to keep him in there for some reason, some strategic reason. He's looking into it. Are you coming in now?"

"Maybe later. I have some other strings to follow up first."

"You won't forget the game? I could pick you up."

"I'm going but not with you. I'll be under the rafters with the screaming hordes."

"You bought a ticket? We never buy tickets."

"Do the reporters and photographers use those seats?"

"Of course not. They're down on the floor, close to the action."

"So these free seats are for the publisher, editors, and friends?"

"Stop, Neva. Don't bark up my tree. Press and sports go together like toast and butter. The press always gets complimentary tickets to sports events just like we always get front row seats at inaugurations, trials, speeches, hog shows, you name it. No players make money off our tickets, and we don't write nice things about the team because of getting free seats. It's a tradition. People want us there, and for good reason. You don't have to get lost under the rafters to save our honor. Sit with me or you won't know what's going on in the game."

"In the game? I don't care what's going on in the game. I'm going to watch the fans. I'm trying to understand obsession, not basketball."

"You can't understand one without the other. But you have that tone in your voice, so I'll save my breath."

The phone rang for the second time when she was cleaning her teeth, wandering around the house as she generally did to keep from getting too bored to brush long enough. She rinsed in the kitchen sink and picked up the phone.

Vera had called back. Splendid.

"Sorry about that," she said. "The office is full of ears."

"You handled it well, very quick thinking. Are you comfortable talking on the phone or should we meet somewhere?"

"I'm fine on the phone now that I'm home. What do you want to talk about?"

"The team."

"I'm not on the team anymore." A low laugh.

"Right, but so much the better. Now you can tell me all their secrets."

"They don't have any. They don't know anything. They think the world's a basketball."

Neva's laughter was echoed on the other end of the line. Her plan to ask Vera all the usual questions about boosters seemed suddenly tedious and possibly wasteful. This bright and talkative young woman not only knew the Boomers from the inside but worked in sports administration, a perspective she was unlikely to find in anyone else so quick on the uptake and ready to chat.

"How long have you worked in the athletic department office?"

"Two years. Too long. I'm looking for a new job on campus."

"Have you ever seen or heard anything that would help explain why someone would want to kill Miles?"

"They wanted to get rid of him. I mean, that sounds stupid, it's not a reason, it's just that they're all glad he's gone. I was kind of shocked, actually. He never made any trouble that I saw, he was never around. He was always going off with Annette. I sure wouldn't want to be her right now."

"Who was glad he's gone?"

"Everybody. Mr. Gregorio, Coach Leonard, even the football coach. He gave a high-five when he heard about it."

"That is shocking. You're sure?"

"Well, he laughed and then saw me watching and went all serious."

"Are you thinking they could have had something to do with the murder, or were just glad someone else had done it?"

"Just glad he's gone. I mean, I'm sick of them but they aren't going to kill anybody, are they? It's just not in the picture. Especially in the season."

"What about Lamarr Duffy? Do you have any particular thoughts or observations on that picture?"

"No idea."

"Did you see any reaction when he was killed?"

"That was a game day so there was too much going on anyway."

"And Frankie's arrest? What do they make of that?"

"Umm, well, I don't know him very well but everybody seems pretty surprised, like not actually believing he did it. What else do you want to know?"

"Since you're leaving the job, would you be willing to snoop around a little, try to find out why Gregorio and the others were pleased by White's death?"

The silence was long, until at length Vera said, "Maybe I didn't say that quite right. Maybe they weren't happy about it. I guess maybe they were relieved."

"Even so, I'd like to know why. He was winning games for them, which is what you'd think they'd want. Just keep your eyes and ears open, how about that? Be alert. But careful. Very careful."

Neva's second visit to Joey Field's apartment did not start with
an open door and big smile. This time he opened it only wide
enough to recognize her and then slammed it, or tried to, but she
got a foot in fast.

"We're not supposed to talk to you," he said. "I'm already in
the doghouse."

"Because of the suspensions?"

"That's right."

"They're really going to miss you this afternoon," she said.

It was a blatant ploy but still Joey appeared to relax slightly.
"Oh, I don't know. I think they'll do all right. Better than
Thursday anyway,"

"Fans are used to a lot better than all right from the Boomers."
Amazed by what was coming out of her mouth, Neva was sure it
must sound as false to Joey as it did to her. But looking almost
friendly, he said, "Was there anything in particular you wanted?"

"You know I've been talking to people. Players, boosters,
campus officials, just trying to understand things. Lyle Crisp, for
instance. We had a pretty good talk on Friday."

"So he said."

"Did he tell you what we talked about?"

"He said you asked about free stuff he gives me and some of
the other guys, but he said he told you he never gave anything free
in his life." Joey laughed with sudden, surprising heartiness. "It's
true. He gets what he wants."

Neva joined his laughter and shook her head with what she
hoped was an expression of rueful appreciation—the fish was
nibbling. "Did you say that to him?"

"Sure. We understand each other."

"Sounds like it. Actually, I've kind of wondered about that, I
mean how a particular player and particular booster get together."

He shrugged and the door opened a bit wider. "Accident, I
guess. You get a lot of different ones coming after you at first and
then it kind of sorts out. Everybody's different."

"It seems you were lucky to get Crisp. He used to coach my
son Ethan in soccer and has always struck me as a very nice
person, and he's certainly dedicated to the team. One thing that

puzzles me, though, is how these guys can afford it. I know Vern Varney's a car dealer, but it had to cost him something to supply cars for both Jim Borden and Dash Clemente."

Joey nodded thoughtfully, no longer hanging onto the open door. Neva withdrew her foot though she did not try to enter.

"And while it doesn't exactly cost Lyle anything for you to live here, he could rent it out and make money."

Joey stopped nodding, looked at the floor, shoved his hands into his pants pockets.

"These aren't cheap apartments, Joey. Eight hundred and fifty dollars is significant income to give up every month."

"I pay two hundred. Didn't he say that? Look, I really have someplace I need to go. Anyway, you already know everything, don't you?"

He picked up a bag that was ready by the door and they walked together to the sporty yellow car that was registered to Lyle Crisp. As he unlocked the door, Neva patted the smooth paint job and reflected, "It's very nice. At least when Lyle gives you free insurance coverage, he's making sure his own purchase is protected."

Joey tossed the bag onto the passenger's side seat, swung into place behind the wheel, put the key into the ignition and reached to close the door.

"Do you get to keep the car when you leave or does it go to a new player?"

He went still for a moment, not looking at her, then shrugged. "I don't know. I never thought to wonder. Doesn't matter, I guess. I'll get another one wherever I play next. That's the way it works. If you're good."

"Oh, Joey, I am sorry. That was a really nasty question. It just popped out and now I feel like a worm." Which was true. Budd still had his car and she could not imagine Lyle asking for this one to be returned. The dart had hit the target but still she regretted having cast it purely for the sake of a telltale reaction. "Listen, just another moment, please. You know there's been another murder, and Franklin Budd's been arrested. This is really out of hand. I feel like an idiot chasing boosters, except there's at least a chance that it's all related somehow. You seem to be one of the most thoughtful players—I'm not buttering you up, really. Could you please think hard, think really, really hard, and if there is anything at all that strikes you as odd, or questionable, or anything particular that links White and Lamarr Duffy, please tell me."

Field gripped the wheel but he made no move to start the car. A low humming like a pensive growl rose from his chest. "Well. Well there is something. Two things. Lamarr had a thing, I mean really a thing, for White's girlfriend, that pilot chick." He paused, cocked his head, and gave her an almost impish look. "I guess she's not really what you'd call a chick. Did you meet her?"

"Can't find her so far but I will. You think there could have been jealousy?"

"That was the idea. I mean I thought about that when Miles died. I don't know what to think with Lamarr killed, too, but you wanted to know."

"Thank you. And the other thing?"

Again the low hum came before words. "You know that car dealer you mentioned, Vern Varney? He hated Miles. I don't know why. All I know is he'd leave the room if Miles came in. But I don't think he even knew Lamarr so that's probably nothing."

"Anything is worth following up at this point. And if you think of anything else, please let me know."

The Willamette Airport had been built south of town during World War II for bomber flight training and now was used mainly by private plane owners, crop dusters, a modest air taxi service, and the small aviation school. An attempt some years ago to raise its fortunes by offering regular flights to Portland and San Francisco had flared and fizzled, and plans to build a proper terminal with a comfortable waiting room and restaurant had gone no further than the drawing board, or maybe just the dreams of investors.

The original hangar was still in use and loomed over a cluster of Quonset huts and other utilitarian structures. South of the buildings at the edge of a runway small planes perched with a ready look like dragonflies about to flit. The flying school and office were in a prefab building in need of paint. In front of it was a graveled wide spot for parking. As she pulled up, the office door opened and a man stepped out. He watched her park, and waited as she got out and headed his way.

"Will Gentry," he said, and gave her proffered hand a manly squeeze in keeping with his air of comfortable fitness.

He was not quite a country club type, but not truly an outdoorsman either despite the down vest and tanned face and forearms. He seemed familiar, though she did not recognize his name and could not place where they might have met.

"Neva Leopold," she said. "From the *Willamette Current*. I'm looking for Annette Octavian."

"Sorry, not here today. Can I help you?"

A telephone rang inside. "Sorry," he said again. "Have to get that. Only one here."

She followed him in as far as the reception counter and turned to study a bulletin board as he vanished through an inner doorway. Along with the usual miscellaneous notices of items for sale and services for hire, the cork board featured a short roster of airport employees, including pictures. Will Gentry was at the top, every silver hair in place, open-collared shirt the same summer blue as his eyes. The professional-looking portrait was striking but still it was outdone by a snapshot just below of a woman tightly zipped into a mechanic's green overall. Billowing red hair framed a white face that was…beautiful? Cold?

The name under the picture was Annette Octavian.

And now she knew why Gentry looked familiar. He and Annette were the couple she'd seen fleeing the coliseum on Sunday.

"Sorry about that," Gentry said for a third time. "Phone didn't ring all morning, wouldn't you know it. Are you writing about our little operation here? How about a coffee?" Rather than head for the small lounge that showed through an inner door, Gentry led the way out of the building and made for the main hangar.

"It's quiet here," she observed, trying to match his long stride.

"Dead, you mean. The economy. At least it gives us a chance to catch up on things."

He opened a normal size door next to the big hangar door and moved aside so she could enter first. The inside was vast, cold, and littered with tools and airplane parts that they navigated through to reach a door at the back. Again Gentry waved her through ahead of him. She took two steps and stopped to take in the sudden shift from winter gray to summer gold. Rich yellow walls, plentiful lamps, polished wood, flowering plants, sunflower-colored sofa and chair, tiled floor in the pink tones of Utah rock. The effect had been so skillfully created she did not at first notice the absence of windows.

"My god," she said. "I'll take it."

His chuckle was satisfied, his expression pleased, though her reaction must have been expected. No one could walk in here and not respond.

"I spend a lot of my life at this place and figure it might as well be comfortable." He laughed with sudden and surprising self-consciousness. "The truth is, I suffer a lot from SAD and this seems to help. I just come in here and forget the rain. Please, sit where you like."

She chose the armchair and for a moment let herself sink into it with closed eyes. Her dream for combatting the winter blues had always been a greenhouse, the real old Victorian glass variety crowded with blooming orange trees, but this was just fine. Why had she never thought of creating a room like this? Might be a great use for the back bedroom, which was now a crisp white with natural wood trim. Mexican colors, bright fabric, lots of plants— and why not yellow window glass to give a sunny cast to the light even in dim January?

"You like it strong, I think," Gentry said. "Afraid my beans aren't home-roasted, but your column a while back almost got me converted."

The electric kettle whistled. As Gentry fussed over the French press, Neva continued to study the room with pleasure. Photos of vintage airplanes in rich sepia. A wall recess full of ferns under grow lights. A banana palm in a huge clay pot. Everything in warm colors and everything immaculate. In fact, there was no clutter, no books or magazines—not even a copy of the *Current,* though he was clearly a regular reader of the newspaper. What did Gentry do in here besides drink coffee?

"Here you are," he said. "No cream, but I hope it's good enough to stand alone."

He sat with athletic grace on the sofa, slipped off his shoes, and put his feet up on the coffee table. "Oof, whew, I needed this. I haven't sat down since about six. Now, what can I do for you?"

"I'm not sure, really. As I said, I'd hoped to see Annette. Nothing to do with the airport, though now I'm here it looks like a good column possibility, including this wonderful room. Would you be willing to be a subject, maybe in a few weeks?"

His shrug was agreeable rather than dismissive. "Whenever it suits, though as I said, there's nothing exciting at the moment. Can I ask why you're looking for Annette?"

"I understand she was Miles White's girlfriend and I'm working on a piece about the basketball team."

This time the shrug was reflexive, without clear meaning. "If White's your interest, then you really had better talk to Annette."

"Can you tell me where to find her? Or give me a phone number other than the airport?"

"I could but it wouldn't be any use. Let's just say she isn't handling things well and wants to be left alone."

"Okay, then how about Mel Pascolini? I understand she flies planes for him and that there's another pilot as well. Is that, possibly, you?"

"It is."

"Is it business people you fly in?"

"Flew in. It's past tense, done with, over. Which means there's no point going into it, and I can't do that anyway. I'm just a pilot. I just fly the plane when needed, same as Annette. Anything else, you need to ask Mel. Though you may have trouble catching him for the next little while. His wife got fed up at last and left with the girls, and he's not the type to take that sitting down. He went after them, and god only knows when he'll be back. Now I'd rather talk about you. You look like a woman looking for a change. How about flying lessons? The first two are free and if you like it, well, we can discuss terms. You won't be sorry."

"You know, I'll think about it," she said. Was she looking for a change? On one level, she'd spent her life looking for change. That's why she was a journalist. On the other hand, this sounded suspiciously like a well-used line. *You look like a woman looking for a change. Come fly with me...* She smiled, let a brief silence pass, then said in a ruminating rather than questioning tone, "You must have seen quite a bit of Miles. It seems he had a special relationship with Pascolini."

"A special relationship. Well, I suppose so."

"It looks like Pascolini may have been providing White's housing."

"Housing?" Gentry appeared genuinely perplexed.

"He owns the apartment complex where Miles lived. I'm finding a pattern with players and boosters, that is, the star players all live in places owned by known basketball boosters."

"Boosters?" Again Gentry seemed lost.

"I'm sorry, I guess I haven't really explained. There appear to be major violations of NCAA rules going on in relation to the basketball team and I'm trying to get a picture of the relationship between specific boosters and their players. White didn't have a known booster but he also seemed to have plenty of money, a nice car and so on. Was Pascolini a Boomers fan?"

"Mel didn't have time for games. Well, not that sort anyway. If it didn't make him richer, he wasn't interested."

"Yet he flew in lots of friends, or business associates, or clients. Whatever they were. That must have been very expensive, to fly in so many."

"So many? It wasn't so many. We only fly Cessna Caravans, not 747s." Gentry drained his cup and swung his feet off the table. "Well, this has been very pleasant but work calls."

"Wait, stop, please." Neva placed her cup on the side table and sat forward. "You don't owe me any information, or anything at all. But I don't understand why you're dodging every single question. No, really, you are. They're simple questions, and if Annette had been here I would have asked her the same. And also what took the two of you to the coliseum the day after White's body was found. I saw you come out."

"Concern for Miles, of course," he said with no sign of surprise or discomfort.

"This isn't the easiest thing to mention, but after you came out you looked around the front corner of the building and saw something that made you clear out of there like the hounds of hell were after you."

"I didn't see you there. As it happens, I saw someone we didn't want to talk to, not right then anyway. No big deal. And now, since you're in the business of tracking things down, I suggest you go find Annette."

"You don't know where she is?"

Gentry didn't answer right away and in that moment something slipped, not quite like a mask coming off but rather a second personality rising into view, a less self-possessed personality. "No, I don't know where she's got to," he said with a tired headshake. "I really don't know. To be honest, I'm a bit concerned. I thought she was getting tired of Miles, but since he died, she's been pretty nuts. I don't want to be rude, but I really don't have anything more to say. Except, if you do find her, please tell her to call me."

So many people making themselves scarce! She'd never followed a story before where one source after another pulled a disappearing act. Budd, Jasper, Annette, Pascolini, and now even Clayton, according to Cal. These were transparent times. Everyone was online and easy to find and easy to find out about—so how could they all vanish down rabbit holes? True, she'd found Budd and Jasper without much trouble, but still it was more trouble than usual.

And there was yet another thing. Families of the deceased were strangely scarce. Over the course of twenty-plus years in journalism, she'd had to seek out parents, spouses, children, aunts—any relative still standing—for information on the dead, mainly accident victims. White had only an uncle in a Texas jail, and so far Cal and his crew had located no one for Lamarr Duffy except a raging alcoholic stepmother. The richest avenue for details about most lives went nowhere for the murdered athletes.

The drive back to town from the airport took about ten minutes on the two-lane highway that ran between wide fields that were already green with the early grass seed crop. It had been far too long since she took a country walk, and watching sudden light sweep across the green expanse through a break in the clouds, she was tempted to turn around and head for the nearest country park.

Her foot backed off the accelerator but pressed down again in the next moment. Later, after this weird chapter in her life was over, she'd go back to trail walking on weekends. Now, every hour counted.

And the name at the front of her thoughts was Vern Varney. If Joey was right that he had hated Miles, she needed to know why.

The car dealership was on the south edge of town six miles from the airport. The same rotund, smiling young man as before greeted her in the showroom. "Vern's out," he said cheerfully. "Game day, you know."

"Oh, right, of course." She smiled and looked about at the shiny new models, or at least made a show of looking as she shifted her own internal gears—it hadn't occurred to her before that Varney's assistant might be a source worth pursuing but this was too good an opportunity to pass up.

"Looks like you're all on your own," she said. "You're not a Boomers fan?"

"One of those is enough around here. Quite enough. Anyway, Saturday shift was a condition of the job. Are you interested in a car? My name's Camden. Camden Hill."

"Neva Leopold. I stopped to chat with Mr. Varney but I wouldn't mind a look at the latest thing. Though I'm not likely to buy it, just so you know. I'm very attached to my old Volvo."

"They're good cars at any age, but one thing you might want to think about is safety. Safe driving features have improved to the point where just about any newer car is going to out-rate the older ones for just about whatever make you want to talk about. As for the onboard computing, well, there's no comparison with even a couple years ago. Just slide into the driver's seat here..."

Neva let him talk on without showing an unfair amount of interest, waiting for the right moment. It came when he said, "Of course, we deal in used vehicles as well."

"That certainly works out nicely for the Boomers. Vern said they go through a lot of cars."

"You can say that again." Camden Hill could not have been more than 30 but his chuckle was old and wise. "Glad it doesn't come out of my paycheck."

"Too bad he didn't get along with Miles White. I wonder if he feels bad about that, given what happened?"

"He wouldn't tell me if he did. But he has been kind of out of it this week so maybe that's why."

"Funny to have such a falling-out over cars."

"Cars? No way—he never offered White a car."

"Maybe that was the sore point?"

"Beats me. Except it was Vern that had no use for Miles, not the other way around. You really should take this little beauty out for a spin."

Two hours later, she was standing in Boomersville with hotdog in hand, though the home-smoked sausage on a custom-made bun was a long way from the old familiar wienie. Burt Thomson had presented it with a whispered "We'll have to talk later. Adam's sick and I'm on my own here." He turned away to tend the grill, while she stood taking in the tailgate carnival that filled half the coliseum parking lot like a giant swap meet or chili cook-off.

"Hey, look who's here," a cheery voice sounded beside her. Gerry Farnes lifted his plastic cup of beer in salute. "You're in the right place anyway. Neva, meet Carol, my one and only daughter and best friend. Only don't tell your mother I said that. She's in town for the run tomorrow. The 25K trail run. We're doing it together and she's promised not to leave me too far behind."

Neva extended her free hand to a young woman in a skirt so short it barely showed below the Boomers sweatshirt she wore zipped over a white turtleneck. Taller than her father, with legs half encased in slim boots with heels, she was not an obvious candidate to beat anyone on a trail run.

"Leave you behind!" The girl laughed and patted his shoulder. "As if, Dad. I've been eating your dust since third grade and it's not going to change any time soon."

"What trail?" Neva addressed the girl but it was her father who replied.

"Calapooia Crest. That hotdog any good?"

"Delicious. Is that the trail Miles White was on?"

"The same. Want a dog, kiddo?"

"You didn't tell me that." Carol was sharply accusatory, her chummy good cheer gone in an instant.

"Didn't think it mattered. I'm starving. How about that hotdog?"

"Of course it matters. And you know it matters or you wouldn't keep going on about hotdogs."

"Did you know Miles?" Neva moved closer to the young woman.

"It's old history," said Farnes. "Sorry, Sweetie, but I really wanted you to do this run. There's nothing to see out there. I checked. Really, it'll be okay."

"It just took me by surprise. I've been trying not to think about it."

"Did you know him?" Neva repeated.

"All the girls had a crush on him."

"Except Carol," Farnes said with quick emphasis. "She's too sensible."

"Out of the running, you mean." Carol spoke directly to Neva now. "But my best friend was a different story. She actually knew him from being on the road with her dad. She followed him around like a, I don't know, not a puppy. Puppies are happy."

"Can I just break in here? I am seriously going to get one of those things on a bun. Yes or no?"

"No. I just ate lunch."

"Did White like your friend?" Neva moved casually to the right just far enough to be in the way should the young woman have decided to follow her father, but her attention appeared to be fully on the question.

"She said he did but I never believed her. There was no evidence, I mean they never dated or anything. She never was on his Facebook page. But she took the pills anyway."

"Pills—you mean suicide?"

"That was the idea but she never took enough. She wasn't very practical, if you know what I mean. But she got sick for a while. They pumped her out. It was disgusting."

"Where is she now?"

"At school. We're not really in touch anymore. Excuse me a minute. Dad!" Now she did step around Neva to join her father, who handed her a steaming bun as he bit into another.

"You haven't changed a bit," he said around a mouthful. And then to Neva, "We're heading inside. Enjoy the game."

Neva watched them move into the current of fans heading toward the coliseum, wishing she'd asked for Carol's contact information or at least for the name of her suicidal friend. She started forward to try to catch them before they reached the door but was hailed by Burt Thomson.

"Come on in," he called out behind her. "I just have to clean up here."

Circling to the rear of his grilling setup, she stood near the back of the van to be out of the way while he organized food and gear, talking as he worked. "Adam's sick but we discussed it last night. He agreed I can't give you clients' names. It's a private business and they're customers. We have to respect their privacy. It's not against the law for one person to pay another person's loan."

"That's true in general," Neva said reasonably. "But this is a bit different, isn't it? Making it appear that players are paying for their own cars when it's really a booster. Very much against the rules, if not the law. And I've already got several names that have been confirmed by the people involved. You and Valley Savings & Loan will of course be named as well. And if I don't have a list of the players, I will have to say something like "Such loans were given to an undisclosed number of Boomers," which may sound worse than an actual number such as four or five."

"Four or five?" Burt did not try to disguise his amusement. "How many years are we talking here?"

"How long has it been going on?"

"Since the year after I was hired. That was eight years ago. I can see you have to use my name. I'm the one who did it. And I will give you the money details for Jasper and Frankie because they said it's ok. You can have that on Monday. But I can't bring other people down."

"I can't see how it would hurt the company, or even boosters particularly. As you said, what you did is not illegal. It's just against the NCAA rules, and sneaky. What about your job? Will you get in trouble?"

Burt was bent over a large cooler and straightened before he said, "I already told them. Right after you left. They weren't happy but, well, you just said yourself I haven't broken any law."

"And the loans?"

"What about them?"

"Will they stay as they are?"

"Of course. Ditto the above. Perfectly legal."

"So that's where we stand, no more information from you, no details apart from Luce and Budd?"

"Sorry. Really. But it's kind of like doctor confidentiality."

Neva had not expected full disclosure but still the offerings seemed puny. "Well, it was a terrific hotdog," she said flatly. "See you Monday."

Bypassing the lines at the six ticket windows, she went straight to the entry door with her home-printed ticket in hand but was stopped by a young woman who asked to look through her shoulder bag and handed her a card that listed prohibited items. Alcohol, glass containers, metal cans, coolers, backpacks, flags or signs on sticks, noisemakers, umbrellas, firearms, knives or weapons of any kind, explosives or flammable material, pets, and beverages except for water in a manufacturer sealed container.

Firearms? Explosives? Crazy…The young woman was tugging on the shoulder bag. Letting it go, Neva looked around with a new kind of curiosity. Had fans really brought explosives into the stands in the past? Or was this yet another unfortunate after-effect of the campus shootings around the country?

The bag was returned and she gave herself up to the crowd. It swept her down the hall, around a corner and down the next hall. Already feeling confined, breathing lightly against the smell of too many warm bodies, she was tempted to find Ambrose after all and claim that free seat.

But she'd reached another corner and here the human current split into strands, one curling right down the adjoining hall, the other curling left up the stairs. She went up.

The bleacher seats were filling fast. She climbed quickly, aiming for an open seat on the aisle, but it was taken before she got there. Onward and upward, a long way upward…she found a spot five rows down from the top and three seats in from the end of the row.

The court was a mile away. Knees shoved into her back, elbows jammed her from both sides. Definitely student territory, though no one appeared to notice her in any way.

The only spot for her bag was between her feet. She settled it there and felt in it for binoculars. Her neighbor on the right also was rummaging in a bag. He pulled out a beer, and before she could ask how he'd smuggled it in, he popped the top and offered her the first swig.

"Very generous of you, but I'm fine thanks," she said. "Did you come in a back door or something?"

"Ve have our vays," he said with a theatrical wink.

Smiling, more at ease, Neva raised the binoculars. First she checked the expensive seats at the base of the bleachers on the opposite side of the court and discovered Ambrose sitting up tall and talking animatedly with a man from the *Current's* advertising department—the free seat had not gone to waste.

Next she found a beaming Tucker Reilly, round as a beach ball in a blue and white Boomers sweatshirt. To his right several seats over were Lyle Crisp and his wife and two boys. Hal Richter appeared to be on his own. Vern Varney was with a gaunt woman who could have been his clone apart from the bright yellow hair, no doubt Elaine Varney, supplier of potted plants to Joey Field.

The mayor, various business owners, a state legislator, one of her neighbors from up the street, a couple of high school teachers, faculty members, President Havesham and his wife, the university vice president for finance—so many familiar faces.

Moving up the stands, scanning hundreds of fans, she focused on a large blue sign with black print that stood still in the sea of waving arms. *What Happened to Miles?* Studying it, she waited, hoping to see the face behind the sign, which must have been smuggled in like the beer. A thunderous cheer erupted and her elbow was struck by the neighbor on her left as he raised his fist in salute, knocking the binoculars sideways. The pep band roared into life and cheerleaders sprang to action. A human pyramid rose without visible effort, men on the bottom tier balancing two tiers of women topped by a beaming blonde who spun a baton toward the high ceiling. She caught it neatly, the pyramid melted, a roar went up from the stands and the crowd leaped to its feet.

Neva also stood up but could see nothing except a large back in a blue jacket. She glanced over her shoulder, noted the height of the young man behind her, and stepped onto the bench seat. On the court far below, players in blue and white loped in a line, circling the perimeter, a few raising their arms in response to the wild cheering.

Arizona trotted in behind the Boomers and the stands went silent as though a switch had been thrown, but then a thin chorus of cheers rose from far down to her left.

The teams went to opposite ends of the court to warm up. The crowd settled again, and Neva returned to the binoculars but the sign about Miles White was gone. Confiscated? She studied the section where it had been but could discover no official picking his way through the crowd with something under his arm, no indignant spectator whose message had been taken away, only beaming fans.

Dropping her view to the court, she found Clemente poised for a practice shot. During their brief exchange in the parking lot, his face had been strikingly mobile, shifting rapidly from suspicion to interest to alarm. Now it was set and blank. He shot, dribbled, passed, dribbled again, as unresponsive to the clamorous crowd and even his fellow players as though he'd been shooting hoops alone in his driveway. The others were the same, their faces as still as carvings, though she caught a silent curse when a player missed a shot. A twist of the lips and then a mask again.

Switching back to the stands, she soon found Gerry Farnes with Carol on his right chatting with a woman Neva didn't know. Carol looked pale but it was probably just the garish lighting. She checked down the line and sure enough just about everyone was pale. Pale and white.

Very white.

She looked at them, she looked at the seated cheerleaders, she looked at the pep band, she looked at the coaches…All white. She looked back at the Boomers. All black except for Kit Mosely. It was just as the statistics she'd looked up had said, but even so, the visible racial imbalance in this saturated space was suddenly the major fact, like a holdover from the jazz era when whites packed clubs where the musicians were all black. In most other communities, of course, the stands would be full of dark faces as well as pale, but here in Whitesville the contrast was extreme.

A buzzer blasted—the game was on.

She found Clemente again but couldn't keep him in the view finder, and soon abandoned the glasses to watch the game properly. Up the court, down the court, up the court, down the court. Players cruised with the ball, pivoted, passed with straight arm-thrusts that appeared automatic and almost off-hand. She had expected an epic battle but the action was workmanlike apart from certain frenzied moments below the basket when players clumped and leaped like fish after the same treat.

Arizona scored. Catcalls erupted all around her. Tucker Reilly shook his fist and scowled. She looked at Clemente, and then other Boomers whose faces she could catch for an instant in the glasses, and all were the same as before, stolid and unreactive.

Up and down the court, up and down the court…Clemente sank a basket. Again she searched for his face and caught a flash of triumph followed by the mask again.

We're professionals, Budd had said. *We learn our job and do it with all we've got. You see some guys strut and put on a big show but most guys are just thinking about the next move and how to get it right.*

"Hey, could I borrow those for a sec?"

It was the young man who had offered the beer.

"You look like you're having a great time," she said.

"You bet. The Boomers rule."

"They win a lot of games."

"I have a good time either way. I mean, when they win you feel good all week. But mostly, you know, it's an outlet. You can come here and scream your head off and nobody cares."

"You like screaming?"

"It's better than tearing my room apart."

"Why would you tear your room apart?"

"Let me put it this way. Some people think being a student's easy. Well, it's not. I never was so worried about things in my life. You know what I mean? I'm working my butt off, going into debt, and for what? I don't even want to think about the job market. So I come here. Everybody screams and jumps up and down, and it's like a, like a, you know, a catharsis. It beats getting drunk. Though that's pretty good too, only, you have the hangover."

"No hangover from a basketball game?"

"Depends." He raised the binoculars and aimed them at the far end of the coliseum. "Just have to find my girlfriend. In the band."

At halftime the Boomers were four points ahead despite being down two key players. The crowd heaved to its feet and flowed out of the stands, again carrying Neva along. Relieved to be moving, she drifted through the packed halls, then went against the crowd to reach the court to try to get a sense of what it was like down in the action. Out on the glossy wood floor, children ran about pretending to dribble balls and shoot baskets. Stepping out onto the court for a better view, she found the posh seats mostly empty.

Across the coliseum where she'd been sitting, the bleachers were about half cleared. She was not quite certain where her spot was, but searching for it she felt suddenly more claustrophobic than she had felt actually sitting up there.

She could not go back up there, definitely not, and Ambrose's extra seat had been taken. What to do?

Working her way out to the hall again, she let herself be carried along for a bit, exchanging greetings right and left but avoiding conversation. Ahead was an exit and it was suddenly irresistible.

As she made for it with determination, a door swung open on the left and party sounds poured out of a brightly lit room. The open door also spilled forth a beaming Tucker Reilly.

"Ms. Leopold!" His delight appeared genuine, with no trace of the stiffness that had ended their interview. "Fine game, fine game. So glad to see you here. I'd suggest a drink but we're out of time."

"The Boomers Den?" she said, reading the sign above the party room door.

"For Court Club members, but you'd be my guest. After the game?"

"I'm afraid I'm on my way out," she said, and confessed to having underestimated the strain of being crammed in with students a mile in the air. "I could have sat with my editor but I wanted to be with the general fans. Atmosphere, you know. But I'm wimpier than I thought."

His chuckle was warm. "You really must stay, you can sit with me. My wife isn't feeling well. Take her seat and we'll have that drink later."

It was past nine when she arrived back home drained and strangely dissatisfied. The game had gone into overtime and at last, shockingly, the Boomers had lost. The defeat had crushed the air out of the coliseum. Even Neva had felt the shock from Clemente's failed free throw that cost the game.

And this time the player's professional cool had dropped away, leaving his face stricken and suddenly younger. His eyes shut, his jaw tightened, his big hands came up to cover his eyes. The next moment the hands dropped and he trotted off the court, alone.

At first tight-lipped and furious, Reilly had seemed to forget her as he prepared to leave, muttering under his breath and yanking up the zipper of his windbreaker, but then he'd turned with a regretful smile. "We can't win every time, I guess. Life must go on. I just hope this isn't how it's going to be until Julian's back."

She had got very little out of him during the game, and had soon given up trying to break into his absorption. And the promised dose of serious gripper immersion in the Boomers Den also had come to nothing—no party following a defeat. It was just as well. She'd had as much noise and crowd as she could manage, and if the other boosters reacted like Reilly, it would have been a bitter crowd at the bar.

At home, she went indoors only as far as the thermostat on the living room wall, turned on the heat, exchanged her light jacket for a polar fleece from the hall closet, and went back out into the clear night. Walking up Spring Street under pale stars, she mulled over the evening, especially her own reaction to the game.

She had cared that the Boomers lost. Amazing.

The air had not only gone out of the coliseum, it had gone out of her as well. For an instant, only an instant, she had felt profoundly disappointed and even let down.

How to account for this? How to explain that moment of deep feeling given that she had never cared a straw for competitive sports? She certainly didn't care about the team's standing in the conference.

What then? Was it simple crowd contagion? Or because she knew the players would catch hell from Leonard and she felt sorry for them, especially Dash Clemente? But someone had to lose— if the Boomers had won, the Arizona players would have taken the knocks.

Would she have felt the same pangs on behalf of a losing Arizona team? It was impossible to know for certain but she didn't think so. She would have enjoyed seeing the Boomers win, and the only explanation that made sense was simply that she now knew some of the players. They had become real people rather than glorified show dogs. It was only a small taste of boosterism but still it was unsettling.

The night was sweetly damp and earthy. She had started off at a brisk pace but gradually slowed to a stroll, savoring the early spring musk of wet earth and new leaves. Her usual loop through the neighborhood took about twenty minutes, and as she returned down Spring Street she felt calm again and ready for a snack, a bit of reading, and sleep.

The contents of the refrigerator were peculiarly uninspiring. As she stood considering whether to fry an egg or make a simple quesadilla, the doorbell rang.

No one visited at this hour.

A mutilated kitten, a skewered basketball, now a late ring at the door…Stepping softly, she crossed the dark living room but stopped at the arched opening to look down the hall toward the front door. The window in the upper half showed an unfamiliar silhouette.

She pulled back sharply. Had she locked the door?

Again the bell rang.

Again she leaned forward only far enough to see the dark shape against the not-quite-dark night. Her visitor was tall and hooded.

The silhouette moved. Impatient pounding rattled the door. A hand lifted and pulled back the hood. Long hair spilled out.

Three quick paces took Neva up the hall. She flipped on the porch light. Annette Octavian looked furiously at her through the window as though considering whether to kick the door in. Neva opened the door.

Octavian up close was every bit as glamorous as she'd appeared on the coliseum steps and in the airport snapshot. She was also strikingly powerful looking, her neck a white pillar, her hands large enough to wear heavy rings, even her considerable cleavage suggesting momentum rather than seduction. Her open black raincoat was elegant rather than sporty, though she wore it over the same green jumpsuit as before.

"You got my messages?" Neva said, moving them toward the living room.

"Afraid not. Lost my phone a while back." The tone was brusque and businesslike.

Neva turned on a lamp and would have invited Octavian to be seated except that the other woman was already settling into an armchair next to the cold fireplace.

Neva took the facing chair and waited while her guest looked sharply about the room as though calculating how much to offer for the furniture. Octavian volunteered none of the sorts of comments that would be usual at such a moment. *Sorry for the late hour. Sorry to drop in without calling first. I hope I didn't catch you at a bad time.*

"You're investigating the team," she said at length, making it a flat statement.

"That's not how I would put it, exactly."

"You're trying to find out who killed Miles."

"As I said, that's not really correct. But first, can I get you a drink? Tea or coffee?"

"No, no. I'm fine." Octavian had not taken off her coat and now pulled it closer.

"I could light a fire."

"Not on my account. I never get cold. And I'm not staying long. I was devastated about Miles. Just devastated."

"Of course."

"I was on pills for three days. It was so shocking. We'd been together for four years, since before he came here. We would have been married. I don't know who could have done such a terrible thing."

She twisted a ring, one set with a fat emerald. The action was energetic rather than pensive, and now she studied Neva as she had studied the room, taking in details. Though she moved only her eyes, Neva felt each shift in glance as though a powerful finger had poked at the hair that hadn't been brushed since before the game, the casual cotton slacks, the favorite gray sweater.

"Where are you staying now?" she said to bring the sizing-up to a close.

"Staying? What do you mean?"

"Will Gentry said you haven't been home for some time and he's worried, quite worried."

Octavian merely shook her head. Silent moments passed. Neva had many questions but resisted asking them, waiting to hear what was on her visitor's mind. At last she said, "Annette, I'm glad to see you but I do wonder why you've come here tonight, so late."

"To find out who killed Miles, of course."

"But I have no idea. Did you think I'd know?"

"The only thing I want in the world is justice for Miles. It was the team, I'm sure it was the team. They all hated him. They were jealous. You have to tell me!"

"I have no idea who killed Miles. Or Lamarr. If I did I'd tell the police."

"But you suspect someone."

"Suspecting isn't the same as knowing."

"You do suspect someone!"

"As it happens, I don't. I don't have the slightest idea. I'm guessing you've heard that I ask about Miles during interviews, but I'm not directly working on the murders. I've been assigned to do some stories about the team, particularly about the players' relationships with the boosters, the so-called grippers."

"Boosters? You're interested in *boosters*? Boosters! Jesus." Octavian threw her head back and laughed, just as Rex Gregorio had done at the mention of boosters. Her amusement did not last. "Excuse me," she said, and stood up in a single forceful movement. "This was a mistake, a complete mistake. So sorry to have bothered you."

"No, wait." Neva raised her hand in a restraining gesture, then also stood. "Please stay. I think you can help me with some information even if I disappointed you. I've just heard that Miles was something of a teen heartthrob. One girl even attempted suicide over it."

"A bunch of twits and losers," Octavian broke in. "Miles thought they were funny."

"He didn't encourage them?"

"They didn't need it, did they? If you'd seen the things they wrote. You don't think that had anything to do with it? Oh, give me a break! No wonder they sent you off chasing boosters." She yanked up her coat zipper and headed for the hall.

Following Annette and talking to her back, Neva gave vent to open irritation, "Annette! This is ridiculous. Just stop for a moment and listen to me."

Octavian turned and held up a commanding hand. "I need time to myself, okay? Like I said, this was a mistake, a big mistake. Forget I was here."

"That's impossible. I have questions—Annette, stop!"

Short of hanging onto her arm like a Chihuahua biting a leg—and no doubt being shaken off with ease—there was no way to stop Annette Octavian from striding out into the night as strangely and abruptly as she had arrived.

CHAPTER
21

Rain fell with steady monotony all day on Sunday. Doing her best to forget about basketball, Neva alternated house chores with reading, but the incident with Annette refused to be put out of sight. And every time it flashed into mind, Neva was irritated and puzzled all over again. The woman was a force, and deeply distraught, no question about that. But her grief had not been convincing. She had put on a good performance but to what purpose?

Above all, what had brought her to Neva's house late at night when, as she had admitted impatiently, none of the telephone messages had reached her? Her dismissal of boosters as worthy of any notice whatsoever could not have been plainer.

Monday morning brought clear skies and the usual lift in mood that came with sunshine. Automatically checking phone messages first thing on reaching the office, she deleted the first two, then sat up with sudden attention at the third.

"This is Gina David at the Motor Vehicles Division. The information you wanted is ready. I didn't want to Fax it until I talked to you."

Gina David answered Neva's return call after the first ring. "You hit the jackpot," she said. "Four moving violations."

"Fantastic. Could you read me the tickets over the phone before Faxing them?"

"I don't know any law against it," the clerk said in a musing tone. "Since there's laws for everything else I guess it must be okay. Are you ready?" Reading slowly, she gave the citations in chronological order, beginning with a failure to stop at a red light two years ago and ending with a speeding ticket dated the week before the murder. For every one of the four tickets, Miles White had been driving the same vehicle—a Buick Regal sedan registered to Mel Pascolini.

"Thank you. Thank you very much," Neva said so fervently she expected Gina David to ask what was so special about ticket information.

But the clerk sounded pleased rather than curious. "You're welcome. It's always great to be able to help instead of making people mad."

The information was better than she'd hoped but also puzzling. Pascolini had not been named as a booster by anyone in a position to know. And a Buick sedan? A long way from the usual choice for an athlete. Clearly, the link between the developer and White had been close but it was not a gripper relationship, she would have bet on that.

It really was time to find Mel Pascolini. Wherever he'd gone, surely he'd be checking messages. First she dialed his home number and left a request for a return call. His company office must have information on his whereabouts, though Charlie had failed to prod it loose. Confident that she could do better, she was seriously let down on reaching a recorded voice that said only that the office was closed. No explanation and no information on when it would open.

Sitting for a moment with her hands folded on the desk, Neva considered what to do next. She didn't want to waste her morning energy on typing notes or getting drawn into a session with Ambrose, who had been on the phone when she arrived but had waved with obvious meaning on catching sight of her.

No, it was not a time for a long Ambrosian chat. She stood up, grabbed her notebook and bag, and headed out with an air of urgency, avoiding eye contact with J.D. as she passed the city editor's desk.

The best direction to aim her energy was at a booster. The only one on Cal's list who remained untackled was service station owner Bill Tunney. He had not been linked to a particular player but was said to give freely to them all, that is, to provide gas, lube jobs, tune-ups, and tires to any who asked, sometimes in exchange for tickets and sometimes as a gift. She did not know Tunney and had never encountered his name until she read it on the booster list.

Sudden unease made her slow down as she approached the largest of Tunney's three service stations, and rather than park out front in full sight she pulled in next to the women's toilet. Though the station was big enough to include a garage it was not one of those that had morphed into a complete stop for travelers like so many on the Interstate. No restaurant, no convenience store, no showers. She'd guessed that Tunney's office would be here, and sure enough she could see a desk and the edge of a filing cabinet through the side window.

That he was not at the desk was a relief.

Giving herself a moment to gather her resolve to face yet another stranger with tough questions, she wrote his name on a fresh page, dated it, and started a list: gas, repairs, tires, towing.

A shadow crossed the page and the next instant the car rocked from a heavy blow to the roof above her head.

Instinctively throwing herself sideways, she landed with her right elbow on the passenger's seat and her left arm shielding her head. A second blow shook the car, but this time it was a hard slap at the window. Twisting to look under her arm, she saw a furious face shoved up close to the glass.

The face jerked away.

She sat up and punched the lock button on the door, then turned to study the man who stood within reach of   the car with his fist cocked back as though to sock her through the window. He was wearing a white shirt with a name in red on the pocket— Bill Tunney.

Neva raised both hands toward him, palms out.

Tunney glared for a long moment without changing his stance, and then dropped his arm.

They stared at each other, Tunney challenging, Neva considering.

She lowered the window halfway.

"You can just forget it!" He bellowed. "Save your goddamned breath and clear out of here. I've got nothing to say to you or anybody else that doesn't mind their own business."

"Mr. Tunney—"

"I said forget it! Get out of here before I call the cops. I heard what you're doing. We know how to deal with troublemakers around here."

Had he turned and stalked away, that would have been the end of it. She would have left without another word. But he stood his ground like a bull, forcing her to react.

"You may not know this," she said as mildly as she could manage after glancing down to see that the door truly was locked, "but you've turned out to be one of the most generous boosters in town."

"What's that supposed to mean?"

"Unlike the others, you don't play favorites. You give gas to one and all."

"That's pure crap."

"The fact is, Mr. Tunney, I am documenting widespread NCAA rule violations by prominent community members. Boosters and players alike have said you provide free gas, tune-ups, and lube jobs for players. Even towing sometimes. It's only right to give you an opportunity to respond."

"Prominent community members? Opportunity! Sounds like you're offering me a chance to join an exclusive club. Thanks but I don't play. Athletes charge gas and services here, just like half the town, and then their bills are paid just like everybody else's. That's the story. Sexy, ain't it?"

"Their bills get paid but who pays them?"

"Go figure. And go to hell while you're at it."

Neva drove only two blocks before pulling over to the curb and shutting off the engine. What if she had not dallied in the car trying to work up her nerve? What if she had gone directly into the station and found Tunney there and had to face him with no locked door between them? Would a man who attacked a vehicle with no real provocation hesitate to hit a woman?

Several silent minutes passed while she went over and over the incident in her mind. Tunney was a different breed from the other grippers, no question about it, the only one so far who had reacted from the gut, without any attempt to dodge or manipulate. It was almost refreshing.

Back at the *Current*, the two-page Fax from the motor vehicle office was waiting in the mail basket. Settling into her chair with the office door closed, she studied the list of tickets issued to Miles White.

Bits and pieces were piling up but did they form a picture? White could be a charmer one moment and rude the next. He "already knew people" wherever the team went. A figure of romance and glamor for teen girls, he had been engaged to a traffic-stopping redhead. He did not generally party with the team. Despite being the star of the court, he was not the pet of any known gripper though he drove a car registered to Mel Pascolini. The car was a Buick. He was not mourned by the very people who had recruited him and for whom he won games. Lots and lots of games.

Murdered for what reason?

Not robbery. Not random.

Sexual jealousy? The only other acknowledged admirer of Annette was Lamarr Duffy, who was now also dead.

Competition? Every credible interviewee dismissed team rivalry as a sensible motive.

Revenge? Varney hated White but with murderous intent? Difficult to believe of an extreme Boomers fan, and Varney looked too feeble to hike out to where White was shot, let alone fire the rifle. Or suffocate Lamarr Duffy with a pillow.

Though she hadn't intended to turn up at Valley Savings & Loan until late afternoon, Neva felt restless and unable to settle, and headed out again, this time on foot. Burt's information would not include anything new, only the details about Budd and Luce, but at least it was real documentation in a sea of claims and denials.

The same effusive young man as before greeted her in the savings and loan lobby but this time he had disappointing news. "Mr. Thomson's ill. He called in this morning and said I was to watch out for you and offer apologies."

No, he had no idea when Burt might return but he'd sounded pretty bad. Terrible cold going around. Did she want to leave a message?

"He left nothing for me? No envelope or papers?" Disappointment was followed by suspicion—this was terribly convenient for Mr. Burt Thomson. On the other hand, his partner had been sick on Saturday, and she had no reason to distrust the man.

Still, it was frustrating, and matters were not improved by a quick walk to the jail where she was told that Budd was not permitted to see general visitors. No doubt Coach Leonard or Rex Gregorio would have been allowed in—with compliments—if Budd had still been an active team member.

CHAPTER
22

Ambrose called a staff meeting for first thing Tuesday morning "so we can all catch up with everybody." After a brief summing up, the editor turned the floor over to Neva. She had already distributed notes on the conversation with Vera, the situation with Burt Thomson and the savings and loan, and the weird visit from Annette Octavian, and now she added details and answered questions. She concluded with an account of yesterday's run-in with Tunney, which drew whistles and exclamations.

"That's the last he'll see of me," J.D. growled. "I've been filling up there for a decade but never again."

"On the other hand," Neva said, "he managed to do what the others haven't. He didn't give himself away one jot. I've been wondering why any of them agree to talk to me. I almost have to respect that."

"He didn't have to be such a jerk about it," said Cal. "And, for my money, he did give himself away—why get so mad if it ain't true? Now I guess it's my turn. Afraid it's kind of dull compared to Neva's tall tales."

He spread a handful of papers out on the editor's desk and held forth at length about full-ride scholarships versus the non-scholarship sports, and the dramatic surge in athletic department earnings with the rise of cable TV. Neva tried but failed to keep her attention on the numbers. It strayed back to White and Pascolini, though when Charlie took over from Cal she had no trouble focusing on his update on Budd's arrest. Still no bail

amount or court date set, and as she'd already discovered, no
visitors allowed apart from officials such as his lawyer.

"And who do you think his mouthpiece is?" Charlie aimed a
Tom Sawyer grin at Neva. "Your pal Hal Richter."

Neva's decision to visit Pascolini's house was in large part an
excuse to get out of the building after sitting through the meeting
in the windowless conference room. What practical use it might
be she didn't know apart from giving her a sense of his situation.
If the house appeared truly closed up she'd have to put serious
energy into finding him elsewhere. If it appeared as though
someone was coming and going she'd leave a note in the mailbox.
And there was a chance she could get more out of the neighbors
than young Charlie had managed.

The contractor lived at the top of a hill where streets wound
among oaks and wide lawns, and where no human life was to be
seen apart from an occasional sturdy figure unloading a mower
from a utility trailer. Pascolini's place was at the top of the hill
where the street turned into a private drive with a security gate.
The gate was open. She stopped to consider this, then drove on
around a bend and discovered a long, low house with a separate
six-bay garage. The wide front lawn was littered with leaves and
twigs that must have come down in last week's storm, giving the
place a neglected air that was out of keeping with its elegant
contemporary lines.

Neva parked at the bottom of a broad brick walkway that led
to the front door, lowered the window, and listened to silence. The
house was unoccupied, she was certain, but still she went up the
walkway and pressed the doorbell button. Sonorous notes
sounded deep within. Twice more she pushed, twice more the
chimes pealed.

To the right of the porch three large windows faced the lawn.
To see in through the nearest she had to step between the house
and an azalea bush in heavy bud. The window gave a clear view
of a kitchen that was not only well-appointed but large, more like
a hotel kitchen than one in a private home. Also unusual was the
placement; the kitchen extended more than halfway across the
front of the house where the living room would typically be.

Better views from the back?

Following a flagstone path this time, she went around the west end of the house to a gate in a tall wood fence. The dangling latch cord invited tugging. The gate swung open and she stepped forward without hesitation into a different world.

From the front, the Pascolini place was notable for its size and location on top of a coveted hill, but the landscaping with dogwood trees and azaleas was so standard and unremarkable that she'd noticed it only because she'd actually looked. The rear of the house was another matter. Somehow, without any rumor of it having reached the all-knowing Neva or the part-time garden writer at the paper, the Pascolinis had conjured a perfect Japanese garden into being. Not a modest backyard version but the real thing, on the quality and scale of public gardens. It covered the back side of the hill, which fell gently away in unfolding levels of terraces, pools, paths, bridges, boulders, and even what appeared to be a small pagoda in the leafy distance.

To come on such a scene with no prior hint was dumbfounding. Everything she knew or thought she knew about Pascolini tumbled into a heap.

The quiet was broken only by a murmur of water that deepened the effect of tranquility and refuge, though signs of recent neglect added a mournful tone. Twigs littered a decoratively raked gravel bed, camellia blossoms rotted on the path, a potted cypress had blown over onto a bed of moss.

Resisting the pull of a path surfaced in white gravel, Neva turned to study the private side of the house. Curving as though to hug the top of the garden, it presented mainly windows. The stone patio that ran nearly the length of the building stood slightly above the garden and was connected to it by several low sets of stone steps.

The windows appeared dark and blank but even so, she studied them for some time before climbing the nearest steps and crossing the patio to peer in. The living room on the other side of the glass was as surprising in its way as the garden, and seemed to stand in opposition to it, or maybe counterpoint. Spacious and spare in its furnishings, the room was almost pure white—white walls, white carpet, white sofas with white cushions. Two large paintings on the opposite wall were so pale she had to look hard to discover off-white geometric shapes arranged in receding layers.

The monochromania was relieved by only one object, a shining black pillar of glass, obsidian or possibly marble, that stood in isolation on the snowy carpet.

A bit of color caught her eye. A fuzzy little yellow slipper lay on its side near a couch.

This small and accidental hint of human presence was disturbing. Could children really have lived here?

Moving to the left down the patio, she found a set of smaller, multi-paned windows that revealed yet another kind of tableau. The room, dark and intimate, suggested an old British men's club, a den of dark wood and leather. A bar at the back gleamed with bottles, round tables filled the floor space and were scattered with cards as though play had just ended. And among the cards were poker chips, heaps of poker chips.

Poker chips…Pascolini was hosting poker games, and the planes had flown in high-stakes players! And White had been the talented dealer. How obvious—why hadn't she thought of this before, after what Lyle had said? *We put on a mock casino night and he was the dealer…We never made so much money.*

White and Pascolini were most certainly linked but it had nothing to do with basketball.

Elated, she scanned what she could see of the room for whatever else it might tell her about the dead athlete, but there was nothing.

A sudden sensation of being observed made her turn back toward the garden. For several minutes she stood facing outward, watching and waiting. Nothing moved apart from an occasional bird, and the only distinctive sound was the distant ripple of wind chimes.

She had no right to be here. She was trespassing. Pascolini was gone, she had gained a valuable bit of information, and now she should leave. Right now. But this might be her only chance to see the garden. The Pascolinis were not likely to agree to a tour when they returned, especially if there there was any suggestion of publicity. This was a private world, a very private world.

And her interest in the garden was private, or at least personal. She wanted to see it out of curiosity and for her own pleasure. Setting aside uneasiness and the nagging voice of guilt, she crossed the patio to the nearest set of steps and descended to a path of fine gravel, not the ubiquitous local gray variety but multi-colored and bright. A side path soon drew her a different way. Wandering without design, meandering downward, she sat on a stone bench, leaned on a bridge railing above cruising carp, lay on her back on a smooth boulder gazing up into budding cherry branches, and tried to out-wait a motionless turtle on a log but gave up before it revealed any sign of not being a sculpture. The various "rooms" of the garden flowed gracefully from one to another, a formal composition in rocks and sand leading to a bamboo forest followed by a grotto with a waterfall and pools descending among white boulders.

At length she came to the pagoda, a tea house with classic curved red roof beams and a sliding door that opened with a light touch on the polished wood handle. The room was simply furnished with a daybed covered in bright pillows, two armchairs made of carved wood, an ornate hat tree draped with fringed shawls, and woven mats on the floor. A stale smell of incense made her want to open windows, but it was not her place to air the tea house or even to explore it further. Without going inside, she shut the door and returned up the main path to the gate.

Back in the office, she sat down without taking time to remove her jacket and Googled Oregon gambling laws. The poker section took a few minutes to find but was brief and straightforward.

Home poker games are legal in any city or county in the State of Oregon, in any format or structure for cash or for fun, as long as the location is a primary living residence. Games outside of homes for any type of monetary or cash value are illegal under Oregon law unless you have applied for a non-profit Monte Carlo license from the department of justice and are granted the license to hold an event for fund raising for the non-profit organization.

Pascolini certainly was not raising money for a good cause. The poker was played in his home, but what a home it was. Add up the scale of it, the commercial-size kitchen, the flying in of players, the special room set up as a gambling lounge, and it shouted business, not fun among friends.

The developer was almost certainly in serious violation of the law, but did this matter? Pascolini had no link to athletics as far as she knew apart from hiring a basketball player to deal cards...but of course it mattered. Gambling and violence in combination were a Wild West tradition. The gambling life might well have killed Miles. For tricky dealing by someone who had lost big? By Pascolini himself to keep him from turning informer after a falling out?

Lamarr Duffy had no connection with the gambling, as far as she knew, but he might have seen someone on the trail—if he really had gone running that day. But was it humanly possible to keep silent after your jogging partner is shot to death in front of you? As far as anyone knew, Duffy had said nothing about seeing what had happened, not even when he told Clayton that he'd gone running with him. If Clayton was telling the truth.

Neva stood up, stretched, sat again. For some time she remained motionless in the chair, thinking. Then she dialed Jerry Farnes to get his daughter's telephone number but there was no answer. She left a message and had no more than stepped out the door in pursuit of tea water when the telephone rang.

"Hello?" said a young woman's voice. "Dad said you were wanting to talk to me? I'm at the airport."

"Good heavens, I just left the message two minutes ago."

"I'm at the airport," Carol said again. "Not much time. Sorry."

"Right. A few questions for you. Your friend who tried to kill herself over Miles White. You're no longer close, you said, but can you give me contact information?"

"You want to talk to Shawna? I don't know, I mean she was upset about other things too I guess, not just Miles. And she might not want to talk about it."

"It's worth trying. She can always refuse. A phone number, email address, whatever you have would help."

"All I've got is email and it's really old. Ready? Shawna dot Varney, all lower case—"

"Varney? Related to Vern Varney?"

"Her dad. Anyway, the rest is at gmail.com. Is that it then?"

"Someone told me Vern Varney hated Miles but they didn't know why. This sounds like a good reason to me. What do you think?"

"Blaming Miles is dumb."

"I'm not sure a parent would be logical about such a thing."

"No, I guess not. My dad would've killed him—oh, my god, I didn't mean to say, I mean, you know what I mean."

"Got it. Did you spend much time with the Varneys?"

"We weren't that kind of friends. We hung out at school, as a group you know. Went to movies. Just a second, oh, they're calling my boarding group. Gotta go. Bye-bye."

Neva wasted no time. Within seconds of hanging up she sent off a message to Shawna. And seconds later she received a notice of delivery failure. She checked the address for typing errors and found none. Maybe she'd recently changed her address?

She could probably get current information from Elaine Varney but how would she explain wanting to contact the girl? *I want to ask your daughter about her near death over a crush on a basketball player who has been murdered.* It wouldn't be much different from saying outright *Did you and your husband blame Miles White for your daughter's near-suicide? Blame him sufficiently to want him dead?*

Dinner was Trader Joe's lamb curry eaten standing at the sink looking out the kitchen window at the early spring dusk. She rinsed the bowl and fork, drank a full glass of water, and collected the empty coffee bean jar from the shelf above the grinder. She had not done a roast for two days. As she started down the basement stairs the telephone in the front hall rang.

Vera's cheery voice said, "Hiya. Have a minute? Or all night?"

"Ah, sounds serious." Neva returned to the kitchen with the phone, plucking the notebook from her bag on the way, and sat down at the table. "I'm all yours for the next week, if you want."

Vera's laughter cascaded merrily over the line. "Nothing that serious. Well, maybe it is, I don't know. Mr. Gregorio is out of town so I decided to have a little look in his office. Last night I went back after everyone was gone. I happen to know his secretary keeps a key to his office in her drawer."

"Vera, you are amazing."

"Dumb, probably. Anyway, I didn't get caught. Part of my job is filing so I'm pretty fast at whipping through files, even messy ones like his. I found one for Miles."

"And?" Neva said after a silence.

"It was empty."

"As in completely empty?"

"Completely empty. Which the others weren't, if you see what I mean. The others who don't play anymore. Clayton and everybody. That didn't seem right so I got to thinking. First I looked in his recycling. Then I went and looked in the shredder bin. It makes confetti, you know, but it's been acting up and sometimes it comes out more like fettuccini. I had to dig a bit but it was in there, the stuff from Miles's folder, with his name on it."

"Did you keep the shreds?"

"No way. I mean, you couldn't read it anyway. It would take a hundred years to put it all back together. But it was definitely his name on a couple of pieces. For sure. I mean it looks funny doing that. Sure he's dead and everything and maybe they don't need the papers anymore, but I've never seen anybody shred information before, not about the team. We had one killed in a car wreck last year, a football player, and they never shredded his stuff."

"This is very, very interesting. They must have shredded the papers in the last few days if the bits are still there."

"That's not all. His computer was on so I clicked on his email. It said he had a phone message."

"A phone message in his email?"

"That's the way it works on campus. You get your phone messages forwarded to email so you can listen anywhere. It's cool. Anyway, I listened."

"My god, Vera. You're worse than I am."

The giggle on the line was girlish but the words that followed were deep and manly. "'Looks like they can't hold Budd. Keep your head down.'"

"That was the message?"

"That was it. The whole thing. They don't say who it's from but it shows the phone number. You want it?"

It was not a number Neva recognized.

"That's it I'm afraid," Vera said as though apologizing.

"It's plenty. Thank you thank you, but please don't do this again. It's too risky. Just keep your eyes and ears open, okay?"

A quick Web search brought up multiple services for tracing phone numbers, all claiming to be free. The first one she tried said the number was in Willamette, Oregon, but then asked for a dollar to provide the name. Resisting the temptation—online shopping had lost its appeal since her card had been hijacked to buy porn videos in Toronto—she tried another site. It gave a street address to go with the number but still not the name.

After a moment's thought, she went to the county assessor's website, typed in the address, and got the full property record. The owner was William Tunney.

CHAPTER
23

Wednesday and Thursday proved a plodding exercise in futility. Clayton Perle was not to be found, Julian refused to talk—this time for real—Will Gentry was distant despite her detailed account of Octavian's late-night visit. Burt Thomson remained sick at home, the Varneys were out of town, and she could not work up the nerve to face Bill Tunney again. She was assured by Kitty Fiori's second-in-command, and then by the police chief herself, that no complaint had reached them of illegal gambling at the Pascolini residence "but we'd be very interested in any such activities."

By Friday morning, she welcomed Ambrose's appearance in her doorway.

"You've earned your little break, I think," he began cheerily. "I brought you some background on Loomis and Borden, but I hope you'll have some fun, too. Maybe check out the spa, get a massage."

"Excuse me?"

"I made the reservations myself, which I don't even do for myself, if you see what I mean. I didn't want any screw-ups. We won't get a second chance like this. The best I could do was a basic queen, but I don't imagine you'll be spending much time in the room anyway."

"What room? What are you talking about?"

"The Montrose Hotel. In Portland, for the games tonight and tomorrow. The teams always stay at the Montrose. We really lucked out—turns out the Mavericks will be in town as well as the Lakers, so you'll get to talk to Julian Loomis and Jim Borden. The Mavericks play the Portland Trail Blazers tonight and the Lakers play tomorrow, but both teams will arrive today. I'd go up myself if I could get away from here."

Neva could only look at him, stunned.

"I'd send Cal with you," the editor went on blithely, "but my gut tells me you'll do better on your own. He knows them too well, and there's history there of the wrong kind. I don't mean Cal's misbehaved, just got into a pattern of blindness, or maybe acceptance is a better word, that he's likely to fall into again. Which isn't to say he's slacking on the academic stuff. That's a whole different ball game, ha ha."

"No. No, Ambrose. No, really. You can't spring this kind of thing on me."

"What do you mean? We agreed on it."

"In your imagination. This is way too far out of my range. For one thing, I can't sleep in hotels. The windows never open and I suffocate."

"So use the climate control system."

"Climate control isn't air. But it's far more than that. I'd be so out of place they wouldn't give me three seconds of their time."

"You want to bet? Somehow, you get these guys talking even when they say they won't. You'll have fun with Loomis. He's smart, real smart. If he decides to talk, you'll get riches pouring out, and if he decides not to talk, well, just be ready to try every maneuver in your bag of tricks. It will be a challenge. These are two of the biggest stars ever to come through this place."

Neva looked at him in silence.

The editor's smile was sly. "You're enjoying this on some level, Leopold. I've got eyes—I haven't seen you so dug into a story in years. These guys were both five star high school players and first-round draft picks and beautiful to watch on the court. They won't be expecting you, which should help. I suggest you get there early and hang out by the desk so you can catch them when they check in."

Alone once more, appalled, Neva sat looking out her narrow window at nothing. Why was the prospect of two nights at the Montrose so dreadful? Plenty of people—maybe most people—would welcome two paid nights in a lively downtown Portland hotel, basketball players or no basketball players. What was her problem? Loomis and Borden were just harmless hoop hotshots, and there was nothing alarming or even all that uncomfortable in the arrangement despite her complaint about bad air. She had no thrilling plans for the weekend that would have to be cancelled and she was sick of blind alleys and closed doors…So why the choked, miserable feeling in her chest?

Trying to corner the NBA stars was bound to be embarrassing.

The two former Boomers would have no interest in talking with an unknown middle-aged woman about favors they'd received in little old Willamette two, three or four years ago. They'd probably laugh and brush her off, most likely in front of fellow team mates, fans, hotel staff, whoever was on the scene.

The prospect sent hot blood up her back, though after further thought she was ready to credit Ambrose with at least the possibility, the chance—a slim chance—that Loomis or Borden would talk to her and would provide just the stick she needed to beat her way out of the woods and into the open at last. Even a slim chance was worth the trip.

The editor's suggestion that she "hang out" near the hotel check-in desk turned out to be practical. The lobby was large, the desk situated midway between the portico entryway and an open cocktail lounge set off by a row of planters. Before claiming a table, she checked with the desk clerk on when the two teams were due. The Lakers should roll in within the hour, he said, looking her up and down—not the usual sort of babe to wait in hotel lobbies for basketball players—and the Mavericks soon after that.

She chose a table near the divider, not only for a clearer view of the desk but to be as far away as possible from the wall-size screen where black men in shorts swarmed up and down a court. With two pro teams in town, this was the basketball capital of Oregon for the weekend, although the only spectators for the silent game on the screen besides her were the stubby bartender and a silent young couple sprawled on a white leather couch in the middle of the cocktail lounge. Not much of a crowd for her to hide in. In fact, she was utterly conspicuous sitting alone in a sea of empty tables drinking gin and tonic at four in the afternoon with two small photos arranged next to the wet cocktail napkin.

Julian Loomis and Jim Borden, both starters for three years, both forwards, both first-round draft picks. Boyish in the freshman mug shots, fuzzy dots for mustaches, faces shy above long necks that gave the only hint of basketball height. Both were men now. She should have insisted on more recent photos. When the teams arrived, she would have scant minutes to identify her targets before they vanished into elevators. And if she missed that first contact they could avoid her all night, refuse to return calls or open their doors. She downed the drink in large swallows and wanted another one. Before she could signal, the bartender was at her side.

"How did you know?" she said.

"Honey, I've been at this game for twenty-five years. I not only know when you're going to order, but what you want and how many it takes to get you where you want to be."

"So how many more do I need?" How many drunken wits had played this game with him?

"You don't need any more." He picked up her glass and tapped the table by the mug shots. "They're here."

He was right. At the other end of the lobby, giants in gray suits were surging in through the revolving door. Extra hotel staff and guests also suddenly appeared from nowhere, calling out, laughing, slapping players on the back. Already it was moving too fast. Neva snatched up the mug shots and hurried to meet the human wave as it hit the desk. In what was clearly an old and familiar drill, players took quick possession of keys and messages and headed for the elevators. Every single one was tall. Every one had a lean jaw. Every one carried a sports bag.

She shoved the useless six-year-old photos into her pocket.

"You need somebody in particular or will anyone do?"

Neva looked up at a young man who laughed down at her in friendly fashion, with no hint of any real intention behind his suggestive words.

"Julian?" She said with sudden hope. "No? Could you please point out Julian Loomis?"

"Hey!" The player shouted as though hailing someone on the far side of a potato field. "Julie! Lady to see you. If that doesn't work out, I'll be around."

Her savior went on toward the elevator but her attention was now on a player who had just checked in. He turned away from the desk with a dazzling and eager smile but when he'd scanned the crowd and realized that she was the lady waiting to see him, he looked severely disappointed.

"I was expecting somebody," he said. "You want to see me?" Though his manner was amiable he did not stop at her side but strode along with team members making for the elevators.

Falling into step, she said, "I'm Jeneva Leopold from the *Willamette Current*. I know you're very busy but I'd really appreciate twenty minutes or so for an interview."

"What kind of interview?"

The group managed to get into one elevator, the players around the edge and Neva alone in the middle. She was surrounded by amused and curious faces that had to look distinctly down to study her. Focusing on Julian, she gave a quick version of her spiel about boosters and rule breaking and too many players ending up with the short end of the stick.

"Hey, Julie, they want you to give back all that nice stuff you got when you were in school."

"You tell this nice lady all about it, Julie. You tell her about the good times you had down there."

"Shut up," Julian said mildly.

"It won't take long," she urged, feeling a fool. "I just have a few questions, mainly from talking to players who are still on the team."

"You talk to her, Julie. She's a real nice lady, you can tell."

"That's right. Only tell her you want to keep the TV."

"Shut up," Julian said, again with no emphasis. "Are you staying here tonight?"

"I am."

"Listen, I'll meet you in the lobby at nine."

The elevator stopped and the group strode out. The last player to go turned back to wink at her. As the doors closed, she leaned against the wall and closed her eyes. The floor dropped under her feet but when the doors opened seconds later she thought the elevator hadn't gone down after all. Six men like the six who had just got off stood looking at her.

"Well, you going to ride it up again or what?"

The elevator had taken her back to the lobby floor and during her brief ride up a new wave of players in suits had arrived.

"Mavericks?" She said as the players crowded in with their bags.

"That's us."

"Jim Borden?"

"That's me. You laying in wait for me in here?"

The laughter was friendly, and this time her pitch about boosters was greeted with smiles and nods but no teasing. Borden listened as Loomis had done, with interest she had not expected, but instead of agreeing to meet her, he said with an almost pompous air, "I don't know what to say. I have to think about it. That was a different part of my life then, and I've got people to see tonight, you know. And a game. This is like homecoming, coming back here, and there are certain expectations of me."

Wordless sounds of derision rose around them but Borden paid no attention. "Tell you what. I'll call you. What's your room number? I might have something to say and I might not."

For two hours, Neva waited in her room assuming that Borden would call before the game rather than after. He did not call. Disappointed but not surprised, she gave up and went out to pace the lobby, the mezzanine, and half a dozen hallways opening onto lounges where the night scene already throbbed. Borden wouldn't have told her anything useful, she was pretty sure of that. Julian, though, might be goaded into indiscretions. Intelligent, and playful like Budd, he was a talker and talkers rarely know when to stop once they get going.

To be less conspicuous, she had changed out of the raincoat and pants into a skirt, and switched her briefcase-type bag for a slim leather purse the size of her notebook. Stopping to check the effect in a mirror on the mezzanine stairway landing, she saw two young women descending behind her. Tall, black, elegant, they paused to scan the lobby below

Hunting for Julian? *I was expecting somebody.*

But the hotel was full of striking young men, dressed now in snappy shirts and slacks and clearly ready to party. The Mavericks were playing tonight so these must be Lakers, each one surrounded by friends, fans…she had no idea what they were, only that most were white, dressed for the prowl, and drunk or fast getting there.

It was an hour until she was to meet Julian, and she was suddenly ravenous. She'd spotted some tables outside what seemed to be the liveliest of the bars, in a hall that was the main route to two other major party spots. If she parked herself there she might catch him coming or going and they wouldn't have to meet in the lobby, plus he'd have a harder time standing her up.

The tables were now occupied, so she settled on a padded bench close by and flagged down a waiter. The BLT came with surprising speed and was very good. Washed down with another gin and tonic it left her in a pleasant mood, a far better mood than she could have imagined that morning. Whether or not she managed to get anything out of Loomis and Borden, simply seeing this aspect of the pro basketball life was worthwhile, though she was damned if she was ever going to admit this to Ambrose.

At ten to nine, she returned to the lobby and found a spot to wait between the desk and the front door, a spot that gave a good view of the lobby and the mezzanine stairs. It also put her in easy sight of the lighted area beneath the front portico where a doorman stood in earnest conversation with a short black man in a green plaid jacket. Behind the man clustered five women in short, tight dresses and fishnet stockings. The doorman gesticulated and nodded, making the towering feathers on his hat dance.

The two young women Neva had seen on the stairs walked swiftly past her and pushed through the revolving door, pausing for a word with the doorman before striding away into the night. Green Plaid called after them and his conspicuous entourage laughed.

A number of guests came and went, including an elderly couple the doorman assisted up the two, low steps to the front door. He looked through the glass at Neva and gave a cheerful thumbs up. An answering smile was already on her face when she realized that he was signaling to someone behind her.

She turned and discovered Julian Loomis leaning into the wall a few feet away.

"Surprise," he said.

"Well, it is a bit," she said, and laughed. "A nice surprise."

She took a step toward him but was suddenly surrounded by the net stocking brigade as it swept past her to reach Loomis. Were these the "someone" he'd expected? It was impossible to tell from his face, which maintained the same look of amused interest as before. Towering above the women like a Maypole, he caught Neva's eye, held up a finger, and stooped to speak to Green Plaid. In response, the man turned to stare at her.

The lobby was crowded now. Guests milled about talking and laughing, engulfing any player who showed up. The seating areas around the edge were full, the tables covered in glasses. Julian scanned the scene, spotted a cluster of chairs in the middle of the room that remained empty—too exposed and uncomfortable, with straight backs and no arms—and headed that way, herding his flock before him. Relieved that they had not simply swept him away into the night, Neva followed, determined to make a scene if it appeared that she was going to lose her chance to get at his mind before they got to his body.

But Julian was no amateur. Clearly unruffled by the situation or the attention it was attracting, he pulled five of the chairs into a line for the girls, while their keeper took up a standing position at one end, legs planted apart, arms folded across his chest. Julian arranged the two remaining chairs face-to-face in front of this extraordinary audience.

"We'll have to talk here," he said and indicated that she should take the chair with its back to the door. "Sit down. I have to see Georgie. I'll be right back."

Rather than sit, she stood with a hand on the back of the chair and watched him stride out the front door to confer with the doorman. Georgie nodded and pointed down the hotel driveway. Julian pulled out some bills, handed them over, and strolled back into the lobby with perfect ease, shaking hands and enduring back slaps with apparent good humor.

As he made his way toward them, Neva turned to consider the line of waiting women, the jutting chests, the short skirts and dancehall stockings, the makeup and heavy scent. Their blank expressions seemed to say *We're not really here*, and it was true—though they stood out like show dogs they were also strangely invisible, that is, no one except Neva appeared to take particular notice.

She smiled at the closest one, barely more than a girl. "Sorry. I seem to be in your way. It shouldn't take too long."

The young woman shrugged. "Same difference."

"Okay," Loomis said, reaching them at last, "Let's sit down."

The chairs were so close together their knees almost touched. Julian's air of being in a normal, comfortable setting was contagious and calming. They might be on stage, they might be part of a singularly strange tableau, but it didn't matter. And maybe the very public weirdness of it would work in her favor.

"You look better without that old coat," Julian said.

"Thank you, and thanks for keeping the appointment. There's obviously better entertainment to be had here tonight."

His deadpan wink was perfect.

"Is it always like this? On the road?"

"More or less. Portland's a friendly town but we seem to draw the action wherever we go. Some guys make it one long party but you can mess yourself up pretty bad if you're not careful. I'm one of the lucky ones. I don't drink, not much anyway. But that's not what you want to talk about."

"No, though it's interesting. As I said on the elevator, what I want to know about are the boosters. But first, I understand you're close to a degree?"

"One term."

"Will you finish?"

"I don't need it. Not for money. But I wouldn't mind having it. You know, people look up to a degree, and you can't shoot baskets forever. I had a good time in school."

"You did better than a lot of your team members."

"I wanted to."

"And you're smart."

"And I'm smart. So what do I pay for the compliment?"

"Ah, nothing in life comes free? That's what Vern Varney said. And Joey Field said the same about Lyle Crisp, that he always gets what he wants in exchange for what he gives. But one thing I've learned already is that not all grippers are born equal. Tell me about your relationship with Hal Richter and his family, and what it was like to be a star in a small university town where the only blacks are eight feet tall."

Julian nodded with an appreciative smile. "At least you talk straight so I will too. I take it you're not talking about the feelings of friendship and mutual regard, or the pleasant times we had. You want to know what was 'wrong' with it. You want me to hang my friends out there in the wind."

"It doesn't sound very nice when you put it like that."

"It isn't nice, is it, what you're doing. Nothing I or my friends ever did hurt that community. And I'd say we did a lot for it. In this way, I just don't get your issue."

"It's not my issue. It's a question of national basketball regulations, and the fact that they're being violated and that players are basically used, with a lot of them ending up holding an empty bag. And that Miles is dead. And Lamarr Duffy as well."

"You know, I'm not ready to talk about that yet, okay? That's not really basketball, and I feel like I need to warm up first."

"That's fine but please don't run off with your friends before we get to it. So then, how about the rest of it, the rules violations and your team members who get stuck with nothing after playing hard for all those years?"

"Why should I care?"

"Can you look me in the eye and say you don't care?"

"I think we're going to have to keep score or we won't know who won. Yes, I care as a matter of fact. If I didn't I might tell you stories that would get you that big journalism prize, the Pulitzer Prize. But I'm not going to do that."

"I'm not sure that's the best way to show you care. Do you care about the guys who played with you on the Boomers?"

"Sure. We were family."

"Some of the members of your family are in the ditch."

"How do you mean?"

"No degrees. They didn't make draft. They're nowhere."

"Like Clayton, you mean?"

"Like Clayton. And Josh Gifford, and others. Josh is taking refrigeration classes at a community college but he still hopes to make it into the NBA."

"Some guys just can't give it up, but what are you worried about Clayton for? He'll go overseas to play. They love us over there. He'll end up playing in Sweden or China and see more of this old world than you'll ever see. Then he'll come back and coach somewhere."

"But he's a zombie. He's lost."

"He'll snap out of it. A lot of guys go through that the first year on the outside."

"He didn't expect people to drop him like they did. One day he was the pampered hero and the next he's nobody, living in a dumpy motel room. You probably can't understand this because you made it, you were chosen."

"Chosen? You make it sound like religion. I worked my butt off, in school and on the team, and I made it. But if you think I don't know what it's like not to make it, maybe you'd like to take a little walk through my old neighborhood. Now, those folks didn't make it. I understand that better than you ever will."

"Okay. Fair enough. So you made it out with basketball and your teammates worked for years expecting to make it out with basketball, they helped bring millions of dollars into the university and the town, and now they're back on the streets or almost, and nobody's responsible for that? Nobody should care?"

"I didn't say anything like that. Damn you can twist words." Julian had been leaning forward with his elbows on his knees to bring his head in line with hers, but now sat back and looked around as though for an exit.

A large man in a baby blue turtleneck and sports coat stepped up and dropped a hand onto his shoulder. "Julian! My man. Damn it's good to see you. You look great."

"Hey, how's it going?" Julian offered a friendly smile along with his hand, which the man clasped and squeezed.

"We don't forget you out here, god damn it, don't ever think we do," he said. "You put this state on the map. Damn it's good to see you. You can bet I'll be there tomorrow. Take care of yourself, hear?"

"Thanks. Same for you."

"Who was that?" Neva watched the man join two others and disappear into the crowded lounge.

"Beats me." Julian shrugged. "Some jackass that thinks he knows me. You think I can keep track of them?"

"You don't like such attention?"

His smile was sad. "It gets old, that's all. I mean the poor bastards all sound so sincere, but you know, I've seen what happens. If I wasn't on a team anymore, he wouldn't even see me. I'm not Julian Loomis to that guy. I'm a high-scoring forward. Do I sound bitter? I'm not. That's the game and the sooner you find out the better. Clayton's just a little slow about things like that. I figured it out in high school."

"Julian, it's obvious you know this is not a nice system. You know that players are vulnerable and have to play a tight game off the court as well as on. You care. Why won't you give me any real information?"

"Okay. Listen up. I'm going to tell you how it is. There are grippers and there are grippers. When a team's hot, grippers break rules like there's no tomorrow. Some do it because they're jerks and some because they get into a real relationship with a player. On the other side, you have the players. Now, a college or professional player is a highly tuned machine. When you're out there on the court with thousands of people screaming at you and TV cameras going, and you know your mother and everybody else is sitting in their living room watching, you can't think about all that. If you think about all that, you're dead. You're screwed. You think about playing ball and you play like it's the last game you'll ever play. Most people go through a whole life never having to concentrate like that, be on the spot like that, okay? Now don't worry, I'm making a point here, I'm not just shooting my mouth off. A player that can do that, that can turn on and shut off, that player has an extra level of awareness, of consciousness you might say, and he can use that off the court, too. He can use it to get people to do what he wants. I'm not kidding. And believe me, for the wrong kind of cat, you can't resist that."

Leaning close again, spilling words faster than she could write, Julian talked as though the thoughts had been ready and waiting for delivery for a long time. "Think of it like this. Think if you had some magic power, could make yourself invisible or fly or something, you'd want to use it. It takes a real mature player not to use it, and you and I know you wouldn't exactly call most freshmen mature, and especially not athletes, not in that way. They haven't had time. I wasn't. I was just a kid, but a kid with a lot of power I didn't know I had at first. When I first moved to Oregon, I'd walk down the street and cars would honk and I was scared. I was the only black dude on the streets, and I was scared. Then I realized they were waving and smiling. They recognized me. I was a hero. I was nineteen and I was a hero to a bunch of whiteys."

He stopped, sat back, took a long breath. "Okay?"

"Great. Just great. Really vivid. No one else has described it so well."

Looking genuinely pleased, he continued in a milder manner, "You know what I liked best in school besides basketball? Debating. But of course I did. That's the same kind of power. Anyway, the point is you have grippers and you have players. You have grippers that use players and you have players that use grippers. And sometimes you have players and grippers that are real friends. And in those cases, what might be done for the player is done out of real feeling. My question for you is, how can that be bad? What gives the NCAA the right to regulate friendship?"

"I assume you're referring to your relationship with Hal Richter?"

"That's right."

"So you're saying that the fact that he gave you a car and paid your rent is in a different category from other gripper activities because it was founded on friendship?"

"That's right. If he did those things. I didn't say he did."

"You don't have to say it. I know it. Every traffic ticket you got for three years was in a car registered to Richter."

Julian whistled and looked around at the silent—and utterly indifferent—fishnet audience. "You hear that? She does her homework." And then to Neva, "You do your homework, don't you? Still, I'm not admitting any of it. If Hal wants to talk about it, that's fine but it's not for me to say. I don't change friends like socks. In a way, I was really lucky. Having a good friend like Hal protected me from other grippers. It's a kind of hands off thing if you're solid with somebody."

"I can see that. Now, if you don't mind, let's talk about Miles and Pascolini."

"What about them?"

"Was Miles dealing poker games for Pascolini? Games for profit?"

"You know, that sounds about right. We did learn never to play cards with him on the road. But that doesn't have anything to do with basketball."

"Why has Franklin Budd been arrested? They're charging him for sure with Lamarr's murder, but he's also under suspicion for killing White. Do you know of anything that might connect White and Lamarr apart from sports?"

"That red-hot girlfriend that Miles had? All the guys wanted her but Lamarr was just about crazy. She's the one that introduced them. I mean Miles and that Pascolini guy." Julian rubbed his big hands on his thighs and looked searchingly toward the door. "She's the pilot, you know."

"Yes, I do know. There are two pilots."

"Two? That's new since my time. They must be doing well."

"So the planes are flying in gamblers?"

"You aren't going to believe this. I don't actually know. I used to think it was betting, that they had some kind of sports betting thing going on with high stakes. And for a while I thought drugs because of the flying. But now you mention poker, that hangs together better. More respectable, you know."

Julian's arm suddenly shot high in an eager wave and he stood up. "Whoa, listen. I have to split, I really do, one of these chicks is the real thing but I kind of blew it last time and I wasn't sure she'd come back. I'm going to ask her to marry me. Listen, how about breakfast? Meet me in the coffee shop at seven. I have to be at the coliseum by eight-thirty for practice. You did pretty good but I think I won. It's fun talking to somebody as smart as me— well, almost as smart."

His laughter was happy and he clasped her hand with friendly warmth. Green Plaid had dropped his guard stance and now moved forward to touch Loomis's arm. Money changed hands, a serious wad of money that Julian pulled from a pocket apparently ready to go. Without another look at any of them, he went to meet the two elegant young women who were now standing just inside the door.

The pimp and his leggy ducklings also headed out and Neva could not help following. The doorman hailed two cabs. The six divided themselves between the cars and left without another glance at Julian, who was walking away with a lovely friend on each arm.

"Nice kid," said the doorman. "Good taste too."

CHAPTER
24

"Chocolate tarts!" Ambrose hooted down the telephone line. "Oh, that's rich, that's really rich."

"Good lord, don't go talking like that to anyone else," Neva said, but she could not help laughing. She was lying back against piled pillows with the phone propped by her ear.

"Sorry, it just popped out. But I mean, five of them. Damn me—maybe I should have been a sports reporter. Did Loomis make a clean confession about Richter?"

"He made the cleanest non-confession you could imagine. Talk about an artful dodger. He treated it like a game and declared himself the winner."

"He's used to winning. Sounds like you're having fun."

"Not fun exactly, but it's certainly entertaining. Don't get your hopes up. I'm not going to get anything useful out of these guys. It looks like I'm not even going to get to talk to Borden. They won the game and are no doubt partying. They're leaving in the morning. I should have sat outside his room like a faithful dog."

"He could still call."

"Right. And send flowers. Any news on Budd's bail?"

"Not yet. You're meeting Loomis at 7? I have half a mind to get in the car and join you for breakfast."

"Great. And I'll just get in my car right now and go home to my own bed and an open window. You can have Julian all to yourself. Or maybe you were thinking more of the, um, tarts?"

Neva had not yet changed for bed, and after hanging up, she sat for several long minutes while an argument raged within: she should go looking for Jim Borden right now all through the hotel; it would be useless to go looking for Borden as he would be deeply into partying after beating the Blazers. She'd rung his room enough times already, and had left messages everywhere they could be left apart from tying one to the doorman's hat. Far better to sleep and be clear-minded for her morning session with Julian.

But once in bed she was unable to sleep and at last gave up trying. She read for two hours and even then did not feel fully sleepy, but she'd finished the book and resignedly turned out the light. The next thing she knew the phone was ringing.

"Hey," said a chummy male voice. "Did I wake you up?"

"Who is this?"

"Me. Jim. I said I'd call. Sorry it's a little late but I lost track and like they say, better late than never."

"Right," she said, and took a long breath to get her heartbeat back under control. "I was asleep but I'm glad you called."

"Julian told me what you want. Like I told you, I don't have anything to say. I only called because I said I would."

"You're married aren't you?"

"Three years next week. How about you?"

"My husband died years ago in a kayaking accident. I still miss him every day." What was this? Dawn confessional? "Our son's in college now. It must be hard being on the road a lot when you have a family."

"It's always hard on the road, family or no family. It isn't a life. People make a big glamorous deal out of it but if you aren't careful, well, you know what I mean. When you're a family man, you can't do like the others and that's a good thing except it's even more boring."

"I talked to Vern Varney a few days ago. He certainly admires you. I got the impression he'd happily trade places."

The chuckle was deep and leisurely. "That's Vern for you. I haven't seen him in a while."

"You don't keep in touch?"

"Not really."

"Will he be at the game tomorrow?"

"I don't expect so. He's more of a Boomers man than a basketball man, if you know what I mean."

"It seems he's taken up with Dash Clemente now that you're gone."

"That's right. Dash can handle him, anyway."

"Handle him?"

"Vern's a good guy but he can be difficult."

"He drinks a lot."

"That's right. Sometimes he's not himself. Moody. You know."

"But he helped you a lot. With a car, housing, and other things."

There was silence and then, "The NCAA doesn't allow that."

"Exactly. That's why I'm doing these stories. Boosters don't pay any attention to the rules. Players tell me they like getting all the stuff but they feel used. Did you ever feel you were being used by Varney?"

"How do you mean?"

"Like he expected things from you in exchange for the favors, and felt that he more or less owned you, like a race horse or something."

"Well, I never actually said he did those things."

"I know he did because I have traffic tickets and other documentation. I'm talking to you because it's all in the past and doesn't affect your life now, and you're free to tell the truth. Although I guess I should be perfectly frank if I'm asking you to be. I said I have documentation but it's mostly innuendo and statements by just a few people, though I do have paperwork that ties specific players to specific boosters without question. Still, it's better to hear it from you, the players. You were an important player and remain a star in the NBA. You have nothing to lose by telling the truth and you might help some other players coming along behind you."

"How so, help other players?"

"All the players who don't make draft and don't get degrees and end up sweeping school hallways."

"I think that sucks, when they don't make it through school. It doesn't matter for somebody like me. I've got investments, but some of these guys, I can tell you I wouldn't want to be in their shoes."

"Don't you think they'd be better off if the system had helped them graduate instead of giving them TVs?"

"Well, shit. Sure. If you put it like that."

"So tell me about it."

The silence was long and ended with another chuckle that raised an image of Borden sprawled on his back on a bed with one hand behind his head and his eyes closed.

"Okay, I'll tell you about it. But only for me, okay? I'm not speaking to what happened with any other players because for one thing, I don't really know. You just don't talk about that stuff, you know what I mean? It's like talking about grades in school, who got a B and who got a C. It's private business. But I can tell you I never went without anything I wanted when I lived down there. Townhouse, microwave, sound system, jewelry, watch, cars—the cars were always used, which I didn't think was fair when other guys got new cars, but what the hell, they were free. They flew us all home for Christmas, and my folks out here for games. Cash was always a problem. They had to be careful about that. But we had a deal where every week I would get a hamburger at McDonald's and while I was sitting in the parking lot this other car would drive up and they'd hand me an envelope with four hundred dollars in it. I can tell you that was useful. Guess who it was."

"Handing out the cash? Varney?"

"No way. That was one thing that scared him was money. He was scared of getting caught and he thought money was dangerous. No. It was Burt Thomson. He works at that savings and loan place."

"Right. I've talked with him about special car loans for players." So Thompson had more to account for than special loans for athletes. Cash was something new in the list of goodies…but Borden was talking freely now and she had to concentrate to get it all down as he supplied detail after detail, confirming and fleshing out the sketchy picture she'd been piecing together for two weeks. And he added new bits, like a house at the coast they had all been free to use, with a liquor cabinet, big-screen TV, game room, hot tub.

"I never had any complaints," he concluded. "Is that what you wanted? I'm feeling kind of beat."

"It's exactly what I need, really terrific. There is just one more thing I hope you can be as helpful on. Did you know that Miles White was dealing poker for Mel Pascolini?"

"I don't have any idea what he was doing. I went off the team when he came on and I never knew him, not to count anyway. We sat around and shot the shit and we did play poker a few times. He always beat me. But I never knew about any business. You might ask Frankie Budd, although who knows what kind of answer you'd get out of him."

"You don't think Budd's reliable?"

"Reliable? Well, let's just say he'd tell you he was a girl if he thought you'd believe it and give him what he wants. You talk to him yet?"

"I did, yes, and so far what he said holds up. He was about as close to a friend as Miles had on the team, did you know that?"

"Sounds like a match to me. Well, it was nice talking to you, really, made me think of the good old times. But I have to be honest here. The only reason I told you all this shit is because it won't make any difference. You could write the best reports in the world and it wouldn't change anything, not for real. It's the system, that's all. Just the system."

Neva fell hard asleep after setting the phone down and didn't wake up until daylight shone full into her face. One look at the clock and she sat up and threw back the covers. "Hell!"

She reached for the phone and punched in the number for the front desk.

"I'm so sorry," a nasally voice of indeterminate sex replied. "There must have been a misunderstanding. It says right here that your wakeup call was cancelled at three this morning."

"Does it say who cancelled it?"

"You did. I mean that's the usual thing."

"As a matter of fact, I didn't. Could the cancellation have been for another room?"

"I don't guess so. I mean, it's your name."

"So it's not just a room number but my name on the cancellation?"

"That's correct. Maybe you were tired and don't remember."

Well. Julian had won this round, no doubt about it.

Standing in the shower with hot water thundering down on her back and neck, she was more amused than bothered by his trick. Given the riches she'd got from Borden, she didn't really need further confessions from former Boomers, and no doubt he would have wasted her time playing more games over breakfast. And he would do the same if she hung around the hotel for another night, would keep up the game of cat and mouse until she declared him the winner.

Nope, no way. She was done here. She had what she needed and she was going home. Ambrose would fuss but she trusted her own judgment on this one.

The lobby was quiet, the chairs neatly returned to their proper order, the daytime doorman wearing only an emblazoned cap on his head. She handed the desk clerk the *Current* credit card and he handed her a folded white paper. It was a note from Julian.

"Sorry about that. I hope you aren't mad. I really needed sleep and I didn't have anything more to say anyway. BTW Dana said yes. We're getting married, probably in May. Looks like I said too much to two women last night!"

CHAPTER
25

The two hour drive down the valley to Willamette was a waking dream despite the triple espresso from Stumptown. It was one of those days when great booms of cloud crowd the sky, first closing up their dark ranks, and then tearing apart to send light sweeping across bright pools of rainwater thronged with geese. She admired, she squinted against the light, she got a headache, and with every mile the events of the night turned more shadowy and improbable. She could not really have interviewed a basketball star in front of five prostitutes and a pimp.

At the second rest stop she parked at the end of the lot farthest from the highway, put the seat back, and closed her eyes.

When she rolled into Willamette just before noon, the temptation to go home was so powerful that she drove three blocks past the *Current* building before self-discipline got the upper hand and she turned around. Ambrose knew she'd left the Montrose and would be waiting. If she didn't show up he'd likely send out the posse, and if she didn't give him at least a general report he might blow a circuit from pure impatience. Half an hour should do it, and then she could sleep.

"Sleep?" Too excited to sit, the editor was pacing his office tiger-fashion. "Are you kidding? It's time to roll on this. We don't know everything, there are still blanks, but you know as well as I do that if we get a story out there it'll knock some more loose."

"Just when were you thinking of running the first story?"

"Tomorrow. Sunday. The whole town reads the paper on Sunday."

"And who's going to write the story?"

"You, of course."

Neva could only blink.

"Did you eat last night? How about breakfast? I mean real food, not carrot muffins. A good feed'll fix you up."

"I'm too tired to chew, let alone write a story. A good story."

"You don't need to write a good story. Just get the facts down and I'll clean up the writing."

"Clean up the writing? *My* writing?"

"You know what I mean. Tie up loose ends, fill in the basketball blanks."

"How can we do the gripper stories with two unsolved murders hanging over the team?"

"The murders aren't a basketball situation, as far as we know or anybody knows."

"We should at least wait until I get the details from Burt Thomson on the sham car loans even if it is just for Budd. And now there's the cash handover as well."

"Time enough for all that by the next story. Remember, this is a series. You begin with the overview, with a general sketch of gripper violations. Then we move on to academics and other issues."

"It's going to look pretty weird to quote Budd as a major source when he's in jail for murder."

"What matters is that everything Budd said that we could check out did check out. It might even help him. And now I'm going to order you a big country feed."

"One request—no pizza."

"What do you take me for? If it doesn't have baby arugula and range-fed tomatoes I won't let it through your door."

Alone in her office, Neva took a deep breath, yawned violently, and dropped forward onto the desk with her head on her folded arms. The next moment she sat up straight, squared her shoulders, let her head roll loose on her neck a few times, stretched her arms overhead with her fingers laced. Then she cleared the desk. Everything went—letters, old notebooks, clippings, press releases, directories, doodle pads, files, all onto the floor in the corner.

On the clean desk she laid out traffic tickets, car registrations, land ownership deeds, grade reports, and team mug shots. She stacked seven full notebooks by her keyboard.

She rested her fingers on the keys and looked into the screen. Nothing happened.

No words rose in her mind. No snappy lead or tidy summary broke the surface, ready to flow out to the world. She had forgotten how to write a news story.

News stories aren't like columns. A column can start any way you want. "Ninety-nine out of every hundred college basketball stars will end up with nothing to show for their dreams but a closetful of Nikes" would get a column off to a zippy start, but a news lead has to be attention-grabbing and full of facts at the same time.

She typed: "For many young men who dream of a career in basketball, college playing is the end of the line. After years of disciplined preparation, they get their four years of glamor, pampering by boosters, and adoration by fans only to finish their eligibility with no degree, no chance at making a professional team, and no skills to see them through life except handling a ball."

She read it over, made a rude noise, hit the delete key. Too many words, not enough punch.

She typed: "Community members who say basketball put this town on the map are jeopardizing the standing of the team by regularly violating national college basketball rules."

This flat bit of work was still on the screen when Ambrose arrived with a white box that he unloaded with somber ostentation. Strawberry-guava juice, local spring greens salad, fresh ravioli dressed with Oregon hazelnut oil and garlic, chocolate raspberry pie.

Suddenly ravenous, Neva shoved ravioli into her mouth. "Bad," she said, standing up and waving at the screen with her fork. "Not the food, it's great. But I can't write news."

Ambrose sat down, read her lead, and shook his head. "No kidding." Without having to think, he typed, "Gifts of money and clothes, free rent and meals, the use of cars—all were available to players on the Boomers basketball team who made their wishes known. 'Anything you wanted—transportation, rent, cash, as far as your imagination could go,' is the way one former player described the benefits provided to some athletes. 'You could let the word leak out that it was going to be tough to pay the rent or you'd like to spend the weekend skiing and presto, no problem.'"

Ambrose straightened. "Take it from there, maestro. It's long for a news lead but we don't have to worry about readers bailing out on this one. You better check that quote. I've read your notes enough to have it just about down but it needs to be exact."

Eleven hours later, Neva pulled into her driveway and sagged against the steering wheel. To walk from the car to the door and then up the stairs to bed was more than she could do. She had worked through the day and into the night, meticulously tapping out a tale that was to take up three-quarters of the front page and then jump to the front of the community section. For the final three hours, Owen Virgil, lawyer and libel guru, had sat at her side reading, checking quotes against her notes, questioning her memory of conversations and events, examining the traffic tickets and other documentation. He pondered and prodded and in the end did not veto a single line.

"It all hangs together," he had said at the end. "Please put these notebooks somewhere secure."

For most of the day, she had run on adrenalin and espresso, her excitement building as she saw that Ambrose was right. They had plenty of material for a story about NCAA violations, for four or five stories, and going back over her notes she had been surprised by the fullness and consistency of the picture that emerged.

Now it was done and so was she. A rag, a shell, a stringless puppet.

With an effort of will she got out of the car, plodded up the walkway, let herself into the dark hall. Home. At last. She drew in an appreciative breath but her breath caught. Something was wrong with the smell. Faint smokiness from coffee roasting, warm wood, toast, a citrusy tang from the grapefruit tree in the dining room—these were right, these were the welcome scents of home. But now there was a different smell in the mix, an alien smell of perfume or unseasonal flowers of a sickly sweetness.

A sudden rumble from deep in the house made her stiffen. The furnace was on. She never left the furnace on even when at work and certainly not during a trip. Someone had spent time in the house since she'd left for Portland yesterday and either they'd neglected to turn down the thermostat or they were still here.

What sort of intruder turns on the heat?

She had slipped her shoes off by the door and now eased her feet back into them again, listening intently. A floorboard creaked. Whoever had got into her house was still here and knew she was home. And it was no surprise visit from Ethan, not with a smell like that on the air.

Facing up the dim hall, she reached behind her, pressed the latch with care, eased the door open, and stepped onto the porch. Ready to run for the car, she called out, "Hello? Hello! I know someone's in the house."

Another creak of wood.

"Answer me! Who's there?"

"Jeneva?" The voice was a woman's.

"This is Neva. Who are you?"

"Annette. I was here before."

Neva reached in and flipped on the hall light. In the glare, she saw a figure in pink cotton leggings and oversize sweater standing in the doorway to the living room. The magnificent hair hung in tangles. In one hand was the fireplace poker. The other flew up to shield her eyes.

"Shut the door," she whispered urgently. "And shut off the light."

Neva hesitated for only an instant. The poker was not meant for her. She turned off the overhead light and locked the door, listening to the other woman's movements. Octavian retreated back to the living room and hung up the poker with a clatter. Following, Neva turned on a small lamp and surveyed the scene, the blanket on the couch, the crumpled tissues scattered over the coffee table, the glass and empty wine bottle, the food wrappers, the magazines and iPod with trailing earbuds.

"Is this house haunted?" Octavian said and pulled the blanket close around her.

"Of course it's haunted." The sudden urge to laugh was a relief. On the evening of the game, Octavian had seemed a ferocious character, hard, cold, manipulative. Now she was afraid of an old house that creaked in the night. She was also afraid of whatever—whoever—might be out there in the dark.

"How did you get in?"

"I'm good at that," she said with a return of arrogance. "Don't worry, I didn't damage anything. I used to date a locksmith. Is there any more wine in this place?"

Though the adrenalin rush had conquered her exhaustion for the moment, Neva felt dazed and overwhelmed by weirdness. The night at the Montrose, the grueling hours at the computer with the lawyer by her side, the discovery of this creature in full occupation of her precious private world…It was too much, really too much. In a trance, she retreated to the kitchen and took her time finding a bottle of Pinot gris, opening it, getting a glass for herself. What was Octavian doing here? What was she afraid of?

Back in the living room, she poured two full glasses, sat in her chair, and made no attempt at conversation. Let this nut explain herself.

"I wouldn't stay in an old house," Annette said, openly peeved.

No one asked you to.

"Don't be mad at me," she continued after the silence had lasted long enough for her to empty her glass and fill it again from the bottle on the coffee table.

"I'm not mad. I'm really tired and really wondering what you're doing here."

"You weren't here so I came in anyway. I didn't think you'd mind."

Again the urge to laugh. Was she verging on hysteria? She was certainly tired of games. "You still haven't told me why you came here in the first place."

Annette pulled the blanket up over the back of her head so only her face showed, and scrunched deeper into the couch. "If everybody'd just leave me alone! And now Frankie's getting out."

"You're hiding from Franklin Budd?"

"I'm not hiding from anybody, okay? I just don't want to see anybody."

"Does Will Gentry know you're here?"

"Don't tell Willie. Don't tell anybody. I thought I could trust you."

"Annette, this doesn't make any sense. You don't even know me. I'm willing to help but I need information. Here you are in my house, uninvited—no, it's okay. But you owe me some answers."

Though no longer so visibly fearful, Octavian looked hollow and spent. She drained the second glass of wine, blew her nose, raised a hand as though to straighten her hair but dropped it again. "You're the one. You know who killed Miles and you won't tell me."

"That's not true. I told you I have no idea. Though did you know that Lamarr went jogging with him that day?"

"Nobody knows that! How do you know?"

"Clayton told me. But then Lamarr was killed. I don't know what that adds up to."

"Nothing! It adds up to nothing, do you hear?"

"Someone told me Lamarr was in love with you."

"So? Most men are. What's your point?"

"No point, just things I've heard. Now I've got to go to bed before I pass out right here. You can use the spare room at the end of the hall if you'd like."

"It's cold back there. I'll sleep right here."

The woman's lack of even basic civility—*Thank you, but I'd rather sleep here if you don't mind; It's so nice of you to let me stay even though I broke in; Sorry if I'm intruding but I really appreciate it*—might have been offensive on another day. Now it seemed merely another bit of craziness in one of the craziest weekends of her life. They would talk in the morning and it would all make sense.

The night, for once, felt too short. She woke to bright day after a sleep so sound she had no memory of it. No restless turning over in bed, no checking the clock, not even a trip to the toilet. For some time she lay savoring the novelty of unbroken rest. Despite the late hour, the house was quiet, with no sound of stirring or hum of the furnace. This was good. A well-slept guest is likely to be a saner guest, even a communicative guest.

Rather than go through the living room and risk waking Annette, Neva went through the back bedroom in order to reach the kitchen through the adjoining utility room. The bedding was lumpy as though it had been hastily straightened after Annette's attempt to sleep in the room, and on one of the pillows was a colorful shawl. She considered it for a moment, then continued to the kitchen. On the counter was a note with no salutation and no signature.

I left ten dollars for all the wine. And I ate two bananas. Don't tell anybody I was here. Watch out for FB—I'm serious.

In the living room the blanket was clumsily folded and the crumpled tissues were in the fireplace. The ten-dollar bill was on the table under a water glass, like a tip. The smell of Annette's perfume hung on the air. Without such evidence, it would have been difficult to believe the strange woman had really been here.

Her absence now made the house eerily quiet, though it was also a relief to be alone, not to have to deal with an uninvited guest no matter what secrets she might have divulged.

Neva went into the front hall to get the paper and saw that the message light on the telephone was blinking. Why had she not heard it ring—oh, hell! The gripper story. In today's paper. She had turned off the ringer before going to bed. She turned it back on and it rang instantly. She did not pick it up, but let it ring as she continued out to the front porch and picked up the newspaper in its winter plastic bag. It felt no different than usual though she knew it was, knew it must already be stirring the community pot with a sharp stick.

The phone stopped ringing as she returned to the hall but started again within seconds. She picked it up almost gingerly, ready to hang up at the first sound of outrage. But the voice was Cal's and his tone was not only jubilant but chummy in a new way.

"We hit it on the nail, Neva! I hope you got a good night's sleep. It's a circus down here. I'm working on part two, the academic story. And talk about timely. There's a new study out about the differences between black and white athlete graduation rates. No surprises there, but it strengthens the whole deal. Are you coming down? I think Ambrose could use some reinforcements although it looks like he's having more fun than two elections and a shootout. Tucker Reilly's in there now."

"Gosh, so sorry to miss him."

"I'm sure there'll be plenty more. Can you give me an ETA? I'll tell Ambrose."

"I'll be there in half an hour."

CHAPTER
26

The spread looked good, with a strong headline that had been J.D.'s inspiration, *Cars, Cash, Gifts, Boosters Did It All*. Mugs of Clemente, Budd, Loomis, Perle, Borden and Field ran under the headline. She'd told Ambrose they needed to run booster pictures as well, but he'd said the plan was to use those with the next story in the series. Now, seeing the lineup of young black male faces, she knew she should have insisted.

Contrary to habit, she read half the story while her coffee dripped, and was just settling at the kitchen table to read the rest of it when the doorbell rang, followed by thunderous pounding.

A livid Rex Gregorio was already shouting as she opened the door.

"Ruined one of the best programs in the country, that's what you goddamn did. Down the goddamn tubes. Call yourself a journalist. I told you to keep clear and I meant it. You'll be sued, the paper'll be sued, every goddamn one of you'll be sued. It's on every TV in the country. Every fucking hotshot newsboy from here to Timbuktu is ringing my phone. I didn't spend ten years of my life, the best years of my life, building this program so you could shit on it. If you don't run a retraction—tomorrow!—you'll wish you didn't live in this town. You dragged the Boomers through the mud, through the goddamn mud, but two can play that game. You must be sick. You make me sick."

Gregorio was gone as suddenly as he'd arrived.

Neva dropped onto the hall chair. Took a long breath. Let it out.

Ambrose had warned her—turn off the phone, lock your doors, too bad you don't have a bullet-proof vest ha ha—but still she had not really expected the anger to blast through her own front door. And finding Octavian camped on her couch had sent her thoughts off in other directions, had in fact distracted her so thoroughly she had failed to brace properly for what the day might bring.

Well, short of actual violence which was not at all likely, it could not get much worse than Gregorio's tantrum. Even so, maybe it would be best not to go directly to the *Current* after all. She wasn't needed there, was not scheduled to write another story today. Ambrose enjoyed being in the line of fire and there was no useful reason to make herself an easy target when he was there to take the shots. She would head for the airport to see what Will Gentry would make of Annette's crazy performance.

The airport appeared as deserted as before, but in the office she found a hefty young woman behind the counter.

"Out at the hangar," she said and pointed with an arm like an overstuffed sausage.

Uncertain of the protocol, Neva tapped on the hangar door before opening it. "Will?" The sound fell flat among tools and scattered parts. She crossed to the inner door and knocked again.

"What?" came the response, muffled but still clearly impatient.

Surprised—Gentry had not seemed the snappish type—she opened the door and stepped into his sanctuary.

"What the hell!"

It wasn't Will Gentry who fixed her with a ferocious look. It was Franklin Budd.

"Frankie! You're not in jail."

"I should have stayed there," he growled, and slapped the newspaper that lay open on the table. "What's my picture doing on the front page? Joey's face is on the front page. Dash and Julian and Josh and Jim, we're all there. Where in hell are the grippers? You said you were out to get the grippers, and what do you have? Six black boys looking stupid as slug bait. What's the matter with you?"

She had seen Budd angry before, on that first day at his townhouse. That outburst had been expected, and had played out like a performance with a cheerful ending. But Budd was different now, hard looking, his skull exposed under a jail buzz cut, his body tensed for rough action. The swagger and playfulness were gone.

"I'm sorry about that, Frankie, really. I said they should run gripper pictures but the editor said they planned to run them with the second story. Aside from the mug shots, the story really is about grippers. They're all in there."

His fierce silence was more than she was up to this morning. *Look out for FB, I'm serious.* She put a hand behind her on the doorknob. "I'm very glad you're out and very very sorry to have disappointed you. I don't know what more to say."

She stepped backwards through the doorway without waiting for an answer.

Gentry was not to be found though his pickup truck was outside the hangar and there seemed nowhere to hide or disappear to in the meager airport setup. She left him a note in the office, then headed back to town the long way up the river. At a pullout with a view of the dark water, she stopped to call Ambrose but could not get through and had to leave a message there as well— just in case—though surely Charlie would already know that Budd had been released.

The athlete's changed appearance even more than his anger stayed with her. Now he did look capable of murder, but was this his true nature coming out or a temporary effect of jail? Had Annette's warning biased her? Whatever the explanation, she felt a sense of loss. Alone among the players Franklin Budd had struck an inner chord that went beyond sympathy. She had liked him, been amused and challenged by him, assumed a reasonable future for him. Now he was an angry stranger.

The newsroom appeared calm when she arrived, with about half the desks occupied by the usual figures bent over keyboards. Ambrose was alone in his office, a phone clamped to his ear, his free hand chopping the air. She slipped into her office unnoticed even by Cal. The phone light was blinking, of course, but she checked email first. Thirty-seven new messages, not so bad, not that many more than had turned up following some of her more controversial columns in the past. A quick reading discovered a fairly equal split between the outraged and the congratulatory, which was a relief. Not a single message from boosters or athletic staff had come her way, though Ambrose evidentally had received plenty of noise from those quarters. Most of the hurrahs were from academic faculty members, with Gerry Farnes in the lead. Nothing had been heard from players apart from Budd's outburst at the airport.

Telephone messages seemed too much to deal with at the moment so she left them for later and checked in with Cal. He was just leaving for lunch.

"Story's done." he said. "I think the information's solid but compared to this morning's piece it's dull as ditchwater."

"Numbers," she said, watching Ambrose charge in their direction across the newsroom. "They can flatten the life out of anything."

"The cop shop's playing games again," the editor fumed. "Giving us the run-around. Luce paid Frankie's bail but it sounds like they couldn't hold him anyway. No evidence. Charlie's still over there. He hasn't been able to find Budd, not at the airport or anywhere. He didn't tell you anything?"

"He was too mad to talk. We really do have to run some gripper pictures."

"We're on it. And I've asked Cal and J.D. to be here at 9 tomorrow to talk through the next round. That suit you?"

"I'll be here."

"I hope you're feeling good, Ms. Leopold. We cracked this one, we really cracked it. I heard from the NCAA this morning."

"I don't feel anything much," she said. And it was true. She felt no pride, or even much interest, only a deep sense of unreality and worry. The real story was only beginning to take shape in her mind. She needed to talk to Gentry. "Actually, I'm out of here. I'll see you tomorrow. Call me only if you have to, okay?"

Five minutes later as she got into the car, her phone rang and she almost said, "That was quick." But it was Gentry on the line, not Ambrose.

"Neva? Will here. Where's Annette?"

"I don't know."

"Your note said she stayed at your place last night."

"She did, but she was gone when I got up."

"Why? Why would she stay with you?"

"I was hoping you could tell me. We'd met only that once before, when she dropped in late at night. This time she let herself in while I was gone. Very unusual behavior, I'd say."

"Welcome to Annette's world. As for why she went to your place, I have no idea. Out of the way there, is it? Your place?"

"Very. She appeared to be hiding, to be afraid of something. Actually, she seemed worried about seeing Frankie. And she didn't want me to tell you she was there."

"Is that so."

It was a statement rather than a question, followed by a silence at both ends of the line until Neva said, "Do you remember telling me that Lamarr Duffy was crazy in love with her?"

"Where are you?" he said rather than answering the question.

Neva was sitting in the driver's seat of the car with the door open and her feet on the pavement. She had wanted to see Gentry this morning, had wanted to ask about Annette and Lamarr, but now the call felt wrong, his tone was wrong. It was none of his business where she was.

"Where are you?" he said again.

"Driving. Where are you?"

"Driving. Listen, if Annette comes back, call me. Promise. This is serious."

"She won't come back."

Neva pulled out of the parking lot, turned the corner and nearly ran into Hal Richter. The lawyer glanced her way but didn't recognize who was behind the wheel—or didn't care. His momentum had a fixed object, no doubt Ambrose, but to see him here at all was a real surprise. Richter was a game player, a backroom dealer, not a gladiator like Gregorio. He wouldn't come out of his lair without serious intent.

To make a deal?

To have her head on a plate?

Her facts were solid and facts aren't libelous…but she didn't really care about Richter. She was not thinking about grippers today. She was thinking about athletes, dead athletes, and about Frankie, Annette, Gentry, Pascolini. Mulling what she knew and what she suspected and what she needed to find out, she drove with no conscious destination, though when she emerged from her thoughts enough to notice, it was clear that her subconscious had not been idle. It had led her back to Mel Pascolini's neighborhood.

A red car was parked in the driveway. She pulled in behind it, got out briskly and rang the bell. No one answered but she had not really expected an answer.

Still moving with quick purpose, she circled to the garden gate, entered, and made as straight for the tea house as the meandering paths allowed. Her single knock on the door was for politeness sake only. Not waiting for a reply she slid open the panel.

Annette Octavian lay against the pillows on the daybed, her body draped in a kimono.

"Aren't you the smart one," she said, setting an open paperback down on the bed and removing iPod plugs from her ears. "So, did I leave tracks or what?"

"The shawl," Neva said and nodded toward the hat rack. "You left it on the bed in the back room."

Later, describing the scene to Ambrose, Neva would keep coming back to the same word. *Apparition.* The powerful but languid body, the red hair once again piled above that white face, the rich colors in the kimono, the cushions, the bed cover, the dark eyes fixed in unblinking scrutiny like a figure on an Egyptian mummy case. The lack of surprise on being discovered.

"I'm not drunk today, if that's what you're thinking," Annette said as though engaged in an ongoing conversation. "Shut the door, would you."

The small room was hot, the light dim. Annette waved toward the chairs. Neva sat on the arm of a chair rather than on the seat cushion, which would have put her below the other woman's eye level. She wanted to say something sharp, even angry, but the words did not come.

"Did you tell anybody I was here?" Annette demanded.

"I didn't know for sure you were here."

Annette shook her head, disbelieving. "I left this morning because I didn't have anything to say. I'm sick of the whole thing."

"What whole thing?"

"All of it."

"Including poker?"

"Everything. I'm done, I'm moving on. Life moves on."

"Why don't you just fly away in your plane?"

"It's not my plane. Anyway, why should I? I'm finally free and I'm going to do what I want for a change."

"Free from Miles?"

"Just free, okay? I wasn't Miles's property."

"How about Lamarr's?"

"Give me a break!"

"I told Will Gentry you were at the house last night."

"And?"

"And he was very interested. He said to let him know if you turned up again."

"So?"

"So I suppose I will. Unless there's a good reason not to?"

"Is Frankie out yet?"

"He got out this morning.'

Annette closed her eyes and dropped her head back against the cushions. They remained like this in silence for several slow minutes during which Neva's energy sank until it vanished like sunshine cut off by clouds. The long day yesterday following a very short night, the angry start to her morning with Gregorio screaming on her porch, and now this disturbing woman.

She needed to be alone, she needed air and light.

She stood up.

Annette's head snapped upright. "Where are you going?"

Not waiting for an answer, she swung her feet to the floor and felt for slippers. "What are you going to do?"

"Go home, leave the phone off, work in the garden or read until I'm ready to sleep. What are you going to do?"

"Depends. If you go telling people where I am I'll have to leave."

Annette found the slippers. She rose to her feet in a dramatic unfolding of body and gown, stretched her arms high with a groan, dropped them, and laughed. "What a funny little woman you are."

The next moment her fingers clamped around Neva's wrist. "It's not your business. It's not your right to tell anyone anything about me. Got it?"

Neva looked up into the other woman's eyes in silence, making no attempt to free her wrist or respond in any way apart from waiting. A frozen minute passed before Annette released her and turned back to the daybed.

CHAPTER
27

Back home again, Neva checked every room for unwelcome visitors, showered, put on sweat pants and a pullover, poured wine, turned off both phones, turned on NPR, settled on the couch with the same throw Annette had used, and fell asleep.

When she woke up the room was in deep twilight and the doorbell was ringing. She switched on the lamp, turned off the radio, dropped the throw on the couch, and went into the hall. Only a silhouette showed outside the window but it was clearly Franklin Budd leaning on the doorbell button.

Her anger and uneasiness of the morning had vanished. She didn't hesitate to let him in and before the door was fully open, he said, "Sorry for being an asshole." He stepped into the hall waving the newspaper. "Whoa, listen to this. 'What gambling is to Las Vegas, basketball is to this town.' Right on—I love it."

"I thought you hated it."

"I hadn't read it. I didn't have time before you showed up. All I saw was the pictures. You shouldn't have used the pictures but the rest of this is really something. Jasper's going to die when he reads this, just die. 'It was like walking around with Madonna.' No shit. Call me Madonna."

"Did I leave anything out?"

"My horse."

"You didn't say anything about a horse."

"Jasper kept a horse for me out at Calapooia Stables for two years. Miles and I used to ride. Shit, we rode that same trail."

From the sullen anger of the morning, Frankie had skipped into excited overdrive. Restless and jumpy, too large for the front hall, he shook the newspaper, read another line, hooted, slapped his leg.

Neva watched him, puzzled. Was he stoned? Drunk? Elated to be out of jail? "Have you eaten? I was thinking of making toast and eggs."

No, he said, thanks very much but he'd stopped on his way for steak and fries and salad piled with blue cheese dressing. "That jail food is shit, just pure shit. I lost twelve pounds. Doesn't that qualify as cruel and unusual punishment or something?"

Their laughter was edgy and was followed by a silence as Budd went back to reading.

"I was up at Pascolini's this afternoon," Neva said. "For the second time. I know what business they were in. Gambling. Poker. They were flying in wealthy players. Miles must have been a brilliant dealer, well, I've been told that he was. I just hadn't realized it was significant."

Budd was nodding. "Yeah, I finally figured that out myself. I had a lot of time to think the last few days. Remember things. Put things together. Annette was here, I heard. Last night."

Neva nodded but looked away. If he asked where to find Annette, what was she to say? Her feelings toward Frankie were far more kindly than any Octavian inspired or was ever likely to, but there were embers here that could explode into fire if she wasn't careful. She needed to think a bit more, check some points of information, and then she'd know what to do.

"You saw her today?" he said.

She nodded, then shook her head. Had Gentry told him Annette had left early, with only a note for parting?

"Here? Not here? Where'd you see her?"

"Frankie, really, I can't say. She said not to tell anyone where she is and made a big deal out of it. Sorry. I'd do the same for you."

Budd grinned, a genuine wide grin. "That's okay, you don't need to tell me." Rolling the newspaper into a tight tube, he turned toward the door, but looked back with a serious air. "Listen. I've got something I have to do, something that might go bad, seriously bad. If I don't call you in the morning, phone Jasper, okay? It'll probably be too late to help, but at least he'll know where to look. Listen, stay cool, you hear?"

He bounded down the steps and jogged out of sight beyond the hedge. A car started and sped away down Spring Street.

The sound had not yet faded when Neva turned back inside, snatched her bag from the hall chair, grabbed a jacket, and ran for her car. What had she set in motion by saying she'd gone to Pascolini's earlier? Budd had put two and two together and now knew where to find four.

It was dark when she eased around the final turn to the contractor's house. Budd's car was recognizable though he had parked in the deep shadow of an oak tree. In front of it was another vehicle, a pickup truck that looked black in the night. Annette's car was still in the driveway, but rather than pull in beside it, Neva came to a quiet stop behind Budd's car and for a moment sat with the window down, waiting, listening. Nothing, not even a breeze in the trees.

The door clicked open, shut softly without fully latching. Rather than cross the open street and front yard, she kept in the line of tree shadow and followed the edge of the cul-de-sac around, pausing for a closer look at the pickup. She wasn't very good at noticing cars but she would have bet it was the same one that had been parked at the airport that morning. Frankie must have called Gentry, though the pilot could not have got here on such short notice, certainly not from the airport. Had he, too, guessed where to find Annette and already arrived here before Budd?

She should call the police, but what would she say? *Three people have converged in a garden and instinct tells me there's going to be trouble.*

The house windows were dark. The gate swung open without needing to be unlatched. After a pause to listen while her eyes adjusted, she followed winding paths toward the teahouse, moving quietly while going as fast as possible in the near-dark.

The teahouse window glowed luminous through the paper covering. No sound disturbed the night as she stood at the edge of the sandy courtyard waiting and watching.

Where was Frankie? Will Gentry? The ferocious Annette?

After some time she thought she could hear murmuring voices inside. She started forward but was stopped by the sudden clear voice of a man speaking with calm authority. "Don't even try it."

A wordless exclamation was followed by a shriek, a woman's shriek, and then a heavy thud.

Moving fast, Neva circled the open patch of sand, felt her way through the darkness at the back of the building, and found the rear door she had hoped was there. Easing it open, she stepped into a small, empty room. The doorway to the main room was directly in front of her and was blocked by a folding screen.

Two careful steps took her to the screen, which stood far enough from the doorway to give a view of the daybed and the room beyond it. Franklin Budd was facing her way with his arms out to his sides and his hands open in an attitude of surrender. Annette Octavian stood mere feet away, a knife with a curved blade in her hand. It looked like a confrontation except that they were not facing each other. They were looking hard toward the front door, which was hidden by the screen.

Neva edged forward to see what made them stare. It was Will Gentry.

Budd was the first to spot her, and reacted with an emphatic, "What the hell?"

"Well, well," said Gentry.

The pilot stood near the door, a man in control and clearly enjoying it. His khaki vest, black turtleneck and black jeans were chicly casual but there was nothing casual about the pistol he aimed at Budd. Ugly and menacing, it was also weirdly primitive, with the head of what looked like an arrow sticking a good two inches out of the long barrel.

"You shouldn't be here, Neva," Budd said. "Don't you think she'd better leave, Will?"

"So you figured it out," Gentry said with a nod. "I had to see them together before I was sure. And what a pair they are."

"What are you talking about?" Annette said, openly irritated.

"You know perfectly well what I'm talking about."

"What is this, Will?" Budd moved slightly forward but stopped at an upward jerk of the dart gun. "Hey, cool it, okay? What's with you? This is stupid."

"Will?" Neva was fully in the room now and, like the others, facing the pilot. "What's going on here?"

"I thought you'd sorted it out—these two are in it together. First they killed Miles, then Lamarr to keep him quiet."

"No way," Budd said. "You know that's not true. I told you already."

"I knew you killed Miles, I never believed you," Octavian said to Budd, then turned a complicit smile on Gentry. "Get him out of here. I can't stand the sight of him. And please take me home."

"Oh, very pretty." Gentry sounded almost amused.

"I never killed anybody in my life," Budd said, disgusted rather than angry. "But she knows that because she did it."

"Annette can't shoot," Gentry said shortly.

"Nice try, guys." Annette was brisk now, and sensibly woman-to-woman as she turned to Neva. "They're obviously working together, but then they always were jealous of Miles. They'll listen to you. Tell them to get out of here and leave me alone."

"Well?" Gentry said.

"Annette didn't shoot Miles—hey!"

One moment Bud had been standing with his hands out to his sides. The next he was behind Annette with her arm wrenched high. The knife clattered to the floor as she screamed and kicked backward. Neva stepped closer, her own hand raised in an automatic stopping gesture.

"Stand back," Bud warned. The words were directed at Neva but it was Gentry he watched and Gentry he addressed with cold ferocity. "Put that damned thing down before I break her arm."

"Frankie—" Again Neva was cut off, this time by Gentry.

"Go ahead and break it." He raised the dart gun as though taking aim.

"You fucking idiots!" screamed Annette.

"Stop!" Neva's voice was as fierce as Annette's but commanding rather than angry. "You're all being absurd. No one in this room killed anyone."

The silence was long and tense. Immobile, watching Gentry for any sign of movement, Neva knew suddenly that she was going to have to step between him and his target. Gentry would not shoot her, she was certain, but still her skin contracted as she shifted weight to the right foot.

"Don't." Gentry's glance merely flickered her way before fixing again on the clenched pair at the end of the room. "First we need some answers here."

Disregarding the caution, Neva took that step to the left. At the same moment laughter erupted behind her.

"Idiots," Annette said again. "It's not even a real knife. And that's not a real dart gun, is it, Will?"

Another long, silent moment passed before she said again, "Well, is it?"

Gentry lowered the gun but his body remained tense, ready for action. "It doesn't change anything."

"It lets us talk like proper human beings," Neva said, and turned to look at Budd just as he raised a foot and stomped hard on the knife. It cracked in half. He released Annette's arm and stepped back out of punching distance.

But instead of turning on him, Annette rolled her shoulder in relief and addressed Neva, "Now you have to tell me. Who killed Miles?"

CHAPTER
28

I don't know who did it. But I know it wasn't one of you.

Lying in bed, unable to sleep, Neva felt again the flush of almost embarrassed regret that had possessed her at Annette's disappointment and even scorn. They had not wanted her there. When the absurd drama was over and they were trying to think of a place to find both food and privacy for talking, Budd said outright that she should stick to "the gripper thing" and leave the murders to them.

But look how wrong you all got it, she had protested.

Driving home wearily, she'd concluded that her appearance on the scene had probably been superfluous. While all three leaned toward personal drama they were not actually violent—witness the silly "weapons".

When she fell asleep at last she slept hard but was up early and at her desk before the lights were turned on in the newsroom. This was just fine. There were stories to write, and write she did for the next several days, working closely with Cal and Ambrose, filling in ever more details. Burt Tompson came through at last with the paperwork on Frankie's car loan, but when asked about the cash handed to Jim Borden, he merely grinned, said *I plead the fifth*, and refused further conversation. She mentioned the money in a story anyway, quoting Borden verbatim.

On Tuesday evening, she turned both phones off and was settling in for a quiet dinner and reading by the fire when there was a soft knock on the door, so soft she wasn't certain it was a knock rather than a squirrel dropping cones on the roof. Only when it came again, more insistent this time, did she go into the hall for a look.

It was Vera, wearing black rather than the sunny yellow of their first meeting. "I did try to call," she said, clasping a gray file folder to her chest.

Neva waved away her apologies for the late visit and urged her to share the meal of pasta with anchovies, but Vera's refusal was emphatic. "Don't feel like eating. This is getting kind of weird."

She set the file folder on the coffee table and opened it to reveal scraps of paper held together with tape.

"You did it!" Neva looked with amazement at the small pile of ragged documents.

"Sort of. I mean I found some big pieces in the bottom but still it took a long time. I never did like puzzles. Anyway, it mostly looked normal to me, the usual stuff, grades, medical records. But there were some other bits that, well, you'll see." She handed Neva a sheet of paper with enough scraps stuck to it to make a paragraph, though one with many gaps.

"A letter, I guess, but a lot's missing," she said almost apologetically.

Neva studied the words briefly before reading aloud, "...refused the money, smug sonofabitch...worried about Bill...pill the beans, you know what I mean? Vern was out...hell to pay...after all these years, you'd think it would be obvious to...don't want to know—don't ask, don't tell—so they're on their own and they know..."

Again Neva considered the words for some time before asking, "There's more?"

"Look at this." Vera was ready with the next taped assemblage. "You take the two of them together, it doesn't look very good."

Again Neva read aloud: "...happened faster...damn trouble now, stupid idiots...wait for the end of the season?! You bet I'm mad but there's no...ong run better for program...witness. Out of our...middle of the night and I can't sle...goddamn spotlight on our program for the wrong...fools think we can really play by...kin off his ass...told him not to make it worse but he's such a...better brace for another one and keep your head do..."

Neva arranged the page fragments side by side on the table, nodding thoughtfully. "Interesting. Very interesting. What do you think it means?"

"If it wasn't in White's file and they didn't shred it I guess it wouldn't mean anything to me, I mean wouldn't be suspicious. But somebody was really worried about something having to do with him, and then something bad happened and they were afraid something else bad was going to happen. Two murders. See what I mean?"

"Mmmm, yes. Bill is Bill Tunney?"

Vera shrugged. "Lots of Bills around, I guess. Vern's got to be Varney anyway."

"And the 'smug sonofabitch?'"

"Miles. I mean, doesn't it look like somebody tried to buy him off from doing something and he wouldn't go along with it?"

"Do you think they ever try to rig the games? I mean lose on purpose?"

"No way. Not. Never. Coach Leonard would rather die." Vera reached for the first fragment. "See here where it says 'pill the beans,' well, that must be 'spill the beans.' In other words, somebody was going to tell something. Maybe Miles was going to tell something, some secret thing that they wanted to shut him up about. And that would explain why nobody was bothered when he died, I mean in the athletic department. I mean he can't talk now, can he?"

"The letters certainly are suggestive, but I can't imagine anyone putting incriminating letters in a general file. And if they were written really recently—which we don't know—then it seems even less likely. Why file risky letters and then shred them immediately?"

"I thought about that. Maybe the letters never were in the file. Maybe they got together everything they had and shredded it all at once. These pieces were in the bottom of the shredder like they could have been done first, like they came off somebody's desk or out of a drawer or something."

"You've clearly thought about this a lot. How about ideas on who shredded the papers?"

"I asked. I mean, not straight out. Just sort of like I was doing my job. They were in the coffee room, some coaches and everybody. I got my coffee and said, 'Anybody know where Miles's file stuff went? I went to file something and it's empty.'"

"Vera!"

"Nobody said anything, and then Gregorio said, 'What did you file?'"

"Uh, oh."

"No problem. I had papers alright. Some routine forms from the registrar's office you have to fill out when a student leaves. Or dies. They hadn't thought of that. I said I didn't actually file them because the folder was empty so I thought they must be putting his papers somewhere else now. Gregorio said to give them to him. But then Alison, she's one of the office assistants, she said that the stuff for Miles was in the files like everybody else's. And I said I already looked and there was a file but there was nothing in it. She said that I must have got the wrong file because she'd put some of the clippings about his murder in there just last week and there was lots of stuff in it. I was watching Gregorio. He had his phone out and was texting somebody. Then he said that the police wanted everything they had on Miles so anyone with more paperwork should give it to him."

"He wasn't suspicious at all?"

"Not a bit. No reason to be. But you see what that means. Either he shredded it or knows who did. He knew it was gone and lied about it."

Neva nodded but said nothing. The young woman was taking serious risks, way beyond anything Neva would have asked for and way beyond good sense. It was impossible to regret having put her up to it given what she'd found but she'd done enough and should stop.

And now the big question was what to do with the stuff? She could not take it to the police, or confront Gregorio, or even show it to Ambrose and Cal at this point. There would be too many questions, including the source of it all. They needed more, but she could not ask Vera to keep snooping. She had to be reined in, not put at further risk.

Now that she'd shifted her load to Neva's shoulders, the young woman was sitting back at ease, waiting with an expectant smile.

"I'm going to have to think hard about what to do with these," Neva said. "Can I keep them? You've done an amazing job, way more than I expected. But it's enough. It's too risky. When I asked you to snoop I pretty much assumed the department wasn't directly involved. Now, well, this is all very suggestive. Leonard's clearly in it somehow, even if it's a matter of knowledge rather than action. Whatever the department's involvement, you really do not want to get noticed by any of these people. Really. Please. Enough."

CHAPTER
29

In the office by 7 a.m., Neva typed up her notes from the conversation with Vera, including the contents of the pieced fragments, and was facing the question of when to give them to Ambrose when the desk phone rang.

"Don't ask me why I'm calling you back," said an unknown male voice. "You left so goddamn many messages everywhere. This has got to be quick. So?"

"Yes, right," Neva said, feeling for notebook and pen. To ask a source to identify himself is to start from a weak position— when, oh, when were they going to get Caller ID in here? "Thank you very much. I know you're busy."

"Busy isn't the half of it," snapped the speaker. "I've come back to a mess. Maybe I shouldn't have come back at all."

The slight note of self-pity was encouraging. It could be worked on to get confidences flowing, though nothing would flow if she couldn't zero in on a name pronto. "I'm sorry to hear that. I once came home from a vacation to find my basement flooded a foot deep."

Silence on the line.

"Not that you found that sort of mess," she added, warm and chatty. *But what sort of mess? Please, give me a hint.*

"Look, my wife left me, a friend's dead, the garden's half wrecked, this goddamned house feels like a morgue. Even my secretary quit. Could you just get on with it? You never beat around the bush before. I can tell you right up front that I'm not going ahead with the hotel project, if that's your beef."

Pascolini! Momentarily thrown, Neva stood up, looked out the window as though for escape, sat down, and said with perfect calm, "I am sorry about all this. Could we possibly meet somewhere? Soon. It's so much easier to discuss difficult subjects in person."

"What difficult subjects?" The old sharp Pascolini was already back in control. "We're not doing the hotel. Period. End of story. Though it has nothing to do with the wetland zoning, I will say that. It's a business decision pure and simple."

"Yes, well, I'm glad to hear this, whatever the reason. But it's not why I called you." She paused for a response, got none, and knew it was time to talk straight. "Okay then. I want to know about Miles White."

"Miles! What the hell—he was shot by some asshole and when they catch the bastard the death penalty'll be too good for him."

"You mentioned a friend who was dead. Was that Miles?"

"Of course. But I don't know what business it is of yours."

"He was your dealer, right? For fly-in poker games?"

Silence.

"I know this is true, Mel, but I'm not interested in the poker, that is, not in your fly-in business as such. I'm working on a series of news stories about the Valley State basketball team, specifically the players' relationships with boosters. Miles did not have a booster. He was a star college athlete without a booster. He—"

Sudden laughter on the other end stopped her short. When the outburst ended, all she could say was, "Excuse me?"

"Well, Christ. He didn't need a booster, did he? Or want one. He had everything he needed, and he hated the sons of bitches. But you know who he hated worst of all? I don't mind telling you or anybody. He hated that big turd of a coach. Leonard. And I'd be happy to tell him to his face. Or maybe you'll put it in the paper in nice big headlines. 'Dead player hated racist turd coach.' That would make my day."

"Racist? How so?"

"Why don't you go ask some of the players that aren't dead yet? Ask them, the black ones, well they're all black aren't they, the ones that count."

"I will ask them, but I'd also like to hear what White said about it."

"I don't remember it all, what all the coach did and said, but a couple of lines stuck in my mind. How about this? 'A pig could handle a ball better than you, even a black pig.' Or 'Get your black ass moving or you can move it right out the door and back to the black hole you came from.' Miles said that kid Perle got the worst of it."

Clayton sitting in his laundry with the sound turned off...*It makes me sick to hear him yell.*

"Was this at practice? Wouldn't a lot of people have heard it?"

"Sure they heard it. I told you Miles hated the boosters too. They thought it was funny. You know what I told him? I told him to rat on the whole lot of them. He could have got the program in real trouble, you know, with all he knew about what was going on. And that's what really bothers me. He said he'd never do it, he had his career to think about, but he got mad one day and threatened to tell the NCAA. What if they thought he really was going to tell? And then he was shot. Are you following me here?"

"Have you told any of this to the police?"

"Are you kidding? Think about it. And I'm a fool to talk to you. I don't know why I am talking to you. I don't even like you. But somebody needs to know and at least you're careful. Surprised? Well, I'm not the nicest guy in the world, my wife— soon to be ex-wife—sure let me know that, but I'm not the dumbest either. I know you could have quoted me a lot worse in the past than you did. You only wrote what you had to, to make your point. I guess that's all I have to say."

Minutes later, walking briskly around Azalea Park in the morning fog, Neva worked first of all to settle herself internally. Mel Pascolini, of all people. Mel, famously tight-lipped and one of her least favorite subjects over the years, in fact an open adversary on development issues, a ruthless builder of cheap apartment complexes, mini-malls, low-end student housing, a dodgy businessman ready to take any shortcut or get around any zoning or environmental rule as long as it was to his profit.

And now he was a significant and straightforward source on a murder.

Really, it was difficult to take in stride. He must have been deeply unhinged by White's death and his wife's departure. With his children.

The big question now was what to do. Pascolini's call had been extraordinarily timely, coming on top of Vera's findings. The two together put the athletic department squarely in the middle of White's murder. He must have threatened to "spill the beans" and then refused to be bought off. And yet she could not imagine Gregorio or Leonard—even a racist Leonard—arranging to have a player killed. Especially not the team star, the player who would surely have taken them to the playoffs again this year.

On the other hand, it was not so difficult to picture those other team devotees committing violence…well, not Vern Varney, at least not doing the actual deed. So that left Bill—*worried about Bill.*

Bill Tunney.

All too easy to imagine him committing murder.

Neva had left the park and was now strolling rather than striding, her mind focused internally. She was within a block of the river when she stopped, puzzled by a feeling that was not quite déjà vu, more like a forgotten memory trying to surface. A familiar smell? She breathed deeply but detected nothing suggestive or unusual. About to walk on, she glanced at the display window to her right, saw rings and necklaces, shook her head—she never had understood the attraction of baubles—and then looked at the name written in elegant gold script at the top of the window. *J.J. Cornish.* Under it was the legend *Fine Jewelry, Oregon Gold.*

Going over the booster list earlier, she had realized that there was yet one more she had not talked to. J.J. Cornish. She didn't know him, he was not connected with a specific player, and the encounter with Tunney had pretty well soured her on such meetings. But maybe the news stories that had run so far would have softened him up already—maybe, like Lyle Crisp, Mr. Cornish was feeling left out.

And there were some new questions on her mind now, starting with racist abuse during practice.

A delicate bell sounded when she opened the door. She just had time to take in the general character of the place and note the absence of Boomer memorabilia when a woman appeared from a room beyond the sales counter. Bright blonde and strikingly tall, she filled the doorway as she smiled in welcome.

Neva smiled in return and stepped closer to offer her hand.

The other woman stiffened, the smile gone in an instant.

Accustomed to sudden reactions—not always positive—on being recognized, Neva said an easy, "Hello. I'm looking for Mr. Cornish?"

The fixed look did not change.

"Is he in today?"

"You're Jeneva Leopold, from the paper."

"That's right."

"I take it you're not interested in jewelry." It was not a question.

"Well, no, not today at any rate. Just a conversation. If he's not in I'll try again later."

"There is no Mr. Cornish and never was," the woman said. "I am J. Cornish. June Cornish. What is it you wished to talk about?"

A she-booster!

Changing gears fast, Neva felt a surge of interest and even relief. No matter how unwilling or unpleasant Cornish proved to be, she at least spoke Woman, a designation that Neva would have scoffed at in her youth but that experience had taught her was real. Cornish must have been a traffic stopper twenty years ago and was still a striking woman, athletic, tanned, long-legged above serious black heels. A woman who had never had to worry about her pants getting too tight, though she'd had a facelift—or two— somewhere along the line. The telltale flesh of her neck was not quite hidden by a knotted blue scarf. Boomer blue, in fact.

"Is there somewhere more?" Neva gestured to suggest, maybe, a retreat to the privacy of the back room.

"It's fine right here." Cornish slid onto a high stool at the counter and Neva hitched herself onto the second stool, feeling like a kid perched on the grownups' seat. Before she could think of a comfortable opener, the other woman took the lead, her chilliness giving way to slight amusement.

"I know why you're here, of course. I read the paper."

Neva waited for more and when it didn't come, she tried a tentative, "You're a major basketball fan I understand?"

"Not a fan, hon. Fans do tailgaters and put flags on their pickup trucks. I don't do flags."

After another wait, Neva asked the obvious. "What do you do?"

"I lived for the Boomers," she said, simple and unapologetic.

"Lived?"

"An era is ending. And you're doing your damndest to bring it down."

"Oh, for heaven's sake. I didn't kill any athletes. I didn't violate NCAA rules like they never existed. I'm not out there on the court screaming racist insults. Let's talk sense here."

Like the outburst at Cal, the angry retort was deeply satisfying—for all of five seconds. *So much for Woman Talk...*Had June Cornish looked offended or ready to snap back, Neva would have apologized, would have admitted to her extreme exasperation that anyone who claimed to "live" for the team could really condone what was happening.

But June did not appear in the least bothered. She drew her lips inward, tapped the counter with a glossy lavender nail, shrugged slightly, and smiled. The smile was not happy. "Jasper told me he spilled his guts to you. I'm not going to do that. What I will say is that I love beautiful things. Look around you."

"And athletes are beautiful?"

Silence.

"This isn't new, you know," Neva said. "Others have said the same. Other boosters. Men."

Rather than reply, June studied Neva, her gaze running up and down the usual crumpled, baggy getup and at last resting on her left hand, which lay on her thigh, the untrimmed nails plainly visible against faded brown pants. The slight shake of her head spoke volumes, though what she actually said was, "You might not understand this but those young men represent perfection. And, I mean, look at me. I'm six-two in my stockings. Hasn't left me a lot of choice in men, but that's not really the point. Of course I was attracted. So did I have sex with them? Sure, when I was younger. I may be foolish but I'm not dumb. Apart from physically, they're just children, emotionally under-developed boys. Well, with some exceptions." She hesitated and looked almost beseechingly at Neva.

Neva nodded.

"Miles," June said sadly. "Miles White. If he'd come along twenty years ago, I'd have completely lost my head. As it was, well, after he met that redheaded pilot I didn't count for much and that was tough, really tough, believe you me. But it was something while it lasted. My god."

Neither woman spoke for some time, until Neva said, "Julian Loomis."

The reply was a mere nod. And then, "Let's leave it there, ok? You have other things on your mind than my bedroom history, I assume."

A wry quality in the other woman's tone felt like welcome encouragement. Neva hitched more solidly onto the stool and took out a notebook. "Indeed I do. For starters, did you ever hear Coach Leonard yelling racist insults during practice?"

"I never went to practice. That was a boy thing, so to speak. But I have heard about this. I'm sure you know by now that a lot of the players don't like Leonard. But he's their ticket to the NBA so what can they do."

"Someone told me that Miles might have threatened to tell the NCAA what the boosters were doing. Did you ever hear this?"

June shook her head thoughtfully. "You mean maybe they killed him to shut him up. Doesn't sound right. As for coaches, verbal abuse is nothing new. And Miles definitely wouldn't have said anything until after the draft, which they'd know, so even if they wanted to stop him from talking they'd have waited. And it's just too crazy. They wouldn't do that."

"I got the impression that it wasn't anyone in the program. It looks like it could have been a booster. One of your lot."

After yet another stretch of silence, June shook her head. "I could accept that easier than someone in the program doing it since you have all kinds of boosters and emotions get crazy. But I can't think of anyone who'd have a reason."

"Vern Varney hated White, I understand."

"Well, sure, he'd leave the room if Miles came in. On account of the daughter. But you don't kill somebody for that, do you? Anyway, he can't shoot. He came out with us once to the Lion's

Club range and he didn't know how to load or handle a rifle, let alone hit something."

"You're a target shooter?"

"I'm single, and that means protecting myself. But it doesn't mean I could hit a man at a hundred yards or whatever it was."

"Of course not. How about Bill Tunney. Is he a gun person?"

"A 'gun person?' Please."

"Sorry, I didn't mean it that way—"

"Oh, I think you did. But I'm used to it. As for Bill, he doesn't need to target shoot, though he is out there sometimes anyway."

"Doesn't need to?"

"Already a crack shot. Former Navy SEAL. To hear him talk, you'd think he was there when they took out Bin Laden. Come to think of it, he wasn't actually a SEAL. He washed out in training. Still, he's a very good shot. But he loves the Boomers."

"Enough to give them free gas, certainly. Did you give them jewelry?"

"Now you're getting personal."

"They all wear gold chains."

June laughed. "As I said, arrested development on a mass scale. I hear the NCAA is all hot and bothered now, thanks to your stories. Nothing will change, you know."

"That's what the players say." Neva's phone chimed, It was a text from Ambrose: "Charlie just heard. Lamarr drugged. Wants to talk to you ASAP."

"Trouble?" June said, not sounding particularly interested.

"Did you know Lamarr Duffy?"

"Only as Frank's roommate. Didn't care for him particularly but I suppose I shouldn't say that under the circumstances. He sure didn't like you. I believe you suffered some childish pranks? Well, that was Duffy's work."

Childish pranks...pins in a kitten's eyes—save us from any child who would do that! But maybe June didn't know the details.

"Did he tell you? No? Who did?"

"Clayton."

"Clayton! Do you know where he is?"

"Don't even ask because I'm not telling you. It's nobody's business, and he is Mr. Nobody now anyway, isn't that how you put it?"

CHAPTER
30

Mr. Nobody.

It was true. She had called him Mr. Nobody in front of the entire town.

Incredible that she had not taken the time or care to think about Clayton himself reading the piece. Frankie was right. She had played straight into the system that victimized the athletes, this time in print.

She was as guilty as the rest of them.

Walking fast, heading for the *Current*, she felt regret and shame wash through her. What was she doing digging and prodding and snooping and poking into this mess? She had done what Ambrose wanted, she had turned up solid evidence of scurvy booster behavior on all fronts, she had made mistakes that she would now have to live with, and that was it. The murders were not her business. The police were hard at it, Charlie was covering it, Gentry, Budd, and Octavian were on some track or other—it was time to step aside.

And that meant passing along all the new pieces of the puzzle to Cal and Ambrose, and Charlie as well, especially the notes from Vera's great snooping...Strange how the brain can be thinking one thing while the body is doing another. Already she was sliding into her car.

The trip to the dealership took less than ten minutes, including waiting for two red lights. No one was in the showroom or the sales office that opened into it. Early lunch for the salesman? In a meeting with Varney?

The deserted showroom did not feel right. Uneasy, unsure what to do, suddenly unable to imagine what she would say to Varney—*Your name was mentioned in a shredded letter found in the athletic department by a snooping office assistant*—she turned to leave. A door slammed at the back of the building. Shouting erupted, not in words but a furious bellowing like an enraged animal.

A few quick steps took her to the connecting door between the showroom and the hallway. The hall was empty but she could hear a voice now, Tunney's voice, loud and accusatory.

"…goddamned weasel! I don't suppose you told them it was your idea, did you? I said did you, you yellow bastard!"

The answer was muffled.

"What? What did you say? God dammit—and I was worried about Lamarr! Where'd you put it? I want it. I want it now. Or do I have to tear this office apart before I tear you apart?"

Neva started forward, hesitated, felt for her phone. It was not in her pocket or shoulder bag. The car. She must have left it in the car. There were phones in the sales office. As she started to turn, the door to Varney's office flew open. Varney half fell into the hallway with Tunney right behind. The car dealer staggered a few steps, hit the opposite wall, and slid to the floor like a rag doll.

Tunney stood over him breathing hard, then drew his foot back for a kick.

"Don't," said Neva.

Tunney rounded on her, red-faced and menacing. "What the hell! I told you to keep out of this."

He started toward her but was stopped by Varney's thin voice. "Leave it, Bill. It's over."

"Over! It was over when I listened to you, you lying bastard." Tunny swung back toward the figure on the floor.

"If you'd waited, like I said." Varney coughed painfully, felt for tissue in his pocket, and spit into it.

"If I'd listened to you, that prick would have wrecked the program and you and me with it. Get up!"

"No letter. Not here."

Tunney grabbed the car dealer by the arm and heaved him to his feet. Varney swayed and put a hand against the wall.

"March," said Tunney, and jerked a thumb back toward the office. "Get it."

"It's not here," Varney said again, his thin lips stained with blood. "I dropped it at the paper. With her name on it." He lifted a hand in Neva's direction, let it fall, and took a few steps toward her with a hand still on the wall. "Call 911," he rasped.

"Right," she said, and backed through the open door to the showroom.

Tunney was fast for a big man in boots. He covered the distance and grabbed her shoulder before she could turn to run. As he pulled her back into the hallway she swung a fist hard into his neck. Her hair had fallen across her face, covering her eyes, but she felt the hit and heard him gag.

And then for a moment she had no idea what was happening. Shouts erupted, the hand was wrenched from her shoulder, she stumbled for balance. But she did not fall.

"Whoopsie!" said a familiar voice as a strong hand clamped around her arm. "You okay?"

Flipping her hair out of the way, Neva looked up into green eyes, Annette Octavian's green eyes. Studying her for signs of obvious damage, Octavian appeared amused as well as concerned.

"Fine, I'm fine," Neva said, and sagged against the wall.

Just in front of her Vern Varney also leaned into the wall, the bloody cloth still over his mouth and nose. Beyond him Tunney lay sprawled on the floor with Frankie on top of him swearing violently.

CHAPTER
31

"Esophageal varices?" said Frankie. "What's that supposed to mean?"

"Varicose veins of the esophagus," said Annette. "That's your breathing thingy."

"I know that much."

"Vern could have drowned in his own blood."

"Gross," said Clayton.

They were in a small sitting room off the workshop attached to June Cornish's jewelry store, Frankie half-lying on a celery green loveseat, Annette sitting with crossed legs in a side chair, Clayton hunched on a footstool with his big hands between his knees. June's voice carried easily from the other room as she ordered pizza from American Dream down the street.

Neva leaned in the doorway though there was an empty chair. She'd spent the morning going over details with Ambrose, Cal, and Charlie for tomorrow's set of stories, the final major set apart from follow-up on Tunney's trial and the NCAA rulings, including penalties for the program. But all that would trickle out over months.

"My part is done," she'd stated yet again as the meeting broke up. The words were aimed at Ambrose, a final Stop Sign for his suggestion that she *do some columns on the players, using the stuff you couldn't get into the news stories. Or how about some features on what it was really like to be a player or a gripper…*Not on your life, she'd said. All that confessional talk would stay right where it was, in her notebooks.

"I can't believe I was doped," Frankie said, sounding more offended than surprised. "No wonder I couldn't get up to go running with Miles. Damn. And I thought it was a hangover from a couple of beers. I guess they never expected Lamarr to go instead. He didn't see them, you know. He would've told me." A pause and then another, softer, "Damn."

"Not your fault," Annette said crisply. "Anyway, he was a dope himself. I'm only being honest. You know it's true."

"Doesn't mean he deserved to die," muttered Clayton.

The three of them had spent the morning under questioning by police, and had picked up at least as much information as they'd been able to give.

"Did they say whether Leonard and Gregorio are being charged as accessories, or at least for withholding information?" Neva asked, looking at Frankie. After checking with Vera on whether she was willing to be named, she had turned over her findings to the police. The response had been an underwhelming *Thanks, we'll look into it.* A far cry from how they'd reacted to Varney's detailed letter of confession when she'd handed that in.

"Didn't say," said Frankie. "Anyone want to bet on it? I'm betting that bit of it disappears."

No one took up the challenge.

Neva's phone rang as the pizza arrived. She saw who was calling and stepped into the storefront to answer, bracing for an attack.

"Jeneva?" said an earnest voice with no trace of anger. "Do you have a minute? I believe I owe you an apology. Of sorts."

Tucker Reilly's tone was richly regretful as he expressed shock, utter shock, at learning that Miles White and Lamarr Duffy had been killed by boosters—*members of our club, members of long standing!*—and thinking back over their conversation at his office he had to say that she'd been right, at least on some counts. Incredible that it was all triggered by a threat to report the program to the NCAA. His confidence in the boosters had been sadly misplaced, which was not to say that one bad apple, well two bad apples actually...

Other than reminding him that the actual shooting and suffocating had been done by Bill Tunney alone, urged on and accompanied by Varney—who was hardly capable of having

done the deeds himself despite his bone-deep hatred of White—
she let Reilly speak his piece. She did not ask for or expect a
reaction to the other revelations about bad booster behavior. With
no specific player as a favorite, Reilly had been one of the few to
come through without a list of definite misdeeds attached to his
name.

She listened patiently until Reilly ran down, then returned to
the back room to find the pizza box empty, June and Annette in
close conversation, Frankie on the phone, and Clayton picking
through a tray of gold chains.

At least June was not a warm weather gripper. It was an oddly
melancholy thought. Time for this old columnist to head home
and see to some early planting of salad greens.

"Buy a plane?" Annette was saying in disbelief.

"I'm looking for something different to do," June said.
"Selling the store, actually. You teach me to fly and we'll see
what happens next."

"That was Jasper," Frankie said, pocketing the phone. "He's
blown away. He never liked Tunney but still. Hard to believe even
a jerk like that would kill Miles just because he threatened to rat
to the NCAA. And then Lamarr to keep him quiet. He said to tell
you good job but he's glad he was out of here before the doors
blew off."

"I still don't get what's the big deal," said Annette. "I don't
mean about Miles and Lamarr. I still can't get hold of that. I mean
about the grippers gripping, so to speak. It's just stuff."

"Thank you, child," June said drily.

"It's not just about stuff," Neva said, watching Clayton lay out
gold chains side by side. "The really bad actors here are the
university, the coaches, the whole lot of them. The program's
being fined and stripped of some trophies but nothing's
happening to Leonard personally. Once the publicity blows over,
do you really think he'll stop humiliating players? And sure, the
board of higher education says it's going to issue new standards
for athletes and academic progress, but it's hard to believe that
will make a real difference, that more players will graduate with
useful degrees."

No one spoke for so long, Neva regretted sounding off. The
killer was in jail, and his accomplice would join him if he lived

long enough to get out of the hospital. Serious problems in the program had been exposed and there were to be some big changes. Frankie and Annette were feeling pleased with themselves for having suspected Tunney and the car dealer before anyone else did, and especially for arriving at the dealership just when they did. Though the timing had been pure luck, Annette had said more than once *I just had a feeling…*However it had happened, Neva could only be grateful and she should just let them enjoy the moment.

"Did you hear about Clayton?" Frankie said at length. He stood up and stretched, brushing the ceiling with one hand. "He's got himself a job. Assistant coach down at some college in the south that nobody ever heard of. Now he can do the yelling himself. He's been trained by the best—why waste it all? Now, I'm for shooting some baskets. Clayton?"

On his way out, Frankie stopped close to Neva and looked down at her with a scowl just as he'd done on that first day at his apartment. He shook his head. "I told my little sister you lied to her. Know what she said? She said, 'So what, you've been lying to me as long as I remember.' And you know what? That bothered me more than anything. I've decided to stick to the straight and narrow. No more lies. It's too easy to play the system. Just so you know, I'm playing straight from here on."

Clayton laughed all the way out the door.

ASHNA GRAVES is the author of two other mysteries, *Death Pans Out* (Poisoned Pen Press), and *No Angel* (Lychgate Press). She has lived in Oregon for the past 30 years.

www.ingramcontent.com/pod-product-compliance
Lightning Source LLC
Chambersburg PA
CBHW020602260626
47157CB00003B/824